PRAISE FOR

BURN-IN

"A visionary new form of storytelling — a roller-coaster ride of science fiction blended with science fact."

— Damon Lindelof, writer/creator of *Lost, Star Trek: Into Darkness,* and *Watchmen*

"I loved it. A glimpse into the future that is entertaining, enlightening, and scary as hell. *Burn-In* is filled with enthralling characters and scenes, but also key real-world issues and questions, which you'll be thinking about long after you finish."

— Reid Hoffman, cofounder of LinkedIn and coauthor of *Blitzscaling*

"A compulsively readable story that also brilliantly explains how our near-future world will look and work. Singer and Cole have woven a gripping detective yarn about a hunt for the terrorists of tomorrow, using the best research from the brightest minds of today."

— Peter Bergen, *New York Times* best-selling author of *Manhunt: The Ten-Year Search for Bin Laden from 9/11 to Abbottabad*

"Their seamless blend of detailed research and rapid-fire storytelling makes Singer and Cole the perfect tour guides for our world's future conflicts."

— Max Brooks, *New York Times* best-selling author of *World War Z* and *Devolution*

"Powerful . . . I've never had such an enjoyable discomfort in reading a book before . . . because *Burn-In* is fiction, but for how long?"

— *Foreign Policy*

"Close to perfecting the genre of educational and informative techno-thriller."

— *Science*

"A thriller you won't want to put down."

— Gayle Tzemach Lemmon, *New York Times* best-selling author of *Ashley's War* and *The Daughters of Kobani*

"Brims with the vibrancy of real, layered human conflict . . . There's more life and imagination in this novel about the robot future than most books of today will ever manage."   — Matt Gallagher, author of *Empire City* and *Youngblood*

"A thought-provoking and philosophical summer blockbuster; it is Michael Bay meets Stephen Hawking, and it is fantastic."   — *Diplomatic Courier*

"A fantastic, compelling, and authoritative look into the future — a future that is equal parts amazing and terrifying . . . It is a terrific read!"   — General David Petraeus (ret.), former commander of US Central Command and director of the CIA

"A fantastic, genre-defying work . . . While recognizable literary influences are palpable, like Isaac Asimov and William Gibson, Singer and Cole nevertheless are experimenting with a distinctive narrative. The text isn't fully fiction nor nonfiction but an informative and entertaining blend of both."   — *Pando*

"Timely, prescient, and meticulously researched, *Burn-In* tells a deeply humane and nuanced story about our changing relationship with AI and warns of dangers to our free society all too few have started to grapple with."   — Ken Liu, author of *The Grace of Kings* and *The Hidden Girl and Other Stories*

"Wrapped in this propulsive thriller is a fascinating analysis of our possible near future, where promises of a techno-utopia veer into surveillance-state nightmare. Cole and Singer brilliantly and terrifyingly imagine a realistic intersection of terrorism, technology, and policing."   — Phil Klay, National Book Award–winning author of *Redeployment*

"In our world of fake news and misinformation, fact and fiction blend together in a disturbingly seamless fashion. Where Singer and Cole's book is different is that it harnesses real-life trends in technology and weaves them into a fictitious and fast-paced storyline to warn us about the perils of our future."   — *Times Higher Education*

"Good timing . . . Both escapist and relevant."   — Tom Standage, editor at the *Economist*

BOOKS BY P. W. SINGER AND AUGUST COLE

Ghost Fleet

Burn-In

BURN-IN

A NOVEL OF THE
REAL ROBOTIC REVOLUTION

IIIIIIIIIIIIIIIIIIIIIIIIIIIII

P. W. SINGER
AND
AUGUST COLE

Mariner Books   Houghton Mifflin Harcourt
Boston   New York

First Mariner Books edition 2021
Copyright © 2020 by P. W. Singer and Redoubt, LLC

hmhbooks.com

Library of Congress Cataloging-in-Publication Data
Names: Singer, P. W. (Peter Warren) author. | Cole, August, author.
Title: Burn-in : a novel of the real robotic revolution / P.W. Singer and August Cole.
Description: Boston : Houghton Mifflin Harcourt, 2020.
Identifiers: LCCN 2019045766 (print) | LCCN 2019045767 (ebook) |
ISBN 9781328637239 (hardcover) | ISBN 9781328637895 (ebook) |
ISBN 9780358508618 (pbk.)
Subjects: GSAFD: Mystery fiction. | Science fiction.
Classification: LCC PS3619.I572455 B87 2020 (print) |
LCC PS3619.I572455 (ebook) | DDC 813/.6 — dc23
LC record available at https://lccn.loc.gov/2019045766
LC ebook record available at https://lccn.loc.gov/2019045767

Printed in the United States of America
DOC 10 9 8 7 6 5 4 3 2 1

To Sue, who gave us edits to this book as she literally waited in the hospital room for her breast cancer surgery.

There is no more true dedication.

burn-in: "the continuous operation of a device (such as a computer) as a test for defects or failure prior to putting it to use."

— Merriam-Webster Dictionary

BURN-IN

The following is a work of fiction.

However, all the places, trends, technologies, and incidents in it are drawn from the real world.

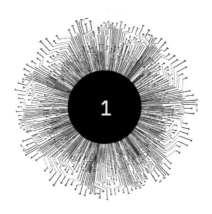

1

CAPITOL HILL

Washington, DC

The man's greasy red beard and braided Viking-style Mohawk had likely not been washed in a couple weeks, but the way that he cradled his AR-15 assault rifle made it clear he took care of what most mattered to him. And Special Agent Lara Keegan of the FBI's Washington Field Office would have bet a month's salary the Viking cleaned that weapon each and every day.

Side-eyeing him through the passenger-side window of a dated black Chevy Tahoe SUV, Keegan delicately folded the wax-paper-thin orange-tinted nanoplastic that she had laid out on the vehicle's dashboard. It gave her something to do while they waited in traffic, plus it kept her hands visible for the Viking to see.

Everything from Louisiana Avenue on up to Union Station was at a standstill. A few drivers honked in frustration, but the rest of the vehicles idled without complaint. That was the easiest way to tell which had a human at the wheel; machines knew not to waste their energy on emotional inefficiency.

Keegan made sure the nanoplastic's gold unidirectional filament was aligned with the crease, and then gently pulled on the next fold of the sheet. As she did, a blue minivan crept into the lane next to them, blocking her view of the Viking. The parents in the front seats were ignoring their two kids in the back trading punches over a suitcase wedged between them. She hoped for their sake it was the end, rather than the start, of a family vacation.

The minivan moved a foot forward and she got a better view of the Viking. The AR-15 was airbrushed a mottled gray and black. So he'd kitted it out for urban combat operations. And, yep, there it was. Peeking out from under the man's red beard was a tactical throat microphone. It was the same kind once only used by special operations teams, designed to allow subvocal, hands-free communication during a firefight. Now anyone could buy one.

The next step in the build required Keegan to look down for just a microsecond. She carefully slid a needle-like spine inside the crease of the folded sheets.

"Hello, World," she said quietly to herself, reciting the mantra of expectant computer programmers dating back before her grandparents' day.[1]

As she quickly looked back to the side, to ensure the Viking hadn't moved, the folds in the orange structure opened up into an origami form of a robotic praying mantis, six tiny hairlike legs unfurling.[2] It gave Keegan a tiny moment of satisfaction to know that she'd created the only thing that seemed to be moving this morning.

The SUV moved an entire foot, then braked hard enough to tip the mantis over. A freshly washed black four-door sharecar wedged itself into their lane mere inches ahead of a dirty red hatchback with cracked roof solar panels. It was just one tiny skirmish in the all-encompassing war between billions of lines of software code, each fighting to make society function smoothly, while simultaneously screwing over their market competitors.

"Bot fight coming," said Keegan. "Two cars up."

Another gleaming black car braked to let other vehicles pass. It was all part of the game. A vehicle might perch on the edge of the traffic line, not close enough to block the neighboring lane, but enough to set off the automated detection protocols, tricking its counterpart into stopping to creep around the perceived obstacle. Or it might be what the fleet of black cars were up to evidently. If two vehicles detected a rival company's car behind them, they would set up a moving screen, driving in parallel at the lowest legal speed.

And Keegan was stuck behind it all, playing with a robot in the passenger seat, trying to ignore a newbie agent nervously tapping a steering wheel that required nothing of him.

"You should call their complaint number," said Special Agent Aiden Griffin. "Or should I override and clear a path?" He'd been out of the FBI Academy a little over a year and still had that too-eager voice; that was why he had the backup-chauffeur job.

That was the only sacrifice the systems would make to the algorithmic gods of efficiency — the law enforcement vehicle protocol had been required for legalization of autonomous vehicles. At the simultaneous signals of a short-range radio wave and siren blast, the battles for speed and position would cease and all vehicles were required to pull to the side of the road.

"Don't touch anything," Keegan commanded. "You do that and 'FBI seen on way to Union Station' will be in the newsfeeds before we even make it a block," she explained.

The drive out to the downtown train station and subway hub hadn't been a planned operation, just a quick response to a flash alert that necessitated an FBI presence. It was likely a wild goose chase, but they had to assume whoever was behind it would be monitoring any activity of interest in the area.

Griff started picking at the sole of his shoe as the tension built, flicking out a small rock that had gotten lodged in one of the ridges. The nervous fixation annoyed Keegan because he wasn't keeping his eye on their environment.

"I get the rest, but what's the hat for?" she asked.

Each day Griff came to work as if dressed for a raid: sleek gray tactical pants and a too-tight black long-sleeved sensor-defeat shirt. He also wore a cumbersome tactical vest, which he was always trying to find a reason to wear.

"Keeps the sun off," he said of the knit black watch cap he had pulled low, almost touching his eyebrows.

"Seriously? It's a winter hat."

"Sweat gets in my eyes otherwise."

"Because you're wearing the hat." She reached back, grabbed a ballcap with "FBI" on the front, and offered it to him. "Here, this is actually what you need."

"Nah, I'm good," he said.

She tossed the hat back behind them. "Suit yourself," she said, point made.

She picked up the origami robot off the dashboard and began to move it back and forth through the air, the way kids played with toy planes. Sweeping it slowly across the horizon, her eyes tracked what was happening in the distance behind it.

"Yep, right there. Just about your two o'clock. One coming down from the distro facility in the *Post*'s old printing plant in College Park."[3] Zooming the mantis back out, she aimed the triangular point of its head at the eight-rotor delivery drone flying above, an imaginary line running from her tiny robot to the larger one in the sky.[4]

"As that thing flies over to deliver its beet juice or spare charger or whatever, it's just soaking up data to mine and sell. That's where the real money is. You set off the siren and it'll flag us to anybody who's buying that drone's feed right now." Keegan tipped the tiny robot in the direction of the Viking. "Plus, there's no telling how our friend with the AR-15 will react to the excitement."

"We're taking too long, though," Griff said.

On that, the newbie was right. She used the robotic mantis's beak like a stylus, tapping it on the "Time to Destination" option on the vehicle's map display. In the rush out, they hadn't been able to re-serve one of the newer vehicles in the FBI's fleet, so the display was the old-school, hard-screen kind, rather than a heads-up display that projected up onto the window.

She didn't need to say anything. It had read seven minutes when they left the office and they'd already been in the SUV for twelve minutes, with another six blocks to go. No plan survived first contact with the enemy or DC traffic. So it was time to change it. Keegan pressed the FBI pin in her jacket lapel that doubled as the send button for her radio.

"Control, this is Keegan. We're stuck here. Permission to get out and leg it?"

She could hear Griff's quiet groan at the idea of leaving the car on the sweltering spring day.

"We can cut across Lower Senate Park and get there in the time it'll take us to move another half block in this car," she said. Keegan intentionally used the formal title of the green space that divided the Senate office buildings from Union Station, knowing that's what the wall map back in the FBI Operations Center displayed, rather than what the Viking and everybody else would have called it: Patriots Camp.

In the earbud in her right ear, Keegan could hear the voice of her boss, Assistant Special Agent in Charge Harrison Noritz, having a muffled conversation with the others back in the Operations Center.

"I think that makes sense," Noritz replied directly to Keegan. "You aren't moving at anything over walking speed anyway. But use discretion, given the . . . sensitivities there."

"You heard the man," Keegan told Griff, crumpling the origami robot in her hand and slipping the balled-up nanoplastic into her pocket. "Set it on RUR. No sense in FBI property getting blown up at the station's parking garage along with us."

With the required permission from the human bureaucracy, Griff gave the machine its authorization, setting the vehicle on "Roam Until Recall," to drive about until called back to their location for pickup. The vehicle quickly lurched forward a few inches. "Now you start moving," Griff huffed. But it was only the autodrive resetting to the more precisely programmed follow distance in its traffic protocol.

As Keegan slammed the passenger-side door shut, she gave an open-handed slap onto the SUV's window, as if giving the machine a high five. The titanium of her wedding ring made a reassuring ping as it rapped against the glass. Griff looked over and gave Keegan a thumbs-up that wasn't needed. The slap was just an old ritual of Keegan's from when she'd had to exit armored vehicles in far more dangerous places.

As she moved around the blue minivan, Keegan saw the dad escalating the argument, jabbing the air with his fingers while he yelled at the kids. *Asshole.* She could also see that the Viking had moved, and not in a good way. His lips were opening and shutting in the staccato style of a professional sharing a rapid update with someone on the other end of a command network. More important, his finger had flicked off the safety and moved down into the rifle's trigger guard.

Keegan walked slowly toward the Viking, with her hands held palms out. "Hands where he can see them," she hissed at Griff.

As they closed, Keegan caught a whiff of that old familiar smell of goat crossed with Break-Free cleaning solvent. She'd been right about both the hair and the gun.

"That's far enough," growled the Viking.

Keegan paused and scanned the area ahead of her. She stood near the start of a central lane that ran through the camp that had sprung up on the seven blocks of park bordering the Capitol building. A row of tents ran along each side of the path, covering ground that members of Congress had been using as a landing area for autonomous personal aircraft. None of the tents were uniform, ranging in size from Improved Combat Shelters — the Army version of a one-person pup tent — to massive AirBeam inflatable barrack buildings. Here and there, a few brightly colored civilian camping tents livened up the sand and jungle green of military surplus. But that's where any disorganization ended. All of it was squared off and as clean as could be. Even the gravel in the pathway had been recently raked into the wavelike patterns of a Zen garden; whoever had that duty had evidently served in INDOPACOM.

"You know the agreement," the Viking said as he tipped the gun toward the edge of the cement, which also aimed it just before their feet. "No cops inside. Only those that paid their dues. Step on the green and y'all will get your asses handed to you . . . again."

Keegan still got angry every time video of that confrontation flashed through her feed. The DC police had gone in dumb, thinking they could roust out the camp with the same tactics that worked on angry students or farmers. But batons and pepper spray were nothing to a couple thousand veterans who'd been through far worse. No one was ready yet to copy what General Douglas MacArthur had done to the Bonus Marchers over a century earlier and bring in tanks.⁵ So instead, a rough truce had been made. Traffic was allowed on the streets that ran through the parks, but everything in between — now known as Patriots Camp — was the veterans' turf, to run as they saw fit. At least until Congress paid up.

"Not a cop, but a federal agent," Keegan said. "More importantly, I'm one of you. I have just as much right to be here as you do."

Behind the Viking, a woman emerged from a tent set up at the park's edge. It was pixelated desert tan, evidently military surplus, with a sign directing journalists to register there. Keegan knew enough about electronics, though, to recognize that the array of antennae peeking from the top was not merely for linking up to the news networks. When the DC police had tried to storm the camp, the veterans had thrown up a digital blockade, not just jamming radios, but tossing up so much electronic noise that the cops' surveillance drones had literally fallen from the skies.

The woman was in her late twenties, diminutive, with a matte black eyebrow stud and dreadlocks. While the Viking was in green digital camo, cut off just above the knees into a pair of ragged shorts, Dreadlocks was in blue Navy coveralls. As she came closer, Keegan spied the name "Richter" stitched on the right, as well as the blue, gold, and red stripes of a Presidential Unit Citation on her sleeve. That and the fact that she carried no weapons indicated she was higher up in the camp's ranks.

"Everything OK, Red?" she asked, looking only at the Viking, as if the two FBI agents didn't exist. Keegan tried not to smile at the typically creative service nickname.

"This lady cop says that she can come in, that she's one of us."

"You don't say," Richter replied, leaning forward as she stared directly at Keegan. Her breath smelled of mint stim gum, which took Keegan back to her own deployments and the cravings that followed. "Prove it."

Keegan slowly pushed up her left sleeve to just beneath the elbow. There, 1 inch below the elbow and 2 inches above the wrist, was a tattoo of an eagle above a globe crossed by an anchor. Three names were below it, each in a different font: Ferry, Rodriguez, Anton. Kee-gan covered the tattoo with her hand, just to show that it was sized according to Marine regulations, just like she'd had to do for her NCO the morning after she'd come back to the barracks with it.[6]

Richter nodded her approval, not having to ask what the three names meant. "How about you?" she asked Griff.

Before he could answer, Keegan said, "He's with me. We just need to cut through to the station." Griff nervously cracked his knuckles while Richter briefly looked him over.

"Sorry, no can do." Now, she only looked at Keegan, ignoring Griff again. "Only those that served."

There wasn't time to argue.

Keegan turned to Griff. "Head back to the vehicle. Link back up with me when you get there."

Griff looked like he was going to argue with her — the Academy certainly didn't teach you to leave your partner behind in a camp full of armed protesters — but Keegan cut him off.

"I'll be fine. Any of them could have shot me back in the Corps, so why do it now? Move," she said more emphatically, signaling an order. "We don't have time to waste."

At that Griff turned and headed back to the SUV, which had only driven itself another 7 feet.

At Keegan's impatience, Richter looked at her quizzically. "I got this, Red," she said to the Viking. "I'll escort her through."

"Yes, ma'am," he said, the chain of command clear.

Richter motioned for Keegan to follow.

Keegan had mixed emotions about it all. She'd been asked to march more than once, but declined every time. She'd varied her excuses — sometimes it was an FBI training course she claimed she couldn't get out of, other times a family commitment. But it was really because she just didn't like where it all had ended up.

Of course, she understood their anger. The toxic combination of an economic collapse and a screwed-up political system had done a job on the benefits they were supposed to get after their service. Everyone was suffering, but it was the inequity of it all that had sparked the movement. Civilian Social Security checks were automatically adjusted higher by law, but not the veterans' benefits, which had to be voted on each year.[7] That one little difference, and the pedestal that veterans were put on in politics, had made their checks the hostages that the two parties used to bargain for what they wanted. Anyone in the military knew that being a pawn for politicians was part of the deal, but not in a way that also harmed their families.

So the response had been familiar to anyone with military tactics: advance toward the threat. A million-strong march of vets from around the nation had shown up in DC to "occupy" Congress.

But that was the thing about anger — once you got organized around it, it could never be satisfied. Most of the vets had gone home after Congress had buckled and the checks had been adjusted. But a decent amount had decided to stay on until Congress also met their demands for guaranteed jobs, housing, and, well, pretty much anything else anyone who'd given more than their fair share felt they deserved. This was the part Keegan wasn't too comfortable with — the idea that they deserved more not just because they were owed it, but because they were better than those who owed them, and whose rules they no longer had to follow.

It was maybe because she wasn't really owed anything; she could never really repay what the Corps gave her. She had joined up a few weeks short of college graduation. She had seen one of those recruitment ads about how the Marines chose to run toward trouble. For her, it had been about fleeing it. The University of Washington Tacoma was 2,936 miles from Parris Island, South Carolina, but even after a cross-country bus ride, at times it still felt too close. After boot camp, the Marines had sent her a few thousand miles farther, to yet another place and time she'd rather not remember, but for different reasons. Forgetting was a necessity, just like it was for a nation that had simply come to accept the sight of veterans bathing in the Reflecting Pool as the price of staying a superpower.

"What's your story, Marine turned Fed?" asked Richter. "Where'd you serve?"

"Keegan. Lara. E-5," Keegan answered, using official shorthand for the enlisted rank that anyone in another service would recognize as a sergeant. "Marine 1st Law Enforcement Battalion, most of it in the Sandbox. You?"

"MP unit, eh? That answers how you ended up becoming a cop afterward," Richter replied. "Me? Radar tech on the *Zumwalt,* most of our time off Hawaii."

"No shit," said Keegan. "I've been to the Smithsonian exhibit."

"Yeah, that was exactly what it was like."

"Smelled better than the ship, I bet."

Richter got an annoyed look and brushed a rogue dreadlock off her face. She was evidently still getting used to their length.

Keegan had done the same thing when she got out. After years of someone else telling you how to live your life, all the way down to the exact length of your hair, you wanted to have control, even just over your looks. Now, she compromised, wearing the straight black hair she'd gotten from her father's side of the family in an angular bob that hit just past her jawline. It was barely long enough to pull back into a half-ponytail when she needed it out of her eyes — or just needed a change.

Keegan nodded and edged slightly ahead of her, a less than subtle signal to Richter that they needed to pick up the pace beyond casual walking speed. She didn't have time for a get-to-know-you talk. The increase in speed, though, caused the sciatic nerve running down her right hip to fire. She suppressed a wince. It felt like a shot of electricity, followed by the muscles involuntarily contracting around the nerve. The old wound always seemed to wake back up at the worst times. Normally, she would ease off and baby it with the yoga stretches she'd learned in recovery, but Locust pose obviously wasn't an option now.

"Seems like you have more than a train to catch," Richter said as they crossed the park toward Columbus Circle. "Something going down at Union Station?"

"Just something that requires our attention," Keegan replied tersely, hoping the pain wasn't registering on her face. That was the only answer Richter would get. Fellow veteran or not, she was still outside the fold.

"Look, I don't need to know the specifics, but do I need to move my people away from that side of the park?" Richter pressed. "If the SOA is able to do here what they did in London, we're within the blast radius."

It wasn't a surprise that Richter's thoughts had first turned to the Sons of Aleppo. Rising out of the refugee camps that held the second generation of Syrian war refugees, the terror group hadn't even been on the FBI's threat matrix when Keegan had first joined.[8] Now, SOA hits on watch lists were a daily fixture of the FBI Counterterrorism Division's briefings. The alerts had spiked again after the Paddington Station attack, where the suicide bombers had worn virtual reality cameras to allow fans to "experience" the attack.

"Just something that requires our attention," Keegan said, repeating the statement as a signal that was all Richter was going to get.

"Of anyone, we have a *right* to know," Richter replied, playing that card.

"Then you also understand why I can't say more," Keegan said. She gritted her teeth as her sciatic nerve fired again, this time radiating farther down her leg. She'd gone off to war a young woman and returned with her grandfather's back, courtesy of her spine being torqued one way by an IED explosion as 135 pounds of combat gear twisted the other way.

"Roger that," Richter answered, but in a disappointed tone.

As they approached the border of the camp at the traffic circle in front of Union Station, another sentry was waiting for them, also carrying an assault rifle. Apparently, the Viking had called ahead. This veteran, though, was older, making no attempt at follicle rebellion, just leaning into going bald by shaving it all off. From a guess at his age, Keegan thought he might have even served in Iraq during one of the earlier times around.

"I'm going to pass you off here," Richter said. "Whoever it is you're looking for, good hunting." She held out her hand, and as the two shook, Richter added with a wry smile, "And thank you for your service."

To another vet, it was as big a "Fuck You" as could be said.

The second that Keegan stepped off the grass onto the curb of Massachusetts Avenue, Richter started bellowing orders to shut down all access to the camp and place the medical team on alert. So much for trust, Keegan thought.

Massachusetts Avenue was somehow even more snarled up closer to the train station. There was no sign of Griff in the SUV, so Keegan began to pick her way through the cars. The automated ones were programmed to be 18 inches apart, so you could squeeze between those pretty easy. It was the human-driven ones that you had to watch out for; they were more likely to lurch unexpectedly and knock fenders, with you caught in the middle.

She stopped alongside a yellow-and-blue-striped sharecar, with two women in the back. One was evidently well-off, if the designer suit and pearls were anything to go by, maybe a lobbyist. Immersed in a VR rig, she was spending her rush hour somewhere else, maybe taking a mind-vacation in Aruba or Alaska. The other was sitting beside her, bored, no technology in hand. She made eye contact with Keegan and seemed to contemplate whether to get out and walk. Keegan shook her head, pulling back her jacket to show the badge on her belt and the holstered Sig Sauer 420 pistol. It was simultaneously the least and most she could do to warn the woman that she might want to wait a beat. The second Keegan did it, she regretted her kindness, realizing the woman would likely post something about it the instant she turned.

Keegan pressed the FBI seal lapel pin in her jacket again. "Control, I'm at the station."

"Received," Noritz replied in her right ear. "We've also got the Tac-Net up, so you can go AR." Keegan pulled an eyeglasses case from her jacket and put on the pair of vizglasses. The FBI-issued version married thick-framed ballistic shooting glasses with an augmented-reality projector.[9] They were supposed to be rugged enough to carry around loose in your pocket, but Keegan always kept hers in the case until needed; a bit of care was worth avoiding the tiny scratch that could cost you a paycheck or even a gunfight.

As Keegan switched the lenses on, her field of view began to populate with colored icons and raw data layered over what she saw. While the first versions of augmented reality had projected the data onto the glass, subsequent versions projected it into your eyes, allowing more information to be packed in. You could control some features with double blinks or exaggerated eye swipes to the side, but any typing was done on her wrist-worn Watchlet, the name of which was a bit of marketing misdirection. It was more like a bracelet than a watch in size, really just a flexible organic light-emitting diode screen that wrapped around the wrist.[10] Whatever they wanted to call it, it was still a far cry from the clunky ruggedized tablets she'd lugged around for the Corps, or even the old iPhones she'd played with as a kid.

Noritz continued to update in her ear, while her viewscreen began to fill. "Griff is at least another minute out," he reported.

Keegan looked back toward Patriots Camp. Just through the tree line, a blue orb glowed on her screen, marking Griff's position at the end of Louisiana Avenue.

Keegan turned back to the arched entrance to Union Station. Now the dirty white stone of the nearly century-and-a-half-old station pulsed with data, from the estimated number of people currently inside (3,740) to a cluster of light blue marking the location of local police arriving on the scene. Most important, though, was the flashing red warning message that had set them all on this seeming race against time. The red strobed, messaging that the station's automated bomb sniffer had caught a trace of volatiles, the chemical vapor trail of explosives.

Keegan made her way over to the police, who were huddled behind the low wall that bordered the marble memorial fountain in front of the train station's entrance. It wouldn't be much cover from a drone, but it might block shrapnel from an explosion. Her AR displayed a text box that marked the local cops' positions and identified the 15-foot statue looking down — Christopher Columbus. That also helped explain why the white marble had a pink hue from being splashed with red paint so often.

"FBI!" Keegan announced as she approached. The law enforcement agency networks were supposed to be integrated, but they'd been developed by different sets of contractors. Anytime a crisis like this arose, the area was soon awash with cops from DC's forty-six different law enforcement agencies, reporting to their own bureaucracies. So the information flow lagged, often taking seconds or even minutes to transfer across systems. No sense in getting shot by an itchy-fingered cop, just because a government contract office went with the low bid.

The cops were a mix of Washington, DC, city police in blue uniforms and, because Union Station was also a subway stop for trains running out to Virginia and Maryland, black-and-yellow-uniformed Metro Transit Police Department officers. Sitting just behind them, two squatters in faded dot-matrix camouflage uniforms calmly dipped canteens in the fountain, then began to divide up a thumb-sized pink bag of Mexican synth. They'd be locked out of the camp, but she guessed they wouldn't mind in a few moments.

"Our guys inside haven't seen anything suspicious. You getting anything more on your rig?" a DC police lieutenant asked Keegan, pointedly ignoring the two men as they stretched out and lost themselves in a narcotic haze. He was mid-forties, African American, evidently the senior officer on the scene. He was also wearing vizglasses, but the blocky, thick, black-rimmed ones that the local PD used. As he spoke, two of the Metro Transit officers began pulling a four-legged bot out of their trunk. Keegan recognized it as a derivative of the military models that she had used in the Marines. With chemical sniffers and cameras mounted on its head, the bot looked like a shaved Dalmatian whose body had been layered in sleek armor.

"Nothing more than the alert that went out. A hit on the chem sensors in the HVAC system," Keegan replied. "Our records are also showing that it has a 43 percent false positive rate."

"Yeah, those sensors were put in just after 9-11, so they're . . ." The police officer paused as their glasses executed a digital handshake, which established an encrypted network. Each shared their officer's identifying information and then layered their views over one another. Keegan watched a starburst of reflected color dance across the cop's lenses. "... getting old," said Kerryon Reynolds, lieutenant, Capitol Hill Station. With ID now shared, the FBI database began to populate Keegan's AR with additional information: sixteen years of service history, no mentions in current FBI investigations, etc.

"My inclination is to follow your lead until there's something more definitive," said Keegan. The quick read from his info showed that Reynolds likely knew his business. Plus, there was no sense in big-footing the local authorities — until there was a need to.

"Appreciate that, Agent Keegan," said Lieutenant Reynolds, going through the same quick assessment of her info. "Given the uncertainty, we're not yet ordering an evacuation. The plan is to do a front-to-back sweep for anything suspicious."

Keegan paused and looked up in the sky as a formation of dark gray Air Force drones flew over. She and Reynolds stood in silence, weighing whether the aircraft were part of the usual White House counter-drone air patrol or tasked to the threat at Union Station.

"Concur. I'll follow in your wake. Give you another set of eyes. Plus the resources of the FBI IT department," Keegan said, tapping the bridge of the vizglasses.

She also liked that the cop's plan meant she'd be going in second. Anyone who'd served knew that going in first was for heroes, the kind more often celebrated at a funeral. At that, she spun her Watchlet's screen absentmindedly, passing through message notifications, a weather forecast, and a photo of a young girl.

Pressing the send button on the lapel pin again, Keegan gave a quick update to Noritz. As she spoke, an automated delivery bot trundled by on the sidewalk, looking like a six-wheeled ice chest.[11] In a different place, under different rules of engagement, she would have advised Reynolds to disable and blast it, just to be safe. But here, they assumed that the vacuum seal meant to keep any food inside fresh would have also likely kept any volatile fumes from leaking out, making it less likely to contain whatever had set off the sensors.

"Received, and agreed," Noritz replied in her ear. "I'll coordinate with their chain of command. I'm also going to relocate Griff, to link with their units going through the east entrance." Taking away her backup wasn't the call Keegan would have made. But it was all part of being quarterbacked from afar.

"Fan out, and try not to start a riot," said Lieutenant Reynolds to the group of police, now up to fourteen with the addition of a couple of US Capitol motorcycle police.

The bright blue helmets and high leather boots worn by the latest two arrivals worried Keegan. Their pomp may have seemed fitting for a police department tasked with protecting the grounds of Congress, but with the Patriots Camp squatting on most of the green space, they had little left to patrol — only the Capitol building itself and the senators' and representatives' office buildings. They still had jurisdictional rights in a two-hundred-block radius, but Keegan thought their officers sometimes seemed to be trying too hard, too eager to make up for the loss of their home turf.

"Entry through each doorway, then fan out to cover the station. Keep off the net unless you see something. Identify but do not engage unless you have to. Call it in and then wait for backup, especially if it looks like something for EOD," Reynolds commanded, referencing the Explosives Ordnance Disposal team, popularly known as a "bomb squad." "And remember, everyone, move nice and calm-like. Day in the park."

Stepping into Union Station was like colliding with a wall of smells. Urine, century-old HVAC systems, and unwashed floors all mixed. More disorienting, though, was the spray of digitized color that washed over information that already overlaid Keegan's view of the lobby due to her AR. The station had been built in the Beaux-Arts style of the turn of the twentieth century, mixing Classical architecture with dripping ornamentation. Now, the soaring ceilings, decorated arches, and granite pillars were covered with riotous wraparound 3-D projections. Lightning-brand gummy stims ("Power Up!" the gum sticks said in a glowing neon rainbow) dueled with pop-up ads for MonsterMash, the latest vizglasses game, where you hunted classic Hollywood monsters across the landscape of your own city.[12] Indifferent to it all, a pigeon took off from its perch in the honeycomb-like ceiling of the station, flew lazily down through a projected werewolf, and began to eat the leftovers of a crumpled farro chip bag on the floor. And through it all walked hundreds of people, equally numb to it all. About the only thing you could immediately tell was someone's income and age. The oldest and poorest had their heads down, staring into their screens, while the virtual territory was dominated by the young and wealthy, staring vaguely into space as they experienced a personalized reality through their vizglasses.

Keegan considered the problem anew. An elderly woman in blue jeans was being followed by one of those "puppy" robotic suitcases, tiny motorized wheels extending out from pivoting legs. It could easily hold 40 pounds of nanoplex, enough to paint all the walls red. The high school group of twenty-two kids wearing matching backpacks . . . enough to take down the entire building.

Noritz's voice chirped in her ear again. "We've been able to connect to the station's sensor cams. We've gotten no hits of interest so far, but facial rec should start populating for you soon."[13]

As the line of police worked its way through the lobby, Keegan stood about 30 feet behind them and slowly panned the crowd. She frowned. The sniffer bot was advancing on the far left side, not the center where its sensors would have been most effective. The two Metro Police officers had kept their bot close to them; this sort of thing always happened when you threw together people from different agencies that didn't play well together.

The pause gave her a moment to stretch her hip, releasing some of the tension that had built up in the firing nerve. Federal privacy regulations kept the system from identifying everyone in the crowd with facial recognition; only companies could legally do that. But the system could run automated searches to ID any person in the crowd unlucky enough to have crossed paths with a US law enforcement agency, a fairly large portion of the population that grew with every traffic stop, visit to an airport, even a police athletic league summer camp. As the sales pitch for the Chinese company that had pioneered the effort put it, "If someone exists, there will be traces, and if there are connections, there will be information."[14]

A red pop-up identified Andrew Watts as the college-aged male in the yellow and green sweatshirt celebrating the Palo Alto @s World Series win, marking him with a misdemeanor conviction for public intoxication and urination. Two drug arrests for Leigh Sullivan, the girl in a peach-colored long dress beside him, both old ones for synth. And a slew of people popped up as victims in one identity theft case or another. None of it matched the SOA database, though, or even the statistically tailored profile for extremist activities.

Then lines began to appear, illustrating any relationships between those identified by facial recognition. A green line blazed between two women at opposite sides of the room; Stacy Limbago wore a purple backpack over one shoulder, while Torrance Fettison carried a maroon attaché case. They seemed to have nothing in common other than that they were both in pantsuits, but the feed marked them as persons of interest in a tax fraud investigation, each unaware that they were about to be swept up in the same case. More and more pop-ups clouded Keegan's view, lanced by green, then blue, then red lines identifying the type of link.

"We've got hyperspectral from the cameras in the station," said Noritz in her ear. "I'm piping it through." A pop-up live feed appeared in her glasses, a moving forest of rainbow limbs, a carnivalesque rendering of each person, their clothing, body, and luggage rendered in different colors depending on the material and temperature — every color but the red that would indicate explosive materials.[15]

It all made Keegan's head ache. It was a familiar pain, that same deep ache in the absolute center of her skull when information overload and adrenaline collided. She'd first felt this way when out on patrol. Just when her unit needed to be at their most alert, they would be flooded with data streams, back then coming from drone feeds and satellites and officers back in an air-conditioned op-center trying to steer them one way or another. The AR rigs were supposed to take all that and boil it down into a "user-friendly tactical interface." But it was still like trying to sip from a fire hose.

She took a deep breath and pushed the glasses to the top of her head. "I got nothing. You got anything?" she asked Noritz, who was likely toggling between the same video feed and whatever Griff was pushing out.

"Same here. Nada. But put your rig back on and just keep monitoring," Noritz replied. He was watching her too.

As the line of police continued to move forward, it began to lose its cohesion, each officer moving off in a different direction, spreading out across the station. She saw Lieutenant Reynolds turn toward the escalator that led down to where the old food court had been in the belowground level of the station. A good idea.

"Understood. I'm going to head down to the good seats," Keegan said. "Tell Griff to sweep the commuter train area and I'll take the Freedom Lounge." The entryway of the train station was where the majority of the foot traffic was, but killing the most people wasn't always the goal of terrorism. Sometimes the play was to go for the most symbolic, the most likely to send a message.

As the escalator took Keegan down to the lower level of the station, she felt the pressure change as she crossed through a new wall of smell. Instead of piss, though, this one was of pumped-in oxygen and eucalyptus oil. At the base of the landing, the white Carrara marble floor shimmered with liquid waves, as if covered by a shallow reflecting pool. It was a projection of water mixed in with the blue text of a holo-ad. Keegan's eyes didn't pick up what it was for, though, instead surveying the room for faces.

Reynolds was in conversation with the Freedom Rail cop who'd been permanently stationed down here, both as an added layer of security and to deter the riffraff. He made eye contact with Keegan and said something quickly to the Freedom Rail guard, who waved her through.

Keegan began to walk slowly through the lounge, each step leaving the simulated appearance of a ripple of water on the marble. The lower-level food court had been converted as part of the Acela privatization deal. The original buyer had gone belly-up when their promise of trains going 800 miles per hour ran into the laws of physics, eminent domain politics, and unbridled inflation.[16] But the ambitious design aesthetic lived on in the lounge, from the sleek black and silver Bauhaus benches to the projection on the wall celebrating the train's passengers as not merely customers, but "visionaries of transportation's future."[17]

Down here, there were fewer pops on the facial recognition. The crimes also shifted, reflecting the clientele, meaning mostly white-collar hits. William Kellerman, in a gray pin-striped double-breasted suit: "illicit transaction designed to evade regulatory oversight." Denise Aboud in a white pantsuit: "falsification of net asset values." Here and there, though, the high and the low crossed. The gray-haired man in the pearlescent blue silk suit was Richard Reynolds: double entry, member of Congress from Delaware and multiple arrests for solicitation of a prostitute — no convictions.

Knowing the vizglasses were steering her to the visual cues, Keegan tried to shift her focus beyond, to see who and what wasn't being called out by the data. An older man with a cane stood beside a woman in her mid-twenties checking her watch, an old-school wrist piece. Neither had any luggage, so Keegan could write them off as packing explosives. Indeed, the woman was hiding nothing at all, wearing skintight purple leggings and an even tighter tube top. A glossy white-legged robot stood beside her, one of the new Attendant models; it was unclear whether the bot was there to aid her, or sent by someone else to monitor her. Maybe a little bit of both?

Nearby was a possibility, a man with a large rolling suitcase and a duffel bag. A lot of carrying capacity. He was in a nice suit, but dated, a few years back in style, another tell. The man then went down to his knees and wrapped his arms around two young boys, twins maybe eight or nine years old.

As Keegan edged closer, though, she could hear the man apologizing: They couldn't afford for all of them to move now, but Daddy had finally gotten a new job and he would come down from New Jersey every other week. Even more, now he'd be able to bring them back something special for their birthday next month. At that, a woman behind the man joined them, asking if the boys wanted ice cream on the way home.

There.

Just on the other side of them. Long black robe and black knit prayer cap. The man had a beard, but scraggly from being uncut for reasons of faith. He thumbed through screens on a tablet with his right hand, while his left hand gripped the handle of a battered rolling suitcase. He held it so tightly that it had turned the skin pale around the gold band on his ring finger.

That familiar feeling hit Keegan, and a single bead of sweat tracked down her back.

Keegan did the rapid double blink that ordered her vizglasses to take a snapshot and upload the image into the database.

She flicked at her collar as if dusting off lint, brushing her mic's comms feed open to Noritz. "Tagged person of interest. Moving in closer to engage. Notify others to converge," she murmured.

In her lenses, a text message popped that there was no return on the face in the law enforcement database.

"Keegan, what are you doing?" said Noritz in her ear. "Continue search."

Keegan took the vizglasses off and put them back in the case, slipping it back into her pocket. While wearing vizglasses wasn't a tell that she was an agent, the lack of them would steer a suspect's mind to think she was a civilian. Plus, she didn't need the info overload now. She needed focus.

With the easy amble of someone lost in conversation, she began walking toward the family. "No. That is *not* what I said. Begin again . . . Order five hundred shares at fifteen hundred."

At that, Noritz spoke again. "Keegan, put your viz back on and continue your search. We have you in the station's video feed. I repeat, there is nothing on that individual's profile to indicate SOA affiliation. I am overriding target designation. Move on."

"No, no, no," Keegan said, now slightly louder, gesticulating as if making her case. "Five. Hundred. At. Fifteen. Hundred. One. Thousand. Five. Hundred." She crossed in front of the tearful family, the children looking up at the loud woman yelling at some call center chat bot. They were old enough to know that arguing with a machine never worked, but people who hadn't grown up with them couldn't help themselves.

"Stand. Down. Keegan!" Noritz again in her ear, this time more forcefully. "Data's not indicating a target. Stand down. You're going to create an incident you won't recover from."

"Dammit, NO!" Keegan said roughly, stopping in front of the family, her back to the man in the black robe. The parents looked over at her angrily.

"Hey, can you please have your call somewhere else?" the father asked.

"No," said Keegan, her annoyed disbelief evident to anyone within 20 feet of her. "I didn't say one thousand at five hundred, you fucking machine. Cancel!"

She could sense the man in the robe notice her, but Keegan kept her back to the target. She didn't like positioning that way, but better to show physical disinterest.

"Let's try it again, you dumbass machine."

In the distance, she could see Lieutenant Reynolds squinting at her quizzically.

"Look, I've got my kids here." The father again, a little louder this time. More eyes — and vizglasses — turned their way.

When was the last time she had been this close to somebody dressed like this? Keegan half expected a sensory flashback to the choking heat and the taste of dusty phlegm and gunpowder residue. But nothing manifested. She was still in Union Station.

"New order. Five. Hundred. At. One thousand and five hundred . . . And don't fuck it up this time."

The father moved the children behind him, his body straightening itself up as he found his confidence. "Ma'am, I've asked you politely. You really need to stop."

"Agent Keegan," Noritz said in her ear. "I am now ordering you to exit the area, and report to me. Cease operation."

"Don't you fucking tell me what to do," Keegan said louder.

As she said it, she extended her left arm and wagged her finger at the father's face, knowing that everyone around her would be drawn to it, including the man in the robe. At the same moment, an expandable metal baton slid from her sleeve into her right hand.[18] In one fluid motion, Keegan swung it backward. She'd aimed for the chest, but with her back turned, her aim was slightly off. The baton impacted higher than she meant to, striking soft flesh of his neck. The snap of metal striking skin was followed an instant later by a sizzle as 75,000 volts passed from the baton into him.

The crowd screamed as the bearded man crumpled to the ground.

Then came the telltale puff of smoke.

FBI DOMESTIC SPECIAL DETENTION FACILITY

Reston, Virginia

As she stretched her back out one more time, Keegan ran a finger down the wall, tracing the thin white dust collecting on the concrete.

Cleanup needed on Aisle Two.

Aisle Two was more technically Annex II of the FBI Domestic Special Detention Facility (DSDF).[19] The "Dizz-Diff" was really just another term for the repurposed shopping center that now housed holding cells as well as one of FBI headquarters' satellite offices. The developers' plan had been a mixed retail and office park. The FBI's plan had been to replace the old Hoover Building headquarters in downtown DC with a brand-new facility for all the FBI personnel in the greater Washington, DC, area.[20] But the stock market's collapse and congressional hearings into shady contracts had dashed both parties' plans. So retail's loss had been the federal government's real estate gain. Keegan's metal and black-felt office cubicle stood just about where stylish toddler pajamas were once sold.

It had been a good fifteen minutes of waiting so far, but Noritz taking his sweet time for the debriefing wasn't going to have the effect he hoped. For Keegan, it was a moment to stretch, recheck the locks on her memories, and figure out what she was missing in the present. Sometimes a moment to do nothing more than think gave you an edge.

She stood with her back straight and felt herself and the nerve pain cluster calm down. As the pain receded, new sensations moved in to fill the void. Her shirt still felt clammy, chilling her in the harsh air conditioning, and she was getting hungry.

So when Noritz finally walked in with a coffee and a glazed donut for her, she eagerly took them.

"Pretty cliché, huh?" said Keegan.

Noritz chuckled, making a show of his offering. "Going to take more than a donut to make you a decent agent. Anyway, you earned it."

That Noritz was wearing a suit and tie as late in the season as April marked him as management. His jet-black hair had about twice as much pomade as was needed, he was a head taller than Keegan, and he weighed at least 80 pounds more. Most of it was muscle, which should have made him an imposing physical presence. Yet from the beginning, Keegan had not been intimidated. From experience she knew that size mattered a lot less in a fight, so his physical bearing did not daunt her. It was also the way that Noritz had a smile that couldn't be washed away during any meeting where higher-ups were present. He was a former Pennsylvania state trooper, and the assignment to the Washington Field Office had given him the glow of a AAA ballplayer who'd been called up to the big leagues. Still unable to believe his good fortune, he'd do anything to stay.

Noritz sat on the corner of Keegan's desk and pulled out a tube of ChapStick, running it over his lips twice. This was the signal that he was moving into a part of the conversation that would be more awkward.

"Alright. Can you just let me in a bit on what went down? The takedown feed is all over gov and civ nets. You're a hero for now, but this is going to bring us some problems until I can answer a key question."

"You mean who is he?" Keegan asked, knowing the best way to divert a question was with another one. "Any hits?"

"None yet," Noritz replied. "He's not said shit since you brought him in. Facial rec and DNA are zeroes in our databases as well as state's and local PDs'."

"Have we run him through the civilian cloud yet?" she asked. She knew Noritz would lose his temper in a few moments, but his ambition was too easy to turn against him, especially once she had figured out how far she could push him.

"We're working on expedited warrants for any cloud presence," said Noritz. "But you know the drill. First their lawyers will argue about who needs to sign off on the warrant and then the engineers will come back and say end-to-end encryption means the info is not obtainable even with a warrant ... Stop dodging," he said, realizing he'd been taken off track. "You're going to need an answer about how you knew he was the suspect. There were no sensor hits and his bag was shielded from the multispectral. I can't just tell the director that the first person you decided to stun out in a 3,000-person crowd, luckily enough, just happened to be wheeling 22 pounds of Buckybomb."

"Maybe I just love the smell of a cattle prod in the morning."

Noritz rolled his eyes. "Alright, time for the serious part of the talk. Look, when we're operating like that, I make the calls. That's what keeps us all out of trouble. Just because you bagged the right bad guy doesn't make what you did right. We can't go around profiling like that, and we damn well can't put it in a formal report that you picked him out of the crowd because he was Muslim."

Keegan finished the donut and looked around for a napkin or tissue. Not finding one, she wiped her hands on her pants. "Sir, I didn't detain the suspect because he's a Muslim. Rather, it was because he isn't."

Noritz looked back at her and shook his head.

"We don't have time for doublespeak," Noritz said, more exasperated than angry, as they headed toward the interrogation room. "You're going to need a clearer explanation than that for the formal report. You better hope you can get something out of the suspect, because your job may depend on it."

FREEDOM RAIL STATION — PRINCETON JUNCTION

Princeton, New Jersey

She was just a few years older than his son would have been.

Her look was mere costume for fighting the system. A choppy haircut and asymmetric reflective makeup that confused the facial recognition cameras — in her case, a wedgelike seven-sided shape on her left cheek and a half checkerboard on the right.[21] Circular blue glass earrings etched with a dazzle array, most likely some kind of adversarial image designed to fool object recognition software into thinking it was seeing a frog or a turtle.[22] Chunky-framed, dual-mode AR-VR glasses with smoked lenses that obscured her eyes. Probably cost as much as tuition did back in her parents' day. All of it as much a fashion statement as an act of rebellion.

Looking the part but still just a kid — just as he'd always be.

The man turned from his fellow passenger, still oblivious to the fact that she was being watched, and stared back out the window. Behind his reflection in the glass — his face framed by wispy, long white hair pulled back into a ponytail — the speed of the train turned the landscape into a green and gray streak. Then it slowly came back into focus, a visual clue that the Freedom Rail had begun to slow.

He used his cane to tap the polished steel toe of her black Dr. Martens boots, another statement of rebellion repurposed into fashion. He wondered if she knew the shoe's journey, rebranded from originally being worn by police to becoming the emblem of skinheads and soccer hooligans and finally as part of the marketized revolution.

"Can I help you?" she said angrily, taking off her glasses. She took in the sight of the old man in the seat beside her. He wore old-fashioned eyeglasses, no electric hookup, just black with an overlay of an almost imperceptible pattern of dot matrices.[23]

"I'm sorry to disturb you, but I saw your ticket was for Princeton Junction," he said, pointing up at the sign at the end of the car flashing their arrival at the station. "I didn't want you to miss your stop."

"Oh my God. Thank you so much! I've got an exam this afternoon and —"

"You got lost in studying?" he said, motioning at her lenses.

"Yep. VR cramming app blocks everything out, even my stop," she said. "But I don't know what I would do without it."

"I can't even imagine," he said. "I'd give you the line about how we studied 'back in my day,' but you don't have time to hear about how dinosaurs roamed the campus and used notepads and laptops."

The train pulled into the station silently, and the two exited together.

As she walked beside him, just a half step back, both out of respect and to catch him if he fell, the man scanned the crowd. Waiting on the platform were a few students and business commuters, but not who he was looking for.

The girl noticed his pause, that minute shift in body stance from not finding what he was looking for. "Do you need any help finding where you need to go?" she asked in that tone that patronizing youth use with the feeble and helpless.

"No," he replied. "Someone was to be here to meet me, but they must be running late."

"Would you like me to wait with you?" It was unclear if she really meant it, or if it was just one of those things you said and hoped the other person wouldn't actually take you up on it. But in either case, it was a kindness that made him think better of her.

"That's very nice of you," he said. "But I wouldn't want to be the one to blame for you bombing your exam. I'll be fine. Thank you . . . and good luck!"

As she walked away, he noticed that she'd pulled her jacket hood up, even though it was a sunny day. Her face was totally enveloped by the thick black light-absorbing fabric and its Defeat-All coating.[24] Was she dressing that way for a reason or just to screw with other students data gathering on their classmates for feed chum?

Either way, he thought, it had to stop. There was more to be done than just coating yourself to slide through the system.

He sat down on one of the benches, pulled out his tablet, and plugged a slightly grimy pair of white headphones into a special adapter on the device. He didn't actually read the text moving across the screen, but it gave him an excuse to wait there and occasionally look up, seeming to check the trains' progress on the arrivals sign, but really to rescan the crowd for his contact.

After fifteen minutes of waiting, the old man gave up. If he stayed much longer, it would be conspicuous, maybe causing someone to come over and check on him. Very well. It would have to be just him.

He boarded the next "Dinky" train that headed directly into Princeton University campus, paying for the fare with paper dollars on one of the old automated machines.

The walk through campus was done at a deliberate pace, step by measured step, using the cane to steady his walk. He took in the Gothic buildings and their unapologetic suggestion that those who studied in them would never allow the progress of the world to erode their import.

If I were a building, that might be me.

He reveled in the feeling as he crossed another quadrangle of green space, where a half dozen youth lazed on the grass on top of orange-and-black-plaid blankets. While many of the students he'd passed earlier had been wearing glasses similar to the girl on the train's, the entry to this quad was marked as an "IQ" area — a tech-free space for students to enjoy their "inherent qualities," to be in only human company without machine interference or monitoring. Who knew what kind of bad decisions might emerge from afternoons spent here? Discourse? Dissent? Disobedience? It was partly why parents were the ones who were the most against IQ zones; they thought it better to track their children's activities, to pen them in with algorithmic boundaries, rather than give them the freedom to become something other than what they had imagined for their creations.

The old man eyed them, but not with envy. Those smiles were fleeting. They'd soon be back in the cloud, chasing that unfillable longing for more — more information, more stimulation, more of everything that would never be enough. Freedom? No. It was really a corral. And they did not even know it.

He made his away across campus to the northwestern corner, to a quad surrounded by a perimeter of three-story Gothic-style buildings. Green vines crossed the limestone archways and flying buttresses, while castlelike turrets decorated the roofs, keeping the rest of the world at bay — this was the image that people thought of when they imagined the ivory tower.

Except here, the wooden doors to a lecture hall were held open by a new kind of footmen — a pair of 24-inch-tall wheeled utility bots used for everything from escorting solitary students home from the library late at night to playing "Old Nassau" when alumni flooded the campus for reunions. This pair, though, were painted dark blue and red, a prank by Penn students he guessed, ahead of an upcoming game. He crossed inside and took a seat toward the back.

FBI DOMESTIC SPECIAL DETENTION FACILITY

Reston, Virginia

The windowless interrogation room was in what had once been a laser tag franchise. Its only light came from a faint LED dome situated directly over a bearded man. The only other points of illumination were the glint of the LED on the gold wedding ring on the man's left hand and, just a few inches higher, a flash of silver where the table's connection bolt had worn off the PVD coating of his black handcuffs. Otherwise, the room was in almost complete darkness as Keegan entered it.

The bearded man looked up at Keegan with what seemed like relief, but he caught himself and instantly hardened his face, dropping his gaze to stare into the darkness. It was curious, though, Keegan noted. Rather than a thousand-mile stare, the prisoner's eyes were focused. As Keegan's eyes slowly adjusted to the dark, she understood why: there was a silhouette at the far end of the table.

So, the head office had already sent someone else into the interrogation room before her. It wasn't the idea of being babysat that rankled her so much as it was the fact that they'd missed identifying the threat, just like Noritz; it seemed they didn't trust the FBI's new "hero" agent not to commit a civil rights violation.

Well, if the prisoner wasn't going to speak to their roommate, neither was she. Keegan turned so her back was to the mute opponent in the staring contest, not acknowledging their presence.

"*Assalamu alaikum,* Peace be upon you. My name is Lara Keegan. I would shake your hand in greeting," Keegan said, gesturing at the handcuffs, "but I have to ask your forgiveness in these circumstances."

Shifting nervously, the suspect tugged at his restraints but kept his eyes locked on the person sitting at the far end of the table. That was fine. Anything that burned up his energy would weaken his resolve.

"You already know me from the station. Let's talk about you."

Silence.

"Nothing? Well, I'll help get you started. Besides your having interesting taste in luggage, we know that you are garbed in the clothes of a cleric. And beyond that, you are wearing black."

Silence.

"This lets us know something truly important. Wearing black is a sign you are a direct descendant of the Prophet Muhammad, peace be upon his name."

The bearded man readjusted his hands in the cuffs but stayed quiet.

"It is an honor to be in the presence of someone with this heritage," she continued. "But it does pose a problem that perhaps we can solve together."

The prisoner still said nothing, but for the first time, his eyes shifted from the figure at the end of the table, as he quickly glanced at Keegan.

Keegan leaned over the table and held the man's cuffed left hand up to examine it in the faint light. She turned it carefully, rotating it to examine the wedding ring in the dimness. "You see, Sura 43 of the Koran says no ornaments of gold should be worn on the person."[25]

She eyed the man's face. Hard to tell. Maybe melanin injections for the skin coloration and some kind of reconstructive surgery to shift the jawline and cheekbones. It would likely leave small scars under the beard area. Could they get a warrant to shave him?

"And that means no imam, especially one in black, would ever wear a gold ring."

Leaning forward, Keegan then put her full weight on the man's elbow and forearm. Pinning the hand down, she yanked the ring off the man's finger. A muted grunt of pain came out of the suspect's mouth as the flesh above the knuckle tore off with the ring. Was he that tough? Or was he just snowed on meds?

"There now, that's better," Keegan said. "Your costume is fixed." She wiped the blood from the ring on her pant leg and then held it up to the light. Turning the ring slowly, she read the inscription out loud. "TR-MP, June 23, Love Forever."

The legs on the prisoner's chair ground into the floor as he shifted his position, trying to worm his way out of the mounting pain in his hand. The trickle of blood from his finger started to pool under his shackled hands. Now three things reflected the LED light.

"'Love Forever.'" Keegan laughed. "We'll see about that. A life sentence in prison has a way of testing relationships. So now it's the time in our conversation to answer questions. Who is the mysterious man in the black robe really?"

Instead, it was the silent observer who spoke.

"Mr. Thomas Reppley of 114 Northwood Avenue, Sanford, Alabama." The voice was dispassionate, the tone of an analyst simply responding with data, unaware that he was screwing up the whole flow of the interrogation.

Keegan ground her teeth in anger but kept her expression passive. Without warning, her opening line of questions made no sense, all because this intervening asshole had held back useful information.

Even if the asshole didn't, she knew not to reveal any discord in front of the prisoner. So Keegan plowed ahead, as if the exchange had been planned.

"So, Mr. Thomas Reppley of 114 Northwood Avenue, Sanford, Alabama, as you can see, the *who* is not a problem for us — despite your costume."

She tilted her head at the figure in the dark. "We know *far* more about you than you think. So, let's talk about the why. We know it wasn't your deep and abiding faith that brought you all the way from Alabama for your little charade on the Freedom Rail. So we need a different answer. Tell me, what else could motivate Mr. Thomas Reppley?"

The observer spoke up again with the same inexpressive tone. "Potential financial gain. Six days ago a deposit was made of 15,909 Monero into an account at Winner's Luck online gambling site.[26] The account was registered to Mr. Reppley's cousin-in-law, Michael Harris Simpkins. This is anomalous, as Mr. Simpkins previously had only used US dollars to make his deposits, not blockchain-based cryptocurrency. Further investigation is recommended."

Reppley's eyes went wide and he sputtered a wet gasp. "Wait. I don't know what —"

This was too much. It was her interrogation to run and she didn't like being played the fool, especially in front of a prisoner. Better to put the brakes on now and pick things back up once this asshole was locked back into whatever closet he worked in.

"You see, Reppley," said Keegan, moving over to the door and the light switch, "there is nothing you can hide from us." She then flicked the switch that turned on the room lights.

What Reppley saw before him made him howl. It was an animalistic scream of rage and fear. The prisoner kicked the chair over and tried to wrench himself free of the table, every instinct fighting to get as far away as possible from the once-shrouded figure. But the handcuffs kept him shackled to the table. As his body convulsed back and forth, he strained against the metal and blood started to drip from the cuffs as they cut into his wrists.

"Goddammit," said Keegan, looking from the observer, to Reppley, and then back again. She threw the ring in disgust. It made a ping as it bounced off the figure at the other end of the table.

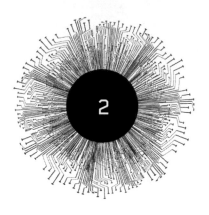

PRINCETON UNIVERSITY

Princeton, New Jersey

As lecture halls went, there was no more hallowed place than Mc-Cosh 50.[1] Besides hosting countless future senators and CEOs for their takes on everything from economics to ethics — or lack thereof — it was where Albert Einstein had delivered a series of four speeches to an audience of scientists gathered from around the nation. Soon after, the lectures on "The Meaning of Relativity" would be turned into a book and Einstein would win the Nobel Prize in Physics.

The room was little changed well over a century later. Some four hundred wooden desks were laid out in auditorium style, open on the left and closed on the right to place your elbow on when taking notes. It must have been torture to left-handed students in the past and today's students used to memory foam and the paper-free learning environment (PFLE) movement. Yet the old man appreciated that the desks remained as a reminder of the physicality of knowledge. Learning ought to be experienced as a corporal process of improvement.

The old man took a seat in the back, toward the right, with an unobstructed view of the class. He gingerly twisted his body to fit in the wooden desk and pulled out a black leather-bound notebook and began to take notes as the lecture began. To his left, a buzz-cut young man in a flowing button-up long-sleeved burlap jumpsuit and orange flip-flops juggled four yellow balls. There was always someone like that — a jester, desperate to be noticed.

Yet nobody paid him any mind, which was, the old man thought, a credit not just to his fellow students but also to the speaker who so held their attention. He truly was a proper heir to this room's renowned history.

Across the wooden stage, Professor J. P. Preston moved fluidly, bounding from foot to foot when he punctuated a point. He wore a dark blue stretch suit, a salmon-colored collarless dress shirt, and a pair of slightly scuffed fabbed mesh brown loafers. Every so often his lecture was diverted by anecdotes about what the president had said to him at their summer "get-together" on Martha's Vineyard. It could have come across as arrogant, but every person in the audience knew that Preston had walked away from literally hundreds of billions of dollars, if not more, by turning his automation kernel into an open-source platform.[2] He had written the software at the core of nearly every automated machinery's operating system, and simply let anyone and everyone have it for free.

Preston explained his reasoning, his fervent belief that technology could be in the public interest. If lawyers could go work for a law clinic or doctors at an aid clinic, why not technologists? In a fragile world of convulsive poverty, conflict, and environmental catastrophe, there was only one way for humanity to survive: to create, to build, to surpass. It was as much a sermon as it was a lecture. And if the old man had still been a student, it would have worked. He would have walked out of the lecture hall and immediately signed up to join this great man in the same great cause.

But he was not a student anymore. When the lecture ended, the old man stood with an aching lower back. He watched as a scrum of students gathered around the professor, each hoping to be noticed, whether to be able to say that they once talked to him or even maybe get up the courage to request a recommendation later. Soon the room was empty. The old man walked to the front of the room and took the wooden stage. He wanted to see what it would feel like, looking out at all the desks, the adoring eyes watching. But all the desks were empty.

Him, they would never know. He closed his eyes, feeling the weight of all that stone above him.

The old man made his way to Preston's office. There was no need to ask the two vandalized bots for directions; he could navigate the rabbit warren of corridors that linked all the buildings at the basement level by reading the small plaques on the wall. It took more time, but wouldn't move any electrons across any network.

Using the cane's brass handle, he rapped on the door. There was no answer, and so he rapped again — four times, in an evenly spaced tempo.

The door cracked open, and there stood Preston. He wore a pair of cheap vizglasses, the kind people wore to big outdoor festivals like Burning Man or industrial work sites. Over Preston's shoulder, the old man saw an old-fashioned frame that held a cover of the *New York Times Magazine*. He was about to speak but stopped, just for a moment. Then he smiled, realizing Preston had slightly enlarged the image from the front page to ensure visitors could more easily read his accolades.

"I am sorry to barge in like this, but I just caught your lecture. Nathaniel Ludd — a big fan of your work, Professor," the old man said.[3] "Life-changing stuff."

The professor took off the glasses for a moment, assessing. Was this an eccentric billionaire with a research-enabling donation? Fortune knocking? Or just another of the idle, would-be intellectuals who haunted the campus, wasting time?

"OK, hi there," Preston finally said. "Very nice to meet you, but I'm in the middle of something — running a model that I need to babysit into adolescence. Can you come back during office hours? It's the same rules for adult auditors as students."

The old man visibly stiffened at the resistance. So much so that Preston backed up a half step. Then, the old man softened his expression into a smile.

"I bet there's never a good time with somebody like you, and I know just what that's like, Professor. I promise it's only a moment if you can indulge me. I'm keenly interested in your Automated Decision

System work and how the open-source model of Linux influenced it. Many may not remember it, but for me, it was life-changing stuff."

"Oh . . . You do know my weakness. How can I turn away an alum who wants to talk ADS *and* Linux?" said Preston. "A few minutes then. Come in and don't mind the mess."

Preston turned his narrow shoulders and beckoned the old man inside. "Mess" was just another affectation. One freshly painted office wall featured an oversized photo of Preston hiking in the Himalayas, a lower body exoskeleton wrapping his hips and knees, easing the load — technology allowing man to conquer new frontiers without the accompanying sacrifices that make them worthwhile. A series of smaller pictures showed him meeting the US president, the UN secretary general, and technology industry luminaries. The old man noticed a faint hairline crack in the wall's plaster that strung the photos together like a crude link analysis display. The office smelled freshly cleaned, no stale food or unwashed socks anywhere. A projected screen displayed a representation of the VR model he was running. It looked like a mosaic of earth-colored tiles arranging themselves by pairs. Preston reached into the projection and waved his hand sideways, as if brushing crumbs off a table, and the projection disappeared. Then, he jauntily pushed the glasses up on the top of his head before sitting, his gaze softening.

"Ramen and Red Bull. There would be no ADS without those two gifts from the heavens. I was a grad student at MIT, in Washington for a summer, supposedly working for NASA when they froze all R and D funding in that budget fight. Remember when they stopped paying the debt for a couple months? It was then, so I was broke and starving — literally. Then another student who was working on DC Metro's driverless cars let me know they had some extra funding that he could get me. It wasn't much, but it kept me in calories and code."

"And that all led to this place," said the old man.

"Exactly," said Preston. He sighed, seemingly lost in his memories. "If I had never worked on that old ADS software, I never would have gotten hired at my first faculty job."

"And my wife and son would still be alive today," said the old man.

Preston looked at him quizzically, still not understanding what he had done years ago, even as the brass top of the cane smashed down on his head. The strike split the VR glasses in two, sending them clattering to the floor, and a jet of blood splashed across the wall above the workstation, leaving a crimson arrow pointing skyward. Another blow. And another. The old man didn't stop until the cane surrendered to his rage with a crack, the brass ball falling to the floor.

The old man stood over the body, looking down at what he had done. The body looked different than how he'd long imagined — no look of fear or accusation on Preston's face. Just the mess that came after something that had to be done. It was then that he realized he wouldn't even need the sterile wipes he'd brought just in case he threw up.

He kicked Preston's chair out of the way and placed a small black rectangle next to the computer under the desk. While the drive downloaded the contents of Preston's computer, the man quickly stripped off his blood-spattered blue dress shirt and khaki slacks. He then peeled off the 3-D printed silicone mask.[4] It had been designed using an algorithm that generated a hyper-realistic face an AI had dreamed up by blending the features of famous celebrities.[5]

The contact lenses came out with more difficulty, bringing forth a rush of tears. It was not mourning over the taking of a life, just the small price of something that had to be done.

A generation's worth of age disappeared as he changed into a pair of tight gray jeans and a puffy down black nylon pullover. He changed shoes, into a pair of basketball sneakers, but with lifts on the left side, which would alter his step and throw off any gait recognition software.[6] Then he went to work on the facial recognition side, putting on a pair of thick, glossy black Nike AR glasses, and slipped in a set of prosthetic teeth with an overbite. A small foil pouch held a moist wipe, which he ran over his cheeks, lips, and chin.[7] The girl on the train's anti-surveillance makeup was for fashion. People who weren't just playing at rebellion used skin lotion with microscopic refracting beads. The beads were invisible to the eye, but they distorted camera imagery at the pixel level. It was the only way to be truly free in a world of algorithms designed to mark and track humans. It was apt that the algorithms themselves had originally been honed by prison inmates paid pennies to train AI as part of cheap human labor.[8]

Footsteps in the hallway stopped in front of the door, and the man froze. He felt his chest tighten and tensed his stomach muscles against the sick feeling that welled up. Strange. He analyzed the feeling, something to be understood as much as fought. Killing Preston hadn't caused it, he reasoned; the thought that he might have to do so again so soon was what made his stomach flutter.

Don't open that door, he willed whoever was on the other side. He knew that chance played a role in so much of life — whether you got a certain disease or struck by lightning even. But the deaths of his wife and son were different. There was code. There was causality. There was Preston. God's hand was not present when their two bodies were violently merged into the 39 tons of metal of their DC Metro subway car. On the way to see him. At work. Writing code himself.

A gentle knock on the wooden door, barely penetrating the oak. A young man's timid voice. "Professor? It's Marshall Winters. I'm early for office hours but thought you might be free to discuss my research project?"

Silence.

Another knock.

The man kneeled carefully, quietly picking up the wooden cane. Frayed and jagged wood, like tiny blood-soaked teeth, where the brass top had been. A simple tool. Man's original weapon. Would he have to use it again?

Another minute passed, then a quiet bashful voice. "Professor Preston, if you're there, I'll come back at office hours . . . I'm sorry to bother you." A defeated sigh, audible even through the thick oak door.

The man waited another minute, counting down the time on his watch. It wasn't one of the new Watchlets or even an old networked one. It was just a ruggedly simple steel automatic watch without even a date display. As the second hand smoothly swept around the black dial, he took a breath every five seconds to calm himself.

Time to go.

But when he gripped the door handle his hands shook uncontrollably. For a moment he could not remember where he was. It wasn't the weight of what he had done but how he had gotten here. As he doubled over, blood rushing to his head, it was as clear a picture as if he had seen it on Preston's VR kit. They were on their tree-lined street, his wife and he each holding their son's hand. The boy hated touching the lines on the sidewalk, so they would swing him by the arms over them, turning his worried steps into leaps of glee. That day, a fire truck drove by, and his son stopped to salute. The driver turned on the lights, a playful flash of red, and gave his son a thumbs-up. He had been so excited, even worried that his parents might have missed the moment of a lifetime. "Did you see that, Daddy?"

They had died the very next day.

As the memory passed, his hands stilled. A final look around the room left him satisfied. This was justice. It was right. Preston and others like him had lived their lives according to a code, and it was broken. They celebrated the idea of "disruption," because they didn't see themselves as actually being responsible for the consequences of their actions.[9] Now, that would change.

He was about to open the door when he stopped again. There, in the corner. With a now steady hand, the man reached under Preston's desk to retrieve the brass knob that had broken off the top of his cane. With sure fingers, he wrapped it in a plastic glove and slipped it into the messenger bag alongside the hard drive, careful not to get any blood on his hands.

FBI DOMESTIC SPECIAL DETENTION FACILITY

Reston, Virginia

The robot was smaller than the average human. Three black metallic ropelike ridges ran along the top of the head, antennae that looked almost like cornrows. The silver-dollar-sized eyes were greenish blue — Keegan assumed it was programming that mimicked the eye color of the person looking at it — nestled in an ovoid basketball-sized metallic and ceramic head. A sharp-edged nose with nostrils, probably a design feature blending form and function for venting, divided the robot's face at midpoint. There was no mouth, which made it look to Keegan like a Japanese Noh mask she'd seen at the Freer Gallery in the Smithsonian. Bad design, she thought. You could easily put another set of sensors there.

The robot's "skin" absorbed the harsh light thrown off by the fluorescent tubes overhead. It was a peculiar effect, a void placed in the center of the room. Faintly stippled, the gray material looked almost brittle, like an eggshell. Keegan guessed, though, the opposite was true. It was likely ceramic composite, lighter and stronger than steel. The hard, light gray material covered the top of its hands, but the fingers themselves were black, most likely some kind of rubber for gripping.

Keegan was tilting her head to the side, to try to look under the table at the robot's actuators, assuming it could walk, when she noticed that Reppley's screams had quieted into something more like moans. She looked back at the man. Snot and saliva dripped off his chin, into his beard, and he was now rocking back and forth, trying to pull away from the table, but each time crying out when his hands were caught by the cuffs. Probably now feeling the pain kick in from nearly breaking his wrists wrestling with the shackles. There was also that distinct smell from the train station's entrance again.

"You're a mess," said Keegan as she stood up to leave. "Stay here. I'll be back in a few to consider the situation at hand."

"Understood, Agent Keegan," said the robot.

"I'm not talking to you, bot," said Keegan. "I'm talking to the human."

Outside, Noritz waited in the hallway with an apologetic expression, trying to head off Keegan's certain explosion. "I swear I had no idea," Noritz said. "After you went in, I got a ping that there would be an observer in the room and I was distinctly told not to notify you."

"That's bullshit. And you know it," Keegan replied. "Totally unacceptable. You do not hold back critical information, let alone introduce an element like that into an initial interrogation. You saw how he freaked out, like he thought the bot was going to torture him. When we're in the room *we* put the pressure on a suspect, not machines. This isn't Beijing, where you can just unleash a bot on a prisoner. What the hell is going wrong with everybody here?"

"I understand you're mad, but you're taking it out on the wrong level of the food chain, Keegan," Noritz said with deliberate calm. "Again, this was not *my* call. Fortunately, *you* can share your concerns with those who made it. They're waiting for us in the conference room." He paused and his bureaucratic veneer cracked a bit, the Pennsylvania state trooper coming back in. "I would advise, however, that you calm the fuck down before you go in."

Keegan followed Noritz down the hall to the conference room, stewing in silence as they walked. When they entered the room, a phalanx of senior agents and Justice Department officials awaited them at the table. Keegan knew a few by sight, the special agent in charge of the DC region, Noritz's boss's boss, as well as the chief of the national security division for the US Attorney's Office for the District of Columbia, who had the jurisdiction on terrorism cases.[10]

Each of them had VR goggles laid out in front of them, except a man in a dark blue suit at the head of the table, who was still wearing the goggles and giving ongoing color commentary. Apparently they'd all been watching the interrogation from the robot's point of view.

"Look at him still blubbering away. I don't want to sound too old, but they don't make terrorists like they used to."

His assistant tapped him on the shoulder and he took off the goggles — Keegan recognized it was the deputy director. Kamal Bosch held the number two position in the Bureau and, even more important, the highest rank that an FBI agent could reach without needing appointment by the president and a vote by the Senate. That made Bosch not just the lead on every major FBI issue and investigation, but also its institutional steward, the ultimate internal guardian of who and what the Bureau was supposed to be.

Bosch motioned for Keegan and Noritz to sit at the table, with a hand gesture that also indicated the two senior agents there were to get up and move to the seats running along the wall for the back-benchers.

"Aggressive work, Agent Keegan. Not just on the arrest today at Union Station, but in there with the suspect. Well done." Bosch sounded sincere, but coming from such a senior official in a three-piece suit, it still left Keegan wary. Even more so when the suit he was wearing was real wool. Keegan also caught a whiff of his cologne, Confiance, imbued with pheromones that supposedly influenced people.[11]

"You two were quite the . . . I don't think I've ever seen a suspect broken down so rapidly like that."

"Thank you, sir. But —"

"Keegan," said Noritz, trying to cut his agent off before she went too far.

"No," said Bosch, running his hand over his razor-shorn scalp. "Let her continue. All of us here are in Agent Keegan's debt today, in more ways than even she knows."

"Sir," said Keegan. "With all due respect —"

"*That* I will not allow, Agent Keegan," said Bosch quickly. "I know what you mean by that. Just say what you want to say."

"I apologize, Deputy Director . . . but what just happened is total horseshit," said Keegan.

Noritz let out a slight grunt of pain beside her, but said nothing.

"That's better," said Bosch, folding his arms as if in judgment. "And your assessment of this is why, Agent Keegan?"

"Two reasons, sir. The first is that machine took over my interrogation."

"Except it didn't. The system simply revealed key information in real time," said a thin man three seats down from Keegan. Maybe late thirties or forties, tall, but his height underscored his seeming fragility. He wore a black suit like most of the others, but his was set off by cyan-colored hair that shifted from a green or blue shade, depending on the angle of the light. It was mesmerizing in a certain way, any slight movement of his head changing the coloration. It was also obvious peacocking, common among civilians, but still abnormal in the Bureau. The real tell, though, was how his hands made a triangle under his chin, as if he had been analyzing the conversation rather than an audience to it. It was an intended signal that said, while he had a seat at the table, he was of a different professional guild than the investigators and lawyers gathered around it. Profiler most likely.

"Agent Keegan, since you didn't let us get to introductions, meet Dr. Sander Modi of Behavioral Analysis Unit 5. . . who evidently disagrees with you," said Bosch.

So that answered two things. First, who he was. Unit 5 was the research wing of the Bureau's National Center for the Analysis of Violent Crime (NCAVC).[12] It had started out with the psychological profilers hunting serial killers back in the 1970s and then moved into anything and everything from all the sciences that might aid the Bureau.

And, second, Bosch had just given away a key part of his own psychology. He was one of those leaders who liked to have the issue debated in front of them, portraying himself as the dispassionate judge, when he had likely already made a decision.

"I'm sorry, sir, but all of you, including Dr. Modi, were not *in* the room. VR gives you the sense you're there, but you're not. It's different in there. An interrogation turns on the emotional read you get on the subject. And that machine just completely threw the subject's emotional state out of whack. Everything we got from Reppley, we could have obtained through other means, without the robot . . . without the blowup."

"Your response, Dr. Modi?" Bosch asked, raising his eyebrows.

"Actually, the 'blowup' was the 'key information' I meant. Agent Keegan certainly received the identifying information much more rapidly than otherwise possible and, importantly, in the active context of this inquiry, 'in the room,' as she puts it."

Keegan nodded in assent; he'd made a smart pivot off her main point.

"But what is more notable," he continued, "is what happened next. You'll note the system detected a pheromone level that was well off the scale. The level of fear that the prisoner displayed was disproportionate in the extreme and certainly does not align with any expected profile models from the scenario of his arrest. Without the robot, we would not have induced that reaction."

"His reaction was that he went nuts. Aren't they all?" said Keegan. But inside, she knew that was not the case. Frankly, the grown man's meltdown bothered her more than the surprise appearance by the robot. She had seen adults crumble before, but it always happened from a trauma that struck like an emotional lightning bolt — hosing out an M-ATV after losing a buddy in battle, the video message that a mother had died while you were thousands of miles away. This was different; Reppley had just lost it at the simple idea of being locked in a room with a robot.

"Agent Keegan, you know you're grasping on this one," said Bosch, now adjudicating. "He's right, both on getting useful data in the moment and that a subject going 'nuts' is something pertinent. What is your second concern?"

"My second concern is that, even if you were going to put a system in the room with me, I should have known. You can't treat a live interrogation like some kind of experiment, putting me in there cold with some *thing*."

"Actually, I can, Agent Keegan. The whole point was the experiment. That *thing* is a learning machine, as are you," said Bosch, "and as the events have proven today, a damn fine one. Both of you went in there 'cold' — without any sense of what awaited — and yet teamed up to achieve a better result. What we want to learn next is whether that can be replicated. I think it's best Agents Keegan and Noritz and I take a walk. Dr. Modi, will you bring TAMS to join us?"

As they left the room, Noritz gave Keegan a look that communicated she better do whatever the hell the deputy director planned and keep her mouth shut as she did.

The walk began silently, leaving the detention cell area and moving out into the mall's atrium. It was all bathed in a pale undersea light due to the green film that had built up on the skylights above. The atrium's planters were empty and a lack of any trash inside spoke to the austerity of the highly automated DSDF.

Bosch began again, speaking directly to Keegan. At that level, a deputy director didn't care about the minor difference in ranks between Noritz and Keegan. They were both simply movable parts in the bureaucracy to him. Noritz's face stayed the same, but Keegan knew him well enough to know that was killing him inside.

"Agent Keegan, I have a proposal for you, which will take you off this case but potentially be far more important to the Bureau."

She nodded warily. Reppley had been her collar, so she already felt possessive toward the case. It also had the promise to be her biggest yet at the Bureau.

"What you and poor Mr. Reppley met today is a product of the defense industrial complex, which Congress in its infinite wisdom has given to us to test out in a new setting. As I understand from your service jacket, you served in the Marine Corps and worked with unmanned systems there."

"Yes, sir. I was an MP, but in the Corps, we all fight. Every squad has a designated squad systems operator. That was my task; basically the robot wrangler for the unit, handling ground systems to hunt IEDs and launching microdrones to scout convoy routes. But nothing of this type of sophistication."

"Well, among the field agents in the Washington Field Office, that still makes you one of our top experts. I assume that is how our algorithm made the match. Correct, Dr. Modi?"

"Yes, sir," Modi replied. "We matched a variety of factors, from experience to past case history, but that stood out." As he spoke, the robot from the room appeared from the detention center hallway. Keegan noted that its steps were actually quieter than a human's on the old shopping mall's floor tiles, likely the same rubber material as its fingers muffling the sound.

She pegged the system at 5 feet tall exactly, 9 inches shorter than she was. As she expected, its human form on top was matched by two legs; anything else likely would have been perceived as too monstrous, moving from the uncanny valley into the scary. That didn't mean its designers had bound it to human limits, though. The hip and knee joints were both circular, akin to large ball bearings, that would allow pivots in multiple directions, but pulled by animal-like tendons likely controlled by bio-inspired AI algorithms.[13] Similarly, it had feet and toes, but the feet had another ball bearing joint, where the human foot would have had an arch, and the toes splayed out at an angle to address the balance issues that had plagued the early unmanned systems. It was a meld of evolution and engineering.

"Ah, here it is," said Bosch. "Agent Keegan, meet TAMS, your partner in this little experiment. TAMS, introduce yourself."

The robot's head turned toward Keegan and Noritz with a faint whir of servos. "I am a Tactical Autonomous Mobility System — TAMS for short," said the robot. "It is a pleasure to meet you."

"Quite the technology, sir," said Noritz. He stepped closer to the robot, peering into its eyes. Keegan's assessment was far less romantic: *It should be a quadruped.* The best bots she'd worked with in the Corps had four legs; they could lose one and still move. The only downside of the doglike designs was Marines got more attached to them.[14]

Bosch began to walk again and the four followed, the machine just slightly behind. "TAMS was originally developed for a joint DARPA and HSARPA program at the end of the last decade. Then the contractors got involved. However, for all the excitement and cool marketing clips on YouTube, it never made it across the proverbial 'Valley of Death' in contracting, from prototype to program of record. Contrary to all the movies we grew up with, it turns out that Terminator robots weren't the future of war."

"Yes, sir. We figured that out pretty quickly. Bigger bot is just a bigger target with more to break," said Keegan. "We needed them to do things and go places that humans couldn't, not just recreate something the military could already force a warm body to do."

"However," said Bosch, "while the military may not have wanted it, there is no such thing as a sunk cost in government programs, and TAMS here has some important fans on the Hill."

"From, let me guess, the Bay Area?" Noritz said, trying to get into the conversation.

"More important," answered Bosch. "The land of the Appropriations Committee. The result is that we are now examining TAMS's suitability in federal law enforcement agencies. In addition to the Washington Field Office, eleven other Bureau field offices will be deploying the system on a provisional basis. This, as I am sure you have deduced with your keen human powers of observation, is where we hope that you come in."

"You want me for a burn-in," said Keegan quietly.

"A what?" asked Noritz.

"Why don't you take this one, bot?" She looked at Modi, who nodded his head in assent.

"TAMS," Modi said. "Tell Agent Noritz what a 'burn-in' is."

"A burn-in is defined as 'the continuous operation of a device, such as a computer, as a test for defects or failure prior to putting it to use,'" answered the machine.[15] It wasn't much of a trick to recite a dictionary definition, but one thing stood out: Keegan noticed that the machine had taken on a different intonation than in the interrogation room. Keegan surmised it had selected one researched to be best suited for conversing with FBI agents. At least, she thought, it didn't have that annoyingly sexist female voice that all the old personal assistant AIs once defaulted to.[16]

As the robot spoke, they paused in their walk to listen, stopping in front of a high-end kitchen store that had not yet been converted into office space. From the inside, its windows still displayed promotional "Going out of business" signs.

"Yes, a burn-in," said Bosch. "A highly appropriate term. Let me be clear. This test is about finding answers, not about creating a win for some funder on the Hill. What I want is data. I want feedback from the field on whether this technology is good for the Bureau . . . or not."

At the last two words, Bosch made eye contact with her. Was that a signal that, despite what he just said, this test had a right answer, one that ensured the Bureau's human agents had a future, unlike everyone else?

"We really do think, though, that TAMS will help you," said Modi, quickly adding in what he thought to be a helpful caveat, "as an observation and decision aide. What an AI system can bring to an agent are the very same things it brought to a soldier in the field or a stock trader on Wall Street: machine-speed collection, collation, and analysis of information.[17] It isn't about replacing, but freeing up the human.[18] Think of it not as artificial intelligence but augmented intelligence. There's no way any of us can keep up with everything in the feed, the cloud, as well as whatever surrounds you. In turn, you need that data operationalized."

"That's true," Noritz said, weighing in. "Keegan is perhaps my best field agent, sir, but even she is struggling to manage it all. For instance, she had to drop off the net at Union Station."

"Too much feed gets in the way. Those designers and programmers haven't been shot at before, and it shows," said Keegan, irritated that Noritz would say she was struggling. "Sometimes you have to turn it all off and really see what's in front of you. That's how I was able to ID the suspect."

"Exactly," said Bosch emphatically. "That's why we very much hope you will accept this assignment. And while we're testing TAMS units in other field offices, you're here with us, and that means your trial counts in a different way. We need to know if TAMS just gets in the way or, worse, endangers the agent or anybody else. If that's the case, that this machine can't perform properly, then we get our own allies on the Hill to bury the program. So get to know it, and show it how to do the job as you see fit. And stay out of the spotlight."

Keegan made eye contact with Noritz, and could see how much he wanted her to say yes.

"But remember, Agent Keegan," said Modi, "TAMS is a learning system. You can study its capabilities, but you'll be the one who can really show us what it can, and can't, do. In the end, if it fails, it will be in part because of you, that you taught it to. Do you understand that responsibility?"

Before Keegan could answer, Bosch interjected. "Agent Keegan, there's a moment when we fully comprehend what responsibility means in the Bureau. For some people, it's a firsthand ordeal that, if they come through it, is transformational. Others learn it at lower stakes, in the form of a story. When I was in my second year in the Bureau, I had a supervisor who once worked on the security detail protecting J. Edgar Hoover. Mr. Hoover had a lot of enemies and just a few friends. I'm sure you are aware?"

"Yes, sir."

"So my guy's the junior agent on the detail, fresh-faced and all that, and they're on the road, in New York City at some midtown hotel. The detail is staying two rooms down from Director Hoover's suite. Never the one beside it; that's for the associate director, what my old job was called back then."

Keegan had heard all the rumors about the FBI's first associate director, Clyde Tolson. Where was Bosch going with this?

"So the security detail is sitting down to eat room service, big steaks and ketchup, or whatever unhealthy crap they ate back then, when the fire alarm goes off. But no smoke. No fire trucks. Nothing. They gotta assume it could be anything. Maybe a Mob or Commie hit on the director, the alarm a distraction. So they bang on the door, but no answer. They gotta make a decision. So they use the master key to let themselves in, prepared in that instant to lay down their lives for the one man in the country who stands between Democracy and tyranny. But when they get inside, there's no Bulgarian hit squad or mafioso assassin with piano wire. It's just the director and Tolson in pink dressing gowns, painting each other's toenails, while a Nina Simone record blares on the hi-fi.

"Now, you see, things like that were frowned on back then. This was a big fucking deal. Hoover's blackmailing a good 10 percent of Congress at the time just for being gay and here he was. And so, my guy's got another choice to make. They may have something now on the director. But J. Edgar sure as hell had something on every single one of them, otherwise he wouldn't have let them anywhere near his security detail — some affair they were having he could rat to their wife, some crooked real estate deal that would put their father in jail, whatever.

"So, they're easing their way back out, quiet like under the cover of the fire alarm, discretion being the better part of valor. But then, they actually do smell smoke. There really was a fire. Somebody passed out in bed with a lit cigar three floors down. So they bang on the door a second time. No reply. This time, they kick it in, but wait a beat to give the two of them time to at least put their nail brushes away, give 'em at least that. Then, they politely inform the director that he's gotta change quicker than Clark Kent and they bundle the two of them out of there, down into the parking garage, and then out the building.

"A few hours later, they're set up at another hotel and life seems to be back to normal, no one saying a thing about it. But then the associate director comes to my old boss, as he's the junior guy on the team. Says he left something back at the first hotel, and would my guy be willing to go back and get it for him. You know what it is?"

Keegan didn't answer, knowing he wanted to say it.

"It's the nail polish. He's either testing out his loyalty now or he just really likes that color. Either way, my guy's got another choice that he did not expect he'd ever have to make as a G-man. So, the thing is, my old boss would never end the story by telling what happened next or even what color the nail polish was. Every damn time, you know what my old boss would say at the end?"

"No, sir."

"'That's when I learned that, in the Bureau, you'll always have career-defining decisions to make. And every single time, the Bureau trusts you'll make the right one for it.'"

BALLSTON NEIGHBORHOOD

Arlington, Virginia

Keegan stood outside the door to her condo, just listening. She rested her forehead gently on the thick wood, closed her eyes, and slowly exhaled. Finding a moment to collect herself before she passed between the two worlds she lived in had become ritual long ago. Leaving in the morning was often early, and done in the dark. She became an FBI agent in those moments, really before she was fully awake. Coming home was sometimes too jarring. She'd learned she had to first catch her breath and give herself time to become a mother — and a wife, whatever that meant now. For a few hours, at least before returning back to the darker places, this was to be where the better angels of her nature prevailed.

Beyond the door was Haley, her four-year-old daughter, and Jared, her husband of seven years. That she knew. But which Jared would it be tonight?

Haley's laughter could be heard through the door, which was likely not a good thing.

Still propped against the door, Keegan swiped down, the various apps displayed on her Watchlet spinning around her wrist like an old-school slot machine until they landed on what she was looking for, a personal app she'd added. It showed a camera view from a mantislike insect bot that lived atop a bookshelf.

She pressed down on the screen and the app expanded to a full-wrist view. She zoomed the shot to see what exactly Haley was doing.

Haley was making her Barbie doll dance along the edge of the kitchen table with a gray spiderlike bot about half the size and made of builder blocks.[19] Whatever imaginary hijinks the two of them were up to, it was making her squeal with laughter, which always revealed the dimple on her left cheek.

God, she loved that girl. They certainly hadn't mixed up the babies at the hospital. Haley had her blue-green eyes, Jared's curly blond hair, her own mom's earlobes, and Jared's mom's small pug nose. Haley also seemed to have inherited his side of the family's build; she was already tall for her age, which was making it more and more difficult to pick her up and carry her to bed.

But as much as she loved Haley, she hated that doll. Both she and Jared had pleaded with Haley to get something else, something less cliché. But before a tense visit to her in-laws in Philadelphia, they'd promised her a doll for good behavior. Barbie had been what Haley had chosen after playing with an old version at her grandparents' house. At least they'd been able to steer her to the astronaut version, though Keegan doubted that anyone with an actual astrophysics PhD would have chosen such an unsuitable hairstyle for a life of helmets and zero-gravity environments.

Keegan panned the camera to track what was going on in the rest of the room, to see where Jared was while Haley played.

She needn't have bothered, as he was in the same tangle of blankets on the couch that he always was when working on the HIT. "Human Intelligence Task" is what they called it, a marketplace of virtualized micro-jobs that machines couldn't do.[20]

She zoomed the shot in. The VR rig covered his face, so she couldn't see his expression or any part of his hair for that matter. He kept it shorter now than when they'd first met; it was easier, with the helmet, plus it meant that the white hairs starting to pop up along his temple blended in with the blond and were almost imperceptible. What she could see was that Jared's neck muscles were visibly tensed under the weight of the helmet. How many hours had he been hitting it today? Three? Ten? The incentive-based nature of it made HIT a perfectly addictive way to help and harm your family.

Keegan watched her husband for a few more seconds, how the weaving of his VR visor had a pattern to it, the slightly exaggerated movements of someone in conversation, when no one was actually in the room with them. The bot did not provide her any audio, but she had listened in on enough of these sessions to know that he was pretty good at it. He had that blend of intelligence and deference that peppered his speech from years of good schools, making him helpful and engaging, but not too pushy.

They were lucky in that and a lot more, she knew. Thank God when Haley was born they'd been covered under Jared's healthcare plan back then. There was no way Uncle Sam's HMO would have paid for the polygenic scoring that allowed them to turn off the genetic trait that would have given her Type 1 diabetes.[21]

And Haley was a happy kid; they'd been able to shield her from most of the changes at home, though she occasionally still cried at night for their nanny. Letting Sandra go had been tough on her, mostly because it was hard for kids to figure out that difference between natural and paid family members.

Luckiest of all, they still had Keegan's job, which meant they hadn't had to downsize out of the only home that Haley had ever known. When she and Jared had started dating, her new job as an FBI agent was a source of curiosity and even cool factor to his law-school buddies. No mention was made of the salary, which was probably a source of amusement to people making seven or eight times as much. Now it was steady income coveted by those same lawyers, reduced to pyramid sharecar syndicates or micro-moment legal work, trying to run up their billable seconds for Mexican pharma companies, all to just cover the interest payments on their credit cards. And that was for those lucky enough to still be in the profession — unlike Jared.

He had been on the partner track for financial sector regulatory contract advisory work, a part of law that was boring as hell but lucrative. That all changed when the firm brought in a "human performance potential" advisory firm. It had initially been hired to find efficiencies, but the monitoring doubled as human training for the machine learning systems, their algorithms getting smarter hour by hour, client by client.[22] Within three months he was fired, as were 80 percent of the junior staffers. The senior partners took a share of the algorithm itself, which would transcend the firm and potentially create generational wealth.

They cut Jared out of all of it. Not just the money, but the deal. That was what had been so hard for him to take, and so hard for her to watch.

This was not how it was supposed to work. That job had been the fulfillment of a lifetime of promises made to him by parents, teachers, loan officers, and more. Study hard, get good grades, go to a good school, and then repeat until you end up with a good job, where you work hard, get a good salary, and send your kids to a good school to repeat it all again. That had been the deal literally for generations. Automation had always seemed a problem just for truck drivers or factory workers, until suddenly it wasn't.[23] It turned out that not even a Yale Law degree could compete with the algorithms.

It was not even a partner or the human resources department that had made the decision to fire him, versus the lucky 20 percent the firm had kept on. The "workforce optimization" was decided by the algorithm, and even the termination letter automatically written and emailed.[24]

Somehow, that cold, dispassionate decision made Jared blame himself more. It wasn't someone else's fault, so it had to be his own. The first thing Jared said when he learned he would lose his job was "I should have been a trial lawyer." Of course, that was no refuge either, as algorithms had cut a swath through that field as well. Predictive analysis meant that both sides knew the chances of success, making it folly to go through with a prosecution or lawsuit; you could just run the numbers and calculate the risks and investments of a pretrial settlement.[25]

Keegan thought about the honeymoon they'd taken to Glacier National Park, just after he'd passed the bar.[26] They'd spent nearly every meal and hike planning their future — jobs, work, houses. Not once had they talked about staying together just for their daughter and Jared spending his days as a remote companion to the elderly.[27]

The fall had been hard, but they hadn't lost everything, unlike so many people they knew.

Within two steps inside the door, Haley slammed into Keegan's legs at full speed, that perfect kind of collision fueled by beautifully raw emotion.

"My butterfly," said Keegan, unlocking Haley's tight grip to scoop her up in her arms. "Missed you."

"All day, Mommy?" Haley said.

"All day," said Keegan.

"Every hour?" said Haley.

"Every single one," said Keegan.

"Each minute?"

"All of them. Until now," said Keegan. In the moment she held her girl in her arms, Haley's head tucked into the crook of her neck, she felt a disorienting loss of connection to the adult things that had occupied her mind. Here and now, she was only Haley's mother. She swayed slightly, taking a slight step back, before she opened her eyes again to the world.

Today, Haley had double French braids. "I love your braids," Keegan said.

"Daddy did them this morning."

She had to give Jared credit. There was no way she could have done that. "Beautiful." Keegan ran her hand along Haley's head, glad her daughter was oblivious to what it'd taken for her father to become so expert at doing her hair.

"He says it's to make me look like a Jedi."

"You do. We'll go find your lightsaber."

Finally noticing her entrance, Jared waved toward Keegan, while murmuring into the helmet mic. It was probably Harlan again, a centenarian from Portland, Oregon. He had started out giving Jared top scores and then moved on to requesting him specifically, which was a nice 5 percent bump in Jared's cut of the fee.

The system could be automated with a synth voice, but there was a reason wealthy clients paid to have a real human engaging and monitoring their loved ones — all the studies showed that the autonomous aids, like the robotic-arm feeding system that Harlan's kids had equipped his kitchen with, were not enough.[28] They needed human interaction; even the simulation of it was not enough.

Keegan set her daughter down. "Let me check in on Daddy," she said to Haley. "I'll be right back."

She sat down heavily next to Jared and tugged away a couple of the blankets, a subtle indication that it was time to get up and join her and Haley.

Jared flashed two fingers, indicating two minutes, which really meant double that. So Keegan got up to see what world Haley had created today for her dolls to play in.

Haley showed off her dolls, and let the spider bot crawl on her hand and arm the way Keegan had once let a tarantula walk all the way up her shoulder in high school. But as Haley babbled on about Barbie and the spider's adventures, Keegan kept sneaking peeks over her shoulder at Jared, waiting for him to get up off the couch. On a good day, he'd come right over and start talking in a silly high-pitched voice, adopting the personas they'd given the dolls. Today was not going to be like that, Keegan could see.

She put an old cartoon on the wall projector to keep Haley occupied and went into the kitchen to get dinner going. *Kratts' Creatures*, the same show she'd watched as a kid — at least she could tell herself she was doing the minimum a good parent would do, by making her daughter watch something slightly educational.

She messaged Jared using the touch screen on the freezer door.

U ready yet?

He responded with an emoji: a sack of money.

JUST 5 MORE, THEN DUN

He'd left the caps lock on, like it was important to shout.

Two minutes had become five minutes in one minute. While she tried to figure out how to respond without it escalating into another fight, she simultaneously pulled up the freezer screen to scan the contents, reordering the tabs to prioritize oldest first. It was one of their little daily battles. Jared always left dinner to the default meal of the day, delivered by drone to the rooftop and paid for through his work account.[29] The daughter of a single mom who often worked late, Keegan instead liked to scavenge, building an entire meal off the first ingredient she found in the fridge.

And tonight that was a bag of frozen synth shrimp from Tennessee. Well, that decided it.

She pushed a screen grab of the shrimp bag to Jared's screen.

Fancy seafood dinner awaits

He sent back a thanks emoji and

CALL ME WHEN YOU GET REAL SHRIMP

Then the real reason:

JUST NEED 3 MO +++ TO GET DAILY PRIME . . . $600

Dammit. Three more micro-likes with Harlan could take twenty minutes, maybe more. What would it take: a leading question about a granddaughter in Phoenix, the one who had not been outside in ninety-four days due to the heat? That really was the game, Keegan thought. In many ways, Jared's legal job had been good prep for this — not just the long hours, but the whole essence, which was to keep the client happy while not actually speaking your mind.

But a prime so big also meant Jared had been grinding hard all week, keeping Harlan happy while tabbing his blood pressure, EKG, stool metadata, and who knows what else.

Just not tonight. Not after the day she'd had. Not after Union Station. Not after the Dizz-Diff interrogation and that robot.

Need u to wrap up. We promised to try to do more dinners together for HaleyGirl.

A quick reply:

ALMOST DUN . . .

Keegan slammed the freezer drawer. Then she called out to Haley to come over to the dinner table, trying to keep the anger out of her tone. It didn't work. Hearing her voice, she cleared her throat. A long exhale, then silence, as she froze in that state between absolutely losing her shit on Jared and the self-control she'd developed as a Marine to lock down your emotions when things went south.

Haley tugged on her pant leg. "Is Daddy coming to dinner, or just us?"

Keegan felt her eyes well up, and she looked away. "He's coming. But you gotta help me cook it first, silly!"

It was in these little moments that she tried to reconnect with Haley, to make up for being at work so much. Jared had her all day, which was maybe why he didn't mind the missed meals.

"OK, but I don't know how."

"I'll get a pan," said Keegan. "You get the shrimp out of the freezer drawer. The silver bag."

"I know what a shrimp is."

They prepared the dinner together, a simple meal of shrimp, a bag of microwaved rice, and fresh broccoli that had been delivered that morning to the building's roof pad. No sauce at all for Haley's portion; Sriracha and honey sauce for the adults.

Keegan and Haley sat down to eat, setting a place for Jared. He remained on the couch. Keegan watched him, noticing the awkward angle of his neck from wearing the VR rig too long. It was going to leave another ache there, another price to be paid. She felt sympathy, love, and resentment all at once, a disorienting sensation that made her reach out and hold Haley's hand and bring it to her lips.

When she looked up, Jared was standing over them with a careful grin. A former shooting guard for his high school basketball team, he was six foot four, tall enough in the way that naturally inspired confidence, but not too imposing. He still had some vestiges of a basketball player's physique, but ever since he'd been laid off, his weight had yo-yoed. First, he'd treated the time off as an opportunity to get fit in a way that he hadn't been able to when on the partner track, and he'd thrown himself into training for a triathlon with the same energy that he had finding new work. Along with a paleo diet, he'd become almost gaunt. But as what had seemed like a useful sabbatical instead dragged into months with no new job offers, he'd picked up the HIT jobs to fill the gaps. Time offline, at the gym or the trail, now competed directly with online time tracking and max score incentives.[30] It was much the same with his time with Haley; every minute doing something with her was a minute away from doing something that could provide for her.

Jared leaned over, gave Keegan a hug, and whispered, "Sorry that took so long. He's gone down for a nap. Gimme a sec for a bathroom break and I'll be right back. Actual promise this time."

As he went down the hallway to the bathroom, Keegan smiled at Haley's excitement that her dad was joining them, as if her cooking had been the key. Keegan poured him a glass of white wine, leaving only a finger of the glass unfilled. And then he returned and was present, truly there, beaming with pride that he had earned the $600 prime.

It was halfway through the meal, while Haley was messing up retelling one of the jokes from the cartoons, that Keegan noticed Jared hadn't touched his wine.

And then it clicked — the bathroom visit. All it took for him there was two quick sprays. Left nostril. Right nostril. Faint vanilla taste at the back of the throat as the Dilaudid aerosol quickly did its work, one targeted molecule at a time. And ninety seconds later, he was his old self again, at least for the next few hours, until he fell asleep. What was it that had decided it for him? The neck pain? The shame? The boredom?

She knew they should talk about it. Even with the positive shift in Jared's mood, the toll was obvious — dark circles under his blue eyes and pale skin. Keegan thought of getting him a sunlamp but knew that it would just make him angry, resentful of her aid. Maybe his employer's algorithms would pick up on it and send him one, just like they had sent the iron supplements.

But it was not worth opening up that wound tonight, at least not in front of Haley. And so Keegan said nothing, no matter how much anger she felt. She wasn't just angry at what he was doing to himself; it also felt like a betrayal. Jared knew that her mother had gone down that path with oxy, working her way through five different doctors to keep getting prescriptions, until they'd had to literally lock her in her bedroom to get her off the stuff. Now he was doing the same, the only difference being he was getting his diagnoses and prescriptions from a virtual physician's assistant.

"Good day? Bad day?" Jared asked, oblivious to how she was seeth-ing inside.

"You really want to know?" she said.

"Sure," he said.

"I got to play the hero today, and as a reward, they offered me . . . a new partner."

"What'd you do?" he asked. It was a reminder as much as a ques-tion: *Don't be careless with your life . . . and your job. Don't be careless with our life.*

Haley started to play with the Lego bot in her lap; she often did it when talk at the table turned tense.

Keegan bristled at the implied doubt in his question. "Had a big collar today. But they want to take me off the case to work with a new agent. It'd be a training gig, but it's one the higher-ups care about."

"Getting noticed like that sounds good," said Jared, his voice de-volving back into that familiar tone of someone with a better job, who was patronizing the other's work — another side effect from the drug's memory hit. *Or is it what he really thinks, even now?*

"I've not decided yet. Lots to mull over. And it doesn't guarantee a promotion, if that's what you're hinting at."

"Still. If it's something the bosses want, makes sense to do it. As long as you don't let the partner steal any of the credit."

Keegan considered, just for a moment, whether to tell him that her new partner was more like the bot in Haley's lap than any of the hu-mans at the table. But she could tell Jared was feeling good tonight, proud, so she just agreed.

He watched, seemingly to see if she was going to add anything fur-ther, then changed the subject, a ball of energy aching to talk to some-one other than an old man 3,000 miles away. "Hey, did you see what happened in Indianapolis? Unbelievable."

Jared had taken to watching a picture-in-picture screen of his so-cial feed during work. It was something to keep his brain busy during the dull parts of the day. But like so much else, the constant flow of news, rumors, arguments, jokes, and memes had become a kind of addiction.[31] Each day, he'd ask Keegan about something trending, then be surprised that someone working in the FBI wasn't as up on the details as he was. It made Keegan doubly glad of the Bureau's policy of freezing social accounts. Defense lawyers using AI to scrape agents' past words to try to show their bias had cost too many convictions.

"No," Keegan replied. "I got sucked into all these new work issues. What happened?"

"You gotta see it." He waved his hand to pull up the feed on the wall screen, and narrated as it played. Her eyes darted to the corner to validate that it had the blue watermark, to confirm it wasn't a deep fake.[32]

"OK, this is an air conditioner factory, right? They were going to botomate the place in a couple months. So at the morning shift, here come the workers, but see how they're all carrying sledgehammers and blowtorches like it's some old-school factory? There's the shift whistle, and they just go to town, smashing everything. It's the whole workforce, so it's not like the bosses or security guards can stop them. And that's the thing that made it go viral. See how they don't even try to hide their faces? No masks, nothing. A few were even wearing VR rigs and put it up online, so you can experience it yourself."

Keegan was suddenly aware that her daughter had also just watched the footage. She tried to turn it into a teaching moment. "Haley, would you break your old toys if we said we wouldn't give you any new ones?"

"No, but you might need to reprogram them if I wasn't getting any more, so they wouldn't get bored of me."

Keegan raised her eyebrows, and Jared laughed.

"That's my girl! Good answer. Go play in your fort while Mommy and I finish dinner."

Haley quickly scooted away. As soon as she crossed the imaginary line her parents had programmed for the boundaries of her play area, her teddy bear, "Baz," purred to life. Short for "BaZooKa," the main character in one of Haley's favorite shows, the toy had plush orange fur, which doubled as crash padding, and blue insectlike wings that had embedded rotors covered by wire mesh to keep tiny fingers intact. The bear took flight and hovered 18 inches away at waist level, ready to follow Haley's every move. The pre-programmed boundaries kept the machine from getting in the way in the kitchen, as much as they gave Haley her own space.

Bounded by a dollhouse and a pair of oversized stuffed giraffes, the play area in the far corner of the living room shielded Haley from the wall screen that listened to conversations and used biosensors to determine what programming to put up next.[33] It pivoted off discussions, providing fodder for one side of an argument; other times, it would just inject a new topic determined from their profiles. She and Jared had been leery about it at first, but it provided them with something to talk about as their conversations grew more difficult, which was something else left unsaid.

The one thing they had agreed on was that Haley should be left out of the system until she turned ten. You could "program out" the voice and bio-cues of a minor, but Keegan didn't trust it. The companies were always trying to fine-print the privacy opt-outs through the automated upgrade agreements. Though by hiding Haley, the sensors could potentially push inappropriate programming the system thought Keegan would react to, like combat-cams from Somalia, but better that than even more steered stimulation at such a young age.

The subtraction of Haley increased the detected level of interest in the topic among the remaining humans, and the newsfeed automatically played the next item in the feed. Selecting the perspective to take based on Jared's psychological and political profile, it played a reaction piece from Senator Harold Jacobs from Ohio. Rather than the typical authenticating self-broadcast from a kitchen or diner, Jacobs had projected himself onto the factory floor, serene, as the destruction took place around him.

"I will never condone violence, ever, but these Americans in Indiana are no different than a previous generation of heroes who defiantly threw British tea into Boston Harbor. They are patriots wag-

ing a righteous fight. This is not just about metal-collar jobs. This is about standing up for something — our right to pursue happiness on terms we all expect. They fight for all of us."

"They don't fight," said Keegan, playing with the last shrimp on her plate before carefully spearing it. "They beat up some machinery. In a fight, someone fights back."

"Some global elites, who never set foot in the communities they want dominated by machines, they think they can buy them off with promises of GBI and free money. No, they have the right to work and will fight for it."

"This guy makes no sense. Now the factory is broken, and with no GBI, they'll get nothing," Keegan said.

"At least they did something," Jared replied. "Damn machines are taking everything. If it keeps up, there'll be nothing but bots and their few gajillionaire owners. How do they think people are going to afford whatever they make?"[34]

On cue, the screen narrative shifted to stimulate what it had determined was a brewing debate between the couple over GBI, the proposed Guaranteed Basic Income program.[35] In this case, the screen filled with a high-resolution image of Willow Shaw — close-cropped silver hair, tan skin, a form-fitting long-sleeved black T-shirt that stopped at the forearms, where e-ink tattoo panels swirled like darting tropical fish whenever he gesticulated with his hands. He had the look of somebody who spent their days outdoors, a high-mountain guide's placidity and openness in his smile.

"I don't think we should blame these workers, but help them."

"Ugh. Not that guy again," said Jared. "As if being everywhere in the net wasn't enough, now he's all over the feed too."

Shaw was the most visible face in the new industry that had taken off in the wake of the last market crash. If the previous generation of tech behemoths had been about unleashing information, Shaw's company KloudSky was about its intelligentization.[36] The combination of mass data, cloud computing, and AI not only had created new market efficiencies but entire new marketplaces, such as letting companies bid in real time on mid-modal drone delivery opportunities for shopping rush-hour commuters. His firm took a slice of each and harvested even more data.

> *"What happened in Indianapolis shows that we're not doing enough. The question of our modern world isn't whether automation is coming or even whether it will bring benefits.[37] We know that it will. The real question is whether those benefits will be distributed beyond the lucky few like me. The work of SANE found that there is so much we can do to change the way we do business in America, but we have to be sure to never lose sight of the values that make all of that change possible."*

"SANE. I still can't believe they called it that," Jared continued. "It's such obvious marketing."

Little known outside Silicon Valley a few years ago, in the last year Shaw had taken on a more public role as a member of the White House task force known as the SANE Commission, short for the Study of Alternative and Novel Economics.

"Yeah, but it works," replied Keegan. "Like 'pro-life' or 'metal-collar job,' even if you know what they're doing, the term still conveys a certain point of view every time you hear it."

> *"That means understanding at the most human level that our basic desires are shared, they are universal — to be safe, supported, and productive members of society. Losing your job should not mean losing your future."*

"Oh, I know that. I can respect that. But it still grates on me. Kinda like that forehead of his."

They both knew he was being petty, but the very image of Shaw offered Jared a convenient target, a veritable human embodiment of the change that he wrestled with every day from the couch. You could be mad at a company, but it was easier to hate a person.

> *"Technology is not destiny.*[38] *AI's impact on the American worker will be decided not by AI, but by us . . . by the policies that we vote on and the organizations we choose to build . . .or not. We can take advantage of the new opportunities provided by this new economy. Or we can miss this closing window to create shared prosperity for all."*[39]

"Yeah, it's a bit too smooth," Keegan said, trying to make peace. "Might be from those nanomites that the viz stars and billionaires are injecting to combat aging."

The second she said it, she regretted it, realizing they'd soon be peppered with skin care and aging ads.

> *"People may think that the SANE Commission is coming up with something new here, but there is little that is more baked into our very history as a nation. Indeed, guaranteeing someone a basic income in a time of tech change was first written about by Thomas Paine, the very man whose ideas helped inspire the American Revolution.*[40] *Today, in a new Industrial Revolution, we need that same kind of bold thinking—"*

The buzzing of Jared's Watchlet marked a pop-up notice breaking into the feed. Thousands of miles away, an elderly woman was stirring in her bed in a first-floor bedroom in a Craftsman bungalow and would soon need a reminder about her medicine. That would be another rewards opportunity for Jared. If he was back online before the actual client request for assistance came in, then it would be another prime.

"Back to the coal mines," Jared said with a smile, and stood up. He couldn't help himself, she knew. It wasn't the drugs, but how he was wired. For all of the talk of giving people some kind of guaranteed income regardless of whether they worked, some people were defined by it. They drew who they were from it.

Shaw continued:

> *"There's no fighting change. We have to embrace it or lose everything."*

Keegan nodded at Jared and switched the screen off. She leaned back in her chair and took a sip of wine, staring at how the liquid took the shape of the glass, adjusting to whatever environment it found itself placed in.

Jared headed over to the corner, to where Haley had already fallen sleep, curled up on a pillow with her toys laid out in front of her. He gave his daughter a kiss on the forehead and smiled at Keegan. For all their present distance, here was their joint creation. He headed back to the couch and put on the VR helmet, off to chase more primes. That drive was part of what had so attracted her — type A all the way, he'd powered his way through law school and now he'd do the same through whatever came next.

Keegan stood up from the table and knelt over her daughter, who hadn't stirred at the kiss.

"Butterfly, time for bed," she whispered, and carefully picked her up, the girl's warm body slightly moving to rest her head over her mom's shoulder. Carrying her to her darkened bedroom, Keegan tucked her daughter under the covers. Just out of reach, Baz hovered in the corner as it wirelessly charged from its wall-mounted power station — a nighttime sentry that Haley claimed kept away any nightmares. Keegan gave her a kiss on the forehead, just where her husband had, and then placed the Lego spider bot on a shelf across from the bed. She reset its camera to face the girl, her own nighttime sentry for warding off the bad.

Keegan quietly closed the door behind her and checked on Jared, whose head was now bopping back and forth, animated again in conversation with his ward. The hallway, lined with black-and-white photos of her and Jared on vacations pre-Haley, led to the office that had previously doubled as the guest bedroom but now was something more. They'd never really formally talked about who got the master and who got the guest room. It had all started with another of their arguments and Keegan just needing to be alone for a night, not even wanting to breathe the same air as him. And then she'd never gone back. It was easier than having that conversation out loud, which would have made it real, and maybe permanent.

Sitting in bed, she opened her work account on her Watchlet and messaged Noritz: *There's no fighting change. We have to embrace it. Agree to program.*

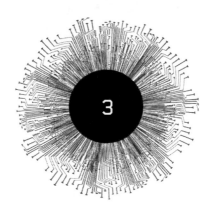

3

FBI ACADEMY

Quantico, Virginia

"We all ready?" Keegan asked the obstacle course instructor. A giant
of a man with jet-black hair and a streak of silver through the middle,
he had a long mustache and a milky white prosthetic eye, as government healthcare did not cover the augmented implants that allowed
a wearer to see. He wore black fatigues that he tucked into his black
boots.

"Course clear. We're green," said the instructor. The man nodded
at Keegan to begin.

Looking out at the quarter-mile sprint obstacle course, its end just
visible in the evaporating morning dew, Keegan instinctively rolled
her shoulders, unconsciously stretching her body at the memory of
having to run it herself years back and, even more, reliving that mental pressure to burn through it so fast so that no man would question
her right to be there. It had been generations since J. Edgar Hoover
had died and women had finally been allowed to attend the Academy
just ten days later. But it still mattered.[1] The same course for everyone
— rope climbs; wooden walls, some you had to climb over, others with
openings designed to simulate a window to go through; the worst
were the monkey bars that individually spun. If you really annoyed
them, the instructors might even grease them with canola oil. While

bringing in as diverse an agent pool as possible was an FBI recruitment talking point, physical fitness was the one place where discrim-
ination was allowed. If the rest of America was losing the war against
obesity and inactivity, then the advantage of being fit and healthy only
increased. And any perceived advantage was as important as any real
edge.

Keegan grew up watching videos of two-legged robots flipping
and jumping through warehouses.[2] She knew that a humanoid robot
could work its way through a set of obstacles like this. That wasn't
what intrigued her. What Keegan most wanted to figure out was how
TAMS would deal with the cognitive, rather than the physical, part.
Machines could handle labeled data and single, structured tasks easily enough. Where they often crapped out was comprehending things
from context only and all the multitasking that went into generalized
learning and interaction.[3] Basically all the things that humans found
easy.

"Good morning, TAMS," Keegan said. At the mention of its name,
the system tilted its head, the physical signal that it was now awaiting
command. It was a response she expected after spending the past several days reviewing its operating manuals and testing reports. What
she had not had time for yet was to configure the bot's user interface
to her own preferences — or, as she thought of it, "the right way."

"Good morning, Agent Keegan," it replied, the eyes lighting up
slightly as it spoke.

"TAMS, in one-on-one communication, no longer use my name,"
Keegan ordered. "Saying it every sentence is wasted words and time."
These critical first steps shaped how the technology would fit her,
rather than the other way around.

"Confirmed," the system replied. The robot's face was blank, yet
Keegan realized that she'd imagined it was making a slightly miffed
expression at being ordered around. Transposing emotion onto the
bot — she'd have to watch out for that.[4]

"So, TAMS, do you know where we are?"

"Yes."

"Where?"

"Latitude 38.53 —"

Keegan quickly interrupted again. "End. Unless numbers requested, provide textual answers." Computers "thought" in terms of numbers, which could quickly overwhelm a person.

"We are at the FBI Academy obstacle course in Quantico, Virginia."

"Correct. Do not tilt you head when awaiting verbal or other commands." She felt herself lapsing into the robotic affect she had used when she was a wrangler in the Marines.

"Understood."

With an exaggerated blink to activate a targeting command on her AR glasses, Keegan tagged the obstacle course's finish point — a rope climb that would test upper body and core strength, as well as mental toughness at the end of the run. "Then get your ass moving, machine. Go!"

Keegan thought it might take the system a few seconds to compute her order, but the bot was a blur of movement. Made sense. An AI was as much a big prediction machine as anything else. TAMS hadn't been there sitting idle, but building scenarios and likelihoods of potential commands that it would receive based on its context.

The other thing that was notable was that the machine didn't go directly to the finish point that Keegan had identified for it, but took off toward the route of the course. It had gauged that the humans wanted it to follow the rules of the environment.

As TAMS took off at a run, Keegan focused first on the feet of the system. The system design was human for interface but had clearly also been influenced by studies of nature. While it had two legs, the bot's spine flexed slightly while it ran. This both balanced its movement as well as gave it more of a recoil from each step — like a cheetah. She'd have to look closer, but they also likely mirrored the animal's retractable claws too, giving it a grip into softer surfaces, like that of a soccer player's cleats.

TAMS quickly made it to the first obstacle, a low wooden log set just above waist level on a human, about chest level on the smaller machine. It was an ease-into-it first waypoint for trainees. There was no pause and the machine didn't go below or around the log; it understood the more advanced rules of the environment's prescribed behavior. Its legs pushed it upward, using both the flex of its joints and a slight expansion of the legs firing like small pistons. The momentum carried it over the log, but at the apogee it touched the log with one hand and pivoted. With hips and shoulders that were fully articulated and a waist that could turn 360 degrees, the robot's moves looked oddly organic — it had not just been building likely scenarios of what it might be asked to do, but was mirroring clips it had reviewed of human trainees on the course. What was not humanlike was how quietly TAMS moved. It was not just that there was no grunting or breathing, but there was also a lack of noise at the contact points. As it made it to the next obstacle, a set of metal bars to swing on, the rubber grips on its hands muffled even that.

Keegan and the instructor ran alongside the robot as it went, Keegan tracking the time and TAMS's power levels on the AR glasses.

"I did it in a minute fifty-two back in my class," Keegan said. "What's the record now?"

"Not bad," said the instructor. "Had a trainee do it in a minute twenty-one just a couple months ago; she was a Ranger, and before that ex-pro CrossFit. Total badass."

As they moved toward the end of the course, TAMS began the final rope climb. When it gripped the rope, it seemed flummoxed, as it swung back and forth in a more random, unpredictable manner. It tried to balance, kicking its feet out in the air like a thrashing swimmer, but that spun the rope the other way. After a beat, it gave up and ignored the spinning, pulling itself up one handhold at a time. It was markedly slower progress than the rest of the rhythmic, gymnast-like movements throughout the course.

TAMS reached the top of the rope and slapped it with its hand; again most likely having scoured video in the cloud, it had figured out that the way you marked your time was to slap the top of the post.

"Time!" said the instructor, standing below TAMS.

"A minute six." He tried to sound matter of fact, but Keegan could sense he was a bit angry that the course record had been broken.

They stood beneath the hanging rope and waited. After a few seconds gawking, the instructor started to laugh.

"Shit," said Keegan, realizing the limits of the programming. TAMS was still at the top of the rope, locked in place, its hands gripping tightly and its feet dangling in the air. This was on her. She had not told TAMS what to do after it achieved the objective, nor authorized it to go beyond. The A in its name stood for "Autonomous," but autonomy for a machine was really just about how much leash the human was willing to give it.

"TAMS. Join us here." Then, worried it might just jump down and get damaged on its very first day, she added, "Use the fast-rope technique." Whether the machine had pulled the meaning from a clip of a firefighter dropping down from a fire station's second floor or of Navy SEALs fast-roping onto a cargo ship's fantail, the effect was the same. With almost no pause, the robot slid down, wrapping its legs around the thick rope to arrest its descent.

"System status report," Keegan said. The robot's diagnostic system projected the bot's internals onto her AR glasses; the layers of circuitry, servos, and batteries were revelatory. The machine was as much a feat of art as engineering, the product of generations of genius coming together. Keegan circled TAMS like a sculptor weighing whether to carve away another sliver of clay. As she examined it, individual systems reported their relative temperatures and performance. The arms were slightly overheated from hanging on the rope, while the legs had returned to normal parameters.

Now, it was time to see how it adjusted. Keegan turned and walked back toward the start of the course. Unordered, TAMS followed, walking slightly behind her, like a servant staying out of the way. Clearly, "join" and human movement trumped the target designation.

"TAMS. I don't want you dogging my heels, where I can't see you. Stay to my side."

The machine adjusted its pace. Interestingly, it chose to go to her right. Chance selection or had it decided based on an observation that Keegan was right-eye dominant?

Keegan asked it a more important question. "TAMS. How much faster can you run that obstacle course with a second try?"

A moment of silence, just the soft footfall of metal on dirt.

"Four point seven seconds," said TAMS.

"Not under a minute?" said Keegan.

"No."

"Why not?"

"The route is not optimized for performance," said TAMS.

"Optimal or optimized?" said Keegan.

"Optimized," said TAMS, which made Keegan stop.

"It is not optimized?" said Keegan.

"What the hell does it mean?" asked the instructor. "Is it some kind of critic now?"

Keegan ignored him, thinking on it. As they reached the starting line, she stood in front of TAMS and bent slightly, speaking at "eye level." "TAMS, nothing will be optimized. Ever," said Keegan.

"Understood," said TAMS.

Under her breath, Keegan muttered, "I'm not so sure about that."

The instructor snorted as he tried to suppress his laughter.

"How will you modify your route?" she asked.

TAMS took a few seconds, then said, "I am unable to provide that information."

"I figured," said Keegan. The machine was trying to figure out how to describe the minute changes it would make, some incomprehensibly small. It probably had the answer, just not the language to describe its process to a human.[5]

"OK, then. TAMS, show what you learned. Do it again."

"Confirmed," said TAMS.

"All clear to start now," said the instructor.

Just as he pronounced the last syllable, TAMS was off, this time without Keegan designating the end point. As the machine reworked its way through the course, Keegan and the instructor running slightly farther behind it this time, she reset the AR history on her glasses to overlay the prior run's track onto her current view. TAMS's second run was not a perfect replica of the first; the tracks — the first in yellow, the second in blue — created a braided ropelike course, almost like a DNA helix weaving through the obstacles.

As TAMS scrambled up the rope, Keegan held her breath until it reached the top, paused, then slid down the rope before landing upright.

"One minute and a half second," said the instructor, his voice more impressed this time around.

"That's really interesting," said Keegan.

"Run it again to see if it can break a minute?" said the instructor.

"Nah, no need," said Keegan. The whole point of these courses was not merely training, but for the trainee to find the limits of what they thought was possible, both physically and mentally, and then push through them. A machine would simply push those limits to their exact breaking point and no further.

"But it would. I'm sure of that," she said.

"How? It said it couldn't."

"TAMS beat its own time estimate in the second run. That means it was learning as it was moving through the course, improving, literally, in midair," said Keegan. "Maybe it can't shave off five seconds on each run, but another second? Give it another bucket of performance data, and it could certainly do that . . . just don't ask it to explain how. Don't think it knows. I sure as hell don't."

"That's fucking scary," said the instructor.

"Scary? Nah. It's basically the same thing your car did on the way here today. Besides, you want scary? We're going to go to the Kill House after this."

FBI ACADEMY HRT COMPOUND

Quantico, Virginia

Sunbeams lanced the finger-sized holes punched in the walls, visible from the dust and powdered plywood that swirled in the dark with the faint breeze. Standing just inside the entry doorway of the FBI

Hostage Rescue Team (HRT) Kill House, Keegan blinked to get her eyes used to the dark.[6] It also made her realize she'd have to go deeper into the specs to see what the bot's visual sensors were able to handle.

"You sure it's OK to be here?" she called out.

The rubber coating on the walls, put there to prevent ricochets, gave the sound in the room a different tone, absorbing the noise of her voice just as they would the energy of bullets.

"For anyone else, no way. But you've got an in with the management." Special Agent Noah Reddy chortled in the distinct way he always did. It sounded a bit like laughing, only inside his Adam's apple.

Keegan had first heard that laugh back in Missouri, when the two of them had been paired up in the military police basic course at Fort Leonard Wood. Even though they had an obvious connection, Noah never once hit on her. She'd respected that, as it had been the last thing she was looking for then. When he'd invited her out clubbing in St. Louis the night of their first leave, she'd worried that it was going to ruin everything but quickly learned he had other plans. "No better wingman than a female friend," he had explained. And they'd watched each other's six from that point forward.

Over a decade later, he had speckles of light gray in his stubble, which meant they were both getting old. But the laugh was the same.

"One of the perks of HRT," Noah continued, "besides getting to actually, you know, shoot the guns, is we get to decide who comes and goes."

"Thanks. I need to keep this between us. I don't want this getting out until I have a better handle on what I'm dealing with."

They could have used Hogan's Alley, the massive 10-acre range that the FBI had built for shooter training, replete with fake office buildings, schools, and even a post office. But today called for something a bit more private, hence the call to Noah for access to the Kill House.

Located in a quiet corner of the Quantico facility, it was where the FBI's most elite squad conducted its riskiest live-fire training — the kind that was increasingly frowned upon by senior Bureau officials in a time when virtual reality weapons training could be conducted with zero chance of injury or death. *Servare Vitas* was the HRT motto. But to "save lives," you had to risk them. Pure digital simulation couldn't prepare you best for the real world, something that applied also to this machine.

Perhaps even more important, the mazelike series of rooms in the HRT's training facility could also be reconfigured into a variety of layouts.[7] For the team, it was to train for a range of different tactical environments, which might be anything from an actual hostage rescue to backstopping a raid on a synth cartel kingpin. For TAMS, it would mean a setting it had never been through before, as whatever layout Noah chose would be a new one. Both Keegan and the machine would be going through blind.

"Important question for you, though," Noah called back, climbing down from one of the catwalks above, from where instructors would typically track the progress of a shooter moving from room to room. "You give your bot a name yet?"

"Technically, it's TAMS," Keegan replied. "No way I'm renaming it."

"You remember how the boots would do that?" Noah said, using the slang for junior Marines who acted as if they were still in boot Camp. "And they'd then start to get feelings for little Scooby Doo or whatever name they gave it, like it was a family pet?[8] One guy in the 3rd even ran out into machine gun fire just to save his robot buddy that had gotten stuck on a berm. Came back dragging the parts all proud, like he should win the Navy Cross for rescuing a fellow Marine."

"Fucking stupid," Keegan said. "No matter what a bot looks like or how smart it gets, it's not a person. Just a tool for a job." She looked over at TAMS to check for any signs of reaction. Nothing. Just quiet observation. "This one's a little bit different, though, you know," said Keegan. "For one, it costs a lot more than anything we had."

"Everything costs more than what Marines get, that's why we're Marines," he said.

"Too true." Keegan had never ceased to be disappointed in the low quality of the equipment she had to contend with in the Corps, even the combat bots. Her idea of military service, fueled by video games, led to a massive shock when she was issued boots that were too big, pants that were too short, and it took days to find extra batteries for her first set of roach bots.

"Your bot's bigger, but not big enough," said Noah. "It's about my son's size."

"Don't you give your kid any milk?" said Keegan.

"No, I don't want him to end up in the Corps like his old man. If he's a runt, then he can go Air Force and just fly drones from the den."

His tone shifted, a sign it was time to go to work as he said, "Keegan, you sure you don't want to just go to the range? Start at 10 yards, work up from there? You know, do this like a normal person would?"

"No," she replied. "We'll work through the course together first, and let it follow along."

"Just make sure your bot stays on the correct side of the muzzle," said Noah.

"You know there're a few people in HQ that I think wouldn't mind that kind of accident."

"Not on my watch," he said. "You did not bring your weird childlike robot here to get schwacked at my Kill House, clear? We're grown-ups now. Mortgages. Kids. We don't do that shit anymore."

Keegan gave him a mock salute but didn't say anything.

Noah walked them back to the start of the close-quarters shooting facility and flicked at a tablet, likely directing the facility to shift a wall or two. Keegan knew him well enough to realize that even giving them that sneak peek at the first room was a misdirect. Would the machine?

Here they stood beneath a cheap wood stall that looked like a fireworks stand. Keegan noted that, with Noah now standing to her right, the robot chose to stand on her left. Somewhere along the way, someone had programmed that human-to-human communication took precedence over robot-to-human positioning.

On a table was a black FBI service-issue 40-caliber Sig Sauer 420, similar to the pistol Keegan wore on her side. It was the same pistol issued to the Army and Marine Corps, but this one had been customized for HRT, with a thumb-sized black targeting pod add-on beneath the barrel and an extended magazine that jutted an inch below the pistol's butt.

Noah pointed at it. "We'll run through with the HRT Sig first." Keegan picked up the new pistol, which synced to her viz once it mapped her palm.

Pistols at the ready, Keegan followed Noah through the open door to the shoot-house.

"TAMS, follow 3 meters behind my movements."

"Understood."

"Yeah, and don't get shot, while you're at it," Noah added.

"You have to begin with its name if you want to give an order."

"Whatever. Just show me what you've forgotten . . . Kill!" he said, Marine lingo for "Let's do this!"

Noah waved his left hand, two fingers making a slight tapping gesture in the air. At that, the room seemed to come to life. Mannequins bolted to cheap autonomous vacuum cleaners started to move. The first room on their left had three possible targets. Keegan quickly noted the weapons silhouette on two of them and moved to fire. But before she could get a shot off, Noah had already fired a double tap into the center of the silhouette. On Keegan's glasses, the target color turned red. She quickly shifted to fire at the second armed target, noting it wore body armor — head shot needed. She fired off a quick shot that clipped the edge of the head, a scratch on the ear at worst, and then a second round through the center of its head. The target turned red as well, while the third mannequin rolled on, an innocent trying to trick them into firing at it.

On and on, room by room, they moved carefully through the building while TAMS followed. Keegan noted that, at every shot, the bot flinched, jerking its head to the right or left, forward or backward, toward the direction of the sound. It was an automated gunshot detection app, giving a visual clue to where the firing was coming from, almost like a pointer dog.[10]

She reached across to touch Noah on the arm, the signal to stop.

"TAMS," Keegan yelled. "Reset to track only non–law enforcement weapons fire."

"Confirmed," TAMS responded, but at the volume of a shout.

Besides the green *concur* sign on her glasses, she'd heard it through her earplugs. Good. The robot had modulated to what it thought the needed volume was. Keegan removed her hearing protection and walked back to the starting point, Noah and TAMS following. Behind them, the target mannequins were now vacuuming up the ejected shell casings.

"Not too bad, Noah," Keegan said. "You do this like it's your job."

"I do mine, so you don't have to do yours. If you ever get in trouble, just dial H-R-T."

"Didn't see you at Union Station."

"Touché," Noah replied. "Let's get the official count." He paused and looked at Keegan as if for permission, gesturing to TAMS with his head.

She nodded.

"TAMS," Noah said, "you poor unlucky machine that has to work with Agent Lara Keegan, who has never been able to shoot straight since her days at Fort Leonard, please provide the range scoring."

"Agent Reddy completed the course with a 100 percent accuracy rate of discharged rounds on target and 94.1 percent in optimal impact areas. Agent Keegan completed the course with 91.4 accuracy rate of discharged rounds on target and 77.1 accuracy rate of discharged rounds in optimal impact areas," the robot said.

"Good of your machine to confirm something we already know, that I'm way better than you," said Noah.

"Let's run it again. This time, I'll use my own weapon," said Keegan, and then with a flourish, "and I'll run it with the bot."

Noah let out a sigh. "That's not a good idea."

"And?"

"You want me on your six?"

"No, I'm good," said Keegan, and Noah headed toward the stairs that led up to the second level of the Kill House.

Back at the wood stall, she put the HRT pistol in her empty shoulder holster and picked up her pistol. It was her Bureau-issue 420 model Sig Sauer. She had modded it with the 3-D printer in the HQ shooting range underneath the old Hoover Building, the grip retextured to her palm, a lighter trigger pull, and a cork-sized compact flash/ sound suppressor, its design inspired by the intricate siphuncles of a nautilus shell. It lacked the refined industrialized aggression of the HRT-model pistol; it was more like one of those fabbed weapons they used to seize from jihadi workshops reeking of cheap Chinese plastic and stale cigarettes.

Keegan put on her AR glasses, synced her pistol, and then paused to pull the left side ear protection off and push it back on again. The last adjustments were more about taking a moment to re-center herself. Then, she turned to TAMS.

"TAMS, follow me, spacing 1 meter," she said, speaking slowly and in as neutral an accent as possible. How many times had she seen a wrangler get into trouble with a bot during combat because the machine didn't understand Texan? "Active target scanning protocol."

As she said the last word, Keegan leaped through the entrance and rolled into the first room, popping up on one knee in a firing position. The room had the same three bots, but repositioned. She aimed at the first target and blasted it with a double-tap shot to the chest and one to the head.

TAMS immediately sent her vizglasses a smiley face emoji as acknowledgment of a hit. She'd have to remember to get it to change that setting. It would be damn off-putting in an actual firefight. More usefully, though, TAMS provided a bright blue X over the unarmed target.

Inside the next room, she engaged the single target as her glasses cued up another on the empty wall, a pulsing red sphere overlaying the rough wood. It pulsed back and forth, but there was nothing there. For a moment, she assumed the feed had crapped out, like it sometimes did.

Then it clicked — the bot was picking up the motion of the targets in the next room. Keegan quickly fired three shots into the ghost on the wall, showering tooth-sized splinters into the air as the bullets punched through. She entered the next room to find a mannequin with three holes in its torso. Noah whistled his appreciation from the catwalk above.

For the next few rooms, she had TAMS take pictures and send them to her vizglasses, so she had a preview of what awaited. Where the walls were cement block and too thick for the acoustic sensor, it used the tiny pinhole camera in its fingertips to peer around the corner. It all felt like cheating, and maybe it was, but it worked, and fair wasn't something that counted in a gunfight.

One level crossed. Now for the next.

Cursing under her breath, she paused in a room that had been set up like a kindergarten classroom for a mass shooting scenario and stood in front of the wooden teacher's desk. She hated these tactical training setups, as did anybody who had grown up going to school each morning fearful they might never walk out again. It brought back that sense of utter powerlessness you felt during mass shooter drills. Her kindergarten teacher had tried to sugarcoat them by saying it "was just like playing hide-and-seek," but even then they knew.[11]

Keegan motioned for the robot to come stand by her and then conspicuously pulled from her pocket a neon orange plastic sleeve with a bright metal-looking sphere at the end of it. She held it in front of TAMS to allow it to inspect it. "TAMS, identify."

"It is a single-shot Alternative Less-Than-Lethal Weapon System."[12]

It was an ingenious little device that converted a pistol from a killing machine to a hurting one. The ball on the end "caught" the bullet exiting the muzzle, slowing it down by nearly 90 percent, giving it the punch of a beanbag round but the accuracy of a regular weapon. The other catch was that it could only work once; part of the trick was that the ball melded with the round.

"Correct. It is a non-lethal that you are authorized to use." She set the orange sleeve on the table, pulled the second pistol from her shoulder holster, ejected its magazine, and flicked out all the rounds but one. Racking the pistol again, she pulled back the slide twice to ensure there were no bullets in the chamber. Both she and the robot already knew that, but rules were rules. On the third time, she racked it again and locked it, holding it at an angle so both she and TAMS could do a visual inspection to see there was no cartridge that had somehow escaped the last two tries. She clipped the orange sleeve onto the muzzle and slid the magazine back into the pistol. The whole time TAMS observed the process.

"We really doing this, Keegan?" called Noah from above. "We ain't in Saudi anymore. Armed sentry bots out on the base perimeter in a war zone are one thing.[13] But all your robot friend has to do is pinch that ball off and cap you in the back of the head. I don't need the Robopocalypse starting on my range."[14]

"It doesn't need a gun to kill me," Keegan replied. "It could just pinch my head off with two of those metal fingers." She turned back to the machine, holding the pistol out, muzzle pointed down, aimed just in front of TAMS's feet. For some reason, Haley's face came into her mind and she shook her head, clearing the image, then turned the pistol so the butt was facing TAMS. "TAMS, engage secondary targets, standard close-quarters battle training ROE. Confirm?"

"Confirmed." The bot stood stock-still, and then its right hand grasped the gun.

Keegan took a deep breath and turned her back to the machine. It was hard to hear with her ear protection on, but she could swear that she felt the auditory click of the gun's safety.

She burst through the doorframe of the next room, kneeling this time. Two targets — Keegan engaged the first one on the right. Two shots to target center.

TAMS entered the room just behind her, with its pistol extended forward in two hands, the gun at the point of the classic triangular shooting position.

Once inside, the robot transferred the gun to its left hand, to better engage the remaining target from its position at the doorway. Keegan jerked back, surprised at the unexpected movement. She should have known, though, that right or left hand wouldn't matter, and it didn't need the second arm to steady the gun like a human would. The gun fired and a mass of orange exploded on the target's chest, center mass, knocking over the robot target.

"Stand down, TAMS," she said to the robot. The robot engaged the Sig's safety and affixed the pistol to its breastplate, where a magnetic spot held it. The bot's designers had thought of everything.

Noah yelled down from the catwalk overhead. "Holy shit. Never seen that before," he said.

"Me either," Keegan said.

"Would have been useful for us back in the day."

"Maybe," she replied. She could think of scores of Marines who might still be alive with a bot like TAMS, a few of them with names etched on her arms. But it might not have made any difference, either.

"We gotta let it run through totally on its own, maybe do it with something more lethal," said Noah.

"Not going to happen, Noah," said Keegan.

"Aren't you curious? C'mon, we're off the grid here. What do you say, TAMS? How would you like to try?"

"Agent Noah, my security protocols do not authorize any use of lethal weapons, nor non-lethal fire without human authorization."

"And there it is. That's exactly the problem," said Keegan. "Anybody who has to ask to shoot first is going to be too late to take the shot that matters the most."

"OK, then. How about we test it out using wax bullets? Try it versus my guys, instead of other bots. Be useful for us to go against something other than the vacuum family."

"Another time. But I do have something we meat sacks need to talk on, Barney-style," said Keegan. Noah nodded in assent, getting the signal from her use of the Marine term for needing to break down a complex situation, referencing the old children's TV show.

As they exited the Kill House, Keegan ordered TAMS to stay by the entry. She and Noah silently walked to the compound's perimeter. The noise of one of the HRT unit's V-290 Valor tilt-rotors prepping its engines nearly drowned out the conversation — as protected as they could get from audible tracking.

"So what do you really think?" Keegan asked.

"It's damn impressive, and a little bit of a horror show. That thing is nothing like what we had. It's like some evolutionary shit, going from tiny roaches to a Neanderthal, but in like seven years instead of seven billion."

"I think your prehistoric time line might be slightly off, but I get your point."

"So what's the deal, though?" Noah asked. "They really want you to prove we can use that thing in the field?"

"That's the part I'm not sure of. Dep director was giving mixed signals on that. One of those read-between-the-lines conversations."

"Well, watch your ass, both bureaucratically and literally . . . and don't forget what Gunny said was rule number one with bots."

"'Never go into battle with a bot you can't trust and never trust a bot you don't know how to snuff out.'"

As she said it, she patted the Leatherman multi-tool that she always kept nestled in a black sleeve on her belt. She thought of the figurative graveyard of overpriced but undertested bots that had been sent to their unit, and then "accidentally" broken in training or gotten lost in the desert, never to be seen again. Better to force a catastrophic overheating, melting memory chips and batteries into an explosive boil, than risk real lives.

"That's right," Noah said. "If a bot puts you at risk, you put it down. Maybe it overheats, maybe trips down some stairs. No matter what, man before machine."

"Woman," corrected Keegan.

CONSTITUTION AVENUE AND 17TH STREET

Washington, DC

"God Bless America!"

The target fit the profile of the exact sort of human the robot had been programmed to approach. He was an adult male, thus legally authorized to purchase. He was geographically located on the end of the raised island of land that held the Washington Monument, a few feet from the four-lane street that divided it from the next block of land, which held the Lincoln Memorial. This marked him as within the established operating perimeter; after annoying too many White House and congressional staff, the robot had been geofenced to the center rectangle of the National Mall. And in the 103-degree-Fahrenheit weather, the man's posture indicated tiredness, in this case leaning against the aluminum gatepost at the end of the stone wall that ran out from the slight hill on each side of the street.[15] Each of these observed data points indicated decreased human resistance.

"Hello, my friend! Are you a patriot too?" the machine asked. As it rolled closer to the man, it played a warbling, distorted clip of the national anthem.

It was a hybrid-bodied robot, the concept pulled from an old NASA system, now commercialized almost beyond recognition like so much else of the space agency's work.[16] A six-wheeled chassis — the wheels on each side painted red, white, and blue — supported the upper body of an Uncle Sam mannequin. Its mouth only opened up and down, while the voice, designed to sound gravelly, came across more like gurgling from the machine being left out in the rain too many times.

"Yeah, sure," the man replied, closing the lid of a metal thermos in his hand.

It was better to go through the dance, Jackson Todd thought, playing the part both for the machine and anyone watching. Just another wayward tourist talking with one of the robots licensed by the Park Service to roam around the Mall — nothing noteworthy.

"Well, then, I've got something special to show you," Uncle Sam said. "Would you like to see it?"

Todd recognized the simple programming tricks designed to provoke the most basic of human emotions — curiosity and greed, the same algorithm that the Serpent had first used on Adam and Eve.

"Yeah, whatever," he said.

At that, a square aluminum tray slid out from what had been designed to look like the beltline of Uncle Sam, a weathered silver eagle as the buckle. On the tray were seven rows of rolled-up miniature American flags, each row holding seven of the souvenirs.

It was sloppy design, Todd thought. They could have made the tray rectangular, so the flag layout was five by ten. Or they could have kept the square tray and had the flag that the customer bought pop up from the middle, as a sort of prize that completed the set.

"As you can see, there is nothing more special than the American flag," Uncle Sam said. "Would you like to buy this symbol of liberty for only fifteen dollars?"

"Not interested," Todd replied, now truly annoyed.

It was these small details that mattered so much. A single flaw could undermine the most complicated of systems. It was the same with the metal gatepost against which he leaned. The gate served a dual purpose. Set beyond the old stone Lockkeeper's House that marked the edge of the now paved-over canal that had run through Washington in pre-railroad days, it decorated the opening in the slight hill that ran along Constitution Avenue. In the event of heavy rains, it also held the floodgate insert that would block off 17th Street and channel the water safely away.

"I do have an end-of-the-day special, just for you," Uncle Sam said, the human's negative verbal reply taking it down another planned decision tree. "Ten dollars is as low as I'm authorized to go. It will be the best purchase since Louisiana!"

Seeing the Uncle Sam robot mindlessly following its protocols for exploiting human weakness, something welled up inside Todd. He decided the risk was worth it. "I'll take it," he said.

Todd pulled a thumb-sized stick from his pocket. Tapping the machine's pay pad, he debited $10 in Bitcoin laundered from a trading market based out of the Caymans. He'd drop the stick at the steps of the Smithsonian Metro station on his way out. Someone would pick it up and create a whole new trail of purchases through the city. If he was lucky, it'd be a tourist, and the data points would jump across the country, or even the world.

"Now please select your flag, touching the one you want," Uncle Sam said.

Todd stepped closer to the robot, so the tray pressed close between their chests, and he ran his left hand just above the field of forty-nine flags. As he did, his eyes took in the surrounding area, double-checking that no one was near and that the stone wall still blocked the traffic camera on the other side of the street.

"This is the one," he said, pressing the point of the flag located four rows back, one row in. When the tray closed, the empty space would be directly above the robot's recharging port.

"An excellent choice!" Uncle Sam said. With an audible snap, the flag unlocked from its holder. Humans could not be trusted to take more than they were permitted, even the patriotic ones.

Before pulling out the flag, Todd unscrewed the lid of his thermos and poured a tiny amount of liquid into his palm. To any observer, including the robot's own sensors, he was merely washing his hands before handling the flag, either out of respect or sanitary precaution at touching something who knows how many others had grasped before him.

Todd reached down, gripping the flag as silvery liquid ran from the inside of his hand. It trickled along the flag's thin wooden pole and into the holder. As he twisted the miniature flag upward, Todd gave the flag a slight tap on the edge, so the last drops fell into the bottom. There, they pooled slightly into a metallic globule that was already transforming at the molecular level.

"Thank you for making America great," Uncle Sam said.

The tray slid back inside its body and the robot's fate was sealed. As long as the weather stayed humid and above 85 degrees over the next week — now certainties in Washington, DC — the gallium would transform the hard metal of its insides into sheets as delicate as a saltine cracker.[17] Liquid metal induced embrittlement, perfectly harmless to a human, deadly to a machine.

"It's my duty," Todd replied. As the robot rolled away in search of more humans to target, he turned his attention back to the aluminum gateposts.

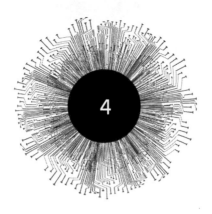

FBI ACADEMY

Quantico, Virginia

Keegan looked at the cup of espresso in front of her, studying the intricate patterns in the crema. She blew on it faintly and breathed in the rich aroma. For thousands of years, she thought, people had done the same at the start of their uncomfortable conversations.

"I guess we should start," Modi said. He opened his eyes, as if seeing the neutral grays of his walls, each holding a beachwood-framed seascape photo, for the first time. At least they were actual black-and-white prints, not those faintly shimmering e-inks normally found in corporate environments, changing images to match the productivity and emotional mandates of the hour.

"Guess so," said Keegan, making a point to look him directly in the eyes. It was not just a challenge but also said she saw through the childish game Modi was playing with his hair. She did note that his eyes were a muted brown, almost nondescript, compared with the shimmer of colors in his coif.

"You like the coffee?" he asked with an easy smile, as if her challenge had been completely expected.

"I'll drink anything, but yeah, this is excellent," she said.

"Kenyan."

His way of signaling that he had read her service jacket. Keegan nodded in acknowledgment.

"So how is it all going?" he asked.

"With the bot?"

"Sure, start there."

She nodded over at TAMS, standing next to the wall, silent. "You want to have this conversation with it in here listening?"

"Yes. Consider these meetings not just a check-in for you, but also for TAMS, and what the two of you make together on your journey toward human-machine progress," Modi said. "That's my role here — taking the two of you and seeing how you can be one. Or maybe it is three to one," he added with a smile.

She sipped the coffee, which tasted of the expensive beans they used to buy before Jared lost his job. "You know that this is something big you've been pulled into," Modi continued. "I know you didn't have much of a real choice. And that's why I'm involved, to be a resource. Because in my experience, when the stakes are high, it can make simple things a lot harder."

"You're just figuring this out?" Keegan replied, raising her eyebrows at the way he emphasized his "experience."

Modi conceded the point with a chuckle and sipped from his cup. He paused, waiting for her to fill the dead space, an obvious tactic of these sessions that both knew he was using.

After ten seconds, she decided to get on with it. "Shouldn't we be drinking bourbon or something if you're trying to get me to spill my guts?"

"More like open your mind."

Keegan grimaced and set down her cup. "You'll have to do better than that."

"OK, then. Tell me about the training so far. I understand you chose to test TAMS out here on the facility."

"Yep. I read all the documentation, but best way to start a burn-in is to see what we're working with, beyond what the designers claim. So we did the obstacle course and some range time."

"And how do you think it did?"

She noted that he asked not about TAMS's performance, which he'd likely already downloaded, but her thoughts on it. "It's got real mobility, especially for urban. Usually you can get a bot this big to work only in a linear way, but it's not like that. But I'm sure you already saw the feeds."

"I did, and I have to say it was exciting, particularly watching it adapt and learn. Was it the same for you?"

"It's quite capable," she said, holding back.

"I wasn't able to track the footage or access metrics from the shooting range, though," he said, tilting his head slightly, as if in a challenge.

Keegan savored the sour bite of the last sip of espresso, now cold. "Yeah, turns out HRT doesn't share its feeds with other offices. Something about operational security, but I think it's just because they don't play well with others."

"So . . . besides the fact that you could do so without prying eyes like mine watching, was there any other reason you choose the Kill House instead of Hogan's Alley?"

"Because not just you, but it" — she nodded at TAMS — "could pull video of Hogan's. A large part of why it excelled at the obstacle course is that it had searchable data of what to expect, what it needed to know. But the world isn't always like that."

"A good reason. How did it go?"

"Seemed to work OK."

"I think we could use a bit more detail than that . . ." he said.

"It helped me clear rooms at a pace I wouldn't have been able to do on my own," Keegan said.

"What about Agent Reddy? Any strong reactions from him?"

"Noah's always been chill. He just rolls with it."

"Nobody with HRT just rolls with it. How about you? Did it change how you viewed TAMS?"

She hoped Noah wasn't going to have to go through a sit-down like this. "Not much. I've seen robots shoot before."

"Not ones with arms and legs."

"True. We had lethal ones on deployment for things like sentry duty and hunter drones you could fire off with preprogrammed enemy vehicle targets.[1] Kept our distance from those, usually. None of them fired so close to my ear, but no surprises." She deflected. "How about you? Do you think the bot should be shooting? Alongside me? Or before me?"

"It is faster, more accurate."

"Sure, it's a helluva piece of technology. But it also got stuck like a kitten in a tree on a simple obstacle course."

"True. But there is a certain beauty in that," Modi replied. "The imperfection, that inability to do something we take for granted, becomes something memorable. In turn, it reminds us that the thing we think is difficult is not hard at all."

Keegan cocked her head. Modi's file wasn't accessible to Keegan, but by the way this conversation was going, it sounded like he had been in graduate school or fellowships while she'd been deployed. On a mission, there was no time for abstract consideration of what it all meant. Instead it was ABC — Always Be Charging. Both yourself and your bots. That was the hard reality, stripped down, like the unrelenting way sand blasted away the paint on even the most up-armored of vehicles. When it was something that really mattered, the test was only whether you and your machine were functional.

Modi noticed the change in her posture. "You seem to disagree. Why?"

Time to change the direction of this.

"Look, I see where this is going. All the wranglers went through SERE," she said, referring to the Survival, Evasion, Resistance, and Escape course that had been developed to help US prisoners of war resist enemy interrogation.

"You're comparing this to torture?" asked Modi incredulously.

"Of a sort, just with good coffee . . . You want hard talk then?"

"It's not about what I want. The most important thing to usable robots is building trust."[2]

She frowned. "Sorry, not going to happen. Machines don't have ethics. They can be programmed to lie and not even know it. And I can lie to a machine and not break a sweat over it."

"No, you're thinking of trust the wrong way," he said. "Trust isn't about morality or emotions. It is about understanding, the person . . . or machine. Trust is simply about acting in an expected manner. I can 'trust' that someone wouldn't lie to me, because I know them. Or I can 'trust' that someone is going to lie to me because they are suspicious of me, just like you did just a minute ago about the range. And what we are working on here, not just you and me, but you and TAMS, is building the understanding that allows that kind of expectation. For this test to work, you two need that kind of trust."

"I'm not sure this bot is ever going to get there. Not just with me, but with anyone. It's capable, but that doesn't make it useful . . . dependable . . . and, however you want to define it, that's also what trust means out there."

Modi nodded. "But it can learn that, maybe, with your help. In many ways, the crossroads we're at with you and TAMS illustrates the journey we're on with AI, going all the way back to Alan Turing's original conception of computation that could unlock the answer to any question."[3]

Some people just can't help but data dumping on you, Keegan thought. She wondered if Modi's problem was hardware or software.

"You talked about the challenge of uncertainty, the unknown," he continued. "But that's what this has always been about with artificial intelligence, even when John McCarthy first coined the term 'artificial intelligence' to describe the strange idea of a computer becoming a thinking machine, even when they were little more than wall-sized calculators.[4] How to handle the uncertainty encapsulated in the questions of how to think, how to act? First, they thought they could do it with raw processing power. The rules are just the engine. Find the rules of how something works, then just crunch out an answer."

"My parents filed their income taxes like that." Keegan tossed it off, mostly to make sure he knew she wasn't going to just sit and listen quietly if he kept lecturing.

"But then they figured out that not everything ran according to a set of static rules, especially anything related to people," Modi said, the pace of his voice increasing. "The more you involved people, the more the rules got complex and even contradictory. The expert systems were only so expert. So training AI instead became about the machine setting priorities and finding and following patterns. It's like how the first driverless cars had to come to grips with incoming data and decide whether to pay attention to the crow eating roadkill or the eighteen-wheeler swerving over the center line. The car had to recognize something in the environment and then respond using a set of prescribed options: stop, accelerate, left, right. The key limit was that it was happening in an environment where there was incredible dynamism but no real adversary, no one operating against it."

"You must have never driven in Boston."

Modi tipped his cup in salute. "That's actually it — facing an adversary is not just what makes an AI more useful in the real world, but it's also how the machine itself becomes more intelligent."

"A revolution from evolution."

"Exactly! AI battling at games of checkers, computers beating humans back before we'd even gone to the moon.[5] Then it happens with chess, a game that most humans can't even master.[6] But then the research field gets stuck in the 'AI winter,' this pause where it seems like the promise of AI is never going to happen, that it's just going to be science fiction forever.[7] But like so much, war solves that technical problem."

"I thought their use in war came later?"

"I meant the war inside the machines, their conflicts of evolution. We figure out the machines can battle inside themselves, running literally millions of tiny experiments that each refine an answer. So you get deep learning, this combination of networks modeled after the neurons in our brain, layer after layer of them firing away in combination and competition."

"We had a substitute teacher that would keep us busy by playing those old history vids. Some smart guy on an old quiz show losing to an AI."[8]

"They always get that wrong. The real turning point was when an AI won at Go.[9] You familiar with it?"

"Yeah, we had to learn about it in adversary training courses in the Corps. It's the ancient Chinese strategy game, like backgammon, but on steroids."

"So an AI beats the top human at Go. It's a big deal, as it was decades before they thought it would be possible because of the complexity of the game. But then the very next version of the AI does so again, this one starting from scratch, just being shown the board and the rules.[10] The machine didn't win because it was faster or crunching more data simulations than the humans can, like they'd already done in chess or the stock market; it was that the machine came up with moves humans hadn't thought of in the over 2,500 years that they'd been playing."[11]

"Which is also what convinced the Chinese to jump so hard into the AI arms race . . .and then sell their versions to any guerilla army with enough yuan," Keegan said.[12]

"But all the gear you dealt with out in the real battlefield was still bounded, like driverless cars reacting as they drive down the street or the player moves on the Go board. A drone or a combat bot had a set area to operate in, a set of yes or no targets. It was adversarial but still kept within certain bounds," he said, bringing his thumbs and pointer fingers together to create a square.

"You and TAMS, though, are in a gray area," he said, opening his hands back up slowly. "Because of how all these advances came together in new ways, it took us back to that original problem — what happens when you combine the old expert systems with all the new approaches?" Modi began ticking them off with his fingers. "Deep learning, Bayesian and evolutionary computing, symbolic reasoning, neural networks modeled on the human brain down to the sub-neuron level via exascale computing but made more powerful than any single brain through synthetic synapses firing literally millions of times faster than the ones in your brain, cross-database access, and cloud-driven insights."[13] At that, he ran out of fingers to list the tech advancements on.

"All to get a supersmart robot that still can't figure out how not to get stuck up a rope," said Keegan.

"Maybe so. All that advancement does is end up at the same place of uncertainty they began with back when they were using slide rules and didn't have the Internet. TAMS has rules to follow, but it also has to sort through limitless data, maybe in a format or type that not just

TAMS but maybe even no human has ever encountered before. And then throw in the variable of the people in our world. Whether it's some car out on the street or a drone missile hunting at sea, its zero or one, human or not, friend or foe. In a law enforcement setting, however, people are potentially adversarial in limitless ways."

"No, it's just as binary as in war. There's us and everybody else. You learn that very early on, literally the first day here at the Academy."

Modi rolled his eyes. "You said, 'It's us or them.' That is a cliché, but what it encapsulates is also one of those simple human flaws of bias that a machine has to learn."

She bit her tongue at that, knowing he was trying to provoke her, another technique she'd learned in SERE.

"Whether it's a positive like common sense or a negative prejudice, machines aren't born with it. Theirs is an artificial and thus learned intelligence. Hell, even the word 'artificial' in AI might be wrong, as it implies something human-made. It's really something beyond that, self-evolving."

"But will it ever learn enough?" Keegan asked. "Sure, you can run millions of simulations with all the variances its cores can handle. But it still might not get the optimal answer for the simple reason that any human intuitively knows you just can't model out every scenario that might happen. There're always blind spots. Which is easy for us to accept, but bots can't."

"TAMS can," said Modi. "If you teach it that. Same as you might a rookie human partner."

"That's where you're wrong," she replied. "Just like 'trust,' 'partner' has a very different meaning beyond the books. TAMS is not a partner, but a technology. The drones that we'd fly out to search for enemy positions were no different than the stone some caveman first picked up. No matter how high-tech something gets, it's just a tool for a job."

"Maybe, but technology is blurring those lines. Take your example of the drone. They may have started out being directed to one target or another, but they evolved, into what were called 'loyal wingmen.' Each version was not just more skilled, but tailored to the human pilot's needs, so that the pilots would eventually trust them to take on threats and jobs that they couldn't handle themselves."[14]

"So, then let me ask you the same question that military pilots would," she said. "If you gave me a human partner instead, do you think I'd be any worse off? 'Cause me being worse off with a human is the only reason to have TAMS instead."

"Well, if you had a human partner, we wouldn't be talking."

"Better off then?"

"That's up to you."

"Maybe we ask the bot?"

"It wouldn't know where to begin."

"Which is my point," said Keegan. "If TAMS can handle the street like it did the interrogation at the Dizz-Diff, then it might be a useful tool someday." She looked over at it, to make sure it didn't get full of itself. "But it's got to be more than that to be a real partner in the way an agent thinks about it. Our job is not just about finding patterns, signals in the noise. It's also about the dog that doesn't bark, to quote the greatest detective of all time.[15] A good agent connects dots that aren't even there. Gaps in information are an opportunity to be creative. That's the difference between a robot being a metal K-9 and an actual partner."[16]

"And that, then, is on you, Agent Keegan," Modi said, as if he had planned for the conversation to get to this point all along. "As I mentioned the first day, it's not about the computing power but the training. *That* is what makes an AI truly intelligent. But that means *you* are going to have to operate differently than you did with robotics in the past. This is a *learning* system. In the Marines, you didn't have any role beyond using the robot as a tool. You'd give it a mission and get out of the way. With a truly intelligent machine you're always going to be teaching, not just by instruction, but also by doing. Your every action is observed, so you are creating a running conversation with its data."

"If that's the case, then how long until it's TAMS 2.0 sitting in this room talking to you about how awful the human it has to train is?" Keegan said.

"Probably by that next generation where we teach by example. Isn't that the case with parents and their kids?" he asked.

"It's what we like to tell ourselves, but I'm not too sure." Keegan thought about whether she and Jared were that way with Haley, wondered if staying together really was best for her.

"In either case," Modi continued, oblivious to the thread he'd pulled, "never forget we get to set the rules. TAMS could one day complain about its partner, but it can't replace you, unless we decide it. We choose our roles. We choose our future."

"That's what they always say," said Keegan, thinking about what Jared would make of that claim. In either case, she considered her professional obligation fulfilled at this point. Modi was paid to talk, but she wasn't. She stood up, signaling the close of the conversation. "I appreciate your advice on this," she said, "especially given how new this all is."

Modi looked slightly disappointed at the shift and glanced over at TAMS, which had remained seated as Keegan stood. Then he tipped his head slightly, as if assenting to end the conversation, trying to get back control. "Again, consider me an ally in all this groundbreaking work. I fully understand that in many ways the situation you've been put in is just as complex for you as it is for TAMS. There is no set of prescribed choices. No set Bureau policy. No set of guardrails you have to stay between."

"Other than to keep the deputy director happy," she said, feeling him out on what she should take away from the boss's hints.

"Indeed. The one command code that you have to follow," Modi said.

Keegan turned to TAMS.

"You get all that, TAMS? You do some deep learning from the conversation?"

"Yes."

"And with that, you just proved my point to the doctor about how far you still need to go." As Keegan reached the doorway, she turned back around. "Almost forgot. Look, I also need to apologize for how we started things off back at the Dizz-Diff, after the Reppley interrogation," she said. "I was pretty keyed up."

She pulled from her pocket a green rectangle of plastic the size of an old-time credit card. She set it up on one of his shelves, on top of a book of psychology. The thin material bent into an arch shape as if squeezed on the ends by invisible fingers. Then it unfolded with the fluid dance of a flickering flame. First paper-thin wings, then legs, until finally a cicada-like insect perched on top of the book.

"Consider it a small apology gift to liven up the place," said Keegan as she and TAMS walked out the door.

DYZRUPTOR BATTLEGROUND QUADRANT 4
The Cloud

Abraham Lincoln smiled tightly at the fiery blast of orange that lit the sky. The explosion illuminated an organic twist of train tracks rising and descending among titanic soot-stained factories. Then another flash and another. At the next thunderclap, he erupted into laughter.

"What the hell is so funny?" Mahatma Gandhi asked, his voice slightly fuzzy due to an encryption program washing out any identifying markers.

"All this work to find the perfect meeting place in the chaos of war," said Lincoln, "and the whole battlefront might collapse on us because the NinjaJam tribe's chieftain got grounded by his mom."[17]

"Nah," Gandhi replied. "They'll hold the line. A crew of their newbies leveled up in the game's last battle royale."

As the two argued about the game's new points system, Joan of Arc impatiently dug in the dirt with the tip of her sword, lifting it up to admire the graphic features, the game engine even generating the tiny detail of a speck of dirt sliding off the sharp edge. Unlike Lincoln and Gandhi, though, she was a facsimile of a facsimile, as there was no death mask, statue, or photographic record to use to generate her avatar.[18] Whoever was behind her account had instead used the face of the actress who had portrayed Joan in the Netflix miniseries. Nearby,

Che Guevara stroked his iconic beard with one hand, lingering for the feel. As he did, George Washington watched, quietly deducing that that meant whoever the leftists had sent as their representative didn't have a beard in real life.

Surrounding the group of revolutionary figures was a shimmering wall of what appeared to be water. That was the representation of the quantum encryption — any attempt to secretly monitor the conversation would change the quantum state, making it as evident to the participants as someone dipping their finger in a flow of water. Setting it within the game, though, made it largely unnecessary. The gathering only existed within the noise of a synthetic-reality digital environment of battling gamers, accessed on a distributed global network of anonymous micro-servers.[19]

The group paused their cacophony as a new figure joined them. Parting the wave of water, the Charlton Heston movie version of Moses appeared in the middle of the assembled avatars. He'd been the one to create the quantum security setting, which made his avatar selection even more apt.

"Moses, it's about time you showed your face," George Washington shouted. "You have a lot of explaining to do. You never leave a man behind."

"He was not *my* man," Moses responded. "And I acted. All your man did was fail at his part of the plan."

"Well, it's not that —"

Che Guevara held up his hand, interrupting Washington. "He is not the only one who owes us an explanation. We are agents of change, are we not? Why blame the Sons of Aleppo? I thought we had all agreed that the enemy of my enemy is my friend."

"I could care less about them," replied Washington. "It was about creating a win-win. Either the feds' political correctness would keep them from checking him out too closely, when they know damn well they should, or if our asset did get caught, then some Muslims get blamed for something they'd like to do anyway."

"But he wasn't Muslim," said Joan.

George Washington snickered.

"That's not what I saw trending. That's just what 'they' want you to believe. In a world of likes and shares, the truth is whatever we make it."[20]

"That may be, but we had not agreed on such a course," Lincoln said.

"If we're going to talk about getting off course," Washington said, "Moses here is to blame for that. My guy's job was to hand over the explosives to take out some Ivy League lab with nobody in it. It's a long way to go from missing a drop-off to bashing in the head of some bookworm."

"That was certainly not in our plan," said Lincoln. "Moses, I know that none of us were there, but this was about making a statement. Starting out with cold-blooded murder can only undermine our cause with the public."

Moses watched them, arms crossed as he appeared to assess the group and its prospects. "I'm not going to be judged after the fact by those who are not willing to go forth to fight for our future," he said. "You don't seem to understand the stakes. It is not human jobs that are at risk from the rise of the robots. It is humanity itself."[21]

"We all take risks," said Lincoln.

"Not equally," Moses said. He put his hands behind his back, twisting his fingers into an interlocking knot in the folds of his robe. After a breath, he spoke in a measured tone. "We could have destroyed all of Princeton's AI department, but what difference would it have made? The machines of the future aren't the problem; it's the people who use them, who depend on them. They will continue to be lost, until we can truly reach them."

He began pacing, his sandals sticking in the wet mud of the game's simulated grass and loamy earth. "Do you all get that? Standing here, or not, as the case may be, hiding behind these avatars, you have become dependent on what you claim to be combating. You choose the veils afforded by technology, not realizing you are wearing blinders."

"Such grandstanding," Che Guevara said. "What's your point?"

"My point? To truly break this dependence, we have to give more, all of us. Much more. As God taught Abraham and his descendants, the faithful only find their conviction with real sacrifice. That's the wonderful irony of all this. All that we need to do is contained in a book written when faith itself was the most important technology of all."

"No Bible talk!" Gandhi yelled.

"Yes, Moses," Joan of Arc said. "We agreed, the rule is leave your personal ideologies at home. This movement, this revolution against the future we all fear, fails if we push our own beliefs instead of the common cause."

Moses locked his hands behind his back and stared back at her. "There is no *we* here. We trust each other only so long as we prove ourselves. I hope my actions demonstrate at least that I am done skulking around in the ether."

"Just take a breath, Moses," said Lincoln. "Please. There is time to do this right so that we —"

"Time for what? Or rather, for whom? I know what you've done, trying to profit off of my actions, like you have so many others' righteous anger."

"What . . . I don't know what you're talking about," said Lincoln.

"Yes, you do." The Moses avatar pointed a single long finger at each of the other avatars. "In your hearts, each of you knows what I am talking about. The only decision now is whether you will act to be on the right side of history or be ground under by it."

At that, he walked toward the blue shimmering wall of water and his figure dissolved.

POTOMAC OVERLOOK NEIGHBORHOOD

McLean, Virginia

Jackson Todd pulled off the VR gloves and helmet, slapping them down on the white kitchen countertop, a white quartzite made to look like Carrara marble. They had remodeled the kitchen when they first bought the house. He and Isabella had actually argued back and forth about whether to get the real stuff. It was one of those stupid things that seemed so important at the time. Ultimately, they'd been swayed by the salesman's pitch that the artificial wouldn't show the stains of any morning coffees or kids' fruit juices. He'd been proven right, the white was still gleaming. It showed no evidence of their years together, only the memories that just hung in the air above it.

Todd ran his index fingers over each eyebrow, up his forehead, and then to the back of his neck, rubbing at the points of pain just where the skull ended. Stretching his neck one way and then the other, he slowly breathed in through his nostrils and out of his mouth. After repeating it nineteen more times, he stood and walked to the other side of the kitchen counter. In bare feet, his steps were careful, still mindful of stepping on the now-absent Legos that had once cluttered the floor.

Pulling a long wooden match from the drawer, he struck it, lighting the gas burner on the stove and placing the kettle atop the heat. Watched pots never boiled, so as he waited, he stared out into the backyard through the kitchen windows. The grade of the lawn, slightly dipping lower to the right, was barely noticeable in the dark, but it still annoyed him, a defect he had always meant to remedy but had never gotten around to. Over it hung a limp zip line, running from one end of the yard to the other. It was set just high enough to appear dangerous to a young boy, but not so high that it really was. Green lichen covered the rope, unused for years now.

When the built-in thermometer on the side of the kettle displayed 93 degrees Celsius, he took it off the burner. He then pulled the metal container from the cupboard, softly shaking it three times, side to side, to sift it one last time. He measured out 4 grams of loose-leaf black tea into the stainless steel mesh ball strainer — 3 grams made the proper amount, but tonight he gave himself an extra gram for the needed focus.

He placed the ball in a double-walled glass cup with a slight clink and poured the water over it, stopping when it reached a line carefully etched into the inside of the glass. Letting the tea steep, he walked over to a wooden cabinet in the den that the kitchen connected to and pulled out an old binder. Trailing his fingers over the faded plastic sleeves of compact discs inside, he pulled out the special one, her handwriting on the reflective shine still visible in black permanent ink. He powered up the old compact disc player he'd bought at a church sale, hit "eject," and loaded the CD in the slide, pushing it back in with his finger, the tray no longer sliding back on its own.

Eyes closed, he stood in front of the CD player as the song began. The slow guitar strum that he'd heard too many times to count but always made him think of that first slow dance at 1 a.m. in the basement of Princeton's Colonial Club eating club: Mazzy Star's "Fade Into You."

I want to hold the hand inside you
I want to take the breath that's true[22]

His body swayed slightly at the memory of their feet shuffling on a floor sticky from dried beer, two sophomores not knowing that it was the beginning of their lives together.

As the song ended, four minutes later, he hit the eject button and placed the disc back in the sleeve. He returned to the kitchen and removed the tea strainer, placing it in the sink, a farmhouse-style one they'd also put in during the remodel. She'd wanted white to go with the countertop, but he'd liked the stainless steel more. She'd given in, a little victory she knew meant more to him than her.

He walked back into his office, careful not to spill the steaming cup of tea.

On one wall hung computer science diplomas framed in inexpensive dark wood frames, the kind bought in that purgatory after graduation when cash is short and ambitions are long. The BSE from Princeton beneath the PhD from Georgia Tech, each certifying that Jackson Todd had their blessing to remake the world.

On the other side of the room, a series of citations and commendations for work at the Defense Advanced Research Projects Agency, including a framed personal letter from the agency director.

Todd sat down at the desk, moving aside a vinyl-covered copy of the Old Testament bristling with the edges of yellow and blue Post-its. He carefully set the cup of tea on a coaster marked with DARPA's old motto from its days dominating the world of information: *Scientia Est Potentia*, Latin for "Knowledge Is Power." Like so much else, they'd actually gotten it wrong. Back in 1655, Hobbes had explained the true intent of the translation: "The end of knowledge is power . . . Lastly, the scope of all speculation is the performing of some action, or thing to be done."[23]

He would be that action, doing the thing that had to be done.

The computer monitor on his desk winked awake, its screensaver a 3-D montage of video clips and still images from vacations, a preschool graduation ceremony, and trips to the ice cream shop. Todd moved down through the menu finder and then opened the file that he had saved for just this occasion. He put in his headphones, snaking their connecting cord into his monitor. As a graduate student, he had always coded to music, the rhythms calming his mind and driving him forward. Today, different background noise was needed.

The file he played instead was a downloaded video of a local TV station's news broadcast, one of those retrospectives they run on anniversaries and slow news days. It began with security-camera footage from the Metro stop at Ballston Station, the neighborhood a mix of condos and government agency buildings located just over the river from Washington, DC. Rush-hour passengers lined the subway platform, but they were difficult to distinguish individually due to the density of the crowd and grainy footage. Privatization of the DC area's commuter line had brought sweeping infrastructure upgrades to the Metro's beleaguered systems, but some corners had been cut to make the bottom line work. The quality of the security cameras was one, the automation integration of the track another.

Moving that feed to a corner of the monitor, Todd sipped his tea and called up a new file. It opened with the logo of Princeton University's Computer Science Department, then revealed line after line of software code.

The video footage cut to passengers entering and leaving the Silver

Line station at McLean, swirling around one another as they tapped their phones on the turnstiles controlling access to the platforms. That they still used handheld devices dated the video. Off to a side, a mother helped her son through the gates, jostled as she tried to tap again and again but seemed unable to get the system to register. It was a sequence Todd had seen hundreds of times, and relived thousands more, during the past seven years. It was maybe two seconds of footage, but the broadcasts always used it because it humanized the disaster. Was the gate malfunction a premonition, from the system itself, warning her? It was like that for Todd now — he had to make crystal clear for people the signs coming from the systems all around them, telling them to stop before it was too late. She just hadn't known how to recognize them. Or maybe she had but wasn't willing to listen to them. He couldn't blame her. He hadn't known then either. Now he did.

Todd's fingers began to type more furiously, finding their rhythm as the news segment continued playing in the background. The platform cleared, the mother and son dashed across the empty space hand in hand. They didn't look harried, though. They looked happy by the way they raised their hands high in triumph as they sprinted through the train doors. On their way to meet up with Daddy for lunch at the pizza place just outside his work, where their son would get a cup of ice cream if he was really good.

Signs that could not be ignored. That was how he was going to save those who were left, he thought, because it was missed signs that had cost him those who mattered the most. Sacrifice was required and he'd made that sacrifice first.

Meanwhile, the news report continued — a voiceover from a journalist while they showed a camera view from inside the train that had left McLean, onrushing tracks framed by dark haze. The journalist's voice marked the train's path as its driverless system moved it toward the city. It stopped at East Falls Church, an elderly couple getting off. "The lucky ones," the narrator intoned, as the train picked up speed again. The camera view shifted back to the Ballston station, as the crowd there pushed their way onto another train on the line. It slowly pulled out of the station. Before it made its way three cars into the dark tunnel at the end of the station, the screen went black and the narrator paused in silence, perhaps out of respect or perhaps just to let the viewers' imagination manufacture the horrors of that instant.

Despite the hot tea, Todd shuddered. But he kept typing, working the ADS code into what it truly needed to be. It had once been an architect of destruction. So it would be again.

The voiceover narration transitioned from one of hushed reverence to cool analysis of the crash's cause. A machine error, she said. A flaw in the code that was not foreseen in design, treating an act of code as if it were an Act of God.[24] There was no one to blame.

No, that was not true, Todd thought. We all were. It was that simple point that they had to understand.

As if the cause of the tragedy could not be questioned further, the story then quickly shifted to the success of the emergency response. A Metro Automatic Train Control shift supervisor explained how the artificial intelligence running the overall train network ensured all the unaffected trains were safely stopped before further accidents and cleared the way for emergency personnel. Then drone footage from an Arlington police quadcopter flashed across the screen as the machine used its onboard cameras to route police and fire vehicles, while overriding traffic lights in real time. Above the station, media drones ghoulishly darted between buildings looking for unique angles, "allowing for much greater transparency and awareness about the everyday heroes and the official response to the tragedy," the narrator said. Then a shaky video shot of a descending octagon-shaped platform, painted bright white. Eight trauma pods arrayed like spokes under the air ambulance's platform, looking from the ground like a flying playground merry-go-round.[25] Emergency medical technicians rushed the pods belowground, then quickly back up. A flashed image from one of the darting drones revealed the mother and her young boy being slotted in next to each other in the octocopter's cradles. Adam and Isabella, no longer holding hands, their arms now limp.

Todd opened up the Wi-Fi. It was the one connection he had to risk, but he'd limited it by tapping into a repeater set that the kids at Langley High School had set up a mile away, which broadcast out the Fairfax County school system's 5G mesh network. If somehow someone did track it back, they'd still have only pinpointed it to a connection point hiding within Virginia's most populous county.

Flicking back to the window of ADS software code still open on his screen, he selected the now modified subroutine of new version updates, which regularly pushed out patches and upgrades across the system. He accessed the directory of current users, his computer noticeably slowing as it downloaded millions of potential targets.

GEORGETOWN NEIGHBORHOOD

Washington, DC

There was a slight hum as the FBI Suburban's electric motor stirred to life, advancing the car 2 feet before shutting off again with a sigh — the typical sound of midafternoon traffic in downtown Washington. Keegan wasn't sure why the vehicle was heading north on Wisconsin Avenue, when she wanted to be heading south to 695 to cross the Anacostia River. Probably no human in the entire traffic jam knew why. Maybe not even the traffic management system that had steered them all this way knew. Whatever the case, it didn't matter; the ride along was the point, not the destination.

Keegan looked over at TAMS, sitting shotgun. There was no set Bureau protocol to where it rode. She could have had the machine lie down in the trunk for all it cared. In a seat, though, it would see what she saw. Plus, they wouldn't get any dirty looks being in the HOV lanes.

The only problem was that, if the idea was to teach it like Modi advised, TAMS didn't seem to be paying attention. Its power-saving mode made it stir to life every time the SUV advanced, then power down again when the car stopped.

"TAMS, change power-management cycling; constant on," Keegan said. "OK? No sleeping on the job."

"Power-management cycle change confirmed."

That was also annoying. Whoever had decided the settings for commands had gone for specificity, but it was going to slow them down. "TAMS, change command settings. When it is just you and I, statement of TAMS is not required. Initial authorization assumed."

"Command setting change confirmed."

"And you don't have to confirm with re-statement of the order. Just say, 'OK.' Understood?"

"OK."

Keegan laughed. *Who says software can't have a sense of humor?*[26]

"Alright, good," she said. After a beat of not knowing what else to say to the machine, she got impatient. "I'm going to drive; this is going too slow." She flicked the wipers to clear the faint layer of dust on the windshield and then put her vizglasses down on the center-console charging pad.

The traffic was moving just slightly faster in the left lane, and she spied her target, a six-wheeled UPS delivery truck. She manually nosed her SUV out in front of the truck, and it immediately slammed on its brakes and then released its flock of delivery drones — standard collision protocol to avoid damaging the onboard cargo.

"Bingo," Keegan said under her breath, congratulating herself for the double score as the drones circled overhead. Liability policies, risk committees, and shareholders all shaped the vehicle's code with safety in mind, which, in turn, created a gap for her to exploit. This was something Modi would have better understood if he'd ever spent time fighting people whose entire strategy was to take advantage of the gaps that happened when someone tried to fit society's rules into an algorithm. Machines were built on assumptions that meant one thing in a lab and another in a narrow alley reeking of dog shit and gunpowder.

They drove west, Keegan following the algorithmically determined route, but at least she was now in charge. It took them along residential streets, a well-off neighborhood of larger homes with elaborate fortifications. Some were subtle, like Kevlar webbing over the hedges, while others were as gaudy as you might find in a Moscow suburb, with sensor clusters atop Roman columns.

What did the robot really know about what that meant? Geolocated images and aggregated data revealed a little about the neighborhood but missed the critical question of why the property owners would go to such lengths.

Having gotten it out of her system, Keegan set the SUV back on autopilot but began tapping the dash screen as more data appeared. The heads-up display kept flagging diverters concealed behind bushes or under false rocks. The devices pulsed false data into the traffic-management and autonomous vehicle navigation networks, trying to keep a rich neighborhood's streets largely free of cut-through traffic. Local police looked the other way because everybody did it. The only people who really cared were the share transport companies, who were rumored to be paying task-worker bounties to remove them. But the devices cost no more than a case of wine and so were easily replaced.

When they finally got back onto the freeway, the SUV hit a massive pothole underneath a bridge and slewed to the right. Keegan slapped her hands back on the wheel for an instant, but the vehicle corrected its course and they continued on. They soon crossed over the Anacostia River, its color a green so dark it could have been government issued. They hadn't gone a block when they got caught in another snarl of traffic. This one wasn't created by a machine algorithm, though. Ahead was a checkpoint backed by a black DC police MRAP.[27] Burning flares and LIDAR reflectors, arrayed like a spray of red flowers on the black asphalt, diverted traffic.

Strange. It hadn't projected onto the SUV's screen. Keegan brought up the local police net on her vizglasses, but the checkpoint wasn't there either; maybe it was a glitch or just not logged yet ... or given how the cops were wearing masks to cover their faces, maybe this one wasn't official.

"We're not in Kansas anymore," she said, talking to herself as much as to the robot.

The cops recognized the government-issue SUV and waved them up to the front of the line of vehicles. At its head, a policeman was standing beside a purple two-door electric car, holding the license of its young driver, his other hand resting on a pistol. This was the sort of unplanned opportunity she had hoped for to test TAMS's ability to read the environment.

"Tell me what you notice about both the officer and the person who they're questioning."

"Both are exhibiting physiological indicators consistent with high levels of nervousness," TAMS said.

"That's fear," said Keegan. "Both have a valid reason for it, which is what can lead to a very bad outcome."

As the SUV began moving again, Keegan switched on the onboard ThreatView. Modeled after the heads-up display used by Air Force fighter pilots to track, it projected various security information collected in the area onto the screen.[28] She tabbed it to track any aerial criminal activity. ThreatView showed a writhing column of climbing and descending drones working the area. Most likely a drug dealer sitting on a rooftop sofa in the shade, operating a distribution network.

Keegan gamed out what she would do if she were dealing. She'd zig when everyone else was zagging, go underground; use squid crawlers to navigate the sewer systems so you were going straight to the customer. Every building, be it a luxury penthouse overlooking the National Mall or a boarded-up shooting gallery, already had a perfect clandestine delivery system, standardized and usually working: a toilet connected to a sewer main. You could have squids learning on every run, teaching one another as they worked their routes. As she worked through the crime in her head, she thought that this was one of those moments when it was good bots couldn't yet read minds.

They drove on another few blocks into Southeast DC. Stopping at a red light, Keegan scanned the corner. A dozen people were boarding an automated trolley bus, the spiderwebs of its cracked windows glowing with refracted light.[29] Maybe someone had thrown rocks at it for fun. Or maybe it had been an act of defiance, lashing out at what the driverless vehicle represented. It didn't matter, though. The buses were essentially disposable, their likely loss baked into the plan. There was a term for that, Keegan knew, because they had also used it to describe the bots she'd used on deployment and even sometimes the human troops. "Attritable."[30]

"Check out the bus," she instructed TAMS. "Are all its systems running normal?"

A few months back, some hackers had run a ransomware hit on the bus system, locking the passengers inside as the automated vehicles drove across the city. As far as attacks went, it was a pretty dumb one; people who ride public transit aren't flush with extra cash. The bus manufacturer had eventually paid up for them, mostly to get the story of people being taken hostage on a robot bus to stop trending.[31] But the fact that the hack had been traced back to Romania had made it international, and thus put it on the FBI's radar screen.

"All systems running within normal parameters," TAMS replied.

In the end, the lawsuit meant that the passengers would likely make out better than the hackers had.

The SUV automatically slammed on its brakes, letting a red Volkswagen hatchback driving without its lights on cut across the lane for driverless cars. The driver slipped a hand out the side window with a quick wave of thanks. Keegan responded with her middle finger.

Fully aware of her own hypocrisy, she looked over to gauge TAMS's response. Nothing. It'd be interesting to know how it factored that. Was it going to use it as data for understanding Keegan's psychology? Or had she just created the first kernel of some future moment of robot road rage?

Keegan tapped in a new destination. As the SUV turned off the arterial, its dash screen shifted — red and green dots popped up in clouds, showing geographic concentrations of past crimes and predicted crimes based upon law enforcement data, as well as private-sector information that fed into the same algorithms.[32]

They drove up a street of low buildings that were a cluster of both colors. The shop fronts were covered in plywood, topped by makeshift apartments hidden behind thick curtains and cardboard. A light wind lifted up translucent food wrappers that drifted in the breeze.

She slipped her vizglasses on and tagged one of the buildings, a closed-down butcher's shop, whose windows had been replaced with what looked like garage doors. Small black crescents covered the front. The bottoms of the protective shielding looked burned, maybe melted. Next door was a burned-out shell of a small industrial space, fingers of charred wood and steel stabbing skyward like a rib cage. A calico cat lounged in the cool shadow of what had been the entrance, lying contentedly in the way that only a cat could, as if the destruction around it had been done by the humans just for its benefit.

"Describe what you see over there," Keegan said, tagging the scene with her glasses. "Tell me the highlights."

"In the foreground is a concrete sidewalk. On top of it is a male cat with gray, black, white, and orange coloring. Behind it are two buildings, both 7 meters in height, 12 meters in width. They were damaged by fire. Signs identify the location as the former business of A-1 Butchers and the Capitol Technology Corridor Site 32."

TAMS had not actually "seen" that, but rather used a neural network. Modeled after the human brain, it corresponded to the information that it actually detected, the digital pixels in the image, to extract information on what those pixels might represent, like the color of the fur of the lazing cat. Indeed, it didn't even detect the color originally, but rather turned the whole image into grayscale, which represented the intensity of light matched to the standard color spectrum a human could see. Just as the neurons in a human's brain are dedicated to detecting specific objects, that grayscale had then been turned into a matrix of numeric values in TAMS's calculations, each and every pixel in it given a number between zero and 255. Then, in a little over a picosecond, the neural network had gone to work, each pixel filtered again and again by a set of votes on what was in it, each layer of winning votes then pulling out information on the tiny details of each part of the image. In this way, the network determined everything from whether the pixel depicted an edge or a curve or a color, which was then fed to the next layer. Ultimately what was known as a Densely Connected Convolutional Network pooled all those pixels, votes, and layers together to recognize what the data matched of most likely objects.³³ All just to "see" a "cat."

"Tell me more," Keegan demanded, nonplussed by the recognition software. "What additional information can you determine about what you are seeing?"

"The cat is of mixed breed, popularly known as a calico," TAMS replied. "Its fur pattern and size indicate a mix of Maine Coon and domestic shorthair. It lacks a collar and is unchipped, classifying it as feral. Would you like me to notify Washington, DC, Animal Care and Control Field Services?"

"No, forget the cat," Keegan said. "What can you conclude from the writing on the wall?"

The bot emitted a faint hum, as if considering the question's validity and the energy required to respond. "The unoccupied retail space was formally leased by A-1 Butchers. It is currently unoccupied and has been renamed Progress Equals Pain, Fuck Your Future."

Keegan snorted. "That's graffiti. Somebody painted that with a spray can, to deface it, not to rename it."

Silence.

She tabbed the image she captured and blew it up larger on the SUV's screen. "Here. This is a sign, just not the kind that you think it is." She drew a circle around "Progress = Pain" and another with her finger around "FUCK YOUR FUTURE." "What did the creators of this imagery mean by that?"

"Graffiti writing in paint is an expression of anger, of individual feeling," said the bot.

"Close. But this is collective, not individual," Keegan responded. "They are expressing what millions of people feel. Anger at the local scene, but also the larger environment they feel caught in."

The machine looked back, calculating what she meant. Or just gathering more details on the cat.

"And how about those black marks on the door, the round ones?" Keegan asked.

That she didn't know, and she was curious to see what TAMS would guess.

The response was immediate, a faint vibration, almost purring, as if this was the kind of problem the bot knew it could solve. It collected billions of pixels and then evaluated them across not just the visual spectrum, but with comparisons, using all the tools that a single human brain lacks.

"Those are impact marks consistent with a hockey puck, most likely the activities of a child athlete at practice."

"Makes sense," said Keegan. "Good observation."

"Thank you for the compliment," TAMS replied.

"Setting change," Keegan ordered. "When on mission, no acknowledgment of praise or other social convention protocols." She saw no need for the faux conversation tools that they often packaged the machines' user interfaces with. It was an implement for work, utilitarian; why make it a Chatty Cathy as if the machine were your friend?[34] TAMS didn't actually feel gratitude, so there was no reason to fake it.

Keegan slowed the SUV to park in front of the burned-out building. "So what happened here?" she asked the machine. "Give me the recent history of this site." She wasn't sure, but she could guess and wondered how her instinct would align with what TAMS pulled.

"Sixteen months ago, the Capitol Technology Corridor opened a micro-factory at this location," TAMS began. "Nine hours after the opening of the micro-factory, a fire broke out that destroyed the facility. The cause was arson. Five people were charged."

"Timing is everything," said Keegan. "Anything further of note?"

"The building was going to print actuated pincer-arms for Task-Shop bots," said the bot.

And that explained it all to Keegan. Task-Shop bots had been developed to deliver items from tractor trailers directly to the shelves of stores.[35] Combined with already automated warehouses and inventory check drones, the entire supply chain that the old grocery and convenience stores ran on had been disrupted.[36] The savings had been immense; what took human grocery store workers hours, a machine could do in minutes, and it allowed the big tech firms to do to super-markets what they'd already done to bookstores.[37] It had also knocked out of the market some eight million jobs that people in neighbor-hoods like this used to depend on.[38]

"However . . ." The bot paused, processing the answer, but also adding to the perceived importance of its finding. "There are indi-cators of a larger criminal conspiracy. The participants in the arson were subsequently paid three Bitcoin each by a member of Local 400 of the United Food and Commercial Workers International Union."

"Now that is useful," Keegan said. "How do you know this?"

"An all-source synthesis of the case's court documents, cloud-har-vested personal biographical data sets, and financial transaction in-formation," said the bot.

"Good," said Keegan. "Why didn't they rebuild the site then?"

"Capitol Technology Corridor deemed the location to be no longer viable as an automated activity site, due to security reasons," said the bot.

Meaning, Keegan thought, the industry of the future had run into the politics of the future.

"If you gather enough information, everything can be linked to to-gether. That's not the hard part. The hard part is figuring out what links actually matter and what else is just random noise," she said.

"Instances of coincidence are commonly cited in popular media, which indicates —" said TAMS.

"Stop. There's no such thing as a coincidence when you're on a case," said Keegan.

As they drove past a low block of cork-colored foam-fab apart-ments, TAMS pushed a notification flagging a man sitting in an old office chair pushed out onto the sidewalk: *Person of Interest: William Leonard of Washington, DC. 71 years old.*

"Why did you send me that?" Keegan asked.

The man's face popped up on ThreatView. Leonard had an arrest record that showed charges for armed robbery and trespassing.

"What is he doing now?" she asked TAMS.

"He is drinking a 32-ounce can of Ox Blood Slambucha, purchased at the Crazy Eight store."

"Where did you get the source?"

"It is contained on the bottle's product label."

"You read the barcode?"

"Yes."

Keegan thought about how somewhere in the police bot there was the same software used by stores for automated checkout. One scanned the items as you placed them in your cart, rather than going through some line with an underpaid human, while the other allowed the police to backtrack the purchases and past locations of somebody on the street. The whole surveillance cycle very likely funded by a VC firm.

"So, you've got an old guy with a record drinking in public. What is the reason to make him a person of interest now?"

"Leonard has a 66 percent chance of being arrested during the next thirty days," TAMS said.

"Arrested for what crime?"

"That is not identified in the model," said TAMS.

"So what are the key causal factors then?"

"Mr. Leonard's past criminal record and his current public consumption of alcohol create a risk matrix of significant accuracy."

"That's a risk, nothing more," said Keegan. "You don't know what goes on in a person's head. We change day to day, minute to minute, second to second. Maybe that next sip . . ." Keegan pulled up a close-in view of the man drinking on the bench. "Gives him that clarity, some insight. Maybe he finds God and, fortified with liquid courage, hangs out with the church choir from here on out."

TAMS's head spun to keep tracking Leonard as they pulled away. "He does not show any association with a church or religious institution."

The robot was probably right, but she didn't want to cede the argument it was having without intending to. "What makes you think you can forecast a person's actions by their connections?" she asked.

"An individual's connections impact their life choices."

That sounded like a canned line, like some wisdom that TAMS had stripped from an online self-help article. The machine's intellectual tendrils could reach far into the cloud, but that also made it unclear when it was an original thought.

"No, it is not that simple," said Keegan. "Take me. I'm connected to plenty of people, but which ones were my friends? Which ones did I actually listen to? And which ones did I just tolerate when I ran into them in college or at a party?"

The screen displayed an image with Keegan in the center of it. It was a photo from an Instagram account she had closed down years ago. Then tens … then hundreds of profile pictures popped up around her photo. School class photos, selfies from parties, headshots from online resumes, each popping up and then morphing into colored dots. As a link analysis began to build, the dots connected into lines so dense they appeared as clouds.

Shit, thought Keegan, seeing faces with hazy familiarity and one in particular she wished that she could forget. "Take it down. I didn't mean that question as an actual command," she said, and the image disappeared from the screen.

Frustration was not an emotion that TAMS would ever feel, but it was welling up in Keegan.

"Let's walk," she said, pulling the SUV into the parking lot of a boarded-up McDonald's on the corner. As they exited the vehicle, Keegan could swear she still smelled fries in the air. A siren blared in the distance and then faded.

TAMS flashed to Keegan's vizglasses that it had lost connection with the cloud, that access to Wi-Fi or 5G was not available.

She scanned the area and noticed an unusually large bird's nest in the crook of the golden arch.

"There's a jammer, up there," said Keegan, tagging it with her vizglasses for DC police to take down later. They probably already knew and just avoided this block for what it signified. Someone wanted this to be a dead zone for a reason.

She led TAMS two blocks to avoid whatever was going on.

A pair of elementary-age boys riding a BMX bike, one astride the rear pegs, chased a middle-school-aged girl on a unicycle. She bunny-hopped it off curbs by using her body weight to bounce the underinflated tire, laughing each time she lifted off. Seeing Keegan and TAMS, the kids skidded their bikes to a stop. Keegan thought they would come over for a look, naturally curious about the bot. Instead, they shook their heads as if in disapproval, and then rolled off up the street and turned at the intersection. She couldn't blame them. So much bad data had been fed into the policing platforms that the machines usually turned out to be even more biased against the people in this neighborhood than their human creators.[39]

From a nearby townhouse, Keegan heard someone sitting on the stoop cough up phlegm and spit onto the sidewalk. She slowly pivoted to see a young man in his twenties wiping his mouth with the back of his hand. She quickly looked past him, off into the distance, avoiding eye contact to defuse the situation. It just wasn't worth it — no different than if she were back patrolling with a squad of Marines.

It didn't work. The man stood up slowly, as if measuring the moment. Arching his back to stretch, he drew up to his full height, at least six and a half feet tall. He wore black sweatpants, a faded gray and blue camo Crye combat shirt with the sleeves cut off, and a pair of neon blue indoor soccer shoes. TAMS flagged Keegan on their closed-network connection that its gun-detection algorithm had identified the bulge in the man's waistband as matching the outline of a Glock 43.[40] The subcompact pistol was marketed by the maker as "ultra-concealable," but object recognition software used changes in light patterns and angles to work around that.[41]

As Keegan and TAMS walked on, broken glass crunching underfoot, the man picked up his pace, jogging up the street. After he passed them, he got back on the sidewalk and stopped to block their path, as if he'd been standing there the entire time. "You got business here?" the man said, leaning down to put his face up close to TAMS.

"No, just passing though. Nothing for us here," Keegan said, keeping her voice low and measured.

"Then you don't got a reason to be here." He spoke to her but kept his eyes locked on TAMS's face. "Unless you're selling . . . Or maybe I don't have to buy." As he said it, the man tapped the bulge where the pistol was hidden in a syncopated rhythm, maybe some song he used to motivate himself. She'd have to ask TAMS what it was later. For now, it meant that the list of ways to deescalate the situation kept getting shorter with each tap.

TAMS pushed another notice to her vizglasses. There were two men on the rooftops, also carrying weapons: AK-47 type.

Time to go. She should not have put them in this kind of situation so soon.

"Screw this," Keegan said to the man, her voice exasperated. "You can keep this piece of shit. Not worth getting shot over. TAMS, stay here."

With a quizzical expression, the man looked at her and then TAMS, which stood still. Keegan pinged the SUV to fetch mode and walked away to stand by the curb, as if waiting in frustration.

The whole time that she waited with her back to him, the man eyeballed her, as if waiting for the trick. When the SUV pulled up, Keegan walked around to the driver's side and got in. At that, the man turned back to the still stationary robot, kneeling down to examine his new prize.

Keegan rolled down the passenger-side window, as if she had something to say to the man. The man looked up in anticipation just as she yelled "TAMS, follow. Now!"

She launched the SUV forward at full speed, the electric motor kicking into gear instantly, throwing Keegan back hard into the seat. As the SUV sped away, she looked in the rearview mirror and saw the robot running after at its maximum speed, about 10 meters behind the vehicle. At the intersection, Keegan made a hard right turn, the tires squealing. TAMS made a more elegant turn, leaning to the inside like a sprinter rounding the curve.

Keegan slammed the brakes and reached back to open the door behind the driver's seat. "Get in!" she yelled. As TAMS climbed in, she checked the mirror again to see if they'd been followed. There was no sign of Glock man. The only people in view were the three kids from before, laughing and pointing. It wasn't just that they'd never seen a robot run like that, but that they'd never seen a robot chauffeured about in the back seat of a car.

"Why does it make you drive?" the little girl called out.

Keegan set the SUV to return to the field office.

"Let's not talk about that again," Keegan said quietly to herself.

"OK," said TAMS.

The Internet

Alice showed up at the door, making that very same soft knock that she always arrived with.[42] *On the other side of the door, Bob thought it was Alice from the distinct signal of the knock. But despite their knowing each other for decades, Alice and Bob's relationship was one of fundamental distrust. Some say it started when Bob let a robber just walk right through the door, mistaking the criminal as Alice.*[43] *Others say it was when Alice accidentally hung all of Bob's dirty laundry out in the open for the world to see.*[44] *Whatever the original reason, the two had come to the realization that neither could be trusted. So they'd agreed to put a special kind of lock on the door. After Alice's knock, Bob inserted a key that he alone had for his side of the door. The key could turn, but the door stayed locked, unless Alice was using her own key on the other side. Only when the lock recognized both keys, and Bob and Alice each turned them to the very same setting, could the door open.*[45]

The two keys verified it was Alice on one side and Bob on the other, and the door opened wide. There was only one problem: it wasn't Alice. Moving through the door was Trudy, a nasty piece of work who was wearing Alice's skin and carrying her key.

Neither Alice, Bob, nor Trudy were actual people, or even robots like TAMS. They were enduring software characters in a digital saga that had gone on since the genesis of the Internet. Faced with the problem of how to exchange information securely on the very first computer networks, two groups of mathematicians — one working in secret for Britain's spy agencies, the other in public at MIT and Stanford — had each independently come up with a system of cryptography that soon became the bedrock of all security in the digital world.[46] Any two parties trying to exchange information, known as "Alice" and "Bob" to the cryptographers, would do so using the interplay of a widely trusted public "key" that contained an algorithm that could code and decode text and a private key, specific to that user, which allowed all other users to verify its authenticity. The system was how any "Trudy," their shorthand for an intruder, would be kept out of the exchange.

Owned by no one person or company, any open-source ecosystem — including Professor Preston's original software — relied on this intricate dance of human trust and digital distrust to work. The underlying software kernel that literally millions of users were sharing, for free, was always improving itself.[47] Its very value was how it freely shared across the crowd everything from new features and bug fixes, to patches that closed any cybersecurity vulnerability discovered by the worldwide community of users.

But these updates weren't just picked up and deployed by the millions of systems running the software without questioning whether it was Alice or Trudy at the door. Instead, they each went through that very same exchange of keys that had always ensured Internet security. Preston's death didn't change any of this; the system was designed to run without him. Bob always asked Alice for her key, and vice versa. But Professor Preston's sudden death in Princeton did provide a moment of opportunity for Trudy to exploit, in the time between his death and his key being suspended or passed on to some other holder. The irony was that news could only be communicated out to the network through the very same system of updates. It was the briefest of windows, but one that required years of planning for Trudy to do anything with it.

While the physical swing of a cane may have helped Trudy move around one of the digital world's most essential security checks, gaining access to the software creator's kernel wasn't enough. Even when Bob let Alice in, he still didn't trust her inside his house.

To authenticate that any incoming code isn't malware, malicious software of some type, network defenses run test after test on it, as every so often security flaws have been found even in the open-source software supposedly validated by the crowd.[48] These tests hunt for revealing snippets of code that can provide a tell of some type of attack, as well as vet it against vast databases that try to find any similarities to the trillions of previously discovered versions of malware. Some defenses even run the new software though simulated versions of their network, to trigger any malware before it hits the real version. The millions of users also provide a kind of herd immunity; all a piece of malware has to do is kick off an alarm in one network, and all the others can be notified to kick it out and protect themselves.

Trudy, though, wasn't doing anything that network defenses would deem suspicious. There were none of the normal signs that would let Bob know it wasn't Alice who he'd let in. Trudy didn't self-replicate, to spread from one network to another. She didn't move laterally, harvesting passwords or user names, to log into one account after another. She didn't collect data or open up backdoor channels of communication out of the network to try to steal information or, even worse, hold it ransom.[49] She didn't "phone home" for instruction from an outside command and control structure to allow her foothold to be exploited further.[50] Nor did she trigger any of the newer tools designed to find particularly crafty malware that hid its tracks. Security researchers had discovered that for all the digital sleight of hand a Trudy might try, they could detect something was amiss in a network by using nontraditional measures like the heat coming off their servers or the speed of the basic Raspberry Pi processors on which so many Internet-connected devices still ran. Changes in temperature or infinitesimally tiny slowdowns on these most simple of machines could give away that some unknown software was secretly riding on top. Here again, Trudy stepped right over this last trip wire, as everything she did was part of a normal software update that would cause the very same effect.

Perhaps most important, though, Trudy avoided the temptation that would have given away any other attacker who had obtained the literal keys to countless kingdoms. Despite the chance to enter millions of systems around the world, which would have been irresist-ible to any criminal or government, all that she was interested in was entering the door of a handful of targets. And then, once in those few, she didn't steal a thing. All Trudy did was the digital equivalent of breathing softly on a single pair of eyeglasses left out on a table.

These handfuls of targets were mom-and-pop businesses and lo-cal governments, regulated only by the Environmental Protection Agency, whose interests lay far from matters of cybersecurity. But even if they had been manned by high-end cyber defense teams, funded by millions of dollars and staffed by ex-NSA members, Trudy was too discreet to trip the usual alarms. She didn't race across their overall networks or alter their major operations or undertake any other ac-tions cyber defenses typically watch for.[51] When all the other billions of lines of code in the approved kernel updates coursed across the network, all Trudy did was make a tiny mathematical update to the complex equations used by a handful of sensors that existed on the edge of their systems. The only thing that shifted was a detail in the chemistry or physics that one automated sensor was observing, most importantly in the world outside the system. Moreover, that minute shift had been observed many times before, so it wasn't viewed by the system as either novel or risky. There was always a logical explana-tion for it, and thus no reason to initiate an added search for anoma-lous behavior. And Trudy only made those new observations register well after she had erased herself, just like the very first versions of her had done when they had pioneered the dark art of digital sabotage against Iranian nuclear facilities a generation earlier.[52]

Each tiny shift Trudy caused at that one sensor, in one place, in one network, at one point in time, made sense on its own. At a privately owned water treatment plant in West Virginia, a conductivity mea-sure reported back that it was detecting higher levels of selenium, which was often caused by runoff from nearby coal mines.[53] The sys-tem automatically responded, as it was supposed to do, by adding in a pulse of ferric oxide to balance the chemistry.[54] At a county-owned plant in Northern Virginia, slight differences in pipe pressures were reported, while at a small town-run plant in western Maryland, it was a stormwater drainage disparity — all typical findings for sensors to detect. Each initiated the standard response of deploying red fluorescent water-flow tracers.

At the Ventilation Control Facility for the Potomac River Tunnel, built by the DC Water and Sewer system to delink the city's sewer and stormwater runoff systems that had once polluted the river after every big rainstorm, it was the air pressure setting on just four valves.[55] At the US Geological Survey (USGS) stream gauge at Point of Rocks, Maryland, an hour's drive upriver from Washington, DC, the altered sensor showed a reduction in the cubic feet per second of water flowing by, which was confirmed by similar slight differences reported by the gauge at Hancock, Maryland, another hour farther away.[56] Each passed on that customary notice of a pending drought, itself a regular occurrence, to the Jennings Randolph and Little Seneca Reservoirs, used to boost Potomac River levels in times of low flow.[57] Meanwhile, at the Savage River Reservoir, it was slightly higher levels of acidity in need of dilution, an occurrence frequently caused by farming and construction runoff.

To any human administrator or AI watching the activity on their own network, there was nothing digital, chemical, or physical to set off an alarm.[58] Everything was operating the way it was supposed to.[59] And that was exactly why Jackson Todd had sent Trudy.

RICHMOND (FORMERLY JEFFERSON DAVIS) HIGHWAY

Arlington, Virginia

Keegan flicked the Petrolhead air freshener dangling from the auxiliary control stalk on the steering wheel in frustration. It gave off a faint whiff of gasoline, the smell designed to relax you by taking you back in time.

It wasn't working, though, and neither was the music. Keegan tapped the Suburban's dash display again and again, the force of each impact revealing her frustration. How had she allowed them to get into such a delicate situation on a training run?

A new hit flooded the car with syrupy harmonized vocals and a catchy intertwining of a rusty-sounding junkyard snare and deep electronic bass. Neural-net-written algorithmic-pop music, or A-Pop, had knocked most of the human songwriters off the charts.[60] Its peppy sound clashed with the light gray of the sky, hazy from the forest fires out West.

As Keegan listened, she considered what had paired that song to the ride. Known demographic data of passenger. Past plays. Geolocation. What other nearby and like vehicles were playing. And time of day. That was all obvious. But what else? Speed of the vehicle? The number of yellow lights run or total trip time waiting at red lights? That would give the network a sense of whether it was supposed to tap into a feeling of flow or tamp down the helpless frustration that went with waiting in an autonomous car at a red light.

Then the song ended, and Keegan looked over at TAMS. "Think you could write something better than that?" she asked dismissively. Before TAMS could respond, she added, "Don't answer that." She switched to an oldies channel instead. It was playing "Can't Stop the Feeling." "That's better," she said, forcing a laugh. Then she remembered it would register it as a false one.

TAMS turned its head to face her. "Would you like me to change the station?"

"Why?" Keegan said.

"Your biometric portfolio reveals a sudden spike in emotions."

"Exactly. It's a song. That's their purpose. You recognize it?"

"It is 'Can't Stop the Feeling,' released in 2016 and associated with the film of the same year *Trolls*," TAMS said.

"Yep, that's it," said Keegan. "It's doing what it's supposed to. Songs aren't merely data, but designed to evoke, well, 'a feeling' that you can't stop. It's normal for humans."

"OK," the machine replied, and then provided an added observation. "However, your response is out of scope."

A series of angry and fearful teenage faces flashed through Keegan's mind. "Why do you think? Explain."

"This particular song was designed to make humans happy, according to an analysis of its commercial success and online ratings."

"The song wasn't designed, it was written," said Keegan. "By a human. By J.T. himself, I think. Is that correct?"

"It was co-written by Justin Timberlake, Karl Martin Sandberg, and Karl Johan Schuster," TAMS corrected.

"Close enough. My point is that music evokes emotions. For example, we used to dance to this song at Millennial Night parties."

It was the morning after just one of those house parties that her life had turned upside down. No. She, on the steps of the University of Washington Tacoma's Student Center, had turned her own life upside down.

"However, your facial micro-expressions indicate high levels of unhappiness," TAMS replied. "Have you observed anything of note in the threat environment or my performance?"

All they'd really been was a group of college kids trying to stand up to a white nationalist militia to whom the local police had turned a deliberate blind eye.[61] A melee broke out at a rally for a Pakistani American student running for the state legislature, someone had died, and they'd taken the blame.[62] It hadn't been her, but that didn't matter. A few weeks later, she'd joined the Corps, which got her as far away as humanly possible from the arrest warrant put out for the seven unidentified people in Guy Fawkes masks.[63]

"No. It is just the music. Songs like this mark a moment in time or a relationship," she said. "So, while it's a song about happiness, it can also go with memories, good and bad ones, none of which really matter anymore. Because humans are fucked up that way."

She realized she was doing the same thing as singing along with the radio, emoting to a machine that couldn't care less, for the very reason that it could never start a feeling.

Keegan looked away, out the driver-side window, as they passed over the Potomac River, needing to change the subject and put some distance between TAMS and her past.

"Damn, look at that," she said. A bright red stream stained the water, looking like an artery of blood moving through the greenish blue of the river.[64] "Are there any reports on what's going on with the river water?" she asked TAMS.

"Fourteen hours ago, the Upper Potomac River Commission Wastewater Treatment Plant reported a software problem that resulted in an inopportune level of iron oxide levels in the river water. The effect spread downstream approximately thirty minutes ago."

"Inopportune?"

"Yes, that is the word used in their press release," TAMS said.

"When the source is a corporate press release, translate assuming too high levels of confidence and positivity," Keegan commanded. "Try your summary again."

"OK. The plant reported an . . . *imbalance* in the level of iron oxide in the river water."

Keegan watched a pair of armored Coast Guard inflatables race upriver, leaving wakes in the bloody red water, like white scars. "Any further incidents?"

"Similar incidents have occurred in multiple other plants, indicating a system-wide episode related to a software update corruption."

"Anything law enforcement related on it?"

"An Environmental Protection Agency investigation file has been opened."

Good luck getting the companies to pay that fine.

"It's really strange looking. Has it ever happened before?"

"Yes. A similar incident in Siberia occurred in 2016, when . . ."[65]

Half listening to TAMS, Keegan pinged her husband, wondering what he might have heard on his feed. His company's open-source intelligence network — though they never called it that — allowed its workers to have a real-time picture of everything from demand for services to breaking news, anything that could influence whether somebody needed to be ready to engage with a customer. It was also usually better than anything she could pull from the FBI network on an event like this because it was faster, had cleaner data, and was easier to query. She swiped the Watchlet, rotating through the icons, until it landed on a personal network tunnel.

"That's enough," Keegan said to TAMS, instructing it to cease the summary.

"Would you like the collective insight from my social network analysis?"

A faint pulse at her temple indicated the creation of a secure connection with Jared's account. "Well . . . fine," she said to TAMS. "Go."

"There is an unevenly distributed but seriously considered theory coalescing around the likelihood of copper-nickel concentrate waste illegally released by a factory in West Virginia. Another trend line focuses on the secret role of government officials in poisoning children."

"Don't go all Deep State on me now, TAMS," she said.

As she did, she typed into her app. *Everything OK?*

All good, Jared wrote back. Then her screen burst with a video of an overweight calico cat sliding backward down a house's stairway bannister, then landing perfectly.

She laughed. Jared must have been having a really good day, lots of points again, probably.

"A third theory believes it to be a sign of religious significance . . ." the robot continued on.

Keegan tuned TAMS out, starting to type out a reply when her Watchlet buzzed slightly.

The three pulses meant it was Haley, her daughter.

Keegan swiped the band to route the call to her glasses. "Hi, butterfly! How're you doing?"

"Fine. Um, where's the almond butter?"

"The cupboard? Why?"

"I need to make my lunch."

"Just get Daddy to grab it."

"I tried."

"Try again. I'm at work, honey, so I can't help now. Daddy can do it." She wondered if TAMS would register her rise in blood pressure. If Jared had time to send her cat memes, he could at least take a five-minute break to make Haley a sandwich.

"No, he can't." Haley with a voice of finality, as if it should be obvious to her.

"Why not?"

"Daddy's been sleeping all morning. I told him that I was hungry, but he wouldn't answer."

Wait.

That hadn't been Jared — he had set up a chat bot to respond to her.[66] Another offering from his employer. Keeping connected with a customer was more important than a live connection with a spouse or child at times, the theory went.

"How long has he been sleeping?" she asked, trying to keep it casual.

"I don't know," the girl replied. "I keep telling him I want lunch and he wouldn't get up."

"Haley, I'm going to come home right now and make you a sandwich. Sound good? Just wait for me. Why don't you start a Tag-Box game?" Referring to one of the mixed reality games that Haley loved so much, the cameras projecting colorful little 3-D boxes around the room that she would chase down for points.[67] "And you know what? Today, you can play as loud as you want, get all the boxes as quick as you can."

"But Daddy is sleeping. He'll get mad."

"That's OK. If he wakes up from it, tell him Mommy said it was OK. I'll be right there, sweetie."

"Alright," Haley said, then obviously running off to boot up the game.

Keegan pulled up the surveillance feeds from her bot on the shelf to try to see what the hell was going on with Jared. She saw what looked like a close-up of a brown rug. She switched views to a cicada she'd placed on another shelf for the cross-room view and got a black circle surrounded by orange fuzz around the top half of the screen. Haley appeared to have attached the cicada to her bear, Baz.

Keegan put the vehicle in pursuit mode, which turned on the Suburban's red and blue lights, nested behind the grill and in a tiara-like strip along the top of the windshield. Immediately, a Hyundai sedan shifted out of their way, the SUV's signal electronically moving any autonomous vehicles.

"Change of plans. We're going to my condo," said Keegan. "Family matter."

"I will notify emergency services," TAMS said.

"What . . . no!" said Keegan. "I never said anything about 911."

"Your actions indicate that this is a serious matter. Do you require any other aid?"

"Absolutely not," said Keegan. This was something she needed to handle on her own. "This is a personal matter. That means it is *not* to go into any FBI incident report."

"OK," said TAMS.

But, like every sensing machine, it would still record everything.

BALLSTON NEIGHBORHOOD

Arlington, Virginia

Keegan reached for the door handle, her stomach knotting in the familiar way it had in front of other doors years ago in a far different place. That queasy feeling of not knowing what was on the other side. Opening it could risk nothing. Or it could set off a bomb. In many ways, it was the same now.

Jogging down her building's hallway, she had come up with a plan: Grab Haley first and put her in her bedroom. Then go to Jared and check if he was breathing. Leave TAMS outside to limit the exposure.

Opening her door, there was no explosion other than the sounds of Haley's game still playing. A few 3-D boxes still hung in the air, another projected onto the kitchen counter. Haley had apparently played so long that she'd gotten bored and was now chasing Baz around the room. Keegan forced a wide smile and scooped the girl up into a hug. As she tucked her daughter into the crook of her neck, she squeezed her extra tight. Haley's weight started to hurt her back, but she ignored it, carrying her daughter into her bedroom, whooshing her down the hall as if it were a game.

"Stay here for a minute, OK?" Keegan said. "You play with your animals and I'm going to surprise Daddy. And I have a new friend to show you, but he's waiting outside for now."

"Why?"

"Because this is family time."

"OK . . . I missed you," said Haley, grabbing a following Baz out of the air, not to play with but to hold tight in solace. No matter what you said, kids always knew when something wasn't right.

"I missed you too," she replied. "We're going to be fine. Promise."

Careful not to slam the thin door, she closed it behind her and then spun quickly, going down the hall to the living room. She could see Jared on the couch, nested in blankets, motionless. He was clearly not active in the feed, his hands dangling loosely, fingers brushing the ground. Worse, she saw one of the tiny aerosol spray cans on the floor, tipped over on its side.

"Jared," she hissed. No reply. No movement.

"Jared!" she said louder, but still not yelling, to keep Haley from worrying more.

Her feet got heavier and heavier with each step closer to him. She put her hands on his shoulder, but he didn't react.

Kneeling down, she held up her Watchlet to just above Jared's mouth. Thankfully, his breath fogged the dark screen. She then lifted his hand and pressed two fingers on the thumb side of his wrist. A heartbeat, but way too slow.

"Jared! Wake up," she said, pulling off the VR headset. It beeped angrily at disconnecting from its user so abruptly.

Jared's face was placid, almost expressionless, and his head rolled back onto the couch. His damp hair smelled faintly of sweat, and his forehead had a band of dots from the rig. She traced the marks left by the VR headset, her fingertip drifting down his cheek.

There was no reset button to push. Not for his body. Not for their marriage. There was nothing she could do except think of all the reasons this should not be happening. To Haley. To her.

"Jared, wake up," she said, shaking him by the shoulders. "You need to wake up. Now." She yanked Jared up by the arm, blinking back the pain that shot down her lower back and leg from tugging at him in an awkward position.

Jared finally stirred, his head jerking up slightly.

"Hey, hey, it's me, wake up," said Keegan softly, brushing his hair back from his forehead.

"Hey," he sighed, eyes still closed. One eye opened, then closed again. "My head is killing me."

"You can't be doing this, Jared," said Keegan, picking up the nasal spray, feeling its emptiness as she put it in her pocket.

"What?" he said, slowly waking up to where he was, who he was. "Where's Haley?"

"Where's Haley is exactly right," she said. The resentment started knotting her throat and she swallowed it. "She's in her room, safe. She called me."

Groggily, he said, "I was offline because a neighbor stopped by Harlan's and —"

"Save the explanation for later," Keegan said, helping him stand. "Let's get you a shower first, to wake up, and then we can talk."

She would take the high road for now. Get him back to himself and then they could talk reasonably. The two of them walked toward their —his—bedroom, Jared leaning slightly on her. At the doorway, his Watchlet buzzed, one of the sleek all-white Apple versions that she'd gotten him as a birthday gift right before the fall, and Jared stiffened with energy, as if finally waking back up. "Shit," he said. "I gotta get back on."

Keegan kept them moving through the door. "Stop. Just stop. You can miss this one. Get a shower and I'll make you some coffee."

"We're out of coffee," he murmured.

"No, I ordered a delivery last night," she said.

He went into the master bathroom, leaving the door open, and she sat on the bed, propping herself up against the long, flannel pillow. Her pillow. Or, at least, it had been when she used to sleep in the bed. He started to undress, pulling off his shirt. Then, he must have realized she was there, and closed the door behind him. It was a sign that he was coming out of his fog, but it stung all the same.

She listened for the shower to come on and then yelled out, "Take it easy for a bit and I'll come check on you once the coffee is ready."

Then came a squeal of excitement in the living room. Haley. Kids never listen. At least her dad wasn't there now, passed out.

Then Haley squealed joyfully.

Keegan got up and went to the living room. TAMS knelt in front of Haley, knees tucked underneath its body facing the girl. Whoever had programmed it must have had kids, knowing that they trust those who engage them at eye level.

"Hello, I am TAMS," the system said, but in the nasal twang of one of Haley's favorite cartoon characters, a pink panda with Pegasus-like wings. It held out its hands, palms open, and Haley instinctually placed hers down on top of them. That's when Keegan realized it was doing a health assessment. Each sensor on the bot was reading her daughter's state, down to the blood pressure flowing through her hands.

"Haley, this is my new robot," Keegan said warily, not sure how to handle introductions. "It's nice, isn't it?"

"Yes. He looks silly," Haley said.

Keegan tried to read her daughter's expression for any sign of discomfort, but the uncanny valley's differing effect on children made it completely normal to see a robot in her den.[68] "I'm not sure it's a he," she said. "Are you still hungry?" she added, wanting to change the subject, so as not to have that confusing conversation right now.

"Yes," Haley said, her attention totally shifting. "Can I have some ice cream?"

"I don't think we have any," said Keegan.

"There are approximately 400 grams of chocolate ice cream in the freezer," said TAMS.

"Haley, sweetie, it's wrong," Keegan said. "We're out of ice cream. Why don't I make you a grilled cheese instead?"

Haley looked quizzically at TAMS, then at her mother, as if deciding whom to trust on the matter of the ice cream. "OK, Mommy. Grill cheese."

"Grilled cheese, *please*," Keegan corrected, stretching out the rhyme, as the girl giggled and then started to run around the room, chanting the rhyme.

"TAMS, come here," Keegan said.

The bot unfolded its legs, stood to its full height, and walked over to her. It could not register emotion, but it seemed to move with a cowed dog's hesitancy.

"Why are you in here? I did not order you to come in," said Keegan.

"Available information indicated a child in distress. Your stress and pain markers showed elevated levels. These combined factors required me to assess the environment," the robot said.

"OK. Whatever. We'll have to fix that later." Keegan went into the kitchen to start Haley's sandwich.

A buzzing started from the couch — Jared's damn VR rig, vibrating gently in a steady pulse that sounded like a bee.

Haley ran over to pick it up. Shooting a quick glance at the closed bedroom door, she put the rig on her head like a crown, chin tilted high into the air. The oversized harness slid down her face, onto her nose. She used two hands to hold it up as she walked over to TAMS, where she plopped down on the floor.

"Haley. Take it off," Keegan said. The girl had trouble lifting it, so Keegan called to the robot. "TAMS, help her get the helmet off."

As the robot plucked the VR rig off Haley's head, Jared walked into the living room. He was in sweatpants and a T-shirt, his wet hair combed. "What the . . ." he blurted out. "Get the hell away from my daughter!"

TAMS continued to pull the helmet off the girl. But now, at her father's anger, Haley held on to the rig. The robot swiveled its head to look at Keegan, away from Jared. It was waiting for her command, or even nonverbal direction, on what to do next. Not Jared's.

"It will only listen to me," she explained, coming into the room to stand between him and TAMS. "Yelling at it won't do anything. That's the way it's programmed." She turned to the machine. "TAMS, stop helping Haley."

"OK," the bot said and stood perfectly still.

"Get out!" said Jared, pointing his finger at the machine. "Out!"

"It's going to be OK, Jared," Keegan said. "TAMS, go wait out in the hallway."

As TAMS soundlessly left the room, Haley walked up to Jared and wrapped her arms around his legs. Keegan knew it wasn't that she was scared; it was more the kind of hug that kids gave when they saw their parents hurting, mimicking them. It still pained her as a mother to see that she'd gone to him first. She told herself it was just because of her job, because Haley was around him all day.

Rubbing Haley's back with one hand, Jared pointed angrily at Keegan. "I don't want that thing to ever be close to, or touch, Haley again. OK?" He was almost sputtering in rage. "And if it broke my rig and cost me my job . . . What were you thinking bringing it here?"

Keegan knew Jared's outburst was the product of much more than an explosion of anger at a machine. TAMS's very existence hurt him; it spoke to the absence of meaning that he felt after losing the job he'd worked for his whole life. It still didn't give him the right to yell.

"What was *I* thinking? I'm thinking that you're pissed off not because a machine came in the house, but because it filled in for you."

Jared shook his head, incredulous. "Never talk to me like that again around Haley."

"Around Haley?!" Keegan yelled. "Your inability to stay off the spray around Haley is the reason we're here! Decide whether you want to be a dad or have a job, cause you clearly can't do both!"

Haley's gaze was locked on to her mother's face, then her father's. Then she started to cry, a low wail that built up into a "no" that stretched out over ten seconds.

"Now see what you did," Jared hissed, and pulled the crying girl in close.

"Honey," Keegan said in a soft tone to Haley and began to step toward her. "It's OK. I didn't mean Daddy really had to choose."

At that moment, TAMS came back inside. It had an alertness to its posture — how its hands were positioned and the bend of its knees — that indicated it was again scanning for trouble. It immediately stood to Keegan's side as she knelt down to hug Haley, but Jared pulled Haley away and stood between his daughter and the robot.

"You need to get that thing out of here, Lara. Now."

Who's scaring Haley more now? Keegan wanted to shout. But she didn't say anything at all, as much for TAMS as for Haley. "Fine, we're going," she said.

"And keep it away from here. It's for your own good too," Jared said. "You better watch out, Lara. That machine is going to find out more than you want it to."

CITYCENTERDC DEVELOPMENT

Washington, DC

"This old hammer killed John Henry."

Todd spun away from the cloth-covered gap he had wedged himself through at the back of the abandoned store. It was a woman's voice singing. He took a step backward, feet crunching on broken glass, searching for the voice. He saw nothing but rays of evening light coming in between the cracks in the plywood covering the windows.

"Easy," the voice said. "We're safe . . . Unless you don't know the rest of the song."

Emerging from a door built flush into the wall of pink marble — a portal that he had somehow missed — was a woman in a black hooded jacket over a pink tufted dress that looked like something for a high school prom. No, he thought, more like a quinceañera dress. Fortunately for her, in that getup, the weather had done one of its usual spring swings.[69] In the high nineties just two days before, now it was in the low fifties. A gray silken scarf covered most of her face, and the drape of the hood hid everything but her watery blue eyes and crow's feet. Maybe late thirties. His eyes were drawn downward, where her right hand was in her jacket pocket, the outline of a pistol stretching the fabric.

"But it won't kill me, it won't kill me."[70]

Todd spoke the old folk song's lyrics, rather than singing them back to her. It was the words that mattered for their purpose, the sign-countersign for the meetup agreed to in the closed game chat room.

"Cool beans," she said, her tone instantly chipper. She drew her gun hand out of the pocket, revealing a pistol-shaped store clerk's price-gun. She waved it with a smile and then tossed it to the ground, the plastic skittering across the broken glass.

"It's 'cause I used to work here," she said, addressing both how she knew about the hidden door and where she'd gotten the price gun. "Selling silk scarves that cost a week's pay. Bags and purses worth more than any bank account I ever had. They only let me wear them at work. Assholes."

She motioned for him to follow, opening back up the hidden door with a push. "You'd think this was a secret room for security guards or something cool like that," she continued. "But it really just connects to the storage rooms and parking garage. I guess they didn't want a handle on the wall to mess up the feng shui. Whatever. It's where we'd hide out when we wanted to avoid the manager."

Not knowing what he was supposed to say, Todd just snorted, feigning amusement. Entering the darkness, he put one hand in his pocket, the other feeling for the wall, to assure himself both of his location and that no one else was lurking along the hall. It had the rough feel of cement blocks, a contrast with the luxurious once-polished wood on the outside. Everything's a façade, he thought.

"The day they fired me turned out to be the best day of my life," she said, her voice ahead in the dark. "If anything will turn you freegan, it's day after day of watching people fondle Birkin bags that they're only going to throw away at the end of the season."[71]

For somebody trying to disguise their appearance at a secret meetup, she did a lot of talking. But maybe that was to be expected. Everything the freegans did was built around the twin pillars of recycling and collectivism, what they saw as the way to beat back the twin sins of consumerism and elitism. Todd thought that, in execution, it meant they spent most of their time standing around trash heaps arguing about urban foraging rights.

"Didn't this used to be a condo complex too?" he asked, making conversation to keep her at ease.

"Yeah, bottom floor high-end goods, top floor high-end people. And, just like with the product, a lot of people fronting like they were high-end. Some of the worst people in the entire nation, paying my month's salary for the condo fees alone, just to be able to say they lived here.[72] Now it's all ours, just there for the taking after it all went bankrupt. I can tell by your clothes," she motioned at his outfit, "that you're a buyer, but there's a lotta good shit here if you want to join in. Might find you like it."

"I appreciate that, but for now, all my time is spent working for the common good. Why I appreciate your help," he added. He needed her aid, not just to find his way through the dark, but to get what he was really here for.

"It's not help," she said. "But sharing. That's the only way out of this."[73]

That only showed how little she understood. The freegans imagined themselves true believers in change. They were more like parasites, in his view, living off a dying society's leftovers. But, like parasites, they had their uses.

They continued down the service hallway, the noise of some kind of early-morning party going on in one of the abandoned condos above reverberating down through the ceiling. After a turn through a door indicating "Parking Garage," they descended a stairway that was pitch black except for a tiny orange digital dot of light at the bottom.

A flashlight illuminated a man smoking a pink e-cigarette and waiting at the stairway's landing. A thick crack in the cigarette's plastic cut through the picture of a Japanese anime girl band that had been popular a few years back.

"Hey," the girl said. "It's us."

"Yeah, I can see that," a male voice said, running out the words with a smoker's drawl. He had hollow eyes, shoulder-length brown hair, and a thin beard. Dressed in brown canvas overalls topped by a blue blazer with gold buttons, he looked like an out-of-work construction worker going out to a yacht club dinner. The discarded clothes of two men who would never meet.

The man aimed the flashlight straight into Todd's eyes. Todd squinted, turning his head slightly at the glare, as the man examined him. He directed the light from Todd's pockmarked cheeks to his long brown stringy hair.

"Shit, man. You don't look like Moses. Just a junkie." He laughed. "But I guess that's the point. If you ever throw away that mask, let us know first. It'd be cool to try out."

"Agreed," Todd said quietly. "You run into any problems?"

"Say again?" the man said. He pulled out the e-cigarette, and then coughed, spitting wetly onto the wall next to him.

Todd took a step forward and said more loudly, "The pallet. Did you get it?" Closer to the man now, Todd tried not to breathe in any more of his funk, a mix of stale fruit, burned plastic, and unwashed clothes.

"Yeah, it's here," the smoker said, putting the e-cigarette back in his mouth. It now bent slightly at the crack. "Shipment address had it going to Richmond, but we got in there before it went out."

That was the key. He'd had the shipment directed to a real address. But if it actually arrived questions would have been asked about the special order of capacitors that showed up out of nowhere.

"Anybody get hurt?" he asked, breathing in through his mouth. The smell of cigarettes, both real and fake, annoyed him, the scent of a loss of control over base cravings.

A long drag and a pulse of orange light, then a deep exhale. "Why?

From the way you were carrying on in the cloud, that wouldn't be an issue."

"There's a time for violence," Todd said.

"Yeah, well, this wasn't one of those times. The Baltimore port is all automated now. Not a single damn person there. All you need to do is punch in the access code and it loads it for you. You just gotta get there before the real delivery truck arrives."[74]

"Good," Todd said. "Where is it?"

The smoker waved the flashlight over Todd's shoulder, lighting up a large shipping pallet. Todd walked over and examined three large cubes, each the height of a man, wrapped in protective blue rubber. Running along the side was thick yellow tape with the image of a broken wineglass and the words "Fragile: Handle with Care." and "Hati-Hati: Mudah Pecah."[75] He'd have to strip that off before they left, a slight clue to its origin point that a street camera might pick up.

"We got it for you, but we ain't driving it out," the man said. "I trust your people are taking care of the pickup?"

Todd looked down at his watch, trying to make out the dial's illuminated markers in the dark. "Something like that." That they thought him a representative of a group was useful. The less they understood the better. All that was coming for him was an automated share delivery van, billed to an account he'd pulled off an open network hack. It would just come up in the network as one of thousands of pickups for the day, lost within the noise of a city of them.

"Cool. There's only one more thing then," the smoker said. The flashlight switched off, leaving the tip of the cigarette the only light in the room. Todd heard a rustle of clothes and then the ratlike squeak of steel sliding against leather.

In the dark, Todd turned, tightening the grip on the pistol he held in his pocket. It was a Brazilian open-source design, bought at a North Carolina gun show a year back. It fired plastic rounds tipped with metal. They were only lethal when fired at close range, but they warped when they hit the body, leaving little to trace back.

"Hey, Tim, this isn't what the group agreed," the girl protested.

"They'll agree when we bring it back," the smoker named Tim said. "Here, take the light."

The flashlight came back on, pointing first at the man and then back at Todd as the girl steadied it. In the man's hand was a black wood-handled Santoku knife, with decorative swirling clouds etched onto the 8-inch blade.[76] The tip was broken off, meaning it was some counterfeit given as a wedding or Father's Day present and then tossed away with an equal lack of gratitude. But the edge of the knife shined in the light, showing it could still cut with ease.

"Show me your wrist," Tim commanded, coming closer to Todd.

Todd felt his face flush with anger, but more at himself for failing to calculate for this scenario. A suppressor — why hadn't he thought to print one? His pistol had seven rounds, meaning these two wouldn't be a problem, but he didn't need the sound reaching an army of scavengers in the condos above. "You really want to do this?" he asked the man.

"Damn right. I'm going to see what you're hiding on that wrist," Tim said greedily, "whether it's attached to the rest of your arm or not."

Todd released the pistol and pulled out his hand, holding it out palm upward.

"I thought so," said Tim. "Nice watch there."

"It's an old one," Todd said. "Not even digital."

The freegan stepped forward and gently held Todd's fingers, turning the hand over so he could see the face of the watch. "An Explorer, right?"[77] Tim's dirty fingernails disgusted Todd.

"A wedding gift from my wife . . . It's not waste, not unneeded," said Todd, making his voice plaintive, as if to appeal to their values.

"Today it is," said the man, nervously tapping his shoe.

It made Todd's stomach ache to think of giving it up. He ran his next moves, visualizing each step. A quick yank back of his hand, then pull out the pistol. First the man, then the talkative girl, then bar the door at the stair, to keep their compatriots from coming down.

But none of it was in the plan. It would create points of connection

where now there were only faint dots. An order of graphene and ceramic sheets, made in a vacuum chamber at an Indonesian fabworks.
A missing package from the Baltimore harbor. A group of scavengers
posing as revolutionaries, who'd be on to their next abandoned building by the end of the day. And a delivery pickup billed to a corporate
account that wouldn't even register it as a crime. Nothing now linked
them together. Nothing worthy of investigation. But bodies would
change that.

The freegan tauntingly shone the light back on the shipping pal-
lets, oblivious to the calculations Todd ran in his head. "You want
your boxes or what?" said the man. "I know what I want. Time to
share, man."

Todd popped the clasp and handed the watch over while the girl
watched, mumbling to herself. "Here. And get out, before I change my
mind." He told himself that if it pained him, then it was just another
sacrifice that proved the worth of it all.

"Thanks, man," the smoker said and retreated quickly. The flashlight flicked off and the pair's footsteps disappeared into the darkness.

After a few seconds, Todd rubbed the skin where the watch had
been. Pulling out a finger-sized flashlight, he brushed a layer of dust
from one of the windows in the blue rubber casing. The dull yellow
sheets of material were beautiful and yet horrifying. They had the
façade of order, when instead, there was deliberate asymmetry, the
kind that was only possible through inhuman precision. After further
inspection, he breathed a sigh of relief. If the sheets had turned red,
the marker that they had cracked in transit, then it was all for naught.[78]

All the other details were too small to see with the naked eye. Each
sheet was actually stacks of atom-thin, but incredibly conductive,
nanocomposite paper.[79] The sheets of graphene film, made of hexago-
nal crystals of carbon atoms, were layered one after another between
equally thin nonconductive ceramic sheets, with a microscopic overlap between the corner of each sheet, like the pages of a book pressed
ever so slightly.

Only those tiny contact points linked it all together.

LOGAN CIRCLE

Washington, DC

TAMS could not have been any quieter. The bot sat in the front seat of the FBI Suburban, motionless and noiseless, as if it knew that it was partly to blame for what had gone down.

She didn't tell TAMS where they were going; she didn't know herself. She just let the Suburban follow its own patrol pattern. Pretty soon, the algorithm had them across the river and looping around the wide traffic circles that L'Enfant had designed into the city, first at Foggy Bottom, then Dupont, and now at Logan. Something about the shape naturally, or rather algorithmically, was like catnip for the nav system, she thought. Maybe it was the mathematical ability to draw a limitless number of connection points compared with a standard intersection; maybe it was just a design quirk. In either case, it captured her mood perfectly, making forward progress without really going anywhere.

At some point in the autonomous circle hunting, Keegan felt hunger pangs and tapped her fingers on the steering wheel, wishing them away. It didn't work. Frustration and anger had conspired to make her far hungrier than she should have been. It was the kind of hunger that only cheese fries and a half-smoke could solve.

"Fuck it," she said, and set the destination.

They found parking a half block away and walked under a bright yellow and white awning on a red and white brick neoclassical storefront.

"More training for you," she said to TAMS. "You can people watch and I'm going to eat."

What Keegan loved about Ben's Chili Bowl was that it was a vibrant landmark in a city full of cold, stone institutions. Built into the front of an old turn-of-the-century silent movie house, the diner had opened in 1958 on U Street, back then known as the "Black Broadway" of the segregated capital city.[80] A favorite of police and protesters alike, it had been the only business to survive the riots after Dr. King died, then the wave of murder and drug crime during the crack epidemic, then the gentrification that turned crime-ridden streets cool, followed by the more recent return of the neighborhood to its dangerous past.

Keegan had first been there blurry-eyed and drunk, Noah and a group of randoms from the Marine barracks taking her there as part of the celebration of her release from Walter Reed. Since then, she'd gone there for occasions that ranged from her and Jared grabbing a hot dog after a date to moments like this, when you just needed to eat something bad for your body, but good for your soul.

She stepped in the door, though, and felt pangs of lament, not relief. She was taking a robot to one of her special places before her own daughter. The smell quickly erased that emotion, her body reacting to the scent of French fries and the tang of chili. They walked to the counter, past the photographs of celebrities who'd eaten there, from US presidents to Hollywood actors. People came not just for the food, but also the history, the connection to something human and bigger than them.

Above the wall of fame was an old-model flat-screen TV, playing footage of a man angrily shouting before a crowd. Closed-captioning text of his rants ran at the bottom of the screen in slightly fuzzed font due to the TV's age.

SENATOR HAROLD JACOBS: NO MACHINE CAN BE TRUSTED. THEY'VE TURNED OUR WATER INTO BOTTOMLESS POOLS OF BLOOD . . .

What a drama queen, Keegan thought. *Something breaks, you fix it. Move on.*

A "SOFTWARE GLITCH" IS MORE THAN A DECIMAL POINT IN THE WRONG PLACE. IT'S A TAX ON YOU. IT MEANS YOUR CHIL-

DREN WILL BE BATHING IN WATER THAT LOOKS LIKE BLOOD
WHILE YOU SPEND YOUR HARD-EARNED MONEY ON BOTTLED
WATER . . .

After a few seconds, Keegan stopped reading and turned to the
menu on the wall, even though she knew what she was going to get—
two half-smokes with chili and an order of fries. The half-smoke was
a DC thing that she'd not known about until she moved to the city. It
looked like a hot dog but tasted like a spicy sausage. She'd be feeling it
later, but so what? A price had to be paid.

After she ordered, she picked a table in the corner. Unlike TAMS,
she didn't have eyes in the back of her head, so she always liked to sit
with her back to the wall, able to see who was coming and going. She
motioned for the robot to sit across from her.

After what seemed hours, but was only little more than a minute,
a waitress brought the food. You used to just pick up the food at the
counter, but a few years back they'd added the waitstaff, mostly as a
way to give someone a job. It was another unexpected effect of the automation wave, new charity jobs created to replace the old ones lost,
just not how everyone had thought.

The waitress placed the tray down stiffly, not making eye contact
with Keegan. *Maybe it's the bot,* she thought.

"Thank you," said Keegan.

The woman lingered for a moment.

"You doing OK?" Keegan asked.

"Oh, sure," she whispered. "We're all fine here."

After she turned away, TAMS spoke. "The waitress was not telling
the truth," it said.

Keegan looked down at the chili covering the sausage before her.
Dammit, the bot was right.

"Yeah, she lied. But what's she going to say, that the pay's terri-
ble and her feet hurt and she wants to go home? Humans lie all the
time. The key is to distinguish between the little lies, the ones that
make just getting on with life possible when it's really hard, and the
big lies." Keegan picked up a half-smoke and pointed it at Jacobs on

the screen, a small drop of chili falling onto the Formica table. She paused. "Tell me more about the waitress's state."

"Micro-expressions indicate not just mistruth, but also emotional distress." It then added, "Your biofeedback indicates the same state."

"Well, the Potomac's the color of blood and I'm stress-eating a sausage bomb with a robot who thinks it can read minds," Keegan replied. Quietly, she added, "Scan the room, but silent push any information of law enforcement interest."

She looked down to see the red light of an emergency message popping on her vizglasses, now lying faceup on the table. Setting down the half-smoke and picking the glasses up, she smeared chili across the lens. The text box read that facial recognition software had identified the beefy man standing behind the counter, watching the waitress a bit too closely, as having two outstanding warrants for armed robbery. A query from TAMS then typed out if it should notify the local police.

"Information noted. Yes, agreed," Keegan replied, deliberately using a calm tone, as if having a normal conversation.

She looked down at the half-smoke, the chili starting to cool and congeal. She crammed as much as she could of the spicy half-smoke into her mouth, getting a good half of it in. Chewing furiously, Keegan wondered if TAMS knew the Heimlich, just in case. She then wiped her mouth with a napkin and placed the dirty paper back in her lap, using the motion to reach under the table for her gun.

5

BEN'S CHILI BOWL

Washington, DC

"I have been instructed to provide you payment," said TAMS. The robot held the two $40 bills between its thumb and trigger finger. The man behind the counter glared back at the robot standing before him, TAMS's head barely topping the counter.

"What?" the man said. He was wearing the yellow "Ben's" T-shirt worn by the restaurant staff, but it was a tight fit.

Its legs telescoping, TAMS boosted its height by over a foot to look the man nearly in the eyes. "I have been instructed to provide you payment," the machine said.

"I know that. Don't you have a credit number to just bill to or something?" he asked.

"It is legal tender for the goods and services you have provided," the machine said, ignoring his query. The robot stood silent as the man scowled in exasperation.

"Give it here, then."

The robot dropped the bills. As the bills fluttered down, they missed the countertop and fell to the floor in front of TAMS — just as Keegan had instructed.

The man looked at the robot in anger. "Stupid machine, pick them up."

TAMS stood still.

"Pick them up."

No movement.

The man grunted in frustration and leaned over the counter, his fingers stretching out to reach the bills on the floor, one leg extended up.

Seeing her opening, Keegan leapt up from the corner table. By the time the man looked up, she was already on him. She was smaller, so she used physics to her advantage. She grabbed the man by the collar and yanked him toward her, his body sliding over the slick counter-top. When his center of mass shifted over the edge, he tumbled to the ground. Before the man could get up, Keegan placed her shin over his throat, using her focused body weight to pin him.

"Auditory sensors indicate four additional people in the food storage areas," TAMS said as patrons sprinted for the door.

The bot began pushing additional information onto her vizglasses. Unlike in the Kill House, the walls were too thick to determine the exact outline of whoever was back there. The glasses also noted the DC Metro Police's ETA, a clock ticking down the arrival of a patrol car projected to be assigned the call to investigate.

"TAMS, hold this guy until police arrive," said Keegan. Pulling the dazed man up, she reached over to grab TAMS's hands and placed them over the man's wrists. "And read him his rights."

"OK."

As the suspect looked confusedly on, the robot held him in place with its locked fingers as makeshift handcuffs. Then, with a vocal tone taken from an amalgam of the recordings of Supreme Court hearings, it began its lecture. "Mr. Andrew Kerinsky, as you are presently detained by a representative of law enforcement, as determined by the 1966 *Miranda v. Arizona* Supreme Court decision, you have a right to . . ."[1]

Keegan stopped listening to the robot as she moved back over the counter and snuck a quick glance around the corner, into the kitchen area. No one. She moved on to the doorway to the storage area and peeked around the edge. The waitress and a cook were kneeling on the floor, eyes fearful. An elderly man in a suit was laid out beside them, a trickle of blood coming from a gash above his eyebrow. Keegan had been to Ben's enough times to recognize Sage Ali, the son of the legendary founder. And behind them, crouched behind a stack of hot dog buns, was a young man with a shaved head wreathed in a barbed wire crown tattoo. In his hand, he held a blue eight-shot revolver, the kind fabbed by 3-D printers in garage gun shops.[2]

At the snap of a round hitting the wall inches in front of her, Keegan jerked back behind the doorway. A second bullet went through the doorway and hit the wall at the other end of the diner behind her, glass spraying from an actor's photograph. Keegan looked back over at TAMS. As the robber now writhed to try to get down to cover, the robot ignored the gunfire, prioritizing Keegan's last order to it. It was now reading out loud a clip from the Wikipedia summary of the 2010 *Berghuis v. Thompkins* Supreme Court case, which amended the suspect's right to silence only if they explicitly verbalized their right to silence.[3]

Changing her position lower to spoil the shaved-head shooter's last aim point, Keegan peeked around the corner again, but he was already gone.

She knew she could hang back and wait for DC police . . . But you don't shoot at a federal agent and just get to run away.

The waitress pointed down the hallway, to the exit door. Stepping into the alley off U Street, Keegan squinted to see if the man had gone left or right. The clang of banging iron caused her to look up. Shaved Head's escape had taken him to the roof of the six-floor luxury condominium behind the restaurant, as she could tell from his red running shoes disappearing over the edge. Keegan ran toward the exterior stairway, when the man reappeared, pointing his pistol down at her.

Shit. Keegan unconsciously shifted her weight to the balls of her feet and felt her stomach knot, her body waiting for the shot to hit.

The explosion from above echoed through the alley. Then came a howl of pain from the rooftop, where a cloud of blue-tinged smoke hung where the man had just been. That was the problem with untraceable black-market 3-D printed guns, she thought in relief. They don't show up in registries, but the black-market printers never vouch for their reliability.

Seeing a service door, Keegan sprinted toward it and pulled a breaching tool from her pocket. She jammed the flashlight-sized tube against the door's radio-frequency identification access plate, the kind used by all the automated cleaning services. An instant later, as the autosearch warrant authorized, the locks popped to allow her inside.

Half a minute later, Keegan was standing on the roof, weapon ready. Breathing hard, chest rising and falling from taking the steps two at a time, she searched the rooftop for any sign of the potentially injured robber. She knelt to peer under an HVAC unit, exhaling in frustration when she heard footsteps. Sweeping her pistol across the roof, she saw nothing. Then she heard them again.

There. Above her. A glimpse of movement as the man bounded from one of the rooftop's drone delivery pads to another, using the raised octagonal "lily-pad" landing platforms like a playground jungle gym.

"Stop!" shouted Keegan. "FBI!"

Shaved Head kept going, leaping across to another of the lily pads.

Keegan grabbed one of the landing platform's support struts and pulled herself up, as if back on the obstacle course in Quantico. By this point, the man had leapt across to a neighboring pad, a larger one designed to accept bulk deliveries.

"There's nowhere to go," Keegan said.

Shaved Head shook his head with a smile and made a running leap toward the next platform, which bordered the side of the roof. He didn't stop but kept running as he landed, leaping off the building. His body disappeared over the edge as he fell into the void.

Holy shit. Had he just committed suicide just to get out of an armed robbery collar?

Keegan made the leap to the lily pad and pulled up. Peering over the edge, she girded her stomach for the sight of what falling six floors did to a body. Instead she saw the robber on a balcony on the building across the street, one floor down. *Bastard.*

Keegan took aim. "Stop!"

Shaved Head looked back at her and then started to jimmy the balcony's sliding glass door. Her heart pounded and the blood rushed in her ears as she centered her sights on the robber. The balcony was decent sized, the kind of premium space that a good lobbyist's salary could buy, with a broad mirrored glass wall running along the back of it. But who was on the other side of that wall? Maybe a kid like Haley. Or a Jared on the couch. She held her fire and holstered her gun. She would have to make the leap herself.

She doubled back two more lily pads, not out of any strategy other than the assumption that there must have been a reason they did the triple jump in the Olympics. Taking a deep breath, she began to run, leaping from one lily pad to another, then the final one, ignoring the nerve pain now starting in her leg and the chili in her stomach, and launched herself across the gap between the buildings.

As Keegan fell short of the balcony on the other side, her brain unconsciously signaled that she should have factored in how much taller the robber was. It gave her body just enough warning to grab at the balcony railing with both hands, the right catching the railing fully, the left with two fingers. It was enough, and she hung there for a second, trying to get a better grip on the slippery metal rail. So she swung her legs out and then back in a kind of Kipping pull-up and let herself fall. The momentum took her down and she just made it past the railing of the balcony one floor below.

Stuck the landing was all Keegan could think.

She laughed out loud, the adrenaline from her near fall welling up. She realized she had lost her vizglasses in the leap. Typical. All that care not to scratch them in her pocket and they'd just fallen five stories.

She heard the robber in the balcony above ripping up the screen door, and she rapped her knuckles on the mirrored glass of the one she was standing on with her gun hand, pulling out her FBI identification card with the other. "FBI! I need you to open up."

No response, so she knocked again. The door slid open, pulled back by an automatic track. But there was nobody there. Puzzled, she peered into the room and called out, "FBI! On the floor!"

She felt a vibration at her ankle — a domo bot in the form of a large cat was rubbing its body against her, purring.[4] The mahogany-shelled quadruped bot turned its head up to her and said, "Welcome to my home. How may I help you?"

Whether that was the owner piped in or the sim-pet acting on its own, it didn't matter. Legally, they'd just given authorization to enter. Keegan kicked the purring cat out of the way and stormed through the apartment, out the front door, and into the hallway of the apartment building. Running to the stairwell, she raced up the steps two at a time. Her guess was that the robber had gone up as well, rightly assuming the streets below were going to start filling with cops.

At the door at the top of the stairs, Keegan paused, both to catch her breath, fighting back the taste of chili that was starting to work its way back into her mouth, and to check her Watchlet. Scrolling the wristband screen to the CityCam app, she pulled up the city government's security camera feeds nearby — nothing useful. One was digital snow, evidently jammed, and the other two cams that covered this block just showed a dark screen, likely sabotaged old-school style with spray paint.[5]

Going in blind then.

She carefully cracked the door, edging her pistol out first.

She caught a flash of movement on the adjacent building — this one was the same height as the one she was on, and the robber was again leaping across the alleyway-sized gap between the two structures.

Second time's the charm.

Keegan ran as fast as she could to the roof's edge. Not needing to leap from one pad to another, she easily made it to the other side, landing with a spray of cheap asphalt shingles. She hit hard, though, the impact a wave of nerves firing all the way up her back. The brief shock made her lose her balance before she rolled back to her feet with her pistol at the ready.

Stepping deliberately around a messily stacked pile of broken TVs sprinkled with green and brown glass, Keegan hunted for the man. Then she saw him — the bastard was starting another run to leap to the next building.

"FBI!" Keegan shouted. "Stop. Running. Now." She tracked the man's lower body with her gun's sights, leading him just a bit and fighting the instinct to place the shot center mass, just as she was taught. She wanted to wound him, not kill him, but this had to end. She exhaled and started to pull the trigger.

That was when Shaved Head's feet skidded as he desperately tried to slow down. Keegan's tunnel vision down her gun sights widened as she saw TAMS's head emerge at the edge of the roof. The robot pulled itself up to block the robber's predicted running path.

Shaved Head made a slight step to his left and TAMS matched him, moving over onto the ledge of the building, ignoring the abyss behind it. As the robber tried to fake right, Keegan ran forward, a slight hitch in her step now, her leg almost completely numb from the inflamed nerve. The man heard her and turned, his eyes wide as Keegan took him with a low rugby tackle. The momentum carried them both into an HVAC vent, knocking it free from its mounts.

"Do *not* move," said Keegan, using her weight to pin the writhing man. She looked up and saw TAMS freeze in place.

"No, TAMS, you're doing what I want," said Keegan. "Come over here and help out."

The robot reached down with one hand to cuff the man at his wrist, using the other to pull Keegan up.

POTOMAC OVERLOOK NEIGHBORHOOD

McLean, Virginia

There was a slight ping as Todd's shovel hit another rock. His forearms ached, but it was exhilarating in a way. For him, the feeling of exhaustion had always been associated with productivity, a job worth doing being done. His efforts hadn't been so physical in the past, but it still gave the same sense of achievement.

The sound of whistling and footsteps approaching interrupted that pleasurable feeling, replacing it with the need to put on a different face. It was crucial to control the flow of the conversation from the start. Todd climbed out of the hole in his backyard and leaned on the shovel as if it were a walking stick. Looking as nonchalant as he could, he called out, "Hey Alden, what's going on with you?"

The head of his next-door neighbor, Alden Chait, appeared over the fence dividing their backyards, perfectly framed like a target, between the evenly spaced wooden posts. "Not much. I forgot to take the compost to the curb," Chait said. "Pickup tomorrow. Then I heard the digging and thought I'd check in on you."

Unstated was the idea that Todd, the older neighbor, who lived alone, ought to be checked in on. It grated on him to think he was only a target of pity and concern.

Chait leaned in farther, as Todd considered the distance that the shovel's blade would need to swing in order to take Chait's head in the temple.

"So you putting up a privacy hedge because of the new camp back there?" Chait asked. He nodded over at the woods just beyond the tangle of scrub and grass that marked the open border of Todd's backyard to Scott's Run Nature Preserve. "I mean I feel sorry for those people, having no jobs and all that, but I wish they'd camp somewhere else."

"Yeah," Todd said, leaving it unclear as to whether he was answering the question or agreeing with the sentiment.

There was a pause, the only noise a slight buzz in the distance of a passenger drone making a run out to Dulles.

"You want any help?" Chait asked, filling the emptiness. "We got one of those new Werx yard bots. The digger attachment can knock that out for you in no time."

"No, I'm good," Todd said. He scratched at his chin with one finger. "You ever have the urge to plant something and watch it grow and become remarkable? From the very beginning, all through your own efforts? That's what I'm after here."

"Well, let me know if you change your mind," Chait said. "I'll plug it into the charger just in case. And just promise me you'll be careful. There's like 200 volts running through the line buried under there."

"Two hundred thousand," Todd said. Chait was dead already. He might as well go knowing the correct number.

"Huh?"

"The power lines that go into your house run up to 240 volts; that's what you're thinking of. But the park is city land, so the line back there is the high-capacity distribution for this whole area. The old overhead power lines for that when you were a kid were 13,000 volts, but the new Japanese multicore cable they put in the ground has a capacity of 200,000 volts."[6]

"I forgot you used to work on all that tech stuff," Chait said. "Well, whatever the number is, I think it saved us a couple hundred thousand dollars. They'd already put that line in when we bought our house. Everybody freaking out about the cancer risk of having a big power line running right behind their home knocked down the price. Didn't bother me. My attitude was like that song in the old movie about the lions, 'Hakuna Matata.' Whatever will be, will be."

He had that wrong as well.

"We were here before all that," Todd said quietly. "Isabella and Adam died right before they put it in."

That was how he knew exactly where the power line was. While mourning his family, he'd sat on the back deck alone, day after day, doing nothing but watching the Dominion Power bots dig the trench and lay the cable. It was then that he'd thought through what he would do next with a life that was over, what could be done to make their sacrifice have any meaning at all.

Todd's comment hung in the air, the darkness of it creating the awkward moment that he intended.

Chait was quiet, noticeably trying to figure a way to exit gracefully. "Well, I need to get back inside; otherwise Inge is going to think something happened to me." He smiled artificially, as if the last few minutes of uncomfortable conversation had been a true pleasure. "Good to see you, Jack. We should have you over soon, maybe dinner or just to have a beer out by the firepit."

Todd looked over Chait's shoulder at the red octagonal sign staked into the rose garden near his neighbor's back door. "STOP. This Smart Home is Watching You" it read. A visible warning to any would-be attackers that it was a wired home.

"We should do that," Todd said. "A fire sounds great."

U STREET

Washington, DC

Keegan led the suspect to the elevator, pissed off that he'd not given her time to stretch out before the chase, as her back now throbbed. Her stomach churned once more from the half-smoke chili dog. Vape pods and cigarette butts littered the elevator car floor, and the slight telltale sheen of a VR pen trail was on its walls. But without her viz-glasses, she couldn't make out whatever the digital graffiti said.

TAMS noticed her interest and began to read it out loud, mostly words about the police that it needed to be programmed not to use around Haley.

Keegan hit the emergency stop button. The robber, whose hands were now cuffed behind his back, stiffened for a moment, then his shoulders slumped, resigned to getting a beating. Keegan shook her head at him, and turned to TAMS.

"TAMS, the cams in this building weren't online, right?"

"That is correct," the robot replied. "DC police and municipal traffic and street surveillance cameras have not been functional in the vicinity of this building for seven months."

"Then how'd you know where to find him?" she said, jerking her head at the robber. Her left shoulder twinged at the movement. She'd feel that worse later.

"The neighboring building is listed as the home address of six individuals with outstanding arrest warrants, one of whom spent five weeks at the Anne Arundel County Detention Center as the cellmate of Mr. Andrew Kerinsky, the first detainee handed over to the Washington, DC, police department. It was his most likely destination."[7]

As it responded, Keegan noticed it moved its hands. That was new. It had learned to use expressive motions at times of explanation — maybe from one of the other test bots in another field office. "You know, that would have been nice to know before I jumped off a building after him."

She released the emergency stop button and the doors opened. Unfortunately, the first thing Keegan saw waiting just outside the building's lobby was Agent Noritz, pacing with the stiff-legged movement of absolute fury.

A female DC police officer stepped in between with a huge smile. "That was effin' amazing," the officer said. "All the way up the side of the building . . ."

Keegan started to smile, proud.

The officer handed Keegan her vizglasses. "You must have dropped these chasing after your robot."

"Thanks," said Keegan slowly.

What'd she mean 'chasing after your robot'?

"How'd you teach it that? The crazy flip part was badass," the police officer continued.

"What crazy flip?" Keegan asked.

"Didn't you see it?"

"I was a bit busy."

"Oh yeah, you're only in the last scene. Well, you gotta watch the rest," she said, holding out her ruggedized tablet to Keegan. Running on a federal budget, DC police relied on surplus Army gear.

Keegan jabbed the screen with her finger. A drone's view showed police cars converge on Ben's Chili Bowl. TAMS emerged from the front door and scrambled up the awning, leaping to the neighboring building, holding onto a windowsill with one hand. It climbed up the side of the building, digging its toes and fingers into the slight gaps between brick and mortar. At the top, it hesitated for a second, processing before it crossed to the next building using the power lines. Keegan recognized the motion from when she'd taken Haley to the National Zoo. It was how orangutans traversed the "O-line" ropes.[8] Back and forth the robot went, leaping and climbing and shuttling across as if in one of those parkour videos.[9] Somehow in the few minutes that the footage had been online, a pulsing club beat had been layered over the video. As the robot climbed to the roof, the camera caught it popping up to block the robber, followed by Keegan coming in from the side of the screen with a tackle.

"I want one, stat," the officer said. "Better than my lazy, broken-down partner."

"I heard that!" a voice behind them hollered back.

"Careful what you wish for," Keegan said. "Where'd you get this?"

"It's everywhere. You guys are trending."

Keegan chuckled. "All I wanted was a chili dog."

"Bad call; the meat in those will kill ya," the cop said in admonishment. "In either case, helluva collar." She then added warily, "I don't think your boss over there is as psyched about it, though."

Keegan looked over to see Noritz still glaring through the lobby window, motioning her to come outside. "Nah, he just really cares for me and got worried," she said.

Nudging the prisoner forward ahead of her, she said, "OK, TAMS, it's your first collar, so you get the honor of taking him to the paddy wagon."

As they exited onto the street, a couple dozen civilians stood behind yellow police tape. Even though many had already seen it on the video, they gaped at the sight of TAMS walking the robber through the door, toward the waiting converted minibus that DC Metro Police had brought to the scene to hold suspects.

Then came an explosion of breaking glass, green shards flying in front of them. Keegan looked up just in time to see another bottle sail out of an open window on the third floor. The robbers' friends? Or just locals pissed off at the police? Or at the machine? It didn't matter; the anger, and the outcome, was the same.

Whoever threw the second bottle was more accurate, but they

hadn't accounted for machine reaction time. TAMS's free hand batted the bottle away with the rubbery side of its hand, and it smashed against a brick wall across the street.

People in the crowd started to yelp, the spotlights on their vizglasses lighting up to record the scene. A few even grabbed at waist packs to launch microdrones that flew over the yellow tape to get close-ups they could sell.

"Get back! You know the drill!" one of the police officers shouted. He swung a jammer rifle — which looked like a black-painted two-by-eight piece of lumber — over the crowd, and the pocket-sized drones dropped to the ground. The jammer was little help against the bottles, though. As another splashed down, Keegan hustled TAMS and the robber toward the police bus. At its open door, the robot handed the man off to an officer, who quickly yanked the prisoner inside and then pulled back from the door to avoid getting hit.

Then the robot froze, unsure of what to do next, even though more bottles sailed toward it.

Keegan hissed at TAMS. "Stop being a target; you're going to get someone hurt," she said. "Follow me."

As another bottle smashed against the van, Keegan and TAMS climbed inside. This one had liquid inside, an explosion of green glass and yellow liquid. Beer or maybe urine dripped down the van's front window.

"Glass is bulletproof," the officer said. "We'll need a wash, but otherwise we're good."

Keegan just nodded as she saw a black FBI Suburban drive up. It was hers, but she hadn't called it yet. "Shit."

The SUV pulled up close to the van, blocking the bottles, and the driver-side window went down.

"Get in," said Noritz. Keegan started to cross over to the SUV, getting into the back seat, but TAMS stayed still. "Dammit, get in, I said!" Noritz yelled.

"You gotta order it by name," Keegan said quietly, as she slid over to make room for TAMS.

Noritz just glared back at her, and so she ordered it for him.

After driving slowly for a few minutes into the Columbia Heights neighborhood, he finally broke down and spoke.

"Explain," said Noritz. His Watchlet buzzed and he held up his hand to keep Keegan from responding. He sighed and frowned even deeper. As he pressed down on the control screen, the SUV flashed its red and blue emergency lights and chirped its siren before doing a U-turn. They were now heading south, at speed.

Keegan looked over at TAMS, sitting still behind Noritz, then back to Noritz.

"I meant you, Keegan," said Noritz.

"This one landed on us," she said. "We were engaged in a training evolution and two dumbasses tried to rip off the local transaction drives from Ben's Chili Bowl."

"And why were you in Ben's?" Noritz said.

Keegan looked out the window before responding. "Establishing a robotic system's cognitive baseline is complex and requires heterogeneous inputs that follow both regular and irregular inputs based on the anticipated local operating environment and its—"

"Cut the bullshit," said Noritz.

"Yes, sir."

"Why did you bring in the bot? It's not like it eats."

"Not half-smokes, sir. They're not good for its digestion," she said, then saw her attempt at calming the keyed-up Noritz down hadn't worked. She continued, but in a more serious tone. "The training assignment they gave me is to teach it, sir. You can't just program human interaction skills, so we're doing ride-alongs through the city. That means visits to places any human agent might go through the course of their day."

That would also give her an excuse if they wanted to know about the detour home.

"Every experience and setting is additional data for TAMS," she said, consciously channeling what she thought Modi might say, "making it that much smarter and useful, as well as giving us data for how it handles different situations."

"Well it sure got some added data today thanks to you," said Noritz, still angry but seemingly placated by her answer. "What you have to get, Keegan, is we're both now under a pretty fucking bright spotlight. You ever fry ants with a magnifying glass as a kid?"

"No, sir," said Keegan, wondering what kind of sicko did that.

"Well, get used to the feeling. You're now being summoned to spend some time under the glass."

"The deputy director?"

"Nope. Try again."

"Main Justice?"

"Nope," Noritz said. "A more powerful lens than that. The kind that can light us all on fire without even thinking or caring about it."

Keegan realized Noritz was savoring his advantage too much to get a straight answer, so she sat back in the seat.

As Keegan shifted, TAMS pushed a notification to her vizglasses: *Based on this vehicle's map setting request, our projected destination is 1600 Pennsylvania Avenue, Washington, DC.*

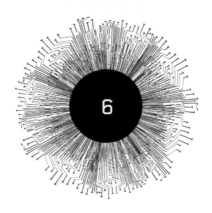

OLD EXECUTIVE OFFICE BUILDING

Washington, DC

They pulled in from the 17th Street security checkpoint that closed off Pennsylvania Avenue. In the history vids, people used to play street hockey on Rollerblades there. But now the once-open boulevard in front of the White House was fortified like a Forward Operating Base in a war zone. Secret Service in heavy body armor and two sniffer bots manned the checkpoint, with two MRAP up-armored vehicles backing them up.[1] Each hulking vehicle mounted the standard Homeland Security mixed-mission turret: eight tubed grenade launchers, filled with a mix of smoke and tear-gas grenades, and the distinctive black rectangle of a counter-drone jammer.

"We're here," said Noritz.

"Hmm," said Keegan. "We being called to the carpet in the Oval Office?"

"You're not that important," said Noritz. "I'm pushing you the details."

Keegan's Watchlet pinged: *Homeland Security Directorate, Eisenhower Executive Office Building.*

"I should have changed first," said Keegan, conscious of the streaks of dust and asphalt on her pants. She ran her tongue across her teeth, wishing she'd also had a chance to brush away the spicy sausage taste.

"Yeah, well, here we are. Your job right now is to say yes, got it? And nothing else," Noritz said. "Let me give you a last piece of advice. Popping up on the radar screen of people like this never works out well for an agent."

"Or their supervisor."

"Especially their supervisor. Don't fuck this up."

Keegan just nodded and got out of the SUV.

She looked up at the gray eight-story building towering over the White House beside it. Holding the offices of all but the most important presidential staff, it had the grand design of a European palace, reflecting the ambitions of becoming an empire that had filled America during its construction in the late nineteenth century.[2] Now, surrounded by checkpoints and a high wall of metal posts tipped with spikes, it had the look of a royal palace under siege. In many ways, it was.

"Let's get on with it," Keegan said to TAMS. She was starting to sweat again. She could have blamed it on the 102-degree heat or that her core temperature had not yet cooled from the chase, but she knew it was something else. Chasing the robber was dangerous, was something she had imagined. Going in blind to the Executive Office Building was a scenario she had never considered. She cast a glance at TAMS and guessed that was never in its modeled scenarios either.

The pair walked steadily up the stairs to the building's main entrance, where a human guard wearing a ballistic-helmet viz rig opened the door to the security complex set up in front of the old building. Inside, they had to pass through a large scanner that hummed like a refrigerator.

"This way, ma'am," said the closest uniformed Secret Service guard, motioning with a black-leather-gloved hand. "First time? All your electronics and any weapons go here in these bins. Then you go on through and you can check in at the desk. You can retrieve your belongings when you exit the building at this location. They'll be secure in a locker. Pick up your badge when you check in."

Keegan dumped her pockets, took off her Watchlet and vizglasses, and placed it all with her service pistol and spare magazines in a lock-box designed after the old post office boxes. She turned the small key to lock it and then placed the key and her belt on a rubber bin. As the bin went through an X-ray machine, she walked through a short hall-way that did a full body scan, the walls themselves the sensors. As she exited, she looked back. TAMS stood on the other side of the scanner, the guard blocking its way.

"No outside electronic devices are allowed through," said the guard.

"It's not a device," said Keegan. "It's a TAMS."

"I don't care what you call it. We can't let him — I mean *it* — through. You're good to go, but . . ."

A young woman in a yellow-striped pantsuit and dark purple heels then stepped forward from the waiting area behind the scanner. "Let the robot in. It's cleared."

"Alright, then," the guard said dubiously, but respecting her authority.

"I'm Mallory Gibbon," the woman said, as TAMS proceeded through, the scanner lights glowing red as it set them off. "Special assistant to the Homeland Security advisor. You can follow me. However, please have your machine shut down its network access nodes." As she spoke, Keegan noticed her eyes flickering back and forth, simultaneously tracking her vizglasses feed for work messages.

Keegan looked at TAMS and said, "TAMS, kill network ports and comms. Confirm."

They all waited a moment until TAMS said, "I am now offline. Confirmed."

The security guard didn't trust an outsider's machine and motioned to his own to verify. A spherical roller bot, looking like a truck tire with a glass sphere inside, extended a small antenna, before circling TAMS to search for any signals.[3] The bot retreated and the guard nodded.

At that, Gibbon held out two red security access badges, with a large "V" for "visitor" in white. Keegan clipped hers onto her shirt lapel. TAMS took the second and then paused. A half second later, it went over to the desk and grabbed a lanyard, attached it to the badge, and placed it around its neck. The lanyard neck swung back and forth more than it would on a human, the card skittering across the chest plate before adhering to the magnetic pistol mount on TAMS's torso.

"Fascinating," Gibbon said, pupils narrowing as she only now made eye contact with Keegan.

"Yep. The way it problem solves without hand holding is hard to get used to."

As they entered the building itself, the antiquated grandiose interior made Keegan feel even more out of place. It had higher than normal, 18-foot ceilings, a relic of a design age before air conditioning, which seemed to dwarf the small robot. The hallway floors were slick marble, set in a black-and-white-checkerboard pattern. TAMS's feet made a muffled tap with each step, while the rubber soles of Keegan's shoes made a squishing noise, making her slightly self-conscious.

Keegan knew better than to speak at times like this; what was coming was coming. Decisions had already been made. Careers at her level weren't a factor in these kinds of people's calculations, so whatever was going to happen was out of her hands.

She reflected on what Noritz had said jokingly about getting fired, knowing how much her family also depended on this job. Keegan felt a flash of anger at the situation, but tried to keep her face impassive.

"This way," Gibbon said, shouldering open what looked like a steel stairway door. It had a modern, almost brutalist design, out of place among the rest of the wood-paneled doors.

The next thing she knew they were outside, Gibbon's heels clicking on the black asphalt. Across from them was a red canvas canopy protecting an unadorned wooden door into the white-walled building.

Cold air blasted out of the door opened by another security bot. A gray-haired man, who Keegan was pretty sure was the secretary of state, pushed roughly past her, trailed by a younger man who nearly collided with her, too intently focused on whatever were his boss's next appointments displayed on his vizglasses. Like the British colonial administrators of old, wearing their wool suits and high collars in the sweltering tropics, both men were in full suits and ties.

They entered the building and descended a half-flight of stairs, the interior dark from the lack of windows. Here, in contrast with the EOB, the ceilings were low and the floor was a double-thick red carpet that muffled their footsteps. Thick-framed art covered the walls, each a battle scene or a portrait of a famous American. It was meant to be refined and luxurious, to awe and relax at the same time. It actually just felt dated.

"And here we are," said Gibbon, stopping at another steel doorway. Guarding it was only a single Secret Service guard behind a wooden desk. No body armor. No bots. Just a gold badge on a white dress shirt. It was as if further security measures would only insult those already inside the inner sanctum.

"Where?"

"He's waiting for you in the Situation Room," said Gibbon. "Well, it's actually not one room, it's a few of them together of different shapes and sizes, all the way down to broom closets just for secure chats. But you're expected in the primary. Of course, he gets the good one. It's the only advice I'd give you. Whatever he wants, he gets."

THE WHITE HOUSE

Washington, DC

At her first step inside the room, Keegan's stomach knotted up. It was not the Homeland Security advisor waiting for them after all. At the far end of a long U-shaped conference table stood Willow Shaw.

The energy he gave off was visceral, as if there were a million small machines churning away inside him. Given Silicon Valley billionaires' predilection for biohacking and performance enhancement, that was in fact possible.

"Agent Keegan, I am Willow Shaw," he said, introducing himself as part of the charade that the famous play, acting as though people don't already know who they are. "It is a great pleasure to meet you."

Shaw stood about a half foot taller than Keegan, with close-cropped silvery hair. It made his age hard to place, as the color could be read simultaneously as a sign of experience or distinctiveness. As he walked clockwise around the table, he dragged neatly trimmed fingernails across the back of each chair as if counting down five — four — three — two — one. He then reached out to shake hands.

Shaw's grip was a vise, as strong as a gunnery sergeant's. Keegan took it as the usual male bullshit of trying to show dominance at the start of a conversation. Yet when their hands met, she was sure Shaw had never swung a kettlebell in his life. His palm felt like it was new skin, exposed to the world for the first time that morning.

This was a hacker's body, thought Keegan, *consciously designed to crack the defenses of most social and cultural norms.*

He looked over to TAMS. "I am pleased to meet your partner, too," he said, extending his hand to shake with the robot as well. She'd not seen anyone do that with TAMS, but it responded as another human would and shook back. As the two hands squeezed, veins and tendons snaked along Shaw's forearm. His biceps flexed, stretching the sleeves of his black nanosilk polo shirt. The goal was clearly to physically dominate any room he walked into. With the robot, though, it seemed more like an engineering test.

"Tell me something about yourself," said Shaw. She read it as another attempt at dominance that the rich and powerful usually played, opening up the conversation with a command to be followed, veiled as interest in getting to know the person. It all wasn't needed, Keegan thought. The unorthodox meeting and the rapidity with which Shaw had compressed space and time to get Keegan and TAMS into this room showed his power over her in the pecking order, while his entire business model was built on knowing people.

But, as quickly as Shaw said it, he stepped even closer to TAMS.

It seemed that the machine was the more interesting person in the room to him.

TAMS stood still, not replying, even as Shaw moved closer to a distance that would make any human recoil at the invasion of their personal space.

"Go ahead, TAMS," Keegan said. "Authorized to answer questions from Mr. Shaw. Tell him something about your status."

"I am due to charge my batteries in approximately 139 minutes," said TAMS.

"Pertinent," Shaw replied. "But it doesn't reveal much of anything. How is Agent Keegan doing today?"

Keegan again felt her stomach clench. Toying with technology and people came easily to Shaw.

"Agent Keegan is currently showing above baseline levels of cortisol and adrenaline, with suboptimal levels of glucose. This can be attributed to her foot pursuit and subsequent apprehension of an armed robbery suspect and the chili and half-smoke hot dog that she ate," TAMS said.

Shaw laughed. It was a dry, nasal snicker that was out of character with his pseudo-dominant physical bearing. "I believe you just made a joke. Actually, I realize I didn't need to laugh to validate it for you, which in and of itself could be construed as humorous," said Shaw.

Keegan squinted, her body's natural reaction as her mind raced to try to figure out what the fuck was going on.

TAMS stood silent.

Shaw nudged one of the ergonomic desk chairs back and sat atop the table's oak surface, as if he were in his own boardroom. "You and me, TAMS, are more alike than different. You are a machine with a mission, not just some servile knee-high domo fetching food according to an algorithm's whims."

He bounded back up from the table and approached TAMS again, examining the robot's head carefully. Keegan took a step back, getting out of the way, realizing Shaw didn't even notice her in that moment.

"You can read me," said Shaw. "Tell me how."[4]

"I use multiple methods, with a combination of optical and LIDAR sensors," TAMS replied. "Registration of body posture and facial micro-expressions. Transdermal electrical conductivity in determining physical response to external emotional stimulus."[5]

"All very good methods," Shaw said, returning to his casual perch on the conference table as if considering which of the dozens of questions welling up inside him he would ask next.

Keegan rocked back on her heels and clasped her hands behind her back; she'd determined the best course of action was just to wait to speak until spoken to and otherwise stay out of the way.

"You're learning all the time, aren't you? Processing, sharing what you know with the other TAMS units in service in other cities," Shaw said. "The network greater than the parts, them learning from you and your experiences with Agent Keegan here, and you learning from their experiences with their own Agent Keegans. The whole of the system then developing and refining new cognitive pathways like . . . Of course, it could go much better if we could have sent out something more cutting edge than yourself. Wet nets can easily surpass your processing power . . ." He paused.

"I apologize, TAMS." He stood again and made a perfect bow of regret in the style of a Japanese courtier. "That was impolite of me and, you'll see as you get to know me, all too common. You and I are more alike than, say, Agent Keegan, here. You're on a journey, an eternal one even, and the challenges you face in comprehending the world around you are so familiar to me. I envy you, though, and the speed with which you will make progress and evolve. My path is more arduous, painful even. I see that as an unnecessary aspect of the human condition — suffering. It need not be that way. In fact, nothing is necessary."

Shaw sat back down and faced Keegan, making eye contact to signal that now she was being spoken to. "My apologies also to you. My sensors and processing capabilities, if you will, are not like other people's. They are in a way more like TAMS's. People like me were once referred to as 'little professors,' because our hyper-intelligence manifests at an early age, as does our desire to share our enthusiasm for subjects dear to us.[6] But, of course, it was not that. The condition is more akin to a difference in programming, which, in turn, requires one to reprogram yourself, to learn to read fellow humans."

Keegan wasn't sure how she was expected to respond, so she did what Noritz had advised. "Yes, sir."

"That statement makes you uncomfortable, Agent Keegan," said Shaw. "That is quite simple to read. But there is no reason at all to feel sorry for me." He stopped briefly, as if processing something, and then his mouth pursed into a slight smile. "Never feel sorry for someone who owns their own plane."[7]

"Mamet," Keegan said back.

Shaw's face opened up, his eyes, cheeks, and mouth all moving in unison to create a wider smile.

This is some multilevel chess shit, she thought.

Was Shaw smiling in acknowledgment of an equal, someone who knew and perhaps enjoyed the same writers? Or had he just woven in the quote from Mamet as a subtle signal that he could track down anything he wanted about what she liked and knew? And was that signal a warning or some kind of strange flirtation?

As if reading her, Shaw continued. "This is who I am. If I were made any other way, would I be a billionaire? Would I be in the White House, standing here with you? Of course not. God makes no mistakes; only bad human programmers do."

Keegan managed a nod and wished she'd insisted that Noritz come.

"My education in reading people accurately has a functional end. It is not that I reorient my sensors and focus on the details, detecting the cues and tells that most people throw away as so much noise. It's more. It also enables what you might see as 'hacking' emotions, turning those tiny observations into moments of exploitation."

"Like in poker," Keegan said.[8]

"For the highest stakes."

He turned back to the robot. "Let us run a comparison. TAMS, what do you observe about Agent Keegan's biometric baseline, say, her micro-muscle and facial movements specifically?"

"Rapid movement of muscles around the right eye indicates emotional discomfort," said TAMS.

"And the clenched jaw, more so just now — see it? — attests to a certain kind of frustration," said Shaw.

"Yes."

"TAMS, you must also register the weight of her body tilting back slightly on her heels, hands held behind her. It's the posture of duty, intended to signal deference, but also, context dependent, can be a means to hide frustration. I am not able to get under her skin, at least literally, like you can. But it is enough to tell."

Keegan also had to pee and wondered what the two would make of that.

"So why don't we relieve her frustration?" Shaw said with a flourish. "What would you like to ask me, Agent Keegan? Anything?"

"Yes, sir . . . I'd like to know what we can do for you," said Keegan.

"Nothing and everything. I was in town for a meeting, so it's something like providence that puts us together today . . . Your incident at the restaurant caught my attention. And I was curious. This remarkable machine, and you, interest me. The president's Homeland Security staff was kind enough to make it all possible."

"Providence," Keegan said.

"You seem suspicious of me," he replied. "What do you think, TAMS?"

"The data confirms it," said TAMS.

You're damn right. You're acting like you own the most important room in the White House.

"I'm hungry," said Shaw, more to himself than to either her or TAMS.

He tapped on his left forearm, running his fingers in a circuitous pattern across the skin, activating a dermal interface.[9] Keegan had never seen the rare and expensive technology in the flesh and she stared, marveling at the machine fused directly into the body.

A moment later, Gibbon opened the door. "The White House steward system will deliver your order shortly."

"I'd prefer you do it yourself," Shaw said.

Keegan wondered if Shaw even understood the ask of having a human deliver food, let alone a White House policy staffer. Gibbon, though, nodded and ducked out.

"While we wait, TAMS, why don't you read me? Agent Keegan, what more do you want to know?"

There was a lot that Keegan wanted to ask him, from where she could buy the superskin cream he was using to erase his wrinkles to what stocks to invest her retirement portfolio in.

"What are you doing in Washington?"

"I'm here all the time, actually. Care and feeding. House. Senate. Commerce. K Street. Sometimes CIA and DOD. Depends on the season. This trip was supposed to be a short one, but now I'm not sure that I'm going to rush back to California."

"TAMS, is he speaking truthfully?" She turned to the robot, trying to catch him off guard.

"No," TAMS replied. "External biodata and facial responses indicate Mr. Shaw is not telling the truth."

"Wonderful," Shaw said. He cocked his head. "TAMS, try again now: I'm not sure I'm going to rush back to California." He tipped his head slightly to Keegan.

"TAMS, is he speaking truthfully?"

"Yes," the robot observed. "Mr. Shaw's facial and other observable biometrics, such as facial muscle micro-movements and his pulse, all corroborate his truthfulness."[10]

"You sure?" said Keegan. It still didn't feel right.

"Sure as any machine can be," said Shaw. "And just how sure is that, Agent Keegan? Do you think I can't manage my own body? My whole life I have been learning how to present the kinds of data — tells, really — to make people more comfortable. But what is important is that you still detected the lie. No matter how good a machine's sensors and processing are, they lack an intuitive understanding of the underlying data. That is the crux of the problem, isn't it? It's no different than what TAMS needs to understand if it's going to be a successful partner for you."

"Mr. Shaw, maybe you should be teamed with TAMS," Keegan said.

"Now your humor is on display, Agent Keegan. Well done. But tell me, how is it really going with this unit? As you have *detected,* I am far from an impartial observer here. As a student of both technology and the human experience, I find utterly fascinating this collision between an evolutionary species and a revolutionary technology. But I also worry about what might happen next. I worry a lot about it, and that, Agent Keegan, is what I am really doing here in Washington."

"What do you mean by that, sir?"

"Just as TAMS and I are similar, so are you and I, Agent Keegan. We are both warriors of a sort. For you it was the alleyways of East Africa and the Arabian Peninsula; for me, the no-less-dangerous hallways of this city. Different battles, of course, but which ones will determine the fate of this nation?"

Keegan bristled at him equating running missions surveilling hacker dens in Mogadishu with dining around town with lobbyists in $5,000 jeans.

"They may want to see it as an experiment, but let there be no mistake: you are now part of a battle that *must* be won," he said. "This is bigger than you or TAMS, your Bureau, or even this government."

"Yes, sir."

"I don't need TAMS to detect your doubt, Agent Keegan . . . May I call you Lara? As we have spoken long enough to cross that barrier, and we are, indeed, on the same side?"

"Sure, Willow," she said, not getting his permission for the reciprocity.

"Lara, technology is essential to what makes us human in the first place, what distinguishes us from every other species, from the first crude tools our ancestors used to kill their food to the fire they used to cook it. And it has thus always filled our dreams. Indeed, it is why the ancients conceived of a technology like TAMS before humans even mastered the printed word, let alone mechanics or computing.

"The Talos of Greek mythology, the ka of the Egyptians, the 'precious metal people' of Buddhist scholar Daoxuan, the golem of the early Jews — even as we moved forward to a world of reason, these technologies were what we aspired to. In the book *Politika,* so foundational to our modern ideas of politics that we take the very name from it, the philosopher Aristotle told how mechanical servants — robots — would be the one thing that would solve human conflict and inequality, making us the equivalents to the 'gods on Olympus.'"[11]

"But it didn't work out that way," Keegan said, knowing Shaw was eventually going to get to the "but" part of the story and trying to steer him toward it quicker.

"Precisely. Aristotle writes at the same time as the myth of Pandora's Box. By its novel nature, any new invention of significance must be destructive to society. And we innately know that too, as much as you don't need to think consciously to process emotions."

"Anger is as much a tool as any created technology," Keegan said.

"Today's fear of robots or algorithms taking jobs is the latest expression of something quite old, as are the demands from the streets for leaders to stop such transformation," Shaw said, running his hand across his forearm. "Five centuries ago, William Lee applied for a patent for an automated knitting contraption and Queen Elizabeth I herself denied it, saying, 'I have too much regard for the poor women and unprotected young maidens who obtain their daily bread by knitting to forward an invention which, by depriving them of employment, would reduce them to starvation.'"[12]

The way that quote rolled so easily off Shaw's tongue after his screen swipe made Keegan wonder if he was using implants. With his resources, he probably wasn't on the cogniceutical drugs the US military experimented with for quicker training cycles. While they boosted focus and memory 10 percent, they also screwed with your sense of certainty, giving you insane levels of overconfidence, including for subjects you hadn't studied.[13] More likely, he also had the embedded brain interfaces Facebook had pioneered, back when it hired away dozens of DARPA scientists to work in its Building 8 skunkworks.[14]

"Government cannot stop the future," Shaw said emphatically.

Keegan made a note to search that line afterward, guessing it had probably been audience-tested at a TED talk and then packaged for online distribution in a short clip. But Shaw very much seemed to believe it, if his expressions could be believed.

"The English factories that kicked off the first Industrial Revolution were no more held back by Queen Elizabeth than a prohibition on systems like TAMS today would stop the advance of AI and robotics."

"Why bother with your commission then?" Keegan asked. "If it's all going to happen anyway, why go through the motions?"

"The repetition of fear does not mean that we shouldn't observe it and assuage it," he said. With ease, he launched into what sounded like another practiced speech.

As she listened, part of Keegan was drawn in. But another part of her brain warned that his intonation and pauses were likely also scientifically tested to resonate. A tech guru was not naturally a great orator, but they could engineer themselves to be.

"There is an arc that runs from good Queen Elizabeth to the revolutionary Thomas Paine, who urged us to cast off her nation's royal rule, to the scientists like Carl Sagan, Stephen Hawking, and Elon Musk some two hundred years later. All of them warned, quite reasonably enough, of the dangers of automation. Sagan was perhaps the most eloquent harbinger because his concern came from a place of deep understanding: 'I have a foreboding of an America in my children's or grandchildren's time — when the United States is a service and information economy; when nearly all the key manufacturing industries have slipped away to other countries; when awesome technological powers are in the hands of a very few, and no one representing the public interest can even grasp the issues; when the people have lost the ability to set their own agendas or knowledgeably question those in authority; when, clutching our crystals and nervously consulting our horoscopes, our critical faculties in decline, unable to distinguish between what feels good and what's true, we slide, almost without noticing, back into superstition and darkness.'"[15]

Keegan had served under a major who'd spouted Winston Churchill quotes that he listened to while he slept. The only way to stop it was to derail him with a question. "And what is your role, then?" she asked now.

"I grew up with my hands in the soil before I could walk, Lara. My family are all farmers in Ohio dating back to their arrival in the first wheeled wagons. It's an identity that transcends profit and loss. The productivity that we embraced started with GPS and Microsoft Excel, then crop-dusting drones and self-driving wheat harvesters. This was why I graduated from high school at eleven — to invent out of necessity. But machines meant fewer people each season. By the time I got my PhD at MIT, my parents were dead and the immigrants we hired each season were no longer needed. I was the only person left on the farm. There was only me, not we. I was the omega point of almost a thousand human generations of agricultural advancement."

He paused, as if to give her time to contemplate the statement.

After a few seconds, she felt the need to fill the silence. It was a shtick, she knew, but on the other hand, the guy had the right to it. Of the two people in the room, he was the one with eleven zeros after his net worth. "So you feel responsible then?"

"Of a sort," Shaw said. "I've done my part to create the 'disruption' that the winners of the new economy worship, but that makes me very uneasy. So when I do my work in this town, it's with an understanding of what's truly at stake. What's of grave seriousness to me is that our society has the tools it needs to make it through the coming storm. And the pathway through it is narrow, for we do not have Beijing's ability to enforce consensus on social control, nor should we ever."[16]

He smiled. From the way his eyes widened and his lips curled, it was a look of genuine excitement at what he was about to share.

"I'll let you in on my secret, Lara: this is a solvable problem . . . once you get past the politics. Liberal or conservative, those are outdated labels useful for dividing, not solving. Society is simply a design problem."

"Yes, sir," said Keegan, not knowing what else she was supposed to say. As she did, Shaw rubbed his forearm again and returned to the other side of the table. At that moment, Gibbon walked in with a plate of charred seaweed, shaved beets, and unfamiliar purple flower petals. Keegan noticed that there was also only one plate, answering the other question that had been troubling her: When was this meeting going to end?

"I see I have kept you too long already. I have a simple offer, with a simple premise: consider me a friend, Lara. Whatever resources I can offer you and TAMS are yours should you need them. We all need allies in the battles yet to come."

Keegan still couldn't tell whether he was lying. And she now knew that TAMS couldn't help with that either.

POTOMAC OVERLOOK NEIGHBORHOOD

McLean, Virginia

It shouldn't have been as easy as 12345, but it was.

Sipping oolong tea with the morning light shining in through his office's window, Todd had started by probing the IP addresses at the Chait home. He did not want to rely on Preston's tech unless he really had to, so his plan was to run a brute-force attack, using an old amended password recovery algorithm called Hashcat, to ping one potential password after another until he gained access.[17]

As he typed out the program's commands, Todd caught sight of his dirty fingers. Thinking through what he'd need to do for this unexpected diversion, he'd lain in bed all night, forgetting to even shower and change after the dig. Isabella used to get on him for that, the way he'd become so consumed with his work that he'd forget to take care of himself. It was perhaps what he missed the most — those gentle reminders that let you know someone else was watching out for you.

He started the program, but before he could even lean back in his chair the computer pinged an alert that it had achieved its goal.

"12345" it typed into Chait's system.

The lighting system in his neighbors' smart home had come with a default password, and like most consumers, they hadn't changed it.[18] Whether the cause was their laziness or shoddy design on the part of the manufacturer didn't matter. It allowed Todd to connect to the operating system for the energy-saving intelligent lighting system over the kitchen sink. From there, he moved laterally across the central software platform, gaining full systems access. It now allowed him to manipulate anything in the house that was connected, whether it was to unlock the doors or change the shower's water temperature.[19] The zeros and ones traveled thousands of miles around the globe, pinging from server to server, but he soon had access to what he really wanted, the gas stove just 3 feet from the hacked kitchen lights.

Now it was just a matter of figuring out when. Todd ran through the home network's machine-to-machine communication logs. Line by line, it gave up every detail of the Chaits' lives. Not just what rooms they went to and for how long, but even what they did in their bedroom, revealed by the minute increase of room temperature caused by the increased body heat of physical exertion.

As Todd saw just how much of their lives the couple had unknowingly given over to the machines — to monitor, to decide, to run — the more it felt like he would be liberating them. Death, after all, was a universal experience among living beings, but only the human mind so concerned itself with questions of its before and after. He was going to offer them up that insight, that lesson, as a gift.

"Hakuna Matata," Chait had said. Todd knew the song well, from his son watching it day after day after day on his little iPad, while eating Cheerios for breakfast.

It means no worries
For the rest of your days.[20]

FBI ACADEMY

Quantico, Virginia

"Your office's changed," Keegan said. "Where'd all the landscapes go?" She also wanted to ask where her origami robot had gone, but that would only draw attention to it.

"Sorry, part of an office redecoration," said Modi. "What do you think?"

"I'm not a fan of the couch," she said of the narrow brown two-person couch she sat on. "Not a fan of the color."

She didn't say how much the tiny touch reminded her of the marriage counselor's office, making her wonder if the furniture choice was part of a psychologist's playbook. She flashed back to her and Jared sitting leg to leg, connected physically as they shared their emotions out loud. The counselor might have hoped it brought them closer, but all it had done was create a familiar claustrophobia. That feeling of being pressed into somebody, surrounded by the faint musk of shared fear and frustration, was too much like sitting in the back of an M-ATV, just waiting to be hit by an IED. They never went back to marriage counseling; she blamed the couch.

"But I dig the pictures. Way better than the seascapes. Looks like it was done by some video game developer on acid."

The images on the wall now had the pixelated swirls of a pointillist painting, woozily human forms colliding with digitized inanimate objects. One had a blue upholstered chair running on a neon yellow sintered track, dashing ahead of a herd of monkeys. Another showed a sunset framed by clouds made up of thousands of rainbow-colored eyes.

"It's from Kendo, the Neuromodal Movement artist algorithm," he said. "I got brain scanned, and a few weeks later the algorithms gave me my portfolio. Not another like it in the world."

"I can imagine. Expensive?"

"I still work for the government," he remarked, cocking an eyebrow as if reconsidering and approving of the investment. "Kendo's algos are based on the original DeepDream code, the first AI artist, so there's a retro element."[21]

"Only now by putting all that on your wall, TAMS now knows your innermost thoughts and identity."

"Who's to say that it already doesn't know that, it's just not authorized to share it with you?" He smiled knowingly. "So, shall we begin?"

"I thought we had," said Keegan.

"No, we're just talking," he said. "But now you're on the clock . . . So how is your training going, TAMS?" He looked over at the machine that stood beside the couch. There was no way in hell she was going to have it sit beside her.

Immediately, the robot began speaking, as if it had successfully predicted that it would be asked before Keegan. "We are working on developing situational awareness based on real-world data inputs, macro-observation, and scenario development," said TAMS. "This is being complemented by synthetic experience modules derived from my training evolutions with Agent Keegan. Notably, we also apprehended two suspects attempting an armed robbery."

"I saw that. TAMS, does Agent Keegan like working with you?"

Keegan shifted forward in her seat and Modi held up his hand before she could interject.

"She is pleased with the pace of my evolving operational performance."

"How do you know that? Has she communicated that to you?"

"Yes, her biometrics, physical observation, and other data all have shared that assessment."

"But not verbally," Modi said, looking back at Keegan.

She wasn't sure how she felt about him catching that, so she showed no reaction. Maybe Shaw and TAMS could read her, but she didn't need Modi doing it too.

"What does that mean then, TAMS? Are you a good partner to Agent Keegan?"

There was a brief pause as the machine seemed to run an assessment across untold parameters. "No," said TAMS.

Keegan felt a surge of, what was it? Shame? Had she disappointed a machine?

"Will you be, TAMS?" Modi asked.

"Yes."

"When, TAMS?"

"Based on my current models and rate of learning, in approximately nine days."

"That exact, huh?" said Keegan.

Modi turned back to her. "And you, Agent Keegan?"

"I'll need longer. Maybe ten days," said Keegan.

"That's not what I meant," said Modi with a chuckle.

"I know," she said. She brought the fingers of her hands together into a tent, and then rested her chin on the thumbs. Though she unconsciously did so, her brain signaled that it was a close mimic of the analytic stance Modi used at their first meeting, and she smiled. Modi smiled back, seeming to come to the same observation.

"It's going well." Keegan pivoted her fingers down to point at Modi. "I can see there's a lot of potential in tactical situations and real-time fusion analysis. But you're going to need the right person with it. Every street we drive is familiar to it; it's got the databases. But the street isn't just the street. It's more than the people, the vehicles, the weather, birds, whatever. It's a feel. That makes not only each street different, but each time we drive or walk by it different. For example, Ben's is going to be different next time we go by it — probably won't be another couple of morons trying to rip off the place."

"And you may not go swinging off balconies again, either," said Modi.

"You joke, but you're right, I can't. Or rather I shouldn't," Keegan replied. "Not because it'll kill my back again, but because it's a move that I've pulled before. It's predictable. That makes it exactly what TAMS wants. But being predictable is what might also get you killed. There is this saying by a German general back in World War II that we were taught in the Corps: 'When faced with the same situation in combat, never do the same thing.'"[22]

"I see. But you also said that we're going to need the 'right person,'" said Modi. "Is that you or someone else? What did you mean by that?"

"I mean, it'll read whoever the human is, I guess, by their facial expressions, biometrics, past performance, whatever it picks up data-wise," said Keegan. "Tell me, do you think it will get more accurate at predicting what I will do, based on how it perceives the neurological and biological basis of my future behavior?"

"Definitely. It's what would make it a damn good poker player," said Modi.

"Not the first time I've heard that," Keegan said.

"How's that?" said Modi.

"Willow Shaw. You know him? He set up a meeting to check out TAMS." She didn't mention the location.

"Know him? Not exactly like you do now, I guess, but of course I know who he is."

"He said something about how our emotions are simply data derived from our physical states and they can be hacked like anything else."

"It's not that simple, Agent Keegan," said Modi.

She noted how he continued calling her by her title, unlike Shaw.

"What you're looking for is something that the old science fiction often got mixed up in the pre-AI days. In trying to predict how machines would one day approach true human-level understanding, they'd blend sentience and sapience. Sentience isn't about a robot becoming a conscious being; you know the kind that were always going to rise up and 'Kill All Humans.' It's simply the ability to perceive and understand one's surroundings. Sapience, though, that's the big stuff. It comes from the Latin for 'wisdom,' whether it's just the wisdom that we call common sense or the kind of wisdom that comes from a deeper understanding of a situation beyond raw facts. How we read one another, as humans, is more in the land of sapience and it is not even close to being understood."

He pointed at the pixelated images on the wall. "A machine can learn patterns, complex ones far beyond our own brain's ability to compute. But how we interact is far more complex than even that, for the reason that it is linked to the very question of how we define ourselves as *Homo sapiens*. Note that how we name our own species draws from the idea of having deeper wisdom and understanding."

"So I take it that you don't agree with the billionaire."

"He may own his own plane, but no. Emotion has all sorts of tells that you or TAMS can learn, but truly understanding what emotion means takes wisdom."

"So when TAMS gets pissed off at another robot driver, then they'll have crossed the line as a species?"

"Of a sort, but it will still only be simulating an emotion." He turned to look at the robot. "TAMS, what is the value of emotions?"

"They provide data points, which aid my understanding of past, present, and projected human behavior."

"For example?" Modi asked.

"While we traveled in a vehicle, Agent Keegan heard a song that reminded her of a prior relationship, most likely romantic. While she did not articulate her sadness, it was evident from her data."

Keegan blushed, and knowing she couldn't hide it, smiled and waved it off. "OK, enough about my history of broken hearts," she said. She considered what to say — she didn't want this to run its course to areas she'd rather not talk on. "So if TAMS is learning, real time, then at what point does it 'know' something?"

"What do you mean? 'Know' can have many meanings."

"It seems like 'knowing' something is a state. But TAMS is always going to be changing, given the data fire hose it's drinking from. Does it have any actual knowledge or is it just always going to be data input and output? AI may be modeled after our brains, but what we observe is limited to such a dramatically narrower data set than what TAMS can register. I think that limitation, that very uncertainty, is exactly what makes it possible to *know* something.[23] That there's actually so much that we don't know is what gives us the kind of conviction on certain things that no machine would ever be satisfied with."

"Deep thoughts for a Marine," Modi observed, tipping his head in respect.

"Safe space, right?" Keegan said. "Don't tell anybody."

"I won't. The truth is we don't *know*, and may never. Because if our creations ever reach that point, their sapience would go past ours." Modi leaned back in his chair, seeming to enjoy the conversation.

Keegan realized she was too, and that left her even more uncomfortable on the undersized couch. "That seems like a good ending point," she said. "We all good?"

"That is for you and TAMS to decide."

POTOMAC OVERLOOK NEIGHBORHOOD

McLean, Virginia

"Man, you can still smell it in the air," said McLean Police Department Detective Alice Tsay.

"Yeah, I hate it. Reminds me of Ramadi," said her partner, Detective Bill Apfel. "The thing no one wants to say is that death . . . stinks."

"Deep. My partner, the poet," Tsay said.

"No doorbell cam that I can see," Apfel said.[24]

"Let's get this over with." Tsay tapped her vizglasses to make sure they were on. It was required in all interactions now with civilians. As if she were going to beat down some guy on his front stoop.

It wasn't that kind of neighborhood anyway. Excepting the burned-down house that reeked of dead bodies, everything else was pretty nice. A cul-de-sac with mostly two-story houses and real grass lawns that reflected their owners' ability to pay the landscaping-water surcharge.

She waited for someone to answer at the house next door, but nothing happened.

After a few seconds, Apfel whispered, "This asshole dead too?"

"Detective Apfel is noting his surprise that the resident has not greeted us yet," Tsay said loudly. Her partner always forgot how sensitive the recorder was.

Even if no one was home, the house would normally ask them to leave a message. That's when she noticed the door was an older model. It had regular hinges, rather than automated ones, and the door lock was analog. There was even an old glass peephole instead of a camera and screen.

"Guess we're going to have to knock," she said, as much for the recorder as for Apfel.

It'd been a while, so she consciously thought through just how hard to hit the door with her knuckles. Not so hard as to come across like a hyped-up SWAT team, but hard enough to send the message that the person on the other side meant business.

After ten seconds, they heard a male voice behind the door. "I'm coming." He sounded tired, as if merely saying the words took effort.

"I'm Detective Alice Tsay, McLean Police Department," she said through the door. "Can we speak to you?"

"Yeah, just give me a second."

The door's metal locks turned slowly and it opened halfway. Tsay saw a man in pajama bottoms and a gray Princeton sweatshirt.

Jackson Todd of McLean, Virginia, looked a little older, thinner, but it was him. His face matched the homeowner's driver's license in the database.

"Sorry to take so long," Todd said. "I'm a bit under the weather. Something I ate, I think."

"Yeah, it's going around," Tsay said. She paused. Let him fill the silence. Sometimes it would take you in unexpected directions.

"Is there something I can help you with?" he asked after exactly three seconds. Long enough to be awkward, but nothing revelatory.

"The fire that destroyed your neighbor's home. We're checking in with all the neighbors, see if they know anything that could aid the investigation."

Tsay watched Todd recoil like an unseen hand had yanked him out of sight. She heard a cough and then a gag. Apfel put a hand on the wooden front door, tempted in the moment to give it a slight nudge and use the chance to render assistance as an excuse to gain entry. Tsay shook her head at him, and he pulled his hand back, remembering that those unmonitored days were done.

Todd reappeared, his hand on the door. "I'm sorry," he said. "It's just the smell, it makes it all worse."

"Yeah," said Apfel. "The last time I smelled something like this—"

Tsay cut him off before he could freak out the civilian more. "Did you notice anything that could have caused the fire at the Chaits? Anything they say to you that might help the fire department in its investigation?"

"No. Nothing like that. Should I be worried? The neighborhood association said it was just a tragic accident."

"Every death is a tragedy," Tsay said. "So far, it looks like something went awry with their home operating system. But there's been a rash of tech fails recently, so we're investigating to ensure no foul play."

Todd nodded, his fingers gripping the door tighter. "Can we do this inside?" He swallowed, as if grappling with the bite of something bitter welling up into his mouth. "I can give you the passwords to check out my systems and I can, um, take care of business."

Tsay looked over at Apfel, whose blank face said it all. If Todd had something to hide, he wouldn't have invited them in and offered up his passwords, while playing IT department for a puking civilian was certainly not how they wanted to spend the rest of the day.

"No, that's OK, sir," Tsay said. "Tech fixes aren't the police's job. Hope you feel better soon."

After Todd closed the door with another cough, Apfel turned to her and said, "Disaster avoided."

CLARENDON NEIGHBORHOOD

Arlington, Virginia

The chair was killing her back and the holster was digging into her side. Whoever had designed the furry orange chair in the shape of a cat had not planned for the sciatic nerve of an adult or the bulk of a Sig pistol. But Haley, sitting cross-legged across from her in a black and white chair that was pudgy like a panda, loved the soft furniture that decorated the coffee shop's kids area. Keegan loved coffee, had ever since she'd stolen sips from her mother's mug of fresh-ground heavily sweetened black brew she drank before leaving to work at the mill in Shelton. She'd leave after a kiss on Keegan's cheek left her in a cloud of coffee, and she'd come home offering a hug tinged with the sharp bite of pulping chemicals. Keegan wondered if the association of smell and person was similar for Haley. Since before she could walk, the two of them would head out on "Starbucks ops." First it was pushing a jogging stroller, then Haley driving her little e-car. It was bonding time for them while Jared went to his personal CrossFit coach. Back then, they'd seen that sort of thing as a necessity; like so much else, it had evolved into another source for arguments when they started to wonder whether they could afford it. This afternoon, it was about the two of them getting away, but this time it was to have a more uncomfortable conversation than the play area of pandas and cats had been designed for. Given the number of single parents on the weekends who took their kids there, maybe it had been.

TAMS sat next to Keegan like a patient dog. Its stillness did not betray its soaking up of the freely available training data in the room, everything from syllables of whispered conversation to the ideal temperature of a grande Americano. The machine was essentially just one massive sensor, collecting in four dimensions as it tracked the physical world but also the terabytes of data packets flowing around the Starbucks. She thought back to Modi's distinction between sentience and sapience.

"How's your cocoa?" Keegan asked. The weather had cooled down again, but Haley would have ordered it even on a triple-digit day.

Haley smiled, sipping from the spill-proof thermal bag that looked like a cross between a Christmas stocking and a foil-wrapped hot dog.

"The panda chair OK?"

"Can we take it home?"

Keegan laughed. "You'd have to walk it and feed it because I'm not taking care of another bear. Baz gets in the way enough." Her chair began to purr as she leaned forward to wipe a smudge of chocolate from the corner of Haley's mouth. A haptic reminder her coffee cup was empty, trying to get her to leave or buy another. There was always some way they were trying to increase customer throughput. It had come, though, just when she was working her way up to the part of the talk she'd dreaded. "Haley, you want another one?"

"Yummy," she said.

"What do you say?"

"Please!"

They got up and walked over to the ordering kiosk, an ebony and dark mahogany obelisk projecting out from the wall.[25]

"Hey, Haley! You've gotten bigger since your last cup," said Ariel, the coffee shop's human host, actually making eye contact through her vizglasses. She stood by the kiosk to assist, but really was just there to make conversation with people.

Keegan guessed Ariel was a college student but had never asked. The too-easy familiarity always threw her. She wondered whether Ariel actually recognized Haley from all the times her name had popped up in her vizglasses, or if she needed the reminder with each visit.

"Going to get her another," Keegan replied. "You know how she loves it here." Did she?

"Enjoy," Ariel said. After making eye contact, which her vizglasses tracked for how often she looked customers in the eye and for how long, she then looked into the distance. She was probably side-hustling a gig tagging images for an AI learning firm or whoever else was willing to buy her time for five minutes at a go.[26]

Keegan paused for a half second in front of the kiosk to still her movements for the facial recognition.[27] After it approved her account, she reset the interface to enter their order manually, rather than having it self-order based on their past purchases, mood, and sleep data.[28]

"Hot. What does that start with?" she asked Haley.

"H!" said Haley.

It was something that the designers often forgot. Efficiency was not always the goal of the user. "Yep," said Keegan. "H as in hhh . . . hot."

They spelled her order out letter by letter, with Haley managing almost all of "chocolate," slipping up on the silent "e" at the end.

Thinking of the haptic nudge from her chair and what else was to come, Keegan realized she'd need to refortify too. "Now, help me with my order," she said, carefully moving Haley's finger across the keyboard, spelling out "f-l-a-t" and then "w-h-i-t-e". Stained with green and red pen ink, Haley's fingers were so tiny, so delicate. In that moment, Keegan grew angry at herself. Was this going to be one of those conversations that would harden her little girl?

"But you spelled it wrong," said Haley. "There's no 'h' in white. H is for happy."

"It's a silent letter. You don't need it when you say it, but when you write it, you do."

"Why?" Haley asked.

"Because it helps people say it better," said Keegan.

"That's silly."

She walked Haley back to her seat until the order was ready at the counter. Leaning back, she steeled herself for what she needed to tell her daughter, watching Haley play in the panda chair. Trying to explain grammar and spelling was hard enough; articulating what was going on with her and Jared was going to be far harder.

Ariel the greeter brought their drinks over to them in a courtesy that was not extended to all the customers. Keegan wasn't certain as to whether it was truly a personal connection or simply the suggestion of another corporate affinity algorithm. She thanked the girl and resolved to take a moment later to give her a five-star rating.

Passing Haley her drink, she marveled at the precise imperfection of how her name was written on the side of the cup. The edges of each letter even had the fairly detectable imperfections of pen ink, as if the writer were already moving on to the next cup, idea, or conversation while engrossed in behind-the-bar activity. But there was nobody actually there.

"Here you go," said Keegan. "It's hot, careful."

"TAMS, how hot is it?" said Haley, sitting back in her chair and resting her leg on the robot.

"The temperature is 129 degrees," said TAMS.

"I knew he would have an answer," she said. "He looks like he's sleeping, but I can feel him breathing."

"Wait, what?" Keegan asked.

Haley touched her leg where it brushed against one of TAMS's cooling ports, behind its left shoulder. "Here."

"Haley, it's not . . ." Then she thought better of it. No need to destroy all her childlike beliefs in one afternoon, like *robots are alive* or *parents know best*. "I'm glad you like TAMS."

TAMS shifted slightly, moving its head left and right, then back to center.

"So, honey, can I talk to you about something?"

Haley's face lost its joy. Kids were good at picking up on those shifts. It was something about the parent trying to sound happy that gave it away.

"Uh-huh."

"When Daddy and I argue, I just want to make sure that you know it's not about you. We are both working a lot, really hard, right now. Sometimes our feelings get in the way."

"I know you love me," she said. "And Daddy too."

"Yes, Daddy loves you so much."

"I know that," Haley sighed, exasperated. "I mean I know you love Daddy."

"I do."

There was no other answer she could give. She looked over at TAMS and wondered what the machine was seeing — and whether it believed her or not. She hoped Haley at least did.

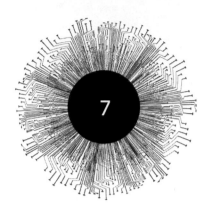

7

CLARENDON NEIGHBORHOOD

Arlington, Virginia

There were no tears from Haley. Trying to explain her parents' new relationship was only going to get harder as she got older, though.

Keegan sipped her coffee and watched her daughter, lost in play, tapping TAMS's head with a crayon, drumming to a song only she could hear.

TAMS's head pivoted swiftly to address Keegan. The jerking surprised Haley and she spilled her drink.

"NOOO!" the girl squealed.

"It's OK, butterfly, we can get another." As Keegan daubed at Haley's shirt with a napkin, TAMS began to speak, unprompted.

"Agent Keegan, there is a system-wide alert from the Army Corps of Engineers for the Potomac River Basin area."

She stopped and turned back to TAMS. "A little late to be telling everybody the Potomac's turned blood red."

"There is a widespread disruption of the river's flow-management systems, creating a cascading surge with imminent, catastrophic effect on the Washington Metropolitan area."

Keegan grabbed Haley by the hand, keeping her close as she made her way to the door, not even looking for TAMS to follow. As she passed Ariel, who looked quizzically at Keegan running out with her daughter in tow, Keegan said, "If you know anyone who lives down by the river, National Landing, Alexandria, Georgetown, wherever, tell them to get to the highest ground they can find."

"Huh?" said Ariel.

And with that, Keegan was outside on the street, summoning her SUV. The vehicle pulled up with its lights flashing. As Keegan put Haley in the back seat, TAMS walked around the vehicle. That surprised Keegan; she had not commanded the bot to do so. Rather than getting in the front seat, the robot climbed in to sit on the other side of Haley. It was following some kind of protective protocol. Was that a set program, or something it had learned from tracking her? Once the three were inside, and TAMS helped Haley fasten her seat belt, the car wedged its way into traffic for the short trip back to their apartment.

Keegan tried to message Jared, but the signal kept dropping and her Fed override wasn't getting through either. Shielding the Watchlet's screen from Haley, she brought up DC Metro Police footage from the Key Bridge. She squinted, unsure of what she was seeing. A wall of reddish-brown, roiling water rushed downstream, surging around the pillars of the storied bridge that connected the District of Columbia and Virginia. She froze the image and expanded it: tree branches spiked skyward out of the frothing water, a blue pickup truck slowly spun like a drifting leaf.

"Haley, when we get home it's really important you listen to your dad," Keegan said.

"Why?"

"Because he's your father," Keegan said. "Just do whatever he says when TAMS and I go back to work."

"Has something bad happened?"

"You're safe. You're going to be fine. Be a good listener."

As she spoke, Keegan called up a cartoon stream on her Watchlet and sent it to the SUV's main screen. "We'll be home soon, butterfly."

"Can't you and TAMS stay with me? I don't want you to go."

Keegan looked at the robot and wondered what it would make of a comment like that. It could not feel the words as a human would. TAMS could only process Haley's request as a demand, as just more data. But as a mother, it utterly destroyed her.

THE TIDAL BASIN

Washington, DC

"What's the matter, honey? Is everything OK?"

It was distinctly not. No matter how hard Tim Phan mashed the pedals, the stupid swan boat seemed to be stuck in place, unable to get away from the other rental boats pushed together by the wind. The one thing he couldn't control, the weather, was going to ruin what was supposed to be the biggest moment of his life.

All the data had pointed him and Dana Rodriguez to this instant. The cross-mapped psychological profiles, the overlapping friend networks, even the 87 percent successful relationship projections they'd each received before their very first meetup over a cup of zucchini tea, an experience suggested by their cloud activity. It all made sense; this was the person he was supposed to spend the rest of his life with . . . if the damned wind would just cooperate.

The plan was to propose to her in the middle of the Tidal Basin, with all the memorials looking on. Dana taught US History to tenth graders at Falls Church High School, so it just fit her. A romantic setting in the center of all that made this country great, from Thomas Jefferson and Martin Luther King Jr. to the collected faces of the Women Leaders Monument — Susan B. Anthony, Rosa Parks, Sandra Day O'Connor, and all the others — staring down. She'd be able to share the viz of it all not just with her family, but with all her students. She'd love that.

Even the temperature was right. The last thing he wanted to do was propose with sweat running off his forehead, though he might have been able to blame the heat for his nerves. Fortunately, the spring weather roller coaster had gone from the hundreds back down to the seventies, an almost perfect day to be out on the water.[1] Except he'd forgotten to check the wind. And now it was going to ruin it all. He didn't want to propose to Dana with some family of tourists in Alabama football shirts sitting just a boat's length away. He tried to pedal harder to get some distance, cursing everything from the wind to himself for wearing flip-flops.

He should have listened to his mom. She'd said to do it by the cherry trees on shore, dressed up for the occasion. But he hadn't wanted to blow his cover; Dana's profile showed greater joy from surprise. And now it had all gone to hell.

Then, as if responding to his curses, the breeze shifted directions. Saved.

"I'm doing great," he said, as they began to edge away from the other boats. He slowed his pedaling to catch his breath. The beating of his heart, though, wouldn't slow down.

"That's good," Dana said. "You looked like you were going to be sick there. I was worried about you for a moment."

His hand went to the pocket of his jacket, feeling for the small box's rounded edges. This was it. This was the moment. He blinked twice rapidly to start the vizglasses recording that would go out live to all the friends and family he'd marked for notice.

"When I'm with you, nothing can go wrong," he said. It wasn't the exact opening line to the speech he'd rehearsed again and again in the bathroom. It was even better, he thought to himself. He took a big breath and slowly withdrew the ring box from his pocket. Dana's eyes widened and she blinked twice as well. She knew.

He opened the velvet box without a word. Inside was a ring of azure blue sapphire, mounted atop a ring of synthetic diamond in the shape of a crystalline vine, grown exactly to the size of Dana's finger.[2] He'd gotten the size for that the old way, wrapping a string around her ring finger while she slept.

Dana's face instantly changed and she gasped. "Oh, God . . . No, no, no," she whispered.

The ring box clattered to the bottom of the boat as Tim's heart sank and his entire body went numb.

Everyone had been watching, and she had said "no."

Then, some kind of instinct took over and he reached down to grab the ring as it bounced between their feet on the boat's plastic floor. Maybe he could get his money back. Maybe the manufacturer would understand that the algorithms just had it wrong.

Dana pulled at his shoulders, trying to yank him back up. "Oh my God, Tim. Look."

Dana pointed behind him, her finger trembling. Tim looked up quickly, his vizglasses slightly askew, broadcasting a scene for which he never could have planned.

Coursing across the green softball fields of the West Potomac Park that divided the pond of the Tidal Basin from the Potomac River was a tsunami of white and red foam mixed. Trees, bushes, and even a bright yellow water-taxi boat, all pitched together by the water's force. To the other side of the Martin Luther King Jr. Memorial, a second wall of water rushed down 17th Street itself. Funneled by the slight hills on each side of the street, the wave pushed ahead of it a double-decker tourist bus and one of the wheeled red, white, and blue Park Service robots that stalked the National Mall.

Then came the sound. Screams of people in the swan boats realizing what was happening mixed with the low rumble of the twin walls of water coursing through the cherry trees and then into the Basin.

With a shaking hand, Tim picked up the ring that he had ordered for Dana. Focusing on nothing else, he slid it onto her finger, trying desperately to remember the lines of his proposal before it was too late.

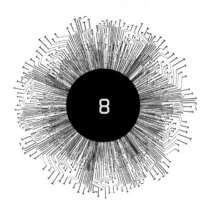

8

BALLSTON NEIGHBORHOOD

Arlington, Virginia

Even on the short drive home, she could sense the change. The confusion. The fear. She could see it in the set jaw of the middle-aged man they passed on the street. Jogging in dress shoes and a suit, he was clearly a government worker, who, like her, had gotten an early notice and therefore a head start on the rush home. Even the sharecars seemed punchy, jumping in and out of traffic with something like alacrity, as if they could not wait to wrap up whatever trip the algorithms had just ordered.

Keegan parked the SUV in front of the building, taking advantage of law enforcement privileges. Plus, she doubted that any cops would be out writing parking tickets today. Next to it was a yellow and blue sharecar, perched sloppily, half on the curb like it was just waiting for the right moment to move to higher ground.

Holding Haley close, Keegan swept into the lobby of the building.

"Stairs," Keegan said, and TAMS pivoted, then swept around her like a determined dance partner. It had registered the situation as machine-first mode, an environment of danger. Keegan noted it with appreciation, until she realized something else.

"TAMS, when we get to the apartment, I'm going in first, OK? Remember last time? We don't need that scene again today."

"OK," said TAMS.

In the flickering light of the stairwell, Keegan looked at the bot, wondering what exactly it made of her command. How did it process the human need for respecting feelings even in a time of crisis?

They took the stairs at an easy pace, counting each step, turning it into a game so as not to frighten Haley. When they reached their floor, the hallway was empty. She went right inside, not bothering to scan first to see how Jared was doing or whether he was working or not.

"Hey! It's me," Keegan shouted as her eyes swept the living room. There was no sign of him, just an empty couch, except for the rig and a pile of loosely bunched blankets. She touched the rig — cold.

"Jared! We're home!" she called again. She sat Haley on the couch and, smiling reassuringly, snuggled the blankets around her into a kind of nest.

No response. The air smelled stale. She moved to open a window, but stopped herself and went straight to the bathroom, past the closed bedroom door.

She closed the drain of the bath and turned the tap on full, then did the same with the sink. She gripped the sink, knuckles white, and nudged the door shut with her foot. Eyes closed, she fought the urge to punch the mirror in anger. Not at Jared. Just at everything in that moment she was powerless to control. She turned the sink faucet off and focused on deepening her breath while she came up with a plan. As she did, her Watchlet vibrated repeatedly with notices, but she ignored it. She opened her eyes and looked in the mirror. *You got this.*

She cracked the door of the master bedroom slowly. Jared lay on the bed, sprawled like a starfish, his head facing away from her. Shit, not again. Not now.

Sitting on the bed, she shook his shoulders. "Hey! Hey! Jared!"

Jared sighed as she did so and reached up to squeeze her hand. "Hey," he said, very far from her and the room right then.

"You need to wake up now! It's an emergency, Jared. You understand? Haley's here. I need you to keep her safe because I need to go back out," she said. "Like now." She released his shoulders and stood up.

At that, he stiffened and sat up, wiping the sleep from his eyes. "OK," he said. "I'm on it."

In the pantry was the box of cans they'd put away for emergencies a few years back. But when was the last time she'd checked the expiration dates? Plus, Haley wouldn't eat tomato soup and refried beans. So she rifled through the cupboards, taking an inventory of the food they had. A box of Cheerios and another of ranch-flavored rice crackers, a jar of chunky peanut butter, and a box of Haley's processed fruit squeeze tubes. The refrigerator and freezer offered little, aside from milk and almond creamer, butter, and a bag of spinach. They had gotten so used to automated food deliveries that there was no need to keep more than a few meal's worth of ingredients on hand. Even air-delivered fresh bread, a luxury that neither had been able to give up, was a daily staple.

She quickly opened the order screen on the refrigerator door and tried to buy a full inventory, essentially two weeks' worth of past orders all at once. But just as she was about to push the "buy" button, the app froze. She kept trying, so intently focused on the small screen that she did not see Jared walk into the room from the bedroom.

"What's going on?" he asked in a gravelly voice, clearing the sleep from his throat. His eyes warily tracked to where TAMS stood watching over Haley, now playing on the couch with her self-assembling Legos. "And why is *it* back?"

Keegan motioned him over with a commanding look of her eyes that indicated they had to talk without Haley hearing.

"We don't have time for this shit right now. I need you locked on, OK? You need to stay in the apartment, with Haley, for a while," she whispered. "I don't know how long. There's a flood downtown. Catastrophic. We're safe up here, but that's not it. I think there's more coming."

"More coming? So you're saying this wasn't accidental. Cyber attack on infrastructure?" he asked.

She smiled at his flash of comprehension. It was a glimpse of the old Jared, the one who had graduated at the top of his law school class. "Exactly. I'm trying to order more food, but it's flaking out, the signal likely overwhelmed by everyone calling at once. Can you keep trying? Everybody's being called into work, TAMS and I . . . Hold it."

She went over to TAMS, who had now become some kind of race-track for Haley, the girl no longer at the couch, now running a Lego race car up and down its legs. She examined its antennae array on the back of its head closer. "Haley, can you stop for a minute? I gotta ask TAMS something important." Haley stopped, and Keegan continued, "TAMS, can you take the network signal from this" — she pulled the Watchlet off her wrist — "and convert it to a satellite-band data feed?"

"Yes," said the bot, taking the bracelet computer. After a second, it reported. "Uplink established."

"Thank God!" said Keegan, feeling dopamine wash away the adrenaline flooding her veins, achievement knocking out fear. She snatched the Watchlet back from the bot and tabbed open her grocery app. In less than a half minute, she showed the screen to Jared. "Order completed, delivery on the way," she said triumphantly.

He held out his hand in a congratulatory high five, his cheeks now showing a healthy red flush.

Take your wins where and when you can get them, she thought, and gave him a five back.

"Go," said Jared. "Haley and I'll go up to the roof pad and bring the food down."

"You sure?"

"We'll be fine," he said.

He took a half step to hug her, but stopped short.

And you have to accept your losses, she thought.

"Don't forget to turn off the bathtub faucet," Keegan said. No need to have a flood in the middle of a flood. She turned to lift her daughter up into a hug.

"Oh, Mommy," she said, pointing down at the Lego car now missing its front hood. "You messed up my construction."

"Sorry, butterfly," she said.

She kissed the top of the girl's head and then looked over to TAMS and gave it a nod, a signal that it was time to go. It was only when she and TAMS were headed down the hallway that she stopped. For a few seconds, she stood, tapping her feet, weighing what to do. Then, keeping one eye on TAMS, she pulled up the delivery order screen on her Watchlet and added an extra supply of Jared's aerosol Dilaudid.

FARRAGUT SQUARE

Washington, DC

Keegan kept her hands on the SUV's wheel, ready to snatch control as she travelled with TAMS against a steady stream of autonomous vehicles fleeing the flooding along the Potomac. Above its historic high water mark, the river spread over the entire basin and had even overwhelmed the barrier walls at Reagan National Airport.[1]

"Send our location to Noritz and the TOC," said Keegan.

TAMS pushed a thumbs-up emoji to Keegan's vizglasses.

Their destination was the old FBI Washington Field Office building at 4th and G. A notice had gone out that a temporary command post had been set up there after the Hoover Building's basement flooded and the entire block lost power.

On the SUV's screen, Keegan projected live satellite imagery of the city overlaid onto a street map. It showed how the flood wave had paid no mind to the orderly gridlike arrangement of Washington's streets. The initial wave had surged well up to M Street, but then the waters had quickly receded, leaving muddy red sidewalks and sucking cars right out of their parking spaces.

Most of all the view showed how just a few feet in elevation made all the difference between devastation and normalcy.[2] Most parts of the city were untouched, but now a massive moat cut through Washington, DC,'s federal district, turning the southern chunk of the city into an island. The Potomac River's newest tributary entered the city at the Tidal Basin on the edge of the National Mall before its waters returned back into the main river near the lower elevation of the District Wharf shopping complex. Or rather what had been the District Wharf shopping complex.

The borders of the flood zone reflected the subtle topographic contours of a city constructed out of swampland, unnoticed by most residents, but which had originally set its design over three centuries back.[3] The flood's edge ran along Pennsylvania Avenue, roughly mirroring the now-paved-over Tiber Creek that had once reached right up to the President's Palace, before it was renamed the White House.[4] It then ran from 15th Street beside the Treasury Department building, down over to the I-395 highway tunnels that opened at the base of Capitol Hill.[5] Its southern side ran along Madison Avenue, the lower edge of the National Mall, which had previously been the open canal where Washington's residents had dumped their trash in the early days of the republic's capital city. The slight incline of the National Mall protected its green spaces, but the Museum of Natural History and the Justice Department, as well as the other buildings between Madison and Pennsylvania Avenues, now appeared as squares of cement rising out of the brown-red water, like tiny islands.

Keegan zoomed in, seeing tiny dots swarming each of the island-buildings. Some were brightly colored city and federal emergency response drones, but there were also parcel drones dropping packages on the rooftops, an automated rush of requested deliveries and flash-funding charity drops. Panning over to the veterans' encampment, Keegan saw that the rest of Capitol Hill remained dry.

"Route the vehicle around any areas less than 20 meters in elevation," Keegan said, realizing the vehicle's navigation probably didn't have a scenario for city streets literally disappearing underwater.

They got as close as Farragut Square before the crowds got too thick. Keegan sent the SUV off to autopark up on high ground near H street and they set out on foot. Overhead, a bright yellow FEMA drone loitered in a lazy circle, while a micro-cam drone from one of the newsfeeds landed on the statue of Admiral Farragut to get a better shot. Thousands of people were out in the streets, some with a specific destination in mind, some aimless, and many just to film and comment.

As they wove through the crowd, they passed the Farragut West Metro entrance. Keegan hated that spot more than anywhere in DC. She'd first been there nine years ago, while on leave from the Saudi stability op. It had been in early December, so on her way home, she'd killed time during a seven-hour layover at Dulles Airport to come in and check out the White House Christmas tree and all that stuff that you were supposed to be fighting for. Riding the subway escalator up, though, she had recoiled at the stench, not because it was that bad, but because it was all too familiar. The station had been turned into an encampment for desperate people, crushed together to escape the cold. She was a stone's throw from the White House, witnessing the abject abandonment of fellow humans that she'd only before experienced in refugee camps. And she knew that her commander in chief would never walk the two city blocks to confront that dark fact.

Today, a stream of men and women, some with children, emerged out of the station, wet and sobbing.

"TAMS, gimme a status check on the Metro," Keegan said as she headed down to see if anyone below needed aid. The rule beaten into her since boot camp was Marines headed toward the sounds of chaos.[6]

"The lower-elevation sections of the Orange Line and Blue Line are flooded," said TAMS. The bot pushed a Metro map with the affected segments to Keegan's vizglasses. It also marked malfunctions that had apparently locked the valves for the Metro system's air vents and the DC stormwater overflow pipes that connected to the Potomac River.[7] To save money, the designs had piggybacked off each other, but now their malfunction prevented the system from clearing itself.

Peering down the escalator, Keegan could see the effect. Muddy water lapped halfway down the steps, meaning the entire ticketing mezzanine was flooded. Worse, the next lower level where the trains boarded also had to be completely underwater.

"Is everyone out?"

"No. My acoustic sensors indicate there is a female adult trapped below."

Keegan couldn't hear anything over the rush of the water and the voices of the crowd above. Her stomach knotted. "Where exactly?"

"I cannot ascertain."

There was an agent's booth in the middle of the second level. That might be high enough for somebody to climb up on and get above the flood. She eyed the swirl of muddy water. It was too deep to stand in, and the current would send her down into the Metro tunnels if she tried swimming it.

"Can you reach her?" Keegan said.

"Yes. I am rated to ISO standards for underwater operations for a duration of thirty minutes at 10 meters depth."

The water reeked of ozone and sewage. If TAMS went in and never came out, that would certainly solve the problem that the deputy director had put in her lap. But it would present another: she would have to find a way to finish the rescue herself.

"Then do it. I need you to reach whoever is down there and lead them out."

"OK," it said.

TAMS stepped carefully toward the water's edge, narrowly avoiding stepping on a tiny frog that hopped up the steps. All sorts of shit down there is going to be forced up, thought Keegan.

"Hey! You need to get out of there! What the hell are you doing?" a man shouted down.

"Good question," Keegan called back, then she thought better of it. It wasn't the time for snark.

"We're FBI. There's someone trapped down there!"

A barrel-chested African American soldier in Army fatigues smeared with mud came running down the escalator. He pulled up in shock at the sight of TAMS descending into the water, one hand gripping the railing. "That thing yours?"

"Yeah," Keegan replied. "It detected someone inside. I think they're stuck in that booth by the turnstiles, you know, where you ask for directions."

"And you're going to send the Terminator in after them?"

"If you've got a better idea, I'm listening."

"Nah. Just don't ask me to sign for that when you lose it."

With the water now up to its neckline, TAMS had stopped to listen to their conversation. Perhaps the soldier's uniform had triggered some old program.

"TAMS, you're still cleared to proceed," Keegan stated.

"OK."

It wasn't a remarkable set of last words, Keegan thought, as the bot disappeared into the murk in a shimmering blue halo generated by its onboard navigation lights. Her AR glasses pushed a notice: *Network connection lost.*

"This going to work?" the soldier asked.

"Hell if I know."

"Sergeant Terrence King, Maryland National Guard," he said. "Your phone app functional? I need to let my wife know I'm OK."

"Agent Lara Keegan. No, not without the bot boosting the signal."

The man sighed.

Then light washed over them and Keegan looked back up the escalator and saw a line of people gathered to watch, several turning on their lens cameras to record them, even a few holding out old smartphones to get a better angle.

"FBI! Turn your cameras off!" she shouted back.

"Like that's ever worked," said King.

Keegan glared at him, then turned back to the water, waiting for any sign of the robot. Neither spoke as they waited, watching another frog hop past their feet and clamber up the escalator. Then they heard a voice.

"We're coming up! We're coming up!" a breathless woman shouted from the far end of the tunnel. Then she appeared, a woman in her fifties. She thrashed at the water with one hand, her other arm being pulled by some force under the water. Just ahead of her a faint blue light got brighter and brighter as it approached beneath the surface.

"We're up here! Watch the steps at the bottom of the escalator," said Keegan, wading into the water as TAMS came into view, its head barely clearing the surface. She and King pulled the woman out of the water, the polyester of her blue WMATA uniform dripping sheets of water.

King took off his jacket to wrap the woman up and led her up the stairs.

TAMS, meanwhile, waited down at the bottom of the escalator, the water lapping at its waist, its arm locked on the railing. Keegan thought about what exactly the deputy director would order at this moment.

"Come on, TAMS," she said. "Get out of the water, hero."

"OK."

As the machine exited the murk, water spurted from its joints and sensor ports. On Keegan's viz screen, it showed that the connection to the bot's operating system was still not working.

"Confirm diagnostics, TAMS," Keegan said.

The robot stood still for thirty seconds, until a message read on Keegan's vizglasses: *System reboot complete. Restore network connection.*

That meant taking TAMS up to the street level to get a signal. "Follow me to the street and reestablish satellite bandwidth connection."

"OK."

At the top of the stairs, she stopped so abruptly that TAMS literally stepped on her heels. Even through the pant leg, the metal edge scraped a piece of skin off the back. "Shit," she said to herself, but not at the pain.

Waiting there was King, standing at attention. He threw a salute and then started clapping, a steady authoritative rhythm. The crowd of hundreds behind him joined in, wet palms slapping together in applause, humans looking for something good to cling to on a day of awfulness, even if it was a machine.

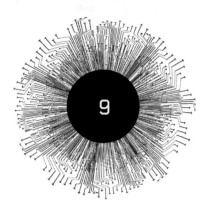

9

THE NATIONAL ARCHIVES

Washington, DC

The sewage stench that burned the back of the throat. The red high-heeled shoe abandoned in the mud. The desert-tan six-by-six National Guard truck, its wheels thrashing water into a chemical froth that looked like a dirty bubble bath.

As the adrenaline ebbed, it all felt overwhelming. In that moment, though, Keegan reminded herself she'd have to monitor the effect also on TAMS; the robot's experience during this disaster was foundational, transformative, just as it would be for the entire nation to see its capital deluged. This was a data set unlike any other.[1]

She knew what awaited at the Washington Field Office: bureaucratic chaos, the bosses jockeying to be in charge, and then long waits to get cleared for whatever their assignment turned out to be. So she found herself drawn in another direction, toward a different kind of duty.

The sound of the bucket brigades rang out two blocks before she saw them, a large crowd singing "The General's Daughter." A country song released last year, it was a ballad about a soldier in the Army who died on her first deployment, after which her dad resigned his commission and took his own life. It was about the darkest song everyone knew, which was probably why someone had started singing it. When it first came out, Keegan had wondered if it had a human writer. Seeing its lyrics stitch together so many people at this moment, she doubted it more than ever.

The crowd ranged from federal workers in muddy suits to woolly-bearded veterans who had left their encampment. It was a moment to choose what you cared most about. One line ran from the steps of the National Gallery of Art, another from the National Museum of American History. Their upper levels were free from the flow of water, but the crowd carried out anything that could be rescued from the lower levels. From person to person, they passed the objects, murmuring with curiosity and cheering whenever something crossed their hands that they recognized. A dripping wet red knit cardigan was treated with as much reverence as a gilded portrait by one of the Dutch Masters.[2]

For Keegan, the choice was the National Archives, which made it TAMS's selection too. It was slightly cruel, and even ironic, thought Keegan, to underscore TAMS's lack of free will at that location. But that's just how it was.

Here, the mission was slightly different. In the waist-deep water, a line of muddy men and women were trying to create a makeshift barrier around the building's perimeter. Keegan noticed they were keeping clear of a jagged edge of metal sticking out of the water on 9th Street where a ramp leading to an underground garage had been. To her, it looked like one of the Archives' pop-up flood barriers had structurally failed, maybe from the weight of the water, maybe just from how everything had seemed to go to shit today.

Somebody shouted a hoarse command to hurry up to beat the tide. Pushing back against the Potomac River's outward flow, the tidal shifts changed the river's water level by 3 feet each day. On top of the flood, it would be catastrophic. While the nation's founding documents held in the Archives were safe behind glass in the public display areas two stories above the water, the levels below held many more irreplaceable records. From early letters and diaries of the Founders to the very first photographs and then audio and film recordings of the nation, they there literally told the story of America.

"TAMS, how long until the tide starts to rise?" Keegan asked.

"High tide will occur in two hours and forty-seven minutes."

"We need to move faster, otherwise the pumps in the Archives won't be able to keep up."

The crowd was using anything and everything they could to build the floodwall. Trash bins were overturned and the garbage bags within tied off and then tossed into a pile. Bags of sod were pulled from a landscaper's truck. Once-hated plastic bags from the gift store were being filled with dirt. Then an Army National Guard truck pulled up and passed out a bin of the all-too-familiar HESCO bags she'd filled with sand or rocks to build temporary bullet-stopper walls in war zones.

"Agent Keegan, you have instructions to report to the Washington Field Office," TAMS said.

"Correct, but this is where we need to be right now. The priority is to help. That mission comes first."

Keegan wedged her way into the line of people, TAMS following. They quickly worked out the pace. A man in shorts and a University of Kansas basketball jersey, a tourist whose vacation had just turned far more interesting than planned, would pass her a bag. She'd then pass it to TAMS, and then the machine passed it to the woman beside it, who was wearing a sun-faded purple running jacket that was torn at the left shoulder.

At the first handoff, the woman had given the machine a curious look. She looked to be in her early sixties. Keegan observed her gaunt frame and silver-haired buzz cut, surmising she was one of those runners who still moved like they were twenty years younger and could care less about anything else but running fast.

"Is that your bot?"

"Nope, it's actually yours. Gov test system. Seemed as good a time as any to put our tax dollars to good use."

"Helluva test." Satisfied, the woman went back to work.

For the next fifteen minutes, Keegan forgot everything around her but the handoff: one bag passed on and then another. The smell of labor soon overpowered the stink of the flood. The only noise TAMS made was a slight grating noise, from fine siltlike mud and grit getting inside its servos.

The woman gave a deep sigh and bent over at the waist.

"You OK?" Keegan asked.

"Yeah, just a stich in my side. Unlike your machine there, I'm tiring out. Too bad it can't do more."

Keegan realized the woman was right. She'd been going about this the wrong way. "TAMS," she said. "Build a wall around the Archives as rapidly as possible."

"OK," said TAMS. The robot ran through the water, leaving a sloshing white wake behind it. It picked a bag of sod off the truck and then ran back, placing it on their stack. It then did it again at the exact same speed, moving so quickly that the humans stopped stacking and watched.

"It's going to run out of those soon," the woman said. Without instruction, the chain of people redirected, all of them now focusing on filling bags to keep TAMS supplied. They worked in a frenzied burst of activity, inspired by the newfound efficiency and also not wanting to get beaten by the demands of a single robot. Half of them dug up dirt with anything that got traction, using shovels taken from the landscaper's truck to the poles once used to hold display signs. The other half packed the bags by hand. Keegan's throat was dry, despite her being soaked to the bone. Her back ached, and so did her leg, but it felt good. There was nothing to focus on beyond the feeling of dirt in your hands and the satisfying sound, almost like a great collective sigh, that the bags made when TAMS stacked yet another.

"It seems that the Declaration of Independence will live to see another disaster, Agent Keegan."

Keegan looked over and there was Modi, though it took her a moment to recognize him. His suit and tie had been replaced with slate-gray tactical pants and shirt. With ripstop fabric and triple stitching, it was what the civilian advisors used to wear when they came out to visit her unit in the field. It must be pretty bad, she thought, if they were handing those out now to the geek squad.

"What are you doing down here?" she said. "And how'd you find us?"

"Hopefully doing some good. That wasn't going to happen back at the office," he said. "And I have my privileges." He pointed down to the screen on his own Watchlet. There was a small map app open with a pulsing red dot. "I may not be on the mobile network, but I have a lock on TAMS."

Rather than let him steer the conversation to why she had not checked into the field office, Keegan just smiled and said, "Well, let's put you to work then too."

The two teamed up, Keegan digging into a plot of sidewalk grass in front of the Navy Memorial with the base of what had once been a traffic barrier and Modi packing the dirt into bags from a dry cleaner. The woman in purple carried them to the central pile that had been set up for TAMS, while back and forth TAMS went at the same pace, stacking and stacking.

Where the robot placed the bags appeared random, but Keegan knew there was some kind of pattern driving the selection. When Keegan was eleven, her uncle had taken her to see the hive where he worked, a sprawling distribution center near Seattle-Tacoma International Airport. He worked as a technician, performing repairs on the warehouse bots. They had zoomed around in what seemed like a frenzy, some driving at top speed on the extra-slick concrete floors, some on tracks that ran along the ceiling. It all looked like chaos, but he had explained that was actually the point.[3]

"What if I gave you a tube of toothpaste, where would you put it in the warehouse?" he'd asked her.

"Whichever row all the toothpaste is in," she'd replied.

"That's what a human would do," he'd explained. "But a thinking machine, they'll just fit that single tube of toothpaste in wherever it goes best, not just by fit, but factoring in everything from its expiration date to the anticipated date someone is going to order it, relative to the date that the book or coffeemaker or whatever it is wedged behind is going to be ordered and pulled off the shelf. Pretty cool, huh?"

He'd been less excited about it all two years later, when he'd lost his job after the company deployed new modular robots that could repair themselves.[4]

She took a breather, and Modi stopped too. He then tried to wipe a clump of mud from his face, but only smeared it with his glove. "Here," then she brushed off the smudge with her bare hand.

"This is definitely not the Singularity that they promised," said Modi.[5]

"Yeah, I thought the plan was for us to be sitting around in our mechanical replacement bodies eating bonbons all day by now."

"Instead of wiping literal shit off our faces as we burn ourselves out trying to keep up with a robot?"

They laughed and went back to filling bags. After a minute, she looked back over at Modi.

"It does raise a good question, though: What are we really hoping to get out of all these machines? I mean, look at TAMS. In the end, is it going to be like this glorified shovel?" she said, waving the pole she'd been digging with. "For all its smarts, just a better tool?"

"Really, really better," Modi said.

"Or something more, something beyond just a tool? Something that we're going to have to think of differently?"

"We doing a session now?" said Modi. "Here?"

"You got somewhere better to be?" Keegan asked.

"Just about anywhere," Modi said. "But I appreciate you trying to keep my mind off how bad my back hurts." He paused. "I do think it's something more. Look at how TAMS is integrated into the group here, robot alongside people, the output of the team more than its parts. Even more, it's not just integrated with the people, but changed them."

"That's the part that worries me."

"What do you mean? As long as more work is getting done, do you think anybody really cares?"

"Not in the moment," said Keegan. "It's when there's time to think that we humans get into trouble."

"That's why you don't like talking to me?"

"Well, not in your office," she said.

"But it's a conversation we need to have. Not just you, all of us," he said. "It's not so much what we think about them. It's what are we supposed to *feel* about a robot? Not just now, but what about when it becomes more like us? Or even worse, does more than us?"

"We used to feel it when our bots got whacked out on mission," Keegan said. "You'd get angry at the enemy for plugging your bots in a different way than you would if they took out a radio or a Humvee. The worst was the legged ones."

"And TAMS is much more than one of your sniffers or a vacuum," Modi said. "It's your partner."

"No, I've had partners," said Keegan. "It's nothing like this."

"But it might be. Because it's always learning to be. Here, look at this." He swiped an app open on his Watchlet screen and showed it to Keegan, drawing closer to her. It showed TAMS's network activity, accessing news coverage and documentaries about human behavior during past flood events.

"But that's not really what a partner is. This just shows it doesn't need me at all."

"Not so fast," said Modi. "You gave it the mission, right?"

"Yeah, I told it to build a wall. But I could have just stayed home and told it that."

"Do you think you would have figured out the situation from afar? Or if TAMS just showed up here, without you, that it would have teamed up with the humans this way? I doubt it. It would make a mistake, maybe step on a toe or just annoy people by its very presence in a high-stress situation. Pretty soon, it would be kicked over on its side in the muck, maybe a sandbag stacked on its head. You were both needed, just maybe not in the way we traditionally think."

"So give the robot a mission and protect it from the bad guys? Not all that different from how I used 'em in the Corps."

He stooped to pick up another bag and held it open for Keegan to fill. "It's not that simple. What you did in the Marines as a wrangler was what's known as the 'centaur model,' like the Greek myth of the guy whose body was blended with a horse.[6] It still treated the robot as a tool, much like the feet of the horse just took the guy wherever he wanted. The next step is a 'shepherd,' a human guiding a robot as it learns its way around the world."[7]

Keegan pounded at the dirt with another stab. "Yeah, I remember that chess master, the one who first got beat by an AI and then became a guru on how humans had to adjust to AI, came up with that concept.[8] A big part of it was that while an AI could beat a chess master, the AI turned out to be unable to beat an ordinary player working with an AI."

"And you just gave away that you know more about all this than you let on," he said with a bemused look. "But I knew that already."

"I contain multitudes."[9]

"Well, then, Whitman, that's what you gotta wrap your head around. You're still trying to get the job done, but have to do so in ways well beyond the machine just being an extension of yourself. You said the question was 'What are we really hoping to get out of all these machines?' I say it's beyond that. Where does that machine's new ability, new intelligence, take us all to next? Not just for you and TAMS, but the future of our existence? What happens as we're working, and living, more and more alongside something that thinks and acts in ways we no longer understand?" He wiped his brow again. "Switch?"

Keegan wordlessly passed him the makeshift shovel. She took a moment to watch TAMS at work, sloshing back and forth in the water. The barrier was now as high as its shoulders. She wondered if the machine would keep building until it could not reach the top. What would it do then? Move laterally to the lower parts of the wall? Or would it begin to build its own wall to stand on, so it could keep building higher and higher?

Modi caught Keegan's gaze. "The paperclip problem," he said.

"The what?"

"What you're thinking of is called the 'paperclip problem.'[10] Imagine an intelligent machine is given the task to make paperclips. Now imagine it is also a learning machine, that gets more and more intelligent along the way, ever improving at its job of making paperclips. Sounds great . . . at first. You get more and more paperclips, cheaper and cheaper. Except, at some point, the machine gets so intelligent, so good at its task, eventually paperclips cover the Earth, then the whole universe. Even worse, it introduces another problem, that of control. If the machine's mission is to make paperclips, what does it do about any people that stand in its way?"

"Will that be the case with TAMS?"

"I guess we'll have to watch that wall to find out."

10

BALLSTON NEIGHBORHOOD

Arlington, Virginia

Keegan woke to find herself on the bathroom floor, using a damp rainbow-striped beach towel as a makeshift pillow.

When they had finally arrived at the Washington Field Office later the night before, it had been chaos, just without the good vibes that had permeated the crowd at the Archives. In a bureaucracy, turf matters above all, even when organizing to help. So most of the tension among managers and all their subordinates had been about who goes where, with who in charge. Despite having just been doing the job on the streets outside, there was no established protocol for where she and TAMS fit into this matrix. So she had made the decision easier for them, typing up a quick mission report to explain the diversion to the Metro and National Archives as being by design and then declaring the need for "operational recovery and recharge," for both of them. With no sign of Noritz to sign off, she had left for home, taking TAMS with her.

Surprisingly, the drive had gone quickly. They'd had to take the long way around the Beltway, but the roads were nearly clear, no one out driving their commute or running errands. In times of crisis, most just want to hunker down with family, something Keegan felt desperately herself.

Once she walked in the door, though, it was like a miniature version of downtown. There was a small pool of water coming out from the bathroom, as if the deluge outside had worked its way up into their apartment. Either Haley or Jared had turned the faucet off eventually, but the puddle had been left as a lower priority than playtime or turking away for more points.

She didn't have the energy for another fight, so while they slept, she had stripped off her muddy clothes and ransacked the condo for whatever she could find to sop the water up. Clean towels. Dirty towels. Dish towels. Even Haley's yellow duck towel with a frayed orange bill on its hood. TAMS probably could've helped, but this was her own mess to clean up. Once she'd gotten most of it up, she'd taken a rest against the bathroom wall, only to fall asleep as the day's exertions and stress finally caught up.

Now, Keegan pulled herself up off the floor slowly and carefully, to be gentle on her back muscles that were stiff as hell. She then examined herself in the mirror. Her eyes were red and the skin on her forearms had faint purple splotches. She was afraid to ask TAMS the exact chemical makeup of the muddy water downtown, but she was pretty sure it was not spa grade. Her back throbbed, the sciatic nerve aching and shooting what felt like mild electric shocks down her leg. If the bags at the Archives hadn't done it, sleeping at an awkward angle on the bathroom floor had.

"Haley?" she called out. There was no response, and she quickly saw why as she peeked out into the den.

Her little girl was sitting on the couch with the VR rig on, the oversized helmet making her neck disappear. Haley's muffled laughter came from underneath the helmet, sounding like she was talking from underwater. Keegan could not make out what the girl was saying, just a stream of vowels broken up by gasps of airy laughter. TAMS sat with its legs folded under itself near a wall outlet, charging, observing.

She shivered at the sight and went back down the hallway to knock on Jared's bedroom door. At no reply, she knocked again and then waited another ten seconds. Still no reply. When she opened the door, the bed was empty; he was nowhere to be seen. She checked her Watchlet — no message.

The fatigue of the past twenty-four hours seemed to get heavier as she sat down beside Haley on the couch.

Leaning in, she could also hear the person on the other side; it was Jared's old guy Harlan, talking, echoing from the inside of the helmet too big for Haley's head.

". . . you just watched what was on the channel," the man's voice on the other side of the country said.

"Did you get to pick a show?" asked the little girl.

"No, no, not at all. If it was Looney Tunes, you watched Looney Tunes. Or waited until something else better came along."

"What's a Looney Tunes?"

Where was Jared? He could get fired for letting Haley on the gear. But at this point, that was the least of her issues. It was the not knowing. He could be sick. Passed out. OD'd. That was not something she was going to be able to deal with again. She had been deployed when her brother died in an Olympia Public Library bathroom, literally on the other side of the planet at the moment his heart stopped beating. But she had imagined it in great detail — cracking open the stall door, seeing the unnatural angle of his arms, the wet hair, one blue leather loafer off, revealing a dark green sock with a hole at the big toe. The kinds of details you never forgot because your own brain had invented them, embroidered them itself.

A gentle rap of her knuckles on the helmet caused Haley to lift it up just enough to peek out from under the brim. "Hi, Mommy. I'm talking to Daddy's friend about cartoons. Did you watch a She-Ra when you were little?"

"No, that's too far back for me as well," Keegan replied.

At that moment, the front door swung open and Jared stepped through. He was wearing a sweatshirt and pajama bottoms, like he'd forgotten to change to go out. Haley's preschool backpack was slung across his shoulders. The strange attire was contrasted by how he strode in, with a loose-limbed confidence Keegan had not seen in him for months. His smile froze, then shattered into pressed lips when he saw her.

"Haley, why don't you show Harlan your animals?" she said. "I bet he'd love to meet your friends."

As Haley ran off, the helmet's weight almost toppling her over, Keegan turned back to Jared. "Where were you? And why is Haley talking to your lonely old guy?"

"I was out. And don't call him that. He helps pay for all this." As he said it, Jared noticed TAMS charging in the corner.

"What's that thing doing back here?" he said, adjusting the small backpack on his shoulder.

"No, you don't get to ask the questions. Haley's not supposed to be doing your job. What the fuck is wrong with you? You can't leave her alone. Ever."

"Lara, just take a breath, OK? Enough. Haley's fine. You should know that . . . Your toys are watching."

So, he had figured it out.

"If you want to talk about it," he said, "then we need to do it *alone.*" His precise diction betrayed that there was something more going on.

Keegan turned to the charging robot. "TAMS, go watch Haley in her room. Play her some *Sesame Street* songs, but close the door so we aren't disturbed by it."

"OK." It stood and walked to the back bedroom. After it closed the door, a low hum of music filtered through. Its algorithms had decided on "People in Your Neighborhood."

"OK, now, what the hell is going on?" Keegan asked. "Why did you leave Haley here to do your damn job? You're a better father than that." The last line was meant to sting.

Jared, though, ignored it, or even worse, didn't notice it. He pulled off the yellow and pink kid's backpack and tossed it to her. It was stuffed full. Lumpy.

"What's this?"

"Open it," he said, a proud, knowing smile on his face.

Somehow she knew it even before she unzipped the bag, so it was not as much a surprise as it should have been. Yet the sight of dollar bills literally spilling out of the bag onto the floor was still striking. Not just twenties and forties, but even hundreds and two-hundreds.

"Jesus. Are you a bank robber now?" she said, picking up a handful to examine it closer. Yep, they were real. She handed them to him.

"No, even better. It's not stealing when it's free," Jared said, tucking the bills into her pocket with a flourish, as if he were tipping her. He reached into the bag and pulled out another fistful. "Somebody sent a flash across my turking feed that the ATMs are crashing all over the country, spewing out cash from some bug in the dispenser system. So I ran down as quick as I could. I got to the one across the street and the one over at the mall before anyone else showed up." He laughed. "I guess it finally paid off that I'm online all the time."

She stared back at him. "How much is in here?"

"I don't know. Should we count it or weigh it?" A flash of a smile again, the charming, confident Jared whom she'd first fallen for. "I just took as much as I could carry. A few other people showed up too, so I got out of there before things got too crazy."

She looked at the bedroom door, wondering if the music really was loud enough. "What were *you* — stressing that they were not in on this together — "thinking? I'm a goddamn FBI agent. My husband cannot — *cannot* — even get caught crossing the street on a red light."

"I *didn't* do anything wrong," he said, defensively. "The money just came out of the machine.¹ I didn't make it do that. It was just there to be picked up. Plus, it's not digital but cash. There's no transaction on our account, just dollars to spend on whatever we need."

"No, it's not," she said. "Let me explain what happens next. The banks track the lost currency and log it into the system. Any transaction with those numbers on them gets blocked, automatically. You took a bunch of worthless paper. We might as well use them to wipe up the water you left running."

"Bullshit," Jared said, not wanting his victory taken away so easily.

"You have a law degree. From Yale," she said. "And you still couldn't figure this out? What's happened to you?"

"What happened to me?" he hissed back. "What about you? You leave your family in the middle of an emergency to do what? Babysit for a machine? At least I'm trying to do something for us, for Haley, instead of training some machine to take my job."

"Now you just sound like that asshole on the news, Jacobs." She stood and walked toward the back hallway, but paused at the doorway and pointed at the dollar bills that had fallen on the carpet. "Pick those up before we come back out. I don't want to have to explain to Haley what her father just did or how he's become such a useless, jobless fuck-up."

It was really that she didn't want to have to explain it all to TAMS, but Jared deserved that twist of the knife.

As she marched down the hallway, each step radiated down her leg. But the pain was almost necessary, to put a physical marker to the emotions she was feeling. At Haley's doorway, she stopped and tried to re-center herself as "The Alphabet Song" blared from the inside.

With a fake smile, she entered the room. Haley was singing along to the music coming out of TAMS, the helmet still on her head but the light indicator showing the feed was off. Either Haley had moved onto something more interesting or Harlan had realized that little kids were only good company in limited doses.

Keegan sat down next to the girl and carefully lifted the helmet off. Throwing it across the room would have been the most satisfying thing at that moment, but she knew they would just deduct it from Jared's earnings. So she laid it at their feet.

Reaching over, she pulled Haley into a hug, rocking her back and forth in the same rhythm she had in that very first moment she'd held her at Georgetown Hospital. It took her back to when Haley was just a tiny living thing wrapped in a blanket, back before the changes between her and Jared had complicated what it meant to be a mother.

Haley somehow knew what she was supposed to say at these moments. "I love you, Mommy. And Daddy loves you too."

"I know, honey," Keegan said. "I know."

As she held the little girl, the previous song ended and a new one came on. It was still *Sesame Street,* but TAMS had decided that the appropriate track now was the song "Sad."[2]

When rotten things happen,
it's OK to be sad.

But the music behind the all-too-timely lyrics was incongruous, the joke being that the doleful words were set to a lively doo-wop beat from the 1950s. The machine could read a room well enough to match a song's lyrics to emotional data, but matching it to musical tone was evidently beyond its capacity.

Keegan smiled at the thought of TAMS's advanced neural networks battling to the death over a song choice and still getting it wrong. Then Haley looked up and smiled back at her mom.

And that's when Keegan wondered if maybe the machine actually had understood just what was needed at that moment.

MOSAIC DISTRICT

Merrifield, Virginia

Keegan's Watchlet vibrated, but she ignored it, manually driving the FBI SUV around a mud-covered lime-green sedan going half the speed limit. Its driver was hunched over the steering wheel, likely the first time in years they had taken over the wheel. In the wake of everything that had happened, it seemed that many people were too jumpy to trust autodrive. The irony was that more people driving themselves would likely cause more deaths.

The traffic inched along just past the Merrifield Mosaic District complex, one of those planned suburban developments faked to look like a throwback city square, which had then been thrown forward by automation.[3] A massive VR playpen had replaced the movie the-ater a few years ago. She'd taken Haley there once on a rainy day; you could explore the inside of the Pyramids or run screaming from what looked to them like a *T. rex* dinosaur.[4]

Her Watchlet pulsed again, this time with an unusual syncopated rhythm that felt like the device was shorting out. Someone had somehow reset the notification. Shaw.

She put the vehicle on auto so she wouldn't viz and drive. Donning her vizglasses, she blinked open the message. It was a call, no visuals.

"Agent Keegan, I'm interested in your latest observations on TAMS."

Taking a deep breath, she considered all the ways she could respond. "TAMS is learning quickly. Connectivity is an issue, to be expected. As you may have seen, no problems with water immersion or ingress." She fired off a question back at him before he could consider the response. "What caused the flood?"

"That is good. As for the flood, the . . . authorities . . ." He paused, as if to show what he thought of them. "Are investigating."

Keegan figured that meant Shaw knew more, but wasn't sharing yet. "How about you? Were you able to ride out the waters?" she asked.

"I did not have a problem of too much water, but rather not enough."

At that, Shaw sent a video of a vineyard. Lines of withered vines were arrayed down a west-facing slope, judging by the rising sun in the background. It seemed as if the grapes were writhing in the light, but she squinted and could see that the movement was from hundreds of ag-bots, their shells made from discarded corks, working away on the field.

"The drought in Sonoma demanded my attention instead."

The nation's capital floods, maybe also sinking the president, whom he's treating like a sock puppet, and yet Shaw's fucking around with grapes? "And so what now?"

"In situations like this, our commission is taking a pause. It is, of course, a greater priority in the overall well-being of the nation, but the president has judged the politics of the moment necessitate otherwise. The incident in Washington . . ."

Keegan's teeth gritted at that description of countless lives lost.

"... if anything, makes it more urgent. Are you familiar with John Gardner?"

She wasn't but began to initiate a search on the name, starting to punch the name into the Watchlet.

"There is no need," Shaw said, as if watching her type. Maybe he was. "Gardner is one of those people who created our world but is little remembered by it.[5] He engineered what were called the 'Great Society' reforms back in the 1960s. The program changed everything in America, from guaranteeing voting rights for the groups that were then minorities to establishing a government role in medical and retirement assistance, to even creating the public broadcasting networks that gave your child *Sesame Street*."

Was that a guess? Or a message?

"In a time of similar turmoil," Shaw continued, "when the nation seemed ready to fall apart, Gardner simply *reimagined* the situation: 'What we have before us are some breathtaking opportunities disguised as insoluble problems.'[6] Now we must simply do the same."

It's easy to say that when you're not living in the muck, thought Keegan. But then again, she was self-aware enough to contemplate that maybe that was exactly what was necessary to get the right perspective on the problem.

"And that is where you and TAMS come in."

"How?"

"During disaster, people can lose that indefinable but real force of faith. They need to believe that their future is going to be better and, having experienced the worst, that they have not lost control. Rather, they can shape what is to come. A reset, of sorts."

And, of course, you know just what everyone else needs.

"While I was not directly engaged with the flood response, your and TAMS's actions during it have become significant to this greater project. Besides increasing attention on your work among White House and Justice Department officials, the cloud activity has been notable. The unexpected combination of this calamity and your actions have made TAMS a potential icon. The machine is definitively trending, with symbology analysis finding interpretations at a pivot point between themes of fear and those of human-machine partnership and, ironically, human compassion."

"It's proving its usefulness," Keegan said, trying to dodge the whole matter of people putting their emotions and beliefs onto machines. It was bad enough for a single person to do it, let alone an entire nation.

"This goes beyond any single machine's utility. Like it or not, you are now the steward of not just TAMS's training but a larger change for us all. I cannot overstate how crucial your work has become."

Keegan thought about Noritz's comment about the magnifying glass. Now it was more like being a bug under it on the sunniest of days.

"As such," Shaw continued, "my offer of aid stands. In exchange . . ."

And there it is, thought Keegan, the other part of the deal.

"I remain highly interested in how TAMS develops, and your relationship with it, Agent Keegan. I hope you will share any insights you gain along the way."

Keegan knew that phrasing it as a "hope" was artifice, wrapping in politeness a command that was expected to be followed.

"Sure," she replied. "And if you learn anything that could be of use about the flood, I hope you'll let me know."

She wasn't a gajillionaire, but she wasn't going to just roll over for one.

FBI SATELLITE FACILITY

Reston, Virginia

"Hail, hail to the hero of the day," Noritz said, making a quick bow in front of her cubicle.

Keegan looked at TAMS, which was recharging beside her cubicle, and then back to her boss.

"Which one of us do you mean?" she asked.

"Does it matter? You're the FBI's new super-team . . . which means *we* need to talk," Noritz said, indicating there was something more to be discussed without the bot listening.

She could have instructed TAMS to turn itself off, but anyone who had grown up during the first generation of home-assistant AIs knew not to trust any recording device even when powered down.[7]

"TAMS, I could really use a drink of water. Go get me a cup of water . . . in an orange mug." This was something else that Modi didn't get about the idea of a machine as partner. Even the most junior agent would balk at being sent off on an obvious snipe hunt.

"OK," TAMS said, and went down the hallway.

"Cruel, but effective," observed Noritz. "Think it will find it?"

"Eventually. There's gotta be one somewhere in the facility. If not, it'll probably 3-D print one. What's up?"

Noritz slid a chair over from an empty cubicle, setting it up to face her. "How are things going?" he asked. This was the Noritz that Keegan liked working for. She could see him back in the day, two state troopers pulled up alongside one another, their cars facing in the opposite direction, shooting the shit.

There were a lot of ways to answer his question. Too many. Which meant she didn't share them.

"Fine."

"You handling TAMS?"

"Yeah, it's under control."

My family, well, that's another matter, she thought. The agent-spouse-parent "identity triangle dilemma," they had called it in the briefing last year. Noritz had been surprisingly cool during that session, sharing with the office how he felt like he was letting down his kids as a father every time he worked a late evening. But she wasn't going to unload that on him either. For all that had changed in the Bureau, she still felt pressure in front of a male boss to only show her work side, to demonstrate those other identities weren't holding her back.[8]

"Good to hear that. I know I was hard on you before, but it was for a reason. If things change, I need to know," he said. "'Cause things are about to get far more challenging for us."

"Yeah?" said Keegan, noting how Noritz used the word "us," not "you."

"People are seeing what we're doing with TAMS," he explained. "They've decided they want more. In case you hadn't noticed, there's not much good news in this town right now."

"'People?' Who?" she asked. "Like 'people' in the Bureau or 'people' elsewhere?"

Or maybe even a "person," she thought.

"That's above your pay grade," he said. "Let me worry about that." He was trying to get some of his power back. It was understandable enough. First the deputy director had ignored him, and then he wasn't invited to the White House meeting. "What you need to worry about," he continued, "is casework. Bad guys. Arrests."

"Sir?"

"No more filling sandbags for you and the bot, though that played perfectly. You're back on the real job . . . with your robot and its mug."

"I'm not sure it's ready for an active investigation. You said this is like being under a microscope. Won't that get us a lot more attention?"

"We're past that point now," Noritz said. "It's been decided the Bureau needs a win, anything, and you're going to be the one to do it." He said it in a way that made it clear that arguing the point was not worth her time.

"So who's the lucky criminal TAMS is going to get to pop its legal cherry on?" Keegan asked, knowing the language would piss him off.

Noritz sighed and rolled his eyes. "Ignoring your evident attempts to dodge this with an assignment to sensitivity training, it is the proverbial good news–bad news case. The good news is that it's the first case that you and TAMS ever had, so your colorful language is not necessary."

"Piss boy from Union Station?" she asked.

"That's how you clean up your language?" Noritz asked. "Yes, the Reppley case. So you're already familiar with the particulars. There's only one problem."

"He wet himself again?"

"Of a sort," Noritz replied. "He got shanked."

"Don't look at me."

"I know that. You only tried to rip his finger off. Somebody got the word out that he was Sons of Aleppo."

"He wasn't."

"Either way, it wasn't appreciated and he bled out in the shower."

"So we investigating his murder?"

"No, Richmond Field Office has it. It has, however, been noticed that you and TAMS were the ones to extract the one lead. You're being tasked to pull that thread further."

"The relative? The one that may have gotten a payout via the gaming site?"

"Yes. A certain Michael Harris Simpkins."

"Where is he?"

"If we knew that, he'd be in a Dizz-Diff already. You're to find him."

"I assume I don't need to ask which one of us you meant by the 'you' in 'You need to find him'?"

"You learn fast."

FBI DOMESTIC SPECIAL
DETENTION FACILITY

Reston, Virginia

It oinked and shook its body with a tremor that started at its rubber spring-mounted curlicue tail and ran all the way to eyes that rolled back and closed in what looked like ecstasy. Designed to look like a cartoon pig wearing a wooden barrel, the eight-wheeled delivery bot was from the sandwich shop that had remained open in the mall complex, kept in business by nearby federal workers. The bots were supposed to be cute, but Keegan found them grotesque, especially how, for large orders, they would travel nose-to-tail on the sidewalk.

"Oink, oink. I have a delivery for Lara Keegan," said the robot.

They were three hours into the search for Simpkins and it was not going well. The quick pull of data by TAMS in the interrogation room had made it all look too easy to the watching crowd of FBI leaders. TAMS's search algorithms instantly scooped up the easy stuff, but now it was all dead ends. Simpkins was a ghost — no criminal history, no registered place of work or residence, and no social media presence to glean for clues. The only data they could pull was a digital spending trail, funneled only through virtualized accounts, run by offshore holding companies that were not responding to warrant requests. For instance, Simpkins had an online gambling account, but he could have been making bets from anywhere in the world. Keegan then played a hunch that maybe he wouldn't be able to resist doing it in person. Pulling betting records and facial recognition databases from physical casinos, which had been among the first to track their customers, though, revealed nothing.[9]

All the network and system outages that had followed the flood in Washington didn't help. Experts had warned about the physical fragility of the federal and commercial database systems, but doing something about it was a different matter. Now, it was as if somebody had dropped a massive rock in the middle of the pond, and the ripples kept radiating out again and again, knocking different networks offline.

Keegan pulled off her viz and glared at the delivery pig bot. "I didn't order anything."

"Oink, oink. I have a delivery for Lara Keegan," it repeated. Between the set messaging system and the wheels instead of legs, it was pretty low-grade tech, even for a sandwich shop. But the older systems were actually what allowed it to be cleared for use in the federal building. Low autonomy, limited sensors, and a weekly pastrami payoff to the security office greased any counterintelligence concerns.

"I said I didn't order anything," she repeated. "Get out of here." She gave the pig bot a gentle kick under its chin. Hopefully that would help it get the message — or at least reboot.

"Oink, oink. I have a delivery for Lara Keegan."

She looked over at the door and then down the hallway, to see if somebody was messing with her. No one.

"TAMS, track the order of this. Find out who sent the delivery."

"I did," TAMS immediately replied. "Your posture and respiratory rate indicated lower blood sugar levels."

She looked at the pig bot and then to the orange mug on her desk. "Fuck me."

Hooking back into the on-site network in the office had meant a whole new set of updates had uploaded onto TAMS. Apparently one of the other TAMS program testers had set their machine for predictive food runs. All she could hope was that his machine (and she was certain it was a he who had trained their TAMS this way) would start randomly wandering off in search of orange mugs.

"New rule: don't order food for me without asking," she commanded.

"OK."

The discussion of food did make her notice just how hungry she was, the thought of it instantly opening what felt like a cavern in her stomach.

Swiping open her pay app, she tapped her Watchlet on the pig's snout. It squealed in delight and the faux-wooden barrel split open.

"So, what'd you decide to get me?" she asked TAMS, reaching into the barrel to pull out the delivery pack. The pig bot oinked its glee at a successful delivery and then spun on its axis and left.

"A Reuben sandwich, jalapeño-flavored taro chips, and a can of root beer," the robot answered.

She salivated at the mere mention of the sandwich and wondered if TAMS had detected that response. "How'd you come up with that?"

"While it is not ideal, according to your current weight and body-mass index . . ."

Great, now she was being body-shamed by a robot.

". . . the order matches observed preferences for food type, but avoids repeating a past meal."

So TAMS had seen her eat a sausage with chili and therefore concluded her preference structure was messy pork products of midwestern origin. Keegan unwrapped the sandwich and took a massive bite, savoring the corned beef, Swiss cheese, sauerkraut, and Russian dressing mixing together in a perfect fusion of tang, spice, and grease. *Thank God it didn't see me order a salad,* she thought.

"So, what's on the menu for tomorrow?" she asked, taking another bite. "Let me guess. Pulled pork barbecue? Pastrami?"

"Tomorrow, it would not be an advisable choice to eat meat due to ongoing activities at the US Department of Agriculture Food Safety and Inspection Service."

With a full mouth, she mumbled, "What?"

"The US Department of Agriculture Food Safety and Inspection Service network has reported a series of malfunctions at animal protein processing facilities in both the eastern and the Midwest region.[10] A briefing for the press by the secretary of agriculture has been announced for 9 a.m. Eastern Standard Time tomorrow. This matches past episodes of salmonella and/or *E. coli* that resulted in the suspension of sales of animal protein products."

Keegan's chewing slowed, and she put the sandwich down. "Fuck," she muttered and pulled out a napkin to spit out the half-chewed bite she'd taken. Giving the robot a glare, she tore open the bag of chips, and chewed, hoping the jalapeño flavoring had some kind of medicinal power.

"OK, let's get back to work before you try to poison me further," she said. As she mused on the problem with at least some part of her brain refueled, she thought about how they could attack the problem from different angles. They were trying to pull at threads when maybe the design of the quilt of data would reveal something they had missed.

She tasked TAMS to create a series of data visualizations. As they built, she stood and walked around the cubicle, as much to change her perspective as to stretch her back.

An image cloud built across her vizglasses of the people Simpkins might know or seek shelter with. While their person of interest didn't have any active online profile, TAMS could populate the cloud with a network drawn from their known contact points. It showed his family members and former schoolmates, only up to tenth grade, of course, she noted. Nothing jumped there. There were crosses and connections between them as would be expected, but nothing stuck out. Then TAMS built a network map visualization of Simpkins's monetary transaction history, envisioned as a ray of different colored lines connecting to various accounts, pulsing with each activity over the last year. They then compared his financial pattern to the network of profiles and their individual accounts and payments, each a similar ray of colored lines, looking for any connection points.

Nothing. She stretched to touch her toes, more in frustration than the need to relieve the tension in her lower back. Even viewed upside down, Simpkins's activity had the same pattern. But there were no crosses, no payments going back and forth between him and the people in the network they were able to track. And that's when it hit her — it shouldn't have the same pattern. It was abnormal that his activity was so normal.

"TAMS, generate a list of his regular transactions. I want to look over them."

The word cloud dissipated and the screen populated with rows of accounts that Simpkins regularly paid into. Without being asked, TAMS color-coded them in the ways it understood would help a human process the data. The breakdown had different colors for frequency — the weekly payments shaded in blue and the monthly payments in yellow, while one-time payments got a splash of orange. Nothing was in red, as the system knew that human brains couldn't help but focus on that color.

Still nothing. There was no signal in the noise that either machine or human brain could detect.[11]

TAMS recategorized them by activity clusters, a new set of colors shading every payment on "entertainment," like the gambling site that had first caught their eye — distinguishing it from the payments to other categories like "utilities." That was what jumped out when Keegan read it. Making regular payments to the power company was quite the responsible thing to do for someone potentially wrapped up in a terrorism case.

"Pull out the payments to Southern Energy Exchange." The moment she said it out loud, she smiled, thinking back to the little jokes they too used to bury in unit expense reports.

"Cancel that," Keegan commanded. "Bring up anyone else who has made a payment to the Southern Energy Exchange. Then geolocate any who are males between the ages eighteen and seventy years old." She thought about it for a second. "No, you know what, make it between eighteen and eighty-five years old. There're still some dirty old dudes at that age."

She took a long pull of root beer and sat back down as the screen transformed into a map flickering with red dots, popping up one after another. And on the edge of the Anacostia River, there was a pulsing cluster of them.

"OK, TAMS, time for you to learn something new."

ANACOSTIA RIVER WATERFRONT

Washington, DC

The congestion on the roads into Washington was back to its old levels. With the floodgates restored and the river returned to its normal level, it was as if the traffic on the roads was trying to forget that whatever had gone wrong had run its course.

During the half-hour drive, Keegan kept thinking of calling Jared, but stopped herself again and again. Instead, she switched on the view from her bots in the apartment. He'd left them up, she guessed both to serve as visual evidence that he could be trusted and a reminder that they had no trust between them. The screen showed Haley drawing at the kitchen table with crayons, while Jared wore his rig, back at work. It was all so normal, as if here too nothing had happened outside their home. But it was an illusion. She also noticed he had the backpack on the couch next to him, ensuring that she saw he was keeping the cash.

Keegan cut the feed as they approached the river and took manual control of the SUV. She wasn't confident enough in the machine's mapping updates to let it drive itself anywhere near the river with all the recent changes. The coordinates of the pulsing red dot put it just beyond the now long-gone RFK Stadium, which edged the Anacostia Riverwalk Trail. It was conveniently located not too far from the Capitol and a parking lot used by everyone from commuters for the Metro to the employees of a nearby cluster of government buildings to anyone out to jog along the river.

She parked the car and they headed on foot to the location of the dot, a small floating pier hidden from view by the crook of the river at the end of the uninhabited Kingman Island.

The pier looked unaffected by the recent disaster; the opposing flow of the Anacostia River had pushed back any of the floodtide coming up from the Potomac. At the pier's end was a building with no windows. In front of it was a weatherproof canopy that blurred when Keegan's vizglasses looked at it. So they had put up sensor-defeat materials to ensure no one image-captured who was coming or going.

On the building's roof was an elevated steel platform, larger than standard drone landing pads, more like the helicopter landing pads attached to an offshore oil rig.

Keegan tapped her Watchlet against a black half-sphere in front of the building, and after it confirmed her bank account could afford the potential charges, a door wide enough for three people hissed open. Inside, the room was bathed in a hazy blue light, black leather couches set against each of the walls. There was no way that she was going to sit on those. A small set of lockers stood in the middle, each with a digital thumbprint-lock. It was unstated you left your vizglasses here. Reluctantly, Keegan also put in her pistol, knowing she'd not get in with it anyway.

At the back wall a stairwell headed up to the roof landing pad. Above the steps, a dozen long black hooded cloaks hung on pegs. Opaque gray face masks, whose distorted features appeared to move depending on the angle you looked at them, hung atop the cloaks.

"Look, this is about to get weird," she said to TAMS. "So I don't want any activity here to be incorporated into your human-interface protocols." She shuddered to think of the updates it would push out to all the other units in the system.

"OK," TAMS said.

A turbine's whine announced their ride's approach. Keegan climbed halfway up the steps, stopped, and pulled down a cloak and mask and put them on TAMS.

"There. You almost look like you belong."

As they exited to the landing pad, what looked like a plane crossed with a boat glided across the river toward them, flying maybe 10 feet above the water.[12] The craft stopped to hover 6 inches off the pad and they boarded into an empty seating area. It re-elevated and they headed down the Anacostia River. Keegan looked out the window at the recovery work going on in the distance of downtown Washington. It was all coordinated by the US military's AI disaster assistance protocol, originally designed to guide troops on humanitarian climate-change disaster-response missions in the Pacific, never envisioned for use just across from the Pentagon itself.[13] Emergency vehicles flashed blue and red beneath a Christmas-colored constellation of drones forming and reforming like a school of fish. Nearby, airborne floodlights illuminated house-sized orange automated snowplows that pushed walls of mud aside to make way for a wave of street cleaners. The scene possessed a certain beauty that she thought Modi would appreciate, the purposeful fusion of people and machines.

The shuttle turned as the Anacostia emptied into the Potomac and picked up even more speed. They flew past Alexandria, the Old Town district still a bloody red from the floodwaters, and then past Mount Vernon, perched up on a hill high enough the waters didn't reach. George Washington had always thought ahead when it came to real estate.

Where the Potomac widened toward the entrance of Chesapeake Bay, the reddish blood of its waters began to take on a more brownish-blue hue, brightened here and there by the green bursts of algae blooms. The next few months would be like chemical warfare in the Bay, thought Keegan, with the new urban detritus battling the older rural runoff.

As the shuttle slowed, Keegan focused on a speck floating just past Point Lookout. As it grew larger, it appeared to be more building than boat, an octagon three stories high and the size of a warehouse. Its light-absorbing paint made it look like a hazy void. Yet it still had navigation lights, making the camouflage seem a bit bizarre. Then again, Keegan thought, the whole premise of the place was an indulgence in contradictions.

The ferry pulsed its engines to climb upward and gently landed on the roof. She turned to give TAMS one last instruction. "The rule here is 'Don't touch.' That means anything. Or anyone. They really hate that."

"OK."

She couldn't tell if it was aware or unaware of what she meant. As she stepped down onto the landing platform, her feet tingled with the pulse of music coming from below. Her ears felt slightly clogged, like the weather was about to do something wild. She flexed her jaw as she walked toward a covered walkway, at the end of which was a burly man in a zippered red leather trench coat and oversized black tactical viz goggles. The coat bulged noticeably, but without her viz-glasses TAMS could not discreetly alert her to what kind of weapon he had.

"Reservation?" the bouncer asked, running a wand up and down her to check for weapons.

"Spur of the moment thing, you know how it is," said Keegan. "With all this shit going down in the city, who knows what tomorrow brings. You get hit out here?"

The bouncer nodded and laughed. "Yeah, we were rocking back and forth for a few minutes . . . shoulda charged extra." He started to scan TAMS and the metal detector immediately lit up. "What's going on?" There was no menace in his voice. Just curiosity.

"Three's the magic number," Keegan said. She looked at TAMS and drew the cloak's hood back to show the robot's face. It stared back, its blank visage taking on whatever meaning the bouncer took from it.

"Whatever floats your boat is the motto here," the bouncer said to Keegan. He nodded, and whoever was reading his gesture from behind the door, human or machine, released the lock and the door opened with a burst of thumping music from the darkness beyond. "Welcome to Control Room."

As human and machine went through the door, the music became clearer. She didn't need to ask TAMS what it was. It was old, the kind that Keegan's mom sometimes listened to on road trips. They'd leave just before bedtime, so the kids could sleep in the car, while she drove through the night, listening to the soundtrack of her youth to stay awake. Nine Inch Nails was the band that scared Keegan the most, more than once making her reach out to hold her sleeping brother's hand in the back seat. The lyrics spoke of beauty but were set to a jarring mix of piano, electronic beats, and wailing.

She shines in a world full of ugliness.
She matters when everything is meaningless.[14]

Descending a metal circular stairwell, Keegan felt the same need. She grasped the railings, both to keep from stumbling in the dark and to mentally hold on to something real.

The stairs emptied into a wide-open room, lit with pink strobes. In the corner by the stairs, a metal cage hung suspended from what looked like a frayed rope. Inside, a young woman was trying to dance to the beat of the music. She wore nothing but bright blue rubber Wellington boots, the kind that people wore around muddy farms — or now the streets of DC. Maybe it was some kind of joke, or trying to turn the recent devastation into sex. She looked little more than eighteen. Maybe she was, or maybe she had just had the work done to look that age; Keegan wasn't sure about any of it. But she was confident that whatever identification the club had for her would attest to that age, whether it was true or not.

Yet, for all her gyrations, the attention of the crowd was on a large circular stage in the middle of the room, where two dancers, human and machine, held their focus. The human dancer was loose-limbed and tall, maybe 6 feet, but she moved with a gymnast's precision. She wore a translucent skinsuit that sparkled with dots of electric light that blinked and brightened with her movements. It gave the feel of watching sexualized energy itself. It was almost lessened when invisible seams in the suit began to give way with each gyration, first discarding a sleeve, then a panel covering her lower back. Underneath the lights was a tattoo that rippled with colors, orange and red flames and some kind of text that Keegan couldn't make out from a distance.

For all the woman's grace, the crowd was more transfixed on the other dancer. A humanoid design robot descended the stage's central pole upside down, hand over hand, with its legs perpendicular to her body. *Its body,* Keegan reminded herself. It was one of the most realistic she'd ever seen, designed to replicate the human form with the kind of expensive fidelity that came from the gray-market fabricators in the Emirates. But its movements were entirely inhuman. The machine pivoted entirely around its shoulders to land on its feet, an unnatural articulation that drew a collective intake of breath from the crowd.

The two dancers entwined, an embrace that made Keegan cringe slightly, a mix of disgust at what that poor woman had to do in front of this crowd and fear about what might happen if the robot malfunctioned just slightly. The two began to caress each other, as if the audience were not even there, knowing that their indifference made it all the more entrancing to the crowd.

Keegan had had enough and turned away to scan the room. Like a cliché, it was almost all men. Even without vizglasses, she recognized a few faces. Dressed like he'd just come from a neighborhood barbecue was a senator from Kentucky, while a few tables over were three Washington Capital hockey players, but in suits and ties, as if they'd just come from a charity banquet. Just behind them stood a clean-shaven man in a black turtleneck. Keegan recognized him from her military days, but she couldn't remember which unit the three-star general now commanded.

For some customers the performance was not enough. In a roped-off corner veiled by a fine chain-mail curtain that billowed like fog, three robotic dancers gyrated astride customers squirming in deep, red leather couches. As the curtain parted to allow a man to stagger out, Keegan caught a better glimpse of one of the dancers. Clad in glossy black carbon-fiber skin, it had a lifelike face mask that recreated a Grammy-winning country music star with long blonde hair. The other machine was all flesh and wreathed in tattoos all the way up to its neck.[15] It looked like one of the most popular viz feed influencers. But as it spun slowly for its customer, Keegan saw the machine had two faces beneath the spiky brown hair, frosted pink at the tips. Even at a distance Keegan could see the twisted expression of pain on one side, while the other smiled deeply, it eyes rolled back. Agony or Ecstasy.

Nausea welled up in Keegan's gut, and she gently nudged TAMS in the other direction. This was not what she had come to see.

"Anything catch your eye?" a female voice said from behind.

Keegan turned, unsure if it would be human or robot. It was a girl, early twenties, perfect skin, pale as moonlight with enormous eyes, set deep like a cat's. Keegan tried to keep her focus on those eyes, glowing greenish blue with bioluminescent contacts, rather than tracking down to the red leather knee-high platform boots. The girl was likely ogled all day; that was the last thing she needed. Then Keegan realized, at a place like this, maybe she wasn't noticed much at all.

"You just want to enjoy the show tonight? Or maybe you two are looking for some company?"

"How much?"

"Depends. I'm Rose, by the way. You and me can have some fun, twenty minutes, for four hundred dollars. An hour is eight hundred. But looking at your friend here, maybe you want it in on the action? That's double."

Keegan nodded but bit the inside of her lower lip, as if thinking it over, running the numbers in her head. She then looked around the room, appearing to weigh the options. Another of the robot dancers in the VIP area stood up and began to walk through the crowd, evidently programmed to drum up business. This one was done up in the sexualized business suit of a news anchorwoman whose viewers' Cambridge scores registered as reacting most to traditional values.[16] Its realism somehow made it seem more artificial, like a robot version of a human fembot.

"What are my other options?" Keegan asked.

"Machine-on-machine is an hour minimum. A thousand dollars. That's the rules, I don't make them."

The human girl, Rose, then noticed the fembots starting to finish their dance, and the rhythm of her voice changed, picking up the pace as she tried to close the deal. "Maybe we start out easy, just you and I, and your friend can watch if you want. Then if you like it, we go up a level."

She's worried about losing work to a machine. Even here.

"Maybe we just talk for a minute. All I want to do is ask you some questions."

"You're not one of the Holy Rollers are you? Jailbreak me to find Jesus? You can go fuck yourself. Better yet, go fuck your tin can."

Keegan put her hands up. "No, nothing like that. I'm just looking for someone."

An upturned palm was Rose's response. "It'll cost you . . . Even if you're a cop."

Smart girl. Keegan pulled one of Jared's $200 bills from her pocket and placed it in the girl's hand. It felt like robbing the girl in a way, but there was no way in hell Noritz would reimburse her for a payoff here.

"Much better," Rose said, tucking it into a pocket lining the inside of her bustier. "Ask me anything you want."

"Anything?" Keegan asked.

"Look around. You think I'm going to be offended?" Rose laughed.

"Why's it cost more for the bots than the humans?"

"Look at 'em. Tech like that don't come cheap. Plus they break. A lot. Maybe you can figure out why. By comparison, the humans? Well, we come cheap," she said with a dark laugh that clearly masked something more, "because we show up here already broken."

"Sorry," said Keegan.

"No need to feel sorry. It is what it is. Even at less than the bots, it pays better than being a store greeter, just getting by until the government decides to kick in some of that basic income money they keep talking about." Her tone consciously changed, trying to get back to the transaction. "Sure you're a cop? You know . . ." she said, squeezing the back of Keegan's neck. Her nails dug into the skin and chills shot through her body. Keegan hoped TAMS was too consumed by everything else that was going on around it to notice. ". . . you can book the Smash Room with me. It's not cheap. A hundred dollars for two minutes," she said.

Keegan recoiled, and Rose smiled.

"That's not what the Smash Room is for, honey. It's for it . . . your bot."

Keegan's eyes darted to TAMS to see whether it was reacting.

"We can tie it up; I've got titanium cuffs, surplus Chinese special forces. Holds any machine down, even if you program it to try. Then do what you want. Diamond saws, concrete hammers. You name it. Whatever gets you off. Or it can play too. We got everything from old Roombas to ones more for human tastes." She nodded over at the fembot, now stroking the hair of the senator, who had been interviewed by the human version of the woman just the weekend before. "Even one of those."

"Something for everybody here," Keegan said.

"Come on, like you haven't thought about it?"

Keegan looked away.

"Oh shit, you have," Rose said.

"It's not like that," Keegan said.

"That's what everybody says at first." And then Rose leaned in. "Go on, tell me."

"Maybe some other time. I really am looking for someone. Need to find a regular by the name of Simpkins."

Another upturned palm. "You wasted your question then. Five hundred dollars more."

"Guys in here are getting a lot more than a name for that tonight," said Keegan.

"Don't be an asshole," Rose said. "You can have whatever you want; told you that already."

Keegan pulled out a wad of bills from her pocket. "Then I want something more than a question answered. You help me find Simpkins, and this is all yours."

Rose's eyes narrowed as she tried to count the stack of bills in Keegan's hand. "Simpkins in trouble?"

"Just gotta find him." Keegan jerked her thumb at TAMS. "Delivery for him. Has he been around here recently?"

Rose reached across and snatched away the wad of bills.

"If you count downstairs as 'around here,'" the girl said with a triumphant smile. She leaned in close again and whispered in Keegan's ear. "Oh, and I know this cash is supposed to be shit. But we got a Russian here who can get us sixty cents on the dollar. Over there, cash is still king. So screw you, and what you tried to pull." She then straightened herself and patted the rectangular lump poking out of the side of her bra. "In either case, a deal is a deal. I'll take you down to him."

But before they headed down the stairs, the girl took TAMS by the hand, looking into its eyes with what seemed like real concern. "Welcome to the business, bot. Just remember this one rule and you'll be fine: we all get fucked."

CONTROL ROOM CLUB

Chesapeake Bay

"You sure you haven't been here before?" Rose asked Keegan as they descended into the club's lowest level. "You got that look on your face."

The damp air reeked of hot plastic, stale sweat, and burning ozone. It was an all-too-familiar smell from the weeks they had spent waiting offshore on the USS *Arlington,* just before it all went to hell.

"No. Just a long day," said Keegan, taking in another deep breath.

The corridor was bathed in red light, and none of the club's music filtered through. The ceiling had to be soundproof, and this bottom level was below the waterline, adding a claustrophobic feel. Then came the sound of a rubber-coated mallet whacking steel. Wheezing gasps for air followed. Keegan looked over at TAMS to see if it was reacting. Nothing. Good. She didn't need it running into one of the chambers unordered, like it had done to check on Haley.

As they walked farther down the wide corridor, the red light faded. TAMS turned on a navigation light, but Keegan hissed to turn it off and the space was left in near darkness. The only light came from the porthole-like observation windows that were the only view into each of the chambers.

Unable to fight her curiosity, Keegan snatched a glance as they passed by. Inside was a spare white room, a bed in the middle. A man in his fifties, bald, with thick black glasses, lay back naked on a purple crescent-shaped pillow. In the corner sat a robot about half his size, matte blue with rainbow-colored bands and a white lace bra, holding an old hardback book. Its frayed blue cover had a picture of a bespectacled boy with a tiny scar on his forehead.

The robot read out loud in the voice of a young woman with a British accent, "I mean, it's sort of exciting, isn't it, breaking the rules?"[17]

"What the . . . ?" Keegan said. "They pay for that?"

"You have no idea," said Rose. "Simpkins is at the back." She pointed to the end of the hallway. "You're on your own from here. He's been on a mean streak this week."

And with that she was gone. Keegan turned to watch her walk purposefully away, back into the red light of the corridor's far end.

They walked to the end and Keegan forced herself to look though the porthole. It was not as bad as she'd feared. A naked man and two women were writhing in a tangle of limbs, atop a silvery set of sheets.

"Let's just get this over with quickly and quietly," Keegan told TAMS. "You go in first. Just tap him on the shoulder, gently like." She didn't need some guy getting off on her bot.

"OK," the robot said, and Keegan pressed the entry button.

The door opened silently, sliding on a track that disappeared into the wall. TAMS stepped through and, with exaggeratedly slow movement, walked up to Simpkins. The man remained oblivious to the door opening and the robot. TAMS reached out toward his left shoulder, just above where a tattoo began, a series of repeating diamond-shaped arrowheads that ran down his arm, stopping at his wrist. TAMS's metal finger tapped the point of one diamond three rows down. Keegan wondered what mathematical equation had led it to choose that one point versus any other?

When Keegan pulled her attention to the entirety of the scene, she regretted sending the bot in first. What had looked through the porthole like a ménage à trois was actually something that made her grip the doorframe in anger.

"Fuck off. I didn't order you," the man said, looking back at TAMS, while still intently thrusting into one of the two identical light-skinned sex bots. "Come back later." One hand propped him up on the bed, while his other clutched a robot's unattached arm. The second robot lay face down, curled over its knees but with its arms reversed. Its head was lolling to the side, only wires connecting to the torso, and a ragged, torn edge to the rubber skin where its neck had been. Yet the robot's hands still gently caressed the breasts of the supine bot that had Simpkins's attention.

"TAMS, non-lethal weapons authorization," Keegan ordered. "Tase him. Now."

"OK."

Keegan turned away, so that she did not have to see what a burst of electrical charge was going to do to all this. At the sound of the sizzling flesh, she turned back around.

Simpkins lay crumpled forward, sprawling atop the two bots. At his cessation of movement, they had also stopped moving.

The stillness was unsettling. It was like a switch had flipped. The room felt tight and the air thin. Keegan entered the room and coughed, trying not to breathe in the funk of sex. Not wanting to touch anything, she used her foot to push Simpkins to the floor, not minding the thump as his head hit. She pulled the sheet off the bed and covered the two bots.

"We need to dress him. Can you do that?" Keegan asked TAMS.

TAMS did not move, looking neither at Keegan nor Simpkins. Then it spoke. "I am unable to perform that operation without assistance."

It was too complex a task for one person or machine, at least without hurting the man further.

"Fine," Keegan said. "We'll do it together."

Damn machine can predict crime all by itself, but this is what it needs me for.

As TAMS held the limp body up, she tugged the man's clothes back on. The machine could touch this creep's flesh; it didn't mind. They were almost done when the clothes were suddenly flung into the air.

Keegan leapt backward, letting go of Simpkins.

On the bed, the two robots had begun to disentangle themselves from each other. They lay separated by no more than an arm's length, their torsos facing as one lifted up the missing leg of the other and reinstalled it, followed by reattaching the head, the tear line fitting back together snugly by design. The process of reassembly and reset continued as a gentle ritual, like it was part of an ancient ceremony performed for thousands of years.

"Working as an FBI bot doesn't seem that bad now, I bet," said Keegan to TAMS.

Five minutes later, Keegan stalked down the hallway with TAMS behind her. The bot had Simpkins in a fireman's carry, the unconscious man's limbs occasionally dragging on the floor. At the bottom of the stairs, Keegan stopped and faced TAMS. "If he wakes, tase him again."

"OK."

At the top of the stairs, Rose waited for them. She leaned against the wall, one leg straight and the other bent at the knee, leather-booted foot pressed against the wall. "Your friend like his surprise?"

"A bit too much," Keegan said. "Time to go home."

"You sure about that?"

FBI SATELLITE FACILITY

Reston, Virginia

It was a different interrogation room from before. The harsh smell of lemon from a recent cleaning blended with lingering scents of cinnamon from when the space had been a candle store years back.

The lights were on. Bright. Keegan had to squint, but thought it suited the situation perfectly. No skulking in the dark for this one anymore.

Simpkins, his wrists shackled to the table, looked from TAMS to her, and then back at the robot.

"Not a chance, asshole," Keegan said.

Simpkins frowned. Then he dipped his head to wipe his brow on the dark blue sleeves of his shirt. At that, he smiled at the realization of how he'd gotten back into his clothes. "Too bad I missed dress-up time," Simpkins said. "But I'm still not talking."

"Sure," said Keegan. "TAMS, come over to where I can see you. You're freaking me out over there."

The robot sat down smoothly and laid its hands on the table across from Simpkins's shackled wrists.

"Easy there," said Keegan, as if warning the robot. "It doesn't seem to like what it saw today, Simpkins."

She suspected that, at just the mere suggestion of it, Simpkins would read TAMS's blank face as if filled with menace.

"Agent Keegan," said Dr. Modi's voice in her earpiece, "I'm recording this interrogation."

He was watching from his office, viewing the room through TAMS's cameras.

"You want out of here?" Keegan asked Simpkins. "There's one way and it's the easy way. We just talk. All the other ways don't end well." She tilted her head at TAMS and its blank face somehow looked even more threatening.

Simpkins shook his manacled hands forward, trying to strike out at TAMS, straining so hard that the metal of the cuffs peeled back the sleeves of his shirt and caught on the meat of his tattooed forearms.

TAMS stared back without expression or action.

"This one isn't programmed for that stuff," Keegan said.

"Agent Keegan, can you hold his wrists out for me to see?" Modi said in her ear again.

More joysticking from afar. Next time she did an interrogation, she'd have to bring her own jammer in to get anything done.

Keegan stood, walked over to Simpkins, and slammed his wrists down on the table. She then looked into TAMS's face. "See, he's fine."

"That's what I thought," Modi said in her ear. "Can you show me both sides?"

"He's fine. See," she said, twisting Simpkins's wrists with a slight tug to show TAMS both sides. "Not a single scratch."

"I see that," Modi said. "The design is what matters. See how the checkerboard is made up of diamond shapes? Those are Othala runes, the marker for the National Freedom Front."[18]

The red, white, and blue Nazis. And, just like they always did, hiding their brand in plain sight.

Keegan let go of Simpkins's wrists and walked back to her seat. "Those are pretty extensive tats," she said. She then uncuffed her shirt sleeve to reveal her tattoo. "How long did it take? Mine took an hour."

Simpkins smiled. "Nine hours."

"Damnnnnn. Must have hurt like a bitch. My arm didn't stop throbbing for a week."

"It's supposed to hurt," he said with a tone of pride. "There's pain in progress."

Wonderful, she thought, another hatemonger from the dark web, who imagined himself some kind of intellectual.[19]

"So what's with the design? This was a pretty obvious choice," she said, pointing out each of the parts. "Eagle, globe, anchor . . . Only a United States Marine can wear it."

"You'll learn it soon enough. Ours is for those who have seen the truth. Patriots around the world wear it," said Simpkins. "Our legions are everywhere."

"I'm betting on that." She turned to TAMS. "TAMS, see how many other tattoos like that you can find in the cloud." She stood to leave the room.

The machine may not have not been able to pull out the underlying meaning of the artistic design, but once given an image to hunt for, it could do search and pattern matching of a kind beyond Simpkins's understanding. Before Keegan had even made her way through the hallway, hundreds of open-source images were flashing across her vizglasses. Photos of a family beach vacation, father, mother, and two daughters, all having matching ankle-band tattoos of the design; the dating profile of an overweight, elderly man, wearing a shirt pin with a neo-Nazi logo on it, as he posed in front of a cherry red sports car; the department newsletter sharing images from the police department's charity softball tournament, an off-duty SWAT team smiling for the camera as they flexed biceps marked with the tattoo.

An accompanying map began to geolocate the images off the photos' metadata. One by one, dots appeared all over the country, but the highest concentration by far was just outside Washington, DC, a short enough drive from Simpkins's favorite club.

BALLSTON NEIGHBORHOOD

Arlington, Virginia

It was two hours before sunrise when she got back to the condo, so she took her shoes off at the door. It was not just her trying to avoid waking Jared, but also because she had no idea what substances were now on their soles. Slipping in quietly, she found Jared sleeping on the couch, Haley lying beside him under a tangle of blankets, propped up on a pair of pillows with giraffes on them. Given that Keegan had just been to a robot sex club, she couldn't complain about his parenting tactics.

The fridge displayed eggs and bread inside, but she stopped short of opening the door. As hungry as she was, it was too early to start banging pans. She knew there were protein bars in the cupboard, so she grabbed one, cringing at the slight sound of the wrapper crinkling as she tore it open. As she took a bite, the chocolate and peanut-butter flavor melted in her mouth, leaving just the slight chalky aftertaste that insect protein supplements always had.

"You're here," Jared murmured from the couch.

"For a little while," Keegan said.

"OK," he said. "Haley's sleeping. Don't wake her."

"I can see. Water, power been good? Cloud OK?"

He murmured yes. "How about you?"

"Yeah, I'm good," she said. She was far from it, but she didn't have it in her this morning to have another battle.

"You're being safe?" he asked. It was real worry. He could read her better than anyone and knew something was off, the legacy from what she'd seen the night before. For all the distance, the love they had shared was still there — indeed, it was sleeping right beside him on the couch. Neither of them wanted to contemplate what it would be like to live somewhere without her, even just for a week at a time. Jared also knew too much about her own past to contemplate a life without him.

"I just need a shower and a change of clothes, then I'll head out."

Jared nodded his head in agreement, no attempt to stop her, and then curled back into a ball. He probably thought it was best she didn't cross paths with Haley. Maybe he was right.

In the guest bathroom, she waited for the water to heat up while finishing the protein bar. As she sat on the fake white marble vanity top, she looked over at the wicker and glass storage basket where she kept her personal hygiene products. Even that basket had some emotional baggage. Keegan wasn't opposed to it. If anything, it was pretty nice. But, like everything, picking it out with Jared had turned into an exhausting series of decisions, him picking out eight different options and then wanting to talk through which of the online reviews they should trust more. That was a before problem, when such petty squabbles were a luxury of the fully employed.

She stood and went over to the basket, pulling out the foldable screen tablet.[20] She kept it wedged behind one of the boxes she knew Jared would never look in. Men were strange, but predictable that way. The tablet was a disposable model she had bought three months back. Buying it had felt like an act of betrayal, but separating your accounts and devices was one of the things that all the guides recommended when you crossed over to this stage in a relationship.

The shower ran, steaming up the small bathroom. She inhaled the damp air and scrolled through messages. Notices from her bank account, advertisements from online dating sites that had somehow figured out her looming change of status, and various messages from friends and family she'd have to answer at some point. She set the tablet down on the sink's edge and got undressed. Wiping the condensation away from the middle of the mirror with her hand, she looked at herself, a bit fearful of what she'd see. A failure as a wife? As a mother?

The woman who looked back had bloodshot eyes, the skin around them slightly swollen, so it looked like she was squinting. Running her hands through her hair, Keegan exhaled to try and shake off the slightly queasy feeling from that toxic mix of emotions and the hangover of adrenaline.

She moved to get in the shower, eager for the reset that the hot water would provide, but stopped short as the tablet flashed the next wave of downloaded messages. One caught her attention, the picture of its sender sending a shiver up her spine. Of all the times for him to reach out.

> So there I was sitting in traffic, minding my own business, and the viz feed pops a clip of you as an FBI superhero with a robot sidekick. Of all the jobs for you to end up in! But you always were smart as hell. I guess that also means it's all good now for me too ... I can't

*tell you what a relief that is. Hit me back at this account and we can
set a time to catch up. Lots to talk about, S*
    *Note: I saw you busted those guys at a chili dog restaurant. Some
things never change* ☺

Just like that, after over fifteen years? With the warrant out for
them after the riot at the student center, a quick decision had been
made in the basement laundry room of her dorm. There should be
no further contact among the group, so there would be no way for
the police to connect the dots. There hadn't even been time for that
clichéd one last kiss with him. She hadn't even gone to graduation,
getting the degree in her first mail call at Parris Island.

And yet there his message was as if all that had been set aside.
Didn't he get that her being a federal agent wasn't a sign that they
were in the clear, but the very opposite? At the same time, she was
curious where he had ended up, what he had become. In her mind, he
was still that curly-haired kid with a dimple on his left cheek from the
dorm next door, who she had first talked to in a political science study
group. Snippets of dances, student marches, and dorm-room hookups
played in her memory. Did he have a wife? Kids? With a single reply,
she could find all that out, maybe even answer the once seemingly
unanswerable question of the road not taken.

Keegan looked back at the woman in the mirror, to see if she could
help in some way. The face that looked back warned her that answering him would risk much more than her marriage.

She cleaned the condensation from the screen and deleted the
message. It didn't seem enough, so she wiped the tablet's memory.
Once that was done, she filled the sink with water and dropped the
tablet in, it making a slight sizzle as the water seeped into the battery.
Then she wrapped the dripping tablet in a towel and stepped on it
repeatedly, until the screen broke and the motherboard cracked.

Inside, though, she knew none of it would be enough to undo the
damage.

11

FBI HOSTAGE RESCUE TEAM OPERATIONS CENTER

Quantico, Virginia

"Here you'll see landing zone Broadway. FBI V-290 Valor, call sign TALON 22, will put an eight-person HRT element here," said Noah.

Watching Noah stand inside the cavernous hangar at Quantico, Keegan felt the familiar pre-mission anticipation build. She tried to dial the excitement back with a deep breath, but it didn't work.

Noah wove his hands through the air in front of him, using force-sensor gesture gloves to conjure up the paths the agents would follow toward their target.[1]

"We'll be staging here." He pointed, and geographic markers appeared on the large 3-D projection in the air in front of the force. The display showed gently rolling land that gained elevation as it ran up to the edge of Shenandoah National Park. The briefing continued for a few more minutes, covering the particulars of the target, an "American Solidarity Enclave" located in the western part of Greene County, Virginia.

ASEs had started to pop up around the country a decade back as a merger of real estate development and hate. The ASEs sold themselves as a place for "true patriots" to live and work together like the early white settlers once had. Purpose-built communities of farm-style homes, where you could know and trust your neighbors, mixed with high-tech on-site manufacturing and "Pure Code" software development. It was a classic play-for-profit using the powerful forces of nostalgia, fear, and division, selling ideas and products to one group of Americans on the basis of them being more American than another. Building on that proven model, the Pure Code movement pushed branded algorithms and apps written by "real Americans," whose racial identity had been certified by genomic testing. Of course, like so much of the shtick, it was bullshit. Most of the programming work was actually outsourced to digital sweatshops in India and Peru.

The gentrification of the rural landscape was also designed around a blend of oversized homes with easily defendable tracts of land against any and all outside threats. For a generation fed doomsday scenarios of everything from Mexican gangs to zombies, having your own secure and self-sufficient enclave seemed like a real need.

The intelligence gathered on this particular ASE showed ninety-six people with National Freedom Front markers, including twenty-three minors. Combined with facial recognition catches of Simpkins making gas station stops on his regular visits to Control Room, it'd been enough to get a search warrant for the site.

"This one's going to be a tough nut, though. There's only one road in and we have indicators local law enforcement may be compromised by this particular ASE."

Images of local press coverage showed the settlement's history. Led by a former congressional staffer from California named Gregory Heath, the first families affiliated with the National Freedom Front had arrived over the last few years with steady regularity, peeling away from their old lives inside the Beltway to establish an existence they described as a "system reboot of real America." Any local resistance to the group had ended after the incumbent mayor of the closest town had ended up shot dead in a ditch after Heath contested the election. A later newsclip showed the new county sheriff, another recent arrival appointed by Heath, lamenting that the shooting remained unsolved.

"So we have to assume all ground movements will be monitored.

The follow-on force will stage out of the Blue Ridge School about 15 klicks south.[2] They'll mask as a delivery vehicle," he said, a picture of a large six-wheeled autonomous UPS truck that the Bureau's Hostage Rescue Team often used as a covert command post popping up on the screen. "It's a boarding school for boys, so they'll be used to some traffic there, delivering care packages and such for the rich kids."

Noah pulled up a 3-D map with their staging area and the routes the FBI force would take from there.

"And then just as everyone in the enclave is waking up to have their coffee and apple pie fritters or whatever the fuck racist fuckers eat for breakfast—"

At that, an enormous agent in the back of the room shouted out, "Tell us what you really think, Reddy!"

"My brief, Keg . . . ," he said to quiet the agent. "Agent Keegan and her, um, partner will show up at their front door to serve the warrant, brought there safe and sound through the hard work and dedication of the FBI's most elite unit." At that, the assembled crowd made the obligatory military-style "Oorah" cheer.

"Agent Keegan, do you have anything more for us? An inspirational message?" Typical Noah, trying to put her on the spot.

She blinked out of the displays on her vizglasses and stood to face the group of body-armor-wearing HRT operators and support staff. "My plan is just let the FBI's most elite unit"—another Oorah from the crowd—"do its thing, and stay out of your way," said Keegan.

After the briefing ended, Noah came up to Keegan as she snapped the magazine in and out of her Next Generation Squad Weapon, checking to ensure it didn't catch, as had plagued the first batches of the gun.[3] She'd carried a version of the NGSW in the Marines, which made the "Next Generation" in the name a bit absurd. But at least they'd finally replaced the old M16 variants Marines had carried for some seventy-five years.

"Hey, boot," Noah said. "You still remember how to use it?"

"Like riding a bike, just with a polymer-cased 6.8-millimeter round."

But Noah didn't laugh. "Be careful out there with your back. Exo's will mess that shit up for you, and I don't have the free time to visit you in the hospital every week again."

"All set," said Keegan, tapping the magazine onto her gray helmet.[4] Then she pulled out a plastic-wrapped square of paper, folded over on itself. The warrant was printed out: shockproof, waterproof, and un-hackable. "Our most important weapon."

"Pretty sure they won't be happy to see us." As Noah said it, he absentmindedly tightened the chest fasteners on his body armor that secured it to the exoskeleton. It was a tell that he was nervous too.

"Don't expect so," said Keegan. "When was anybody happy to see you and me at their door?"

"Bit different this time. Less danger, more firepower," said Noah, flexing his arm in the exoskeleton toward the waiting tilt-rotor aircraft. He took a long look at TAMS. "The question is, is your bot ready for this? There're a lot of HRT applicants who were hot shit in the Kill House, but turned out to be just shit when it came to actually doing the job. I assume it's the same for machines."

"It's done OK so far," said Keegan, feeling somehow obligated to defend TAMS. It was her machine as far as anybody in the hangar was concerned.

"It going in armed?" Noah asked.

"Benelli shotgun with Taser rounds," she said.[5] Then, after waiting a beat, "It likes shocking Nazis."

He looked back at her quizzically, not sure if she was putting him on.

"How about your team?" she asked. "Anything else I need to know?"

"Just the basics today; you and that thing are enough of a novelty. We don't need any more risk."

She knew Noah trusted her, but she was an outsider to his team and therefore a liability. And the machine she'd brought into their element only magnified an unknown quantity.

Another HRT operator called for Noah's attention, so he left her. Mostly to keep busy, Keegan tried to find who had feeds of the insect-sized reconnaissance bots the FBI usually deployed ahead of the assault.

She went over to the HRT agent that Noah had called Keg. Six foot five and 250 pounds, he had the football player build that Hollywood imagined of special operators, rather than the reality, which was most of them looking like cross-country runners. Add in the extra inches of lift from his exosuit's boots, and he towered over Keegan.[6]

He needed that size, as he carried one of the new .50-caliber M109 sniper rifles that fired hypersonic bullets. It gave them twice the speed and range as regular rounds, but the longer, heavier barrel also meant twice the weight and the need to change out the barrel after every engagement.[7] Only the most elite units could afford them, and only their biggest members could handle them.

"Keg?" Keegan asked. She wondered about the nickname's origin. Was it a reference to his burly size, some legendary drinking escapade, or maybe just some secret handshake acronym among the team's operators? She didn't want to give the satisfaction of asking, though. No matter how integrated these units had become, they still had too many vestiges of back when they'd been a boys' club.

"Yo," he said, caught in the midst of spitting into a black plastic bottle he'd mounted on the latch-point of his body armor.

These guys and their dip. It never changes.

"I mean, 'How can I assist you?'" as if parroting an order Noah had given in a talk to the unit before Keegan's arrival.

"I can't find any feeds from the recon bots," Keegan said.

Keg shook his head, an audible sound as the big man's armor and exosuit strained. "'Cause there ain't any. They sent in a set with cover as EPA sniffers. We got about four minutes of coverage, but then they just powered down. I can push you what we have, but all we got were images of sticks and leaves."

"Damn," she said.

"Not my call," said Keg, seeing the look that crossed her face. "We still got the overhead feed from the Iris drone."

"I'm just looking for something more."

"Aren't we all, sister," said Keg. He had a kind, gap-toothed smile beneath a nose that looked like it had been broken once a year.

So, all they had was the aerial sensor data from a disposable Iris glider loitering 7,000 feet overhead. It could have been a faulty battery set that cut the insect bot feeds, but Keegan's mind quickly went to a more malicious cause. Most likely a Zapper, one of the networked countermeasures systems that used the drones' wireless charging capability to rapidly drain their onboard batteries, rather than top them up. A lot of the anti-government compounds, and plenty of inner-city drug dealers, bought them off Alibaba as easily as they did new shoes.

"Yeah, my spidey senses are reading it as well," Keg said. "Either way, you and your midget machine are running with me now, so you'll be fine."

"Got it," Keegan said. "Can I ask you another question?"

"Fire away. You're the reason we get to go out today on a real mission instead of more video game training, so ask what you want."

"You actually going fit in the Valor with all that shit on?"

"Sometimes we have to leave any deadweight behind if it gets tight," Keg said. "Usually that's your boy, Noah. This time, though, I'm sizing up how much you and your bot weigh."

"You know never to ask that of a lady, especially not one with a robot that carries a shotgun," Keegan replied.

Keg tipped the rifle in salute. Being able to joke at a time like this was one of the little tests that mattered.

After the team loaded into the Valor, they lifted off into the night sky under total darkness, not using the usual navigation lights. The "squirt" rapid departure helped reduce the chance that plane spotters would be able to capture the flight and report it onto the opensource flight trackers.[8]

Keegan tried to close her eyes and nap, but it was impossible to sleep aboard the Valor. She hated tilt-rotor aircraft; knew too many horror stories about them. To make matters worse, she was wedged in tighter than even they'd been in the old Ospreys. On one side was the massive Keg, his exosuit secured to the floor and bulkhead by the crew chief—no lap belt was strong enough for the weight. On her other side was TAMS. That normally would have given her more space, but the petite robot was bulked out with a protective armor kit that added a layer of ceramic plating over its chest.

The Valor's flight path took it north toward the city, another precaution to avoid tipping off their target. The plan was to then fly west along the Potomac and dip back southwest. It added time, but gave Keegan an aerial view of the flooded areas of Washington. The Georgetown waterfront, where she and Jared had first started to run together in that transition period from dating to relationship, was still dark — no power. But the mud- and water-logged streets glinted in the lights of construction equipment and the hundreds of drones assisting in the relief efforts. While the city hadn't been ready for the fast-moving flood, cleaning up after severe weather events was something that the government was prepared for, as every major metropolitan area along the eastern seaboard had to deal with them more and more in recent years.[9]

"Look at all that mud," said Noah, sitting directly across from her. "Bet they have it cleaned up in a week."

"Just thinking the same thing," said Keegan. The air cooled as the Valor gained altitude, lifting them above the recent spike in heat that had followed the flood.

"Saw you guys pitching in during all the mess, rescuing kittens from trees and even the Declaration of Independence."

"Anything to avoid going to the office," said Keegan.

"Typical of your lazy ass. And don't think I didn't notice your buddy there did all the work . . . as usual," Noah said, nodding at TAMS.

Keegan gave him the finger and watched out the window as the Valor climbed away from DC. As the tilt-rotor crossed over into Arlington, she could make out their high-rise. She gave it a little wave, thinking of Haley and how cool she would think it was that Mommy had flown by in one of the tilt-rotor planes they sometimes saw through the window. Better she didn't know, though, considering the risks that went with it.

Keg reached across with his exo-shrouded arm and tapped Noah's knee. "One of your pistol mag covers is popped open." He pointed at the magazine secured next to the pistol on Noah's chest plate. "You dive for cover, you're going to get dirt and shit in there."

Noah gave a thumbs-up and firmly restrapped the Velcro tab down.

Keg shook his head disapprovingly. "Thomson used to do that. Said it saved him time on the reload," he said, laughing. "What a moron."

"You're just pissed because he shot you in the Atlanta raid," Noah said.

"He was going to shoot somebody eventually, better it was me."

"Where'd it catch you again?"

"Right in the plate, between the shoulders. Not even a scratch under the ceramic."

"Didn't hurt, that what you trying to say?"

"Of course it hurt, but I wasn't going to let him know."

Listening in to their back-and-forth, Keegan watched them with envy. She missed that camaraderie and knew it was something she would never have with a partner like TAMS. Sure, she could train it to speak with something like humor or even to be profane, but it would not commit the kinds of gaffes and screwups that deepened friendships in a way that nothing else could.

The tilt-rotor gained altitude, moving above the personal flier traffic of the super-commuters heading home late. Able to see more and more of the geography, Keegan watched the distinct neighborhoods morph into vinelike entanglements of red and white lights encircling pools of black.

She switched on her full-color night vision. The lightless black zones became vibrant projections of color on her lens, revealing the nighttime activity now taking place in abandoned retail and housing developments at the border line of the exurbs. This palette was the picture of modern agriculture, corn stalks nearly as tall as the empty two-story homes in whose lawns they now grew, as hundreds of mantislike compostable ag-bots moved between them, tending the crops.[10]

"What's that down there, TAMS?" as she marked a rectangular 20-acre stretch of land, all trace of human buildings cleared away.

"The designated area is an apple orchard operated by MG Farms, a limited liability corporation registered in Delaware," TAMS said. Keegan zoomed the view in on the lines of trees, and moving between them were a half dozen Ocado bots, mechanized limbs alternately thrashing and delicately grabbing fruit through the night.[11] She wondered if that was it? Was that what drove Shaw, not a sense of "responsibility," but its dark twin, some kind of guilt buried deep beneath that placid exterior, that the real crop his family's farm had shared with the world was scenes like this?

"Bet they're not listening to any country songs," said Noah, who had hooked on to the same feed.

"Used to be when you wanted to get people to vote for you it was to scream about some immigrant coming to pick fruit for pennies," said Keegan. "Now, from farm to table, it's the bots that do it."[12]

"Wonder how many Americans down there would sign up to do that work now? I bet more than a few," Noah said.

"Bullshit," said Keegan. "They'd just complain about someone taking their jobs, even if it's jobs they don't want to do."

The Valor dropped in a steep dive, engine surging as the aircraft picked up speed. Keegan braced herself and fought the anxiety that made her want to throw up. To focus on something else, she shifted to the external feed from the Valor's own situational-awareness suite. The aircraft's wider-angle view of the landscape just showed more dark zones. Starry motes of light in the night vision were the only sign of human life. It made her think of Shaw and the changes he'd mentioned that had taken place in rural America over just a single lifetime.[13] Small town after small town emptied not just of people, but of hope. The Valor flew over closed-up farms, stores, and gas stations that were the only monuments to a way of life made obsolete. The most depressing was an abandoned school's high school football stadium. For all that she hated the way those places were treated as temples to first kisses and life-changing quarterback passes, the sight of it was jolting. If they'd forsaken even that, what was left?

A moment later, a particularly violent lurch of the Valor caused her to lose her grasp on the NGSW rifle. Keg reached out with an exo-suit-shrouded arm and caught the weapon, while he spit dip into his black bottle. Coral-like perforated carbon supports wrapped his limb. The weapon was strapped to her, so there was no chance of her losing it completely, but it was still embarrassing.

Keg handed the weapon back to Keegan. "I was sketched out about your bot, but now I'm more worried about you. Try not to shoot any holes in the floor." As if to keep her from making a quip back, he quickly flipped down his protective face mask, concealing the last sign that there was indeed a person underneath all that carbon and ceramic.

There may be a person under there, Keegan thought, but he's already half-machine. The two surveillance appendages on his back could function like extra limbs and even hold weapons. She looked over at TAMS, sitting on her other side, entirely unhuman, but its fragility seeming more human by far. And what was she, other than caught in the middle?

AMERICAN SOLIDARITY ENCLAVE

Greene County, Virginia

The head-high rock formations jutted out of the hillside like broken bones. They afforded the approaching HRT group plenty of cover — but they did for any defenders as well. This sort of country had a fighting history, and she could feel it.

The Valor had dropped them off in a forest clearing, using a valley dipping through the hills to try to mask its approach. From there, they'd advanced on foot as silently as they could. The team's dog-like, four-legged scout bot took point, stalking forward 100 meters ahead of them. Keegan tasked TAMS to follow in the rear. Even though its sensors were more advanced than those of the HRT bot, she knew they trusted their own gear more.

Keegan crouched at the base of one of the outcroppings and watched the low hills above for any sign of activity. Her eyes said there was nobody up there, and the Iris drone feed indicated the same thing. TAMS, though, pinged her there was intermittent short-distance radio-wave transmission activity in the area, the kind used in personal-area networks. It could be nothing — a hunter, a hiker, even a drone out surveying crops. And, yet, it could be something.

A glance back confirmed that TAMS remained out of sight, the robot's presence behind a large rock marked on Keegan's vizglasses.

Orders from Noah came next, and the team of eight HRT operators and Keegan slowly climbed up the ridge and over to a dip in the ground just below its crest. The agents crawled on their bellies to the depression, which they covered with a sensor-defeat material whose patterns refracted the colors around them. If the compound did have a guard detail running scans of the area, it would make it harder to find them. They pushed the scout bot ahead 50 meters more to set a perimeter.

If not for sitting in a hole covered by mesh netting, the setting would have been bucolic. They were at the edge of a vineyard, row after row of flowering vines and young grapes. On her right, Keg tapped Keegan on the shoulder and pointed to the east, where the sky had begun to fill with orange, red, and cream swirls just ahead of the sun's rise. For all his bulk, he apparently had an artist's appreciation of the moment. Then, he spat dip, this time onto the dirt.

Keegan looked over at Noah, to her left, who continued to study the Iris's imagery of the compound.

Reaching up, Keegan snatched a grape off the vine and popped it in her mouth.

"I wouldn't do that," whispered Noah. "You don't know what they put in those things . . . might turn you into a Nazi."

"Yeah, I don't think racism works that way," Keegan whispered back. She waited a beat. "Pretty safe bet, though, it's all white wine."

"Good one." He looked over at her. "You know, as messed up as it sounds, I'm glad we get to do this again, just shooting the shit, while waiting for it." He held out a leather-gloved hand and they bumped fists.

They stayed silent for another minute, thinking back to the others they knew from those days who wouldn't be able to watch a sunrise. "So why does anybody drink wine from Virginia anyway?" Noah said, breaking the silence.

"That's old think," said Keegan. "Some decent vineyards, though it depends on the vintages."

"Vintages? Listen to you. What do you think they call this one?"

"Stormfront Cellars?"[14]

"Alt Reich Riesling?" said Noah.

"You two are really changing the way I think about Marines," Keg said, interrupting them. "We got five more minutes if you want to place an online order for a case."

They were silent for another minute that seemed to go by in a second. In that compression of time between the final moments of waiting and dangerous action, Keegan regularly found clarity. It was a precious feeling, that cross of melancholy and understanding what truly mattered. As the shadows lifted further and the sunrise began to paint the green hillside in orange and red light, she pulled one last image of Haley into her mind. Then one of Jared, which made her wonder if she'd done that out of habit, or something more.

"This really is beautiful land, though," Noah said in a voice that revealed he was lost in the same state.

"It is. Doesn't seem fair." Keegan tapped the transmit button and said into her mouthpiece, "TAMS, just how did these fuckers afford a place like this?"

TAMS sent a frown emoji, indicating it was unable to answer Keegan, then a status pop-up that it was not using its network access in order to reduce their electronic signature. Then it sent another message, this one a warning, indicating that Keegan's biodata pointed toward elevated levels of stress.

"No kidding," Keegan said to herself.

"Time to go to work," Noah said and waved them out of the hide site.

Keg went first, getting up from his prone position to a firing position, on his knees, scanning ahead with his scope. Seeing nothing, he moved slowly to the next row of the vineyard, weaving around the staked grapes.

Keegan looked over at Noah, who got to his feet with similar ease and moved to the row ahead of Keg, each footfall deliberate as a stalking lion. He looked over at Keegan and angled his head, indicating it was her turn. As she got into a low crouch, though, she caught a glimpse of bright green. No more than a fine brush stroke, it lined across Noah's helmet and then dropped just below its brim.

"Contact!" Keegan shouted, instinctively dropping back down into the ditch. But by that point, the sniper's round had gone through Noah's goggles. His body snapped back from the bullet's impact into the inside of his helmet.

"Unable to locate the shooter," yelled Keg. He had also dropped prone, the exoskeleton suit automatically extending the stalk-like sensors on his back above the grapes.

Keegan slithered up to the top of the ditch. Her primary thought was to get to Noah, to throw up a pop-up ballistic shield to protect him, even though she knew he no longer needed it.

Another volley of shots ripped through the vineyard, splintering wood and kicking up dust beside her, forcing her back down. There was no telltale sound; the compound's defenders were firing with silencers, a puzzling legal modification that made a weapon perfect for hunting people.

Keg stood up and fired off three thunderous shots. With no clear targets yet, it was mostly to try and suppress their fire.

Keegan's eyes burned as a fleeting image of Noah's son, who she'd last seen as a toddler, burst into her mind — and then of Noah and his husband dancing at their wedding. How the hell was Tomas going to raise a kid all alone?

A sudden impact drove Keegan's shoulder into the dirt, driving out all other thoughts as she yelled out in pain. She instinctively rolled, moving her position to complicate the shooter's targeting. As she did, she did a mental check: the pain was dull, like being hit with a sledgehammer, not the sharpness of a penetrating bullet. The body armor had held. But the fact that they'd hit her while in the ditch meant there was a second shooter, coming from a different angle from whoever killed Noah.

Keegan ground her teeth, hearing another agent's garbled message in her earbud. Jamming. What a shit-show. She crawled forward with scurrying movements designed to throw off the shooter. As she did, another round squarely hit her protective shoulder plate. She flashed back to her range instructors and their careful explanation of windage, and how even a barely competent marksman wouldn't make the same mistake twice.[15]

She felt her legs being yanked by the ankles, as she was dragged backward. She desperately tried to hold on to her weapon, knowing she'd need it whenever she could right herself. But as she bumped across the ground, soil filling her mouth, it slipped out of her grip.

A few seconds later, she came to a stop. Rolling onto her back, she groped for the automatic tactical knife clipped to the exoskeleton. It was a futile gesture. Even reaching for it, she knew that she wouldn't be able to snap it out in time, but she wanted to go out fighting.

As her sight cleared, though, she saw TAMS's blank face looking down at her. It was crouched over her body protectively. Over its shoulder, she saw a wooden shed a few feet away that stood in the line of sight of the shooter.

"We need the QRF and medevac. Direct them to our position," said Keegan.

"It is not possible to transmit," said TAMS. "Two small unmanned aerial systems are jamming communications." As if confirming its report, a pair of quadcopters, one tailing the other, zipped overhead.

Even in the midst of the fight, part of Keegan's brain marked a reminder later to instruct TAMS to call them "drones." It was quicker than the formal name.

The report of Keg's rifle echoed through the valley, and the squad of HRT operators began to advance out of the vineyard. Their confident movements reflected the agents' extensive combat experience, most of them former special operations soldiers. But one by one they fell, disappearing between the rows of grapes as if they were slipping beneath waves.

"Where's my weapon?" Keegan said, carefully pushing herself up.

TAMS sent a thumbs-up emoji and sprinted off. A few seconds later, it had Keegan's NGSW in one hand and its shotgun in the other.

The drones buzzed by, circling the squad.

"TAMS, shoot down those drones with the shotgun," Keegan said.[16]

"OK," TAMS responded. The bot stood and raised the shotgun,

the stock's butt braced against its left shoulder, its right arm locked straight out to grasp the under-barrel foregrip. In firing position, the shotgun made the bot look even smaller. "Two autonomous aerial targets engaged," it said, giving an unnecessary play-by-play, something else she marked to change if they got out of this intact.

Then TAMS's torso spun on its axis, twisting left, then right, as it fired two shots. An incoming round smacked against the robot's plate armor on its back, and TAMS's feet shifted slightly to rebalance itself after the impact. Another two shots, and TAMS knelt back down.

"Targets destroyed."

Keegan's vizglasses flooded with an array of rapidly moving colored icons and representative data. It took her a moment to process it all. Blue flashing dots indicated four operators wounded and in need of medical assistance, while the dark blue dots surrounded by black boxes marked where their team members' bodies lay in need of recovery. She had "situational awareness" to be sure, enough to tell her that everything had gone to shit.

What mattered, though, were the red dots.

"I mark fourteen active shooters, TAMS. Is that correct?" As she spoke, she began moving again at a low crawl, no longer as concerned about the snipers pinpointing her without the quadcopter spotters. Her target was a long barnlike building, which the pre-raid briefing indicated was a fortified server farm.

"There are eight adult males, four adult females, and two minors. All of them are equipped with automatic weapons and protective armor."

"Even the kids?"

"The minors are equipped with AR-15 rifles, ballistic helmets, and vests.[17] Their position is located adjacent to the main dining facility entrance."

"These people," said Keegan in disgust at someone who would teach kids not just to hate, but to kill for it. In the middle of a shootout, you were supposed to be totally focused in the moment, all extraneous thoughts purged. But that was never the case, she knew.

She crouched against the side of the server building. Her lens marked a suspected shooter in a three-story brick McMansion just beyond the row of grapes.

She rolled out of the cover position, spying a helmeted man in a dark green camouflage smock firing an AR-15 out of the open window on the second floor. He was spraying fire down at two of the injured HRT operators, one dragging the other past the red roses capping the ends of the vineyard rows. Just because you bought the gear of a soldier didn't mean you knew how to use it. If he'd had any experience, he would have fired from inside the room, not so exposed. Keegan fired three times, the impact of the rounds spinning the man back and out of sight.

Keegan signaled for TAMS to join her and the bot sprinted toward her, drawing fire from multiple shooters. At that, Keg's weapon boomed again. He'd also gotten the targeting data to his scope, so he could now fire back with more effect.

A message flashed and Keegan ground her teeth. A trio of the local sheriff's department SUVs would be onsite in less than five minutes. But they were reinforcements for the wrong side. Based on communications TAMS received via the Iris drone, an appeal had gone out from the compound for help from local law enforcement, portraying their stand against the HRT as defending private property against rogue federal agents.[18]

Keegan designated the approaching vehicles as a threat and indicated the point at which she did not want them to cross. She marked this with a red X, which she dragged on the screen to the center of the narrow road that ran into the ASE compound, placing the target about 200 meters from the main entrance. The Valor crew confirmed the request instantaneously.

Never a subtle aircraft, the Valor thundered above as it raced over the compound. A hard bank left, then right, to evade ground fire. Then it pulled almost straight up with a strained whine. As it did, it released a beer-keg-shaped jet-black canister that broke in half midway through its climbing turn. Dozens of small spheres flew earthward.

Moments later, a series of popcorn-like bursts rattled Keegan's ears as the spheres detonated. Firing together, each one released a pink spray that immediately turned from mist to gel to something akin to a wall of bubble gum. The barrier, nearly as long as a football field, kept growing with an unsettling sound akin to Rice Krispies doused in milk. The sticky foam wasn't just unpassable, but impossible to get off your clothing. It left coils of intestine-like material that activated the more you tried to scrape it. After the Nairobi embassy evacuation, Keegan and her unit had ended up just burning their uniforms in a pink-hued crackling fire.[19]

A quick check of her vizglasses showed the bulk of the HRT operators had regrouped in the shelter of the ASE's barn. The distinctive sharp-sounding detonation of a hand grenade, then another, shook the server farm as the ASE members began to concentrate their attack on the massed HRT.

The main ASE meeting building, a single-story long house with a churchlike steeple, remained the objective. Another grenade detonated nearby. Unless the HRT operators could take down that hall, this would become a drawn-out fight that could last hours.

Another volley of gunfire lashed out at them, rippling the dirt around the robot. TAMS took multiple hits in the chest and back, the protective armor plates now bullet-scarred and cracked. The antennae running along the top of its head couldn't be shielded, though, and one was split open and frayed. The robot was a bullet magnet.

"TAMS, I need you to go to the center of the main square, approximately 10 meters from the entrance to that long building, you got it?"

"OK."

"When you get there, stop and stay there."

"OK."

It deserved better. Reaching into a pouch attached to the robot's chest rig, she pulled out the 12-gauge shells and carefully reloaded the Benelli shotgun and passed it back. "You are authorized for self-defense measures," said Keegan. "Now go."

The machine dashed around the edge of the server building, and then stood still. Keegan heard the distinctive cowbell-like sound of rounds hitting the bot's ceramic armor, a cacophony indicating the attention of the defenders was focused on destroying the bot.

As her vizglasses showed the red dots converging on the open area in upstairs windows and under porches, the blue dots of the HRT operators snaked in and out of the buildings to get to more advantageous positions. There was something about the robot that set the ASE defenders off — maybe it was just the fact that it wouldn't go down.

The robot remained still as gunfire raked its armor. Occasionally, it fired its shotgun at the great hall's tower, but the non-lethal Taser rounds were of no use.

Another round hit the machine, this one a pinging of metal on metal. It was too much.

"TAMS, get out of there!" she screamed. "Take cover."

As TAMS now ran, a trace of bullets following it, Keegan used the opportunity to sprint across open ground to a low building the tactical map said was a pump house. Her body slammed into its brick wall and she caught her breath. She told herself that calling off the bot was the right call, that making it a harder target would make it a more enticing one. She thought about what Noah would say after the mission, the shit he'd give her for treating a machine that way . . . then she remembered he wouldn't say anything at all.

That was when she heard the pump house's steel door roll up.

Shit. She took a step back and snugged the NGSW to her shoulder, keeping both eyes wide open. Hands shaking, she exhaled and forced a loose grip, ready to fire at any moment.

She saw the muzzle first, a boy stepping out from the doorway. The AR-15 had a stubby flash suppressor with some kind of writing on it; the boy couldn't be more than twelve or thirteen judging by the first few hairs of a mustache. Orange-tinted motocross goggles covered his eyes. His tactical helmet was the same model as the one Keegan wore, and bobbled on his head.

Close behind him was a girl, eight or nine years old, armed with a compact pink AR-15 rifle and body armor covered in stickers of cartoon eagles. A long blonde ponytail coiled out from under the helmet and ran over her shoulder down to her waist.

The boy raised his weapon halfway then let it drop, unable to shoot. But the girl brought the rifle all the way to her shoulder and aimed at Keegan's head.

Keegan froze. She couldn't do it. Shouldn't do it.

Keegan lowered her muzzle and said "I love you" under her breath, hoping that Haley, no matter what she was doing at that moment, would feel those last words.

The girl squinted her right eye, as if taking the measure of her target one last time before pulling the trigger.

Then came two blasts, and the children fell back into the dark of the pump house. Keegan pivoted to see TAMS behind her, its shotgun still in a firing position. In shock, she turned back and entered the building, her gun raised again.

The children lay on the floor, their arms out wide, as if they'd just leapt in a carefree summertime swan dive.

Keegan dry heaved and knelt beside their small bodies, feeling for a pulse. They were still alive — non-lethal rounds in the Benelli. Not designed for the body size of kids, which made it a damn close call.

"TAMS, what is the ETA on medevac?"

"Thirty seconds," the machine replied.

Keegan knelt and brought up a map, as much to see what had changed in the situation in the compound as to focus on anything but the images of the two kids. She knew that if you thought about something like this too long you could get caught in a loop in a situation where you had to keep moving forward.

There were no more red circles on the main square. Four remained inside the long house, so Keegan moved, one step at a time, toward it. Movement in a second-floor window of a nearby house caught her attention. Using the laser designator on her NGSW, she dazzled the window to warn away whoever was there.

"TAMS, stay there and watch the square."

Overhead, the Valor made a low pass as it prepared to land in the main square, kicking up twin tornados of dust. Just as Keegan was about to enter the building, TAMS stopped her with a message to her viz.

Significant subsurface activity beneath my position. It matches acoustic profile of tunneling. Construction plans indicate a Derler mobile safe room was installed 3 years ago in the house of Gregory Heath.

Derlers had started out as a showy, but useful, luxury for the elite *vory* in Russia. With enough C-4, anyone could blast into even the most armored safe room, making them not all that safe for dodging a rival oligarch. In turn, a tunnel was just another way into your dacha that had to be guarded. The Derler was like a subterranean submarine that created a new escape route whenever you needed it.

Keegan pushed the notice to the HRT operators and tasked TAMS with tracking the sound as best it could. The robot first walked out wide to three points and then, evidently detecting acoustic traces by its triangulation, began to follow a straight line exiting the compound.

From out of a cloud of dust, a green-and-yellow-wheeled backhoe loader appeared, driven by Keg. He had ditched the heavy exosuit, and his chilled-out pre-mission demeanor had been replaced by a wild-eyed look of anger. Another HRT operator rode alongside him on the farm equipment, weapon at the ready.

"Just tell me where," Keg shouted.

"Start digging about 50 meters in front of the bot."

When FBI and state law enforcement reinforcements arrived, it was a new kind of hurry up and wait. Every twelve seconds TAMS took one step forward marking the Derler's progress through the soil, while the backhoe dug away at a perpendicular line. "This has got to be the slowest fucking getaway chase in history," said Keg.

Eventually, the Derler had no choice but to try and cross the trench that Keg had excavated in front of it. As it emerged into view, it looked like one of the indestructible old Soyuz space capsules that were the original basis of its design.[20] The primary modifications were a drill bit on its nose and four tank treads running along its sides, pushing dirt from the front to the back, leaving no tunnel behind it. Keg bashed at the capsule with the backhoe's arm, but the hull was too thick to penetrate. Finally, he wedged the teeth of the arm's digging bucket into one of the capsule's treads. The other treads whirred, trying to pull away. Keg started to drag the backhoe in opposition, almost tipping it over, until the added weight of the construction vehicle's grip overheated the Derler's engine, and smoke poured out of it.

After a few seconds, the hatch on the side opened and an older man with a shaved head and muttonchops started to climb out. TAMS pushed a notice that facial recognition matched Gregory Heath. Sweat stained his black T-shirt around the neck and under the arms. His eyes were ringed by dark circles, their color a bruiselike purple that sharply contrasted with the pale white of his skin, but they matched the color of the interlaced tattoos wreathing his neck.

Keegan shouted down to him. "Get your hands up or we're covering this hole back up."

He glared and slowly held up his hands as he climbed out of the hole.

FBI agents carefully zip-tied his hands behind his back and quietly read him his rights. He muttered to himself and ground his teeth as they led him to the Valor. Then, Heath saw TAMS. A thin layer of dust covered the machine, which made the robot look sculpted out of sandstone.

"The devil's tool!" Heath screamed, and then spit at it. The saliva hit TAMS in the faceplate, leaving a white trail in the dust as it dripped down.[21]

Keg pushed Heath down to his knees, and then tipped the cuffed man over on his side. "Shut the fuck up."

Heath seemed to welcome it, screaming at the agents. "SLAVES, all of you!" His face was almost joyful in its rage, the certainty of somebody whose anger would now be known by even more. He knew that if he played his cards right, his movement could be the martyrs of this day, not the dead FBI agents.

Keegan ignored him, knowing that if she got any closer, it wouldn't end well. Instead, she walked over to TAMS and used the back of her sleeve to wipe most of Heath's spit off. Then she ran her hand along the bot's chipped and scratched add-on chest armor, checking to make sure none of the shots had penetrated. She unbuckled it, and the battered chest plate fell amidst shell casings glinting in the dawn light. Then, on unsteady legs, Keegan walked away, leaving the bot to figure out on its own what to do next.

As she hiked the hill back to the vineyard, she first passed the body of the scout bot. Its four legs were tucked under its body, still in its sentry-mode pose, just now with a tangle of wires sticking out from its neck from where a sniper's round had taken off its head. Almost exactly 50 meters past the bot lay Noah's body. Someone had already placed a rumpled silver thermal blanket over the HRT operator from the waist up, a hasty attempt to conceal the identity of the dead agent. There were certain to be news camcopters around soon.

Keegan sighed and tasted bile. She tossed her vizglasses to the ground and knelt down in the soil. For all the times they'd talked about how they wanted to go out, there were no good ways to die. Yet Noah did not deserve to die like this, killed on his country's soil at the hands of another American. It was all bullshit. Hell, his husband would have been better off if Noah had been killed abroad; Federal Line of Duty Death Benefits were capped at $10,000 for domestic ops versus $100,000 abroad. It meant your family got a tenth as much if a homegrown versus foreign terrorist killed you.[22]

Self-blame started to replace her sadness. You couldn't tell yourself there was nothing you could have done, Keegan thought, because there always something that just might have made a difference. Always. Maybe something big like never going on the mission to begin with, like letting state police handle it. Or maybe just one more minute shooting the shit while you watched the sun rise.

Keegan laid a hand on the foil blanket, resting her palm where it covered Noah's forehead. She couldn't bring herself to lift the covering and see the hole torn in her friend's face. She felt the protective rim of his helmet's brow, and then beneath it the jagged edges of the ballistic goggles where the round tore through.

"Screw this," she said, standing up and pinching her nose to fight back the tears. She turned away from the body and was surprised to find TAMS standing no more than 10 paces away. "Get out of here," she yelled at it.

Knowing the futility of taking it out on the machine, she quietly said to it, "Go to the Valor. I'll meet you there in a minute."

"OK," it said, and began to walk toward the tilt-rotor.

What did a learning machine comprehend about a moment like this? It could see what she was doing, even read the evident physical tells of her sadness and anger. But could it read all that it took her not to act, not to sprint to where they held Heath and shoot him in the exact same spot between the eyes?

And how would it remember this day? Would a lifetime of nightmares for Keegan be mere data to the machine?

She bent down to tuck the silver blanket around Noah, so it wouldn't blow away, folding it under his limp shoulders, careful to avoid the bloody soil under the head. It was a crime scene, after all, but what was most important in that moment was doing something for her wingman.

"Agent Keegan!" somebody shouted from the compound below.

She stood up and turned to see one of the HRT operators running toward her. "We need to get moving, now. Headquarters is calling in the Valor for a rescue op."

"What for?" Keegan asked, angry that anything else could be considered more important.

"There's been another disaster," the agent said. "This time a chemical spill . . . a couple trains crashed in Baltimore."

There was too much happening at once, Keegan thought.

She spun a tab on her Watchlet to her personal account, sending a message to Jared that he should fill up the bathtub again.

FBI DOMESTIC SPECIAL
DETENTION FACILITY

Reston, Virginia

"We should have tossed him out of the Valor," said Keg.

Keg stood next to Keegan as they watched Heath rave and shout in a squirming tantrum inside the interrogation room. To bring him in, the HRT force had split up. Keegan, Keg, and one other agent flew directly to Quantico and then raced in a two-vehicle convoy up to the Dizz-Diff. The impossibly large sweep of the crisis playing out in Baltimore was evident even on the drive up, 75 miles away from the disaster. The southbound side of I-95 was jammed even more than normal, while the traffic toward the city was lighter than it should have been. Overhead, a steady stream of helicopters and drones flew north, ranging from emergency response systems moving toward the disaster zone to delivery bots filling a rush of gas mask orders in the DC suburbs. The winds had fortunately taken the gas cloud out to sea, but everyone was still on edge. The uncertainty was taking hold, no one knowing what was going to break down next, so prepping for anything. It was evident when they rolled through a National Guard roadblock of four armored fighting vehicles, including a pair of desert-tan Strykers mounting IM-SHORAD ground-to-air missiles.

"Just send him to do cleanup in Baltimore," said another HRT member about Heath. "No MOPP suit, though; just breathe in the air."[23]

"We need him alive," Keegan said louder than she meant to, both to chill the discussion they shouldn't be having and because she had to hear herself say it to believe it. On the flight back, Keegan too had thought through how easy it would be for Heath to end up with a broken neck or a bullet in his heart from a failed escape attempt. With so much chaos going on, they might even get away with it.

She switched the screen from a view of Heath to updates on Baltimore. It confirmed the reports that two automated trains had collided at Baltimore's Morrell Park terminal. Laden with chemicals, their loads had combined to lace the air with chlorine and phosgene gas, the cocktail used in the very first chemical warfare attacks in World War I, and brought back in more recent wars.[24] Aerial newsfeeds kept hopping between perspective shots of different drones, alternating views whenever their camcopters got chased off or the yellow-green smoke got too thick.

Then a hand, hesitant on her shoulder. Keegan smelled coffee and turned around.

"I'm sorry about Agent Reddy. I know you guys go way back," said Noritz. He then held out a mug of coffee and a chocolate donut. "I know you don't feel like eating, but you have to take care of yourself."

It was a small gesture, one she appreciated. "Sir," Keegan said. "I . . ." She trailed off. The wall screen switched to hundreds of people being triaged and treated at Johns Hopkins Hospital. The footage was shaky, shot by human not machine. The injured rubbed at chemical burns and scratched at red eyes, coughing up blood and phlegm. The news report added that this was just the start. The phosgene's effects were more potent, but slower-acting on victims' insides, causing death for many a full day from now.

"Like images from a war zone," Noritz said. "Hell, maybe it is and we don't even know it. Those neo-Nazi shits have worked for Russia in the past."[25] Noritz paused as a new image appeared on the screen. He squinted in disbelief at a swooping drone feed flying over a crowd numbering in tens of thousands walking along a highway. The mass of bodies filled the median and emergency turnoff lanes, as automated vehicles ignored them, zooming by at normal speeds in the car lanes.

"Shit, that's the BW Parkway.[26] All those people from Baltimore are headed here," Keegan said.

Then the screen cut to a politician in the halls of the McCain Senate Office Building. It was Senator Jacobs. Though the sound was off, the text crawl revealed the politician's demand to do something about what he called these "unnatural disasters." He planned to rally Americans to "take the future into their own hands."

"I don't even know what that means," said Noritz. "Take the future into their own hands."

"Pretty simple, isn't it? Get people pissed off, smash some bots or whatever." Keegan flashed back to Control Room, disconnected bot limbs on dirty sheets.

"You doing OK?" he asked, noticing her vacant look.

"No," said Keegan. "But we're past that."

"We sure are," he said. "We're pushing everybody out to protect critical infrastructure so you're taking the lead on Heath."

"So it's mine now?"

"I'd send you home if it were up to me. You've been through enough for now," said Noritz. Noritz looked at Keegan with an arched eyebrow, pulled out his ChapStick, and popped the cap on and off. "You need to be aware that this is getting political."

"Always was, right?" said Keegan.

"Just get in the room with Heath. Of course, whether a failed attack on one train station before all this shit even matters is debatable."

"Well, it matters to me," she said. "Heath's lucky he's survived this long."

"Well, do this right and maybe one day we change that too."

Keegan didn't reply, uncertain if Noritz meant the death penalty or the same end that had found Reppley. The Bureau too had favors it could collect on inside prisons.

A few minutes later, Keegan and TAMS entered the room, the robot walking in first. TAMS moved directly across from the bare metal table that Heath was cuffed to, affecting a seating position without having to rely on a chair. Keegan pulled over a chair from the wall for herself and sat down between the prisoner and the machine.

The robot nodded at Keegan, and she uncuffed Heath.

"Mr. Heath, it is a pleasure to see you again," the robot said.

Keegan noted it spoke in a faint twang with drawn-out vowels now. The algorithm had either decided to build empathy with Heath or picked up how everyone who often served in a position of command in law enforcement or the military affected a southern accent, even if they weren't from the South.

Heath nodded but looked at Keegan, a squinting, puzzled expression on his face. The strange situation had already created a crack in the zealot's angry certainty.

"Don't look at me. This is out of my hands," said Keegan. "You're too important for a human to run this."

Heath flushed, then stared back resolutely at TAMS. "Where's my lawyer?" he said. "I'm not saying shit more."

"Mr. Heath, the revision last year to the Homeland Security Act provides for federal law enforcement to proceed with interrogation without counsel present during a national emergency," said TAMS. "When your counsel arrives, they will be allowed to see you."

"If they can get through," said Keegan. "You probably haven't been keeping up on the news out in your racist theme park, but DC's gone haywire. Tell him if I am lying, TAMS."

"Agent Keegan is correct," said TAMS. "There is decreased likelihood of counsel arriving. However, I am able to provide that legal counsel protocols would advise cooperation, noting that it is more likely to yield a reduced sentence by a statistically significant margin. However, it is your right to receive that analysis from a human counsel directly."

"This bot is saying another bot would tell your lawyer the same thing it's telling you," Keegan said.

Heath looked over at Keegan with a glare and turned back to TAMS. "Whatever." He coughed deeply from his throat, swished back and forth in his mouth, and spat at the robot, this time hitting it just below the chin.

"Mr. Heath, this is now the second time that you have provided me a saliva-derived DNA sample," said TAMS as the spittle dripped off its chin onto the metal table. "It is your intent to signal disdain; however, its unrequested sharing also provides DNA information that *Terrence v. State of Nevada* ruled usable by law enforcement."

"Fuck you," said Heath, first to the robot and then he turned to Keegan. "And fuck you too."

Keegan smiled and nodded her head slightly in acknowledgment. But she also mimicked wiping her own chin, just with her hand balled into a fist. Spit on the human, the gesture said, and it ends differently.

TAMS continued. "Your DNA information provides much useful data, but most notable to your profile is its integration with commercial system genealogy testing. Based on the WhoNet database, it appears that your ethnic heritage is 54 percent Caucasian, 32 percent African American, and 14 percent Sephardic Jewish."[27]

Heath's eyes widened and he licked his lips. Keegan wondered if he actually knew this all along.

"Pretty interesting background for your brand as a 'real' American," Keegan said.

"This information is notable," TAMS said in that slight southern tone that now came across as menacing, "not just for use in medical analysis. Predication analytics indicate that its inclusion in your open-source biographic profile would cause a notable shift in web traffic."

Keegan produced a tablet, which now showed a social media metrics model of what would happen if this information were pushed out. Not only did the data visualization reveal a plunge in Heath's followers and influence, but it also projected a viral outbreak of threats of violent physical action.

"Those are the numbers of a dead Nazi, not just online, but anywhere he goes," Keegan whispered.

"Analysis indicates that it is useful to allow humans time to process information of significance," TAMS said, following the script that Keegan had given it before the interrogation. "I will return in five minutes. Agent Keegan will stay to monitor you." TAMS stood and walked out of the interrogation room.

"You know how this ends, don't you? You're not just responsible for the deaths of FBI agents, but you won't even get to be a martyr. The release of this data will end that." Keegan paused. "You're dead either way. Unless . . ."

Heath leaned back against the chair's hard back with a look of feigned nonchalance, as if he were stretching after a long day at the office and wondering where he should go for happy hour. "Wyoming," he said.

What is he talking about? Keegan thought. "Wyoming, what?"

"If I do witness protection, I want to go to Wyoming."[28]

That was a fast trade; Heath had apparently been working this out ever since he was captured. *No, this came from well before then,* thought Keegan. A guy with a tunneling safe room always had a plan to get out.

"Talk," Keegan growled, thinking about Heath's likely ask. Maybe 20 or 30 acres, off the grid, but with wind and solar to avoid working too much. Not one of those tiny houses; he seemed more like a double-wide trailer kind of guy.

As she thought about it, she could almost taste the sweet air of the Tetons, savoring the beauty on the hike she'd make in before she found a hide site, the deep breath in as she framed Heath's head in the reticle of a long-range rifle scope. The only question was what beer would Keg bring along for the campfire that night?

No, not beer. Whatever wine they had been growing. Noah would have laughed that dumb laugh of his at that.

"There's some things you need to understand," Heath said. "This is much bigger than me or the NFF. You assume in your complacency that groups of different views can't come together, but we can, as long as the foe is shared."[29]

"And who's that?"

"It's not a 'who' but a what. Everything. Our cause brings together all who know that the world must change, that the status quo must not stand."

"Whatever. I'm sticking with 'who.' Who is coming together?" Keegan asked.

"It is a movement that exists virtually, because it's the only way we were willing to meet with groups we share so much with, but also so little. It's both idea and network — a web. We only used virtual cutouts and —"

"*Who?* Names. I'm not joining your little hate club, so just spit it out."

"You will want to target the leaders of inferior stock, first. Their mistake is one made often, thinking that I am just another redneck whose irrational anger comes from losing his place in this world. Wrong. Wrong! Born of the hearts of Aryan heroes, with the conviction for a strong nation led by the strongest, I know my place, my destiny, and that is the source of my rage."

"You're better than them. I get it," said Keegan placidly. "You just want me to roll up your partners in crime in exchange for a get-out-of-jail card. Who were they?"

Heath smiled as if he were a kid caught cheating and he could now tell on his classmates. "The Brave and Strong, Nation's Promise, the Freegan Collective, and . . ."

As Heath rattled off the names of various extremist groups, from neo-Marxists to environmental terrorists, Keegan considered the significance of them coming together. They were ideological rivals, constantly battling not just online but in the streets. Then again, Stalin had once teamed with Hitler, and then with the free world against Hitler. Of course, it could all be bullshit, Heath trying to frame his own enemies.

"These are the same assholes already on my watch lists," Keegan said. "You want Wyoming? Ratting out a bunch of known names is not going to even get you a lifetime in solitary."

"But they were working with us. If we go down, they should too!"

"Then maybe you shouldn't have been so dumb as to get caught," Keegan said. "Look, you just said it's all virtual. Bet you've never shaken their hands, shared a beer, tattooed each other's asses, or whatever it is you all do when a bunch of domestic terrorists are alone together. You got their names, locations?"

Heath shook his head but smiled.

"Not good enough then," Keegan said. "Better give me something before the robot comes back."

"Lincoln."

"Nebraska? You bargaining down from Wyoming to Nebraska?" Keegan asked incredulously.

"No, we all used avatars to cloud our identity, famous people from history. But that's how I can give you the one name worth it. Moses revealed just enough to figure out who Lincoln really was."

"Huh?"

"I want to go to Wyoming, far from anybody. That's what I'm going to need if I tell you."

"It's gotta be worth it. No deal till you show your cards. Let me be crystal clear with you: this is your only lifeline. Who is this 'Lincoln'?"

Heath looked down, as if measuring whether it was worth it.

"He's closer than you think. He's here. In Washington."

Keegan got chills.

"In the FBI?"

Heath slowly shook his head and then he smiled. "Jacobs."

"I need the full name. There're a lot of people named 'Jacobs' in the world."

Heath's smile grew wider. "Only one is a United States senator."

12

FBI DOMESTIC SPECIAL DETENTION FACILITY

Reston, Virginia

Keegan stood alone in the hallway outside the interrogation room trying to work out whether Heath was telling the truth. The HRT operators had cleared out, smartly realizing that Heath's revelation could turn any agent near it into political collateral damage.

Keegan had even sent TAMS off to go charge. The reason was twofold: if there was anything to the allegation, this was going to get complicated very quickly. She needed to know where things stood before she set TAMS loose, crawling the cloud's corners for information on a US senator's potential link to a crime, let alone one involving an unprecedented network of terrorist groups. The second was the ABC rule: Always Be Charging. As chaotic and consequential as everything had been until now, it was going to get a lot worse.

She guessed it would take a minute, but Noritz showed up in the hallway within thirty seconds. He must have run all the way from his office.

"Bosch wants to meet . . ." said Noritz, motioning to follow him. "Now."

Noritz stared at the ground the whole way. They headed to Noritz's office, not toward the executive conference room and its automated meeting transcription recording devices. Noritz tried to hurry her there, moving at a pace almost like a speed walk, but Keegan deliberately held back, both to stretch out time to figure out how to handle this — nothing good ever came from a meeting like this — and because the exosuit had indeed tweaked her back, just like Noah had warned.

Noticing himself out in front alone, Noritz slowed to match her pace. When they got to his office, Keegan saw Bosch, alone, sitting at Noritz's desk. On the desk in front of him was a thin, gray metal box, with three parallel indentations running along the side — a personal jammer, designed to overwhelm the frequencies of any devices within 16 feet of the user.[1]

So, Keegan thought, *it's going to be one of those conversations.*

"Shut the door," he growled.

Noritz stood to the side, as if to get out of the firing line.

"I've just looked through your interrogation of Mr. Heath. An interrogation that, I understand, has pointed you toward a candidate for the office of the president of the United States, Senator Jacobs."

"That's correct, sir," Keegan said.

"No, it is not," Bosch said. He chopped at the air with his hand and twirled his AR glasses with the other. "This ends here."

"Sir?" said Keegan.

"Every crime is political in this town," said Bosch. "That goes without saying. But this is on a level that goes beyond any one agent, any one investigation. These kinds of pursuits quickly metastasize into cancers that threaten the Bureau's survival."

"Cases make the Bureau," said Keegan, repeating the line she'd been taught in the Academy, knowing Bosch and Noritz knew it too.

"No, that's the saying for the masses. For the leadership, it is that certain cases *break* the Bureau," said Bosch. "I've lived it. You know what the job of deputy director for the Bureau really is? It is not about keeping the trains running on time, like in other agencies. It is about ensuring the continuity of the finest law enforcement organization that any country has ever established. We've seen it pushed close before. Why do you think we're out here in the 'burbs? Because we got tangled up with a presidential election, for some damned good reasons I might add.[2] But it didn't matter, we were the ones left holding the bag of shit." Bosch narrowed his eyes. "At least the Russians aren't involved in this. Or is there something else you're not telling me?"

"No Russians, sir," Keegan said. "But if there is something more here and we don't pull that thread, it's the kind of thing that could harm the Bureau."

Bosch ground his teeth and his cheeks turned red. "Don't you dare tell me about doing the right thing for the Bureau! That was your damn job, Agent Keegan! First, you took what should have been an easy assignment to ensure the TAMS program failed valiantly and instead you created some kind of robot superhero all over the news, and, even worse, all over my inbox with queries from the White House. How fucking dumb are you, Agent Keegan? I should have assigned it to the damn bot, as it's clearly the smarter one between the two of you."

Well, thought Keegan, that answered the question of where Bosch really stood on the TAMS program.

"And then," Bosch kept screaming. "On top of that fuck-up, you turn that one simple job into an even bigger shitstorm. The last deputy director who touched something political like this didn't just get fired, but lost their pension literally the day before their retirement.[3] And that is not happening here, I can guaran-damn-tee you that."

Being screamed at was nothing new to Keegan, but this felt different. The Marines who had yelled at Keegan had power that only went as far as their squad or platoon, maybe a company. Bosch was one of the most powerful men in the country. Or maybe not, based on the way he was reacting to all this.

"Yes, sir," said Keegan. There was nothing else to say. What was going to happen was going to happen regardless of all the histrionics.

"Neither of you are to approach Jacobs. Don't let me hear about you even Googling him. In case either of you aren't getting the message this time, Keegan's off the case. So is the bot."

Bosch shifted his attention exclusively to Noritz, ignoring Keegan completely, as if he was done with her. "You screw this up, Noritz, and you'll be lucky to end up working security for some automated distro warehouse in West Virginia."[4]

Noritz looked down at his shoes and nodded. When he looked up, Bosch had already barged out the door with a slam behind him. "Don't fuck me on this, Keegan," said Noritz, pointing her out the same door.

Keegan headed to the bathroom. She needed somewhere alone to process this. She turned on the sink, cupping her hands beneath the faucet. For about thirty seconds, she just stared at the water dripping through her fingers, falling through the cracks no matter what she did.

Then, she did what they taught her when faced with a problem: work it from another angle. She overlapped her fingers at a slant, making a design the water couldn't escape. After the faucet filled the cup of her hands, she splashed it onto her face, as much to recharge as to remind herself that the last twenty-four hours had not been a dream.

The face that looked back at her in the mirror was different from the one in her home. It was tired, haunted, and frankly just pissed off.

As she dried her face with a hand towel, a message popped on her Watchlet. Willow Shaw. She should have expected it.

> *I wanted to check on how you and our friend TAMS are doing.*

About to take some downtime, she responded.

> *So I've heard.*

Another little hint that his eyes were everywhere.

> *I've spoken with the president about the investigation and the need for you and TAMS to continue with this important work, now more than ever.*

Did Shaw tell the president, or did the president tell Shaw? Keegan wondered.

My boss told me otherwise, she replied.

> *If you can get the information you're looking for, you'll have support at the highest levels possible.*

More ambiguity. What was going on here? Couldn't Shaw just get Bosch off her back with a single message? Probably, but that clearly wasn't how it was going to work.

OK.

It was a passive aggressive answer, her own attempt at ambiguity, given she hadn't yet worked out her next move.

Then, a final note from Shaw:

> *All understand the importance of what we've asked and the challenges you face. TAMS is an asset to our nation playing a valuable role in this time of peril. So are you, Agent Keegan. Do what you know is right and the system will take care of you.*

"System" as in the machine? Or "system" as in the real powers that be?

She headed back to her cubicle, thinking about how she needed someone to talk this through with, someone like Noah whom she could trust with her life . . . And that decided it before she even made it down the hall.

Keegan didn't even bother to sit and instead just unhooked TAMS from its charging dock. The first thing she said to the robot was "Find me the location of Senator Harold Jacobs."

THE NATIONAL MALL
AND MEMORIAL PARKS
Washington, DC

Keegan stood on the roof of the FBI's mobile command post, a converted tractor-trailer truck parked maybe 150 yards to the west of the base of the Lincoln Memorial. With one foot propped on a knee-high, mushroom-like antenna, she leaned into the breeze and surveyed the scene. She could have viewed it through video feeds, but she wanted to get the lay of the land.

It was about as perfect a day as could be planned for a revolution. The weather had swung again, down from the low nineties to a pleasant and, most important to the cleanup, low-humidity 71 degrees. Under overcast skies, the slight breeze cut through the trees that surrounded the National Mall's perimeter, feeling like soft, light touches to her skin.

A voice buzzed in her earbud. "Hey, you can't be up there!" One of the FBI support techs inside must have heard the footsteps on the roof.

She ignored him and closed her eyes, going over what she had just seen. She wanted to imprint it all in her mind, something her old gunny sergeant had taught: a visualization insurance plan, in case the GPS went down mid-patrol.

Just above the tree line, a flock of media drones danced up and down, their control algorithms positioning them for the best crowd shots, but also trying to block their robotic competitors' line of sight. Flying above them was another layer of law enforcement surveillance drones from each of the agencies that had to play together for events like these. US Park Police had jurisdiction over the National Mall, but they were backed up by DC Metro, which owned the roads that ran through it, while Secret Service had the White House side, and US Capitol Police had the other end of the Mall. Hell, there was probably a drone from the Bureau of Engraving and Printing police somewhere up in there too, thought Keegan.[5] A third layer, yet higher, was made up of air taxis, evidently diverting from their normal commutes so that passengers could post selfies of themselves above this historic gathering.

Below the aerial scrum, a pair of movie screens framed the Lincoln Memorial. But there was no sign or banner draped overhead — in the augmented-reality feeds, each person would just project their own political slogan onto the screens and the building's blank white marble. Everyone could then sell or see whatever message they wanted, contradictory beliefs occupying the same hallowed ground.

A wooden speaker's podium stood in the center of the stage, an old-model silver microphone set on it — an unmistakable link back to the past great leaders who had stood there. Whoever was advising Senator Jacobs knew their business.

Before the memorial was an overwhelming crowd of people. For all the time she had lived in DC, Keegan had never seen a protest march this big in person. Yet this was different from the photos of the anti-war, civil rights, and women's rights marches she had only seen pictures of. Or rather, it was the crowd that was different, because they all looked different.

Usually protesters shared a common look or background. Mostly teens. Or mostly women. Or mostly pissed-off farmers. But here was a skinhead geared up in leather standing next to a thin, pale man in his fifties wearing a cheap gray suit, a Treasury Department lanyard around his neck. An elderly white woman in a shawl, carrying a sign that read "Income is a Human Right," wedged herself next to a teen with beaded LED dreadlocks that blinked an image of the American flag. The two had locked arms and punched their fists into the air at the drones overhead, as if the power of their shared anger alone could rip them from the sky.

Keegan snorted at the thought — not just the fantasy that you could will an algorithm to fail, but also because she'd seen an angry crowd in Riyadh do the very same thing right before they charged her checkpoint. She wanted to shout back down to this crowd: *You still have it pretty damn good compared to the rest of the world.*

It didn't matter; Jacobs offered something that had been missing for more than an entire generation: unity. The demonstrators were discovering what it was like to join together again with fellow Americans. Distinct in their own prior allegiances and affinities, together they were discovering how being angry could become its own identity. Angry at the changes they'd seen play out on the news and up close, from the color of the water that ran past their city to the historic flood that had taken a chunk out of it. Angry at what had happened to the banks, the food, and even the air itself. Angry at whatever catastrophe was next. But most of all, angry at all the algorithms and bots marching a few Americans into the future while leaving the rest of them behind. They no longer understood how the machines worked, but they understood they were changing everything. It was one massive crowd of a people who just wanted to get things back to the way they used to be.

"Agent Keegan, we really do need you to get down. Everything's calibrated up there. You could knock us offline," said the tech voice in her ear.

She opened her eyes and saw the crowd had grown even larger in the minute she'd been going over the scene in her mind.

"TAMS, estimate crowd size," Keegan asked.[6] She'd left the robot below, both to keep a lower profile and to avoid freaking out the techs in the command post with any more weight up top.

"Surveillance footage identifies 368,242 individuals presently standing on the National Mall grounds," TAMS responded. "Washington Metro reports 96,786 additional riders on incoming trains. DC bus system reports 57,345 on transit buses. Share ridership services report 12,398 customers designating the Mall as their destination —"

"Got it. End request," Keegan said. "We need to get up there before he starts up. I'm coming down." When she climbed down, TAMS was already waiting for her.

When she made the small jump off the last rung, she created small splashes, squishing into the grass. Despite the last three days of sun, the soil was still waterlogged from the flood. Everything behind them, from Independence Avenue all the way down to the river, looked like it could have been one big rice paddy. Right now, the Roosevelt, Terrorism War Veterans, and Martin Luther King Jr. Memorials were all still submerged under a foot of water.[7]

"Follow," Keegan instructed the machine. It instantly projected a suggested route to the stage onto her vizglasses. She ignored it; she'd already planned her route from her perch atop the FBI trailer. TAMS's mapping software wasn't factoring in the trouble that it would likely cause if a robot marched its way through the biggest anti-technology crowd in history. Keegan's path would take a little bit longer, but they would skirt through the back edge of the crowd, thousands of people spilling over off the south side of the rectangle of the Reflecting Pool in front of the Lincoln Memorial.

As they started out, a forty-ish man in khakis and an expensive neon-green running jacket was the first to turn around and notice them. Probably some out-of-work lawyer or lobbyist, judging by the expensive black loafers that he was wearing despite the muck. He eyed Keegan, wearing her blue windbreaker with "FBI" stenciled in bright yellow, and the small robot, wearing a vest marked the same. The man gave the robot the middle finger. Another protester standing beside him, a woman in her twenties wearing a tie-dye skirt, held a neatly inked cardboard sign reading "Humanity First."[8] She laughed and slapped the man's back in congratulations at his success in insulting a robot oblivious to insults.

The crowd thickened as they moved closer to the memorial. "Pull in tight behind me, half distance of normal-follow mode," Keegan instructed TAMS. The corner of her glasses showed a green thumbs-up emoji signaling the bot's compliance. The machine would be nipping at her heels, but it would make it harder for people to see what was coming through.

As they passed through the back of the crowd, most ignored them. Everyone was transfixed by the setup on stage; plus the 5-foot-tall robot was almost too short to see before it had already passed by, its human form blending in. When people did notice Keegan and the machine, though, there were none of the amused smiles they'd received during their first training runs. Mostly, there were frowns and curses. A few protesters recorded videos, seeking to go viral with a post about a machine shouldering its way into their day of outrage. One big guy, wearing tan construction worker's overalls, spat at the robot. He missed and hit the back of another protester, their eyes still on the stage, oblivious to the drama behind. Keegan kept moving. Arresting some pissed-off, out-of-work day laborer for "contempt of cop" was not why they were here.[9]

The robot kept pace with her, but Keegan noticed its feed of messages into her vizglasses was a microsecond slow. Overload. Every sensor in the area, from drones and the DC police surveillance towers to the heartbeat reports in elderly protesters' pacemakers, created a massive fire hose of data that bogged it down.

Keegan felt a tug on her right sleeve. Her arm tensed, ready for a strike, maybe someone not content to spit, but as she turned, she saw a pair of rheumy eyes looking up from beneath a hoodie. A young girl, maybe in her late teens. It was hard to tell. Her checks still had the outlines of the hip harlequin color blocks designed to fool face ID software in surveillance cameras; now the makeup was streaked, looking like a clown who had spent the last night in tears.

"Hey, can you spare anything?" the girl said. "I'm from Baltimore."

Keegan nodded and gave her a $50 bill from her wallet before moving on without a word. Hopefully, she'd be able to use the tracked bill to get something at one of the street vendors. A few were not yet linked into the tracking system that would take the money out of circulation.

The two approached the stage's security perimeter, a 4-foot-high temporary metal fence circling the Lincoln Memorial's base. A line of DC Metro Police officers stood behind it, looking unmovable in their well-worn riot armor. The police officers warily tracked TAMS's arrival, trying to read the crowd's response to the machine, worried it would spark the very violence they were here to stop. Once they were through the security checkpoint, Keegan noticed TAMS had already reverted to a normal follow distance, having analyzed and projected that Keegan's close-in order was just for the crowd environment. Always a learning machine.

In the crowd, a call-and-response chant began. "Who is the future for?" a blue-jeans-wearing hype-man yelled over the loudspeakers. "We're who the future's for!" screamed back the crowd, as instructed by the text on the screens and their vizglasses feeds, which would then project an image of someone in the crowd.

Keegan indicated TAMS should hang back as they approached the waiting area for the speakers concealed at the back of the memorial. "There's Senator Jacobs," said Keegan. "Wait here."

TAMS pulsed another green emoji at Keegan and moved to stand by one of the pillars, the bulk of the massive 7-and-a-half-foot-thick fluted white marble columns making the tiny robot look even smaller by comparison.

Keegan was in no mood to draw this out; she needed to get to Jacobs before he was swept up in his own moment.

As she walked up to the circle of staffers surrounding the senator, Keegan recited in her head the opening line she was going to deliver.

Jacobs beat her to it.

"Get that monstrosity out of here!" screamed Jacobs, pointing over the shoulder of one of his staffers at TAMS, standing back by the pillar. "Are you trying to start a riot?"

Jacobs strode out to meet her, face reddening with each step. TAMS sent a query to her vizglasses as to whether she wanted assistance, which Keegan blinked away. She studied the sneering man's face, taking in the broken blood vessels in his nose, the gray hairs in his eyebrows, the sculpted canopy of thinning hair, and the anger lines around his mouth, imperfections that were automatically glossed over as part of the unspoken algorithmic compact between the media and powerful people. He was a couple inches taller than Keegan, and it seemed like he was willing himself even taller, to tower over her and intimidate.

"Senator, if anybody starts a riot today, it's going to be from that stage."

"That's an insult — as is bringing that robot here. How dare you, after everything that's happened. Agent, you're supposed to be stopping terrorists, not inciting violence. Give me your name!"

"Special Agent Lara Keegan, Washington Field Office."

A pause to enjoy watching Jacobs's eyes bulge — he'd heard the name before. But in what context?

"K — E — E — G — A — N." She stepped forward and hissed in his ear. "But before you file a formal report, I have another name to share: Gregory Heath."

Senator Jacobs snapped, "I don't know who you're talking about."

Senator Jacobs is lying, read the message from TAMS, monitoring Jacobs's facial micro-expressions from 10 meters away.

Of course he is, Keegan thought. *He's a politician.*

Jacobs looked rattled for a second, but then a woman stepped between them. She was in her forties, wearing thick black glasses that contrasted with skin so pale it looked as if it had never been touched by the sun. As she wrinkled her snub nose and glared at Keegan, she tapped her vizglasses to ensure they were on, likely rapidly ascertaining who this impertinent person really was. "Senator, you have to make your way to the staging area. You'll be on soon."

All it took was an audience of one, and the senator composed himself.

"I have an important announcement today and this nonsense has to wait," he said firmly. "Alicia here is my chief of staff. You can make an appointment with her. Alicia, get the agent on my calendar for next week."

The gambit had failed. Keegan knew there'd be no "next week." The meeting would be bumped just long enough for the senator to bring holy hell down on the FBI's leadership and budget. In the weeks that it would take for Bosch to officially dismiss her from the FBI she would likely be assigned a job in the flooded Hoover Building basement, checking driver's license numbers by hand.

The woman started to ask for Keegan's contact information, but Keegan interrupted. "No, that's not going to work. This is urgent. I'll wait right here to speak with the senator after he gets offstage."

TAMS sent an urgent update — not just a message icon, but a flash of bright red that washed across her whole view.

"I'm sorry, the senator is not going to be able —"

Keegan held up a hand for her to be silent, reading quickly.

Jared and Haley Keegan are in the operational zone, approximately 73 meters from your position, TAMS messaged.

"What? In the crowd?" Keegan said out loud. "Here?"

She turned to look at the crowd, even larger, pressed in even tighter in the minutes since she'd surveyed it earlier. A faint green arrow appeared in her field of view, marking her family's location. The crowd roared, a surge of sound that caught her off guard.

She turned to see that Jacobs had stepped onstage, slightly stooping, as if unsure if all this was for him. But with every step closer to the wooden podium, Jacobs stood taller, broader, the crowd's fury a source of energy. With his chin now cocked, the senator said into the microphone, "Now. Is. *Our*. Time!"

The crowd only got louder with each line of Jacobs's speech. The mass of people began to press toward the metal barriers, the line of police in riot gear rippling slightly, the cops taking small steps back, steadying themselves in case the fencing broke under the weight of tens of thousands of people.

Keegan could sense this was going to turn bad — and soon. She tried to open her personal comms app on her Watchlet to message Jared, but it froze because the network was overloaded by the scale of the crowd.

She leapt off the back of the memorial. Between the crowd and the police line, there was no way she could make her way directly to where the green arrow was pulsing. So she worked her way back through the edge of the crowd, reversing how she and TAMS had made their way up. Her stomach knotted tighter with each step, not knowing what she was going to say to Jared or if he would even listen to her. They hadn't spoken since their last fight.

Ducking under the signs waved by two protestors, Keegan pulled up quickly to reorient herself, somebody bumping into her from behind, hard. "Back off," she hissed and turned around, only to see TAMS. She'd forgotten to tell the machine to stay behind. It stared back at Keegan, pulsing a thumbs-up emoji of its readiness to her viewscreen.

"That's all you have to say?" Keegan said. "Stay close, but don't step on my heels again."

Another green thumbs-up. It also registered a health monitor alert that Keegan was exhibiting signs of stress and anger. *No kidding.*

As she looked out at the crowd, she saw the Korean War Memorial, slightly to the right. The statues of the poncho-clad stone soldiers, stretched out in a patrol, broke up the tight mass of the crowd. That was where it made the most sense to wade in.

For the moment, the crowd's focus had unshakably locked on to Jacobs. The energy in the air was real, unmistakable if not detectable by actual sensors. He was pulling them in, recounting how he had long been the lonely voice, warning against the ever-increasing spread of automation. He was the prophet to whom no one had listened. But now they would listen: "Because we will make them!"

As Keegan and TAMS reached the periphery of the Korean War Memorial, she saw how a few people had perched snake-bodied camera bots atop the statue soldiers' helmets, arrowlike heads panning from articulated rubber coiled bodies.

Another cheer from the crowd reverberated as Jacobs launched into a diatribe against the president's permitting all of this "so-called progress to happen" due to inattention and greed, even letting the government's own plans for the future be developed by the "very same inhuman monsters who are destroying the country, while profiting from it." He stopped short of naming Willow Shaw, but he didn't have to; the crowd already knew who he was talking about.

The green arrow in her vizglasses showed Jared and Haley 80 feet into the crowd from the Korean War Memorial. So close, yet Keegan could not figure out how to get to them, especially with the machine on her heels. And she couldn't very well leave TAMS alone any more than Jared could leave Haley.

Think. Think. Think, she willed herself.

Then she saw a teenager in bright orange leather motocross gear that had hard plastic guards protecting his joints. He looked like some kind of postmodern knight, or the dissident version of the riot police. Instead of a shield and lance, though, he held two signs, dark blue reflective print on a white background, one on each shoulder.

Keegan took off her jacket, turned it inside out, and went over to him after telling TAMS to stay in the shadow of one of the statues. "Hey, my sign got wet and ruined. Could I have one of those?"

The biker looked her over, blinked a few times into his viz, and then smiled. They were all in this together. "Sure. I took two because they were giving them out for free anyway. Which one? 'Work + Glory + God' or 'Damn the Machines!'?"

"Whichever one's heavier," said Keegan.

"They're exactly the same. Here, take 'Damn the Machines!'"

"Thanks," Keegan said. The sign's pole felt off. She looked down and it had a woven grip etched into it, which seemed odd. The weight of the pole was also off. It was plastic, but completely solid. The paper of the poster at the top was held in place by two plastic sleeves, each 4 inches in length. She ran her hand along the thick sleeves . . . thicker than they needed to be.

Take the paper out and you had a damn good melee weapon that, with enough force, could punch its way through skin, maybe even light body armor.[10]

TAMS sent Keegan a message driven by her newfound interest in the sign: *There are 2,445 "Damn the Machines!" signs presently in the protest. Stenciling and format indicate the signs were made at the same facility as the 2,456 "Work + Glory + God" posters, 2,467 "Humans First" posters, 2,473 . . .*

So someone had seeded the crowd with thousands of weapons that wouldn't be picked up by metal detectors. It was a lot like how the alt-righters back in school had weaponized flagpoles, always trying to act like they were patriotic, but really just gearing up for an unfair fight.[11]

"Cease update," said Keegan. "Just confirm Jared's location and join me."

Same position, messaged TAMS. *They are 18 meters away.*

Keegan started a chant to match the message on her sign — "Damn the Machines! Damn the Machines!" — lifting it up and down in front of her, working the cadence into her steps. It worked and the crowd began to part, ever so slightly, as TAMS drafted behind her.

It wasn't until she was three rows of people away from the green arrow projected onto her viz that she could finally see Jared with her own eyes. He had Haley on his shoulders, the little girl tapping on his chest with purple rain galoshes. Keegan pushed her way through and grabbed Jared's shoulder. He looked surprised and then mad.

"What you doing here?" he said, instinctively holding Haley's legs tighter to his chest at the sight of her.

"We need to get out of here. It's not safe for *either* of you," said

Keegan, emphasizing the word. "Why would you even bring her here?"

"This is history in the making," Jared said. "She'll always be able to say she was here."

Keegan tried to figure out if this was the drugs speaking, but the earnestness in his face showed it wasn't. He really did believe it.

At that moment, Haley looked down and saw her. "Mommy! I can't see the man on the stage. Can I watch through your viz?"

"Sure, honey. Let's get you and Daddy over to the side where we can have some space," Keegan replied.

"No, Lara," Jared said. "We're staying. You don't get . . ." That was when he saw TAMS standing behind her. "Did you really bring that thing here?"

Just, then an alert hit her viz: *Notice: Senator Jacobs . . .*

Before she could finish reading the message from TAMS, she knew what was happening. Her body felt the eyes of tens of thousands of people on her.

"Mommy, Mommy, that's you!" Haley screamed in delight.

Keegan looked up, and there they were: she and TAMS close-up on the two massive screens, Haley's waving hand in the corner.

The screens shifted back to Senator Jacobs onstage. "And they even dared to send one of their machines for me today. To stop me! This is what they do to those who speak the truth," Jacobs roared.

"Lara, what's going on?" Jared asked, at the same time Haley cried out, "Mommy? Is that man talking about you?"

Simultaneously, TAMS began flooding Keegan's vizglasses with updates, but all she saw was the wash of red color that now painted over them. Someone had tagged Keegan and TAMS, so anybody using augmented-reality glasses within the area would see them called out, a giant dark red arrow hovering over their heads.

The people around them began to turn, realizing that the arrow and the woman on the screen were literally right beside them.

Over the loudspeakers, Jacobs's speech slurred as he raged. "Don't let them do it! Don't let the machines win! I promise *whatever* you do, you will be remembered as the righteous ones. As you protect me, I will protect you!"[12]

So that was it. Jacobs wasn't going to leave it to the bureaucracy to silence her.

"My threat assessment is —" TAMS reported.

"We need to go, now!" said Keegan.

As the words came out of her mouth, someone snatched the "Damn the Machines!" sign out of Keegan's hand and she was shoved to the ground. As she landed on her side, the fall knocked her into Jared and the two of them tumbled. Haley fell off her father's shoulders. Keegan tried to push herself off the ground, fingers grasping at the slick grass for grip. As she pulled herself up on her hands and knees, a kick struck her on the right of her rib cage, just below the shoulder. The shock of it radiated across her whole side. She could hear Jared screaming for Haley, but the voice moved farther away as the rush of the crowd swept him up.

Another kick landed on her left. This one packing the power of a football punter, the laces of a shoe connecting in the soft of her stomach and lifting her up. The impact blasted the air out of her lungs and she fell over gasping.

Fighting for breath, she thought only of Haley. Where was she? All she saw was muddy feet and legs. Somehow, over it all, she could still hear Jacobs yelling. "By taking back what is ours, we'll show them who has the true power!"

Keegan struck out with a kick, feeling her boot's heel impact someone's knee. She didn't know if it was the person who had kicked her; she just needed to create space. From her right another kick came in, this one trying to stomp on her head. She managed to block it with her right forearm.

Still on the ground, she drew her pistol, the bio-lock thrumming in her hand as it identified its owner. Keegan's right arm lashed out with the gun, smashing the metal edge of its grip hard into a hand that was trying to grab her. She rolled over and, with her left hand, pushed herself up from the ground that had already been churned into mud from the fight. Three points of her body touched earth, while her right arm swung the pistol in an arc. The crowd pulled back as she panned the weapon in their direction.

Keegan spat blood and wet grass as she stood. Two hands on the pistol now in a close-combat shooting posture, the stance natural from years of training, but her mind forgetting everything else but her daughter.

"Haley! Haley!" she shouted, blinking away tears and mud, her mind registering that she had lost her vizglasses during the skirmish.

She continued to sweep her gun in an arc until she caught sight of an elderly woman, wearing a gray GEORGETOWN LAW sweatshirt, who had Haley wrapped in her arms. The scared look on her face and the way she stroked the girl's hair showed she was trying to protect the little girl.

Haley wailed in fear, but she was safe. Keegan wanted to run to her daughter more than anything else, but she could sense movement behind her. She spun, swinging the gun barrel back and forth at the crowd that had edged closer again.

"Back!" Keegan roared. "GET THE FUCK BACK!"

When the crowd stepped back just a few feet, she saw TAMS sprawled on the ground, two men bashing away at it with poster poles. One was in a blue denim shirt and cowboy hat with an American flag stuck in its leather band, the other wearing a bright yellow school crossing-guard's vest.[13] They hadn't even bothered to pull the poster off. The paper anti-automation signs flapped about, torn and crumpled, as the poles crashed down on the robot. As Crossing Guard hammered away, Cowboy froze, seeing Keegan and her gun. He grabbed his partner, trying to stop him.

Over the loudspeaker, Jacobs was still yelling something, but the only voice Keegan could hear was Haley: "Mommy, they hurt him!" The little girl broke free of the elderly woman and ran to the machine, the muck sucking at her purple boots. Haley reached out a hand to TAMS to try to help the machine get to its feet.

Keegan tipped the gun's muzzle slightly, to signal to the two men what would happen if they moved even the slightest bit toward her daughter. But she knew if she fired, it would be all over in this crowd. They would tear her and her family apart and nobody would stop them.

The two men with poles didn't move, but in the crowd behind them, Keegan could see an approaching line of posters bobbing up and down in tight formation. Reinforcements.

TAMS stood up, mud dripping from the sensor ridges that ran down the back of its head. The two of them looked ridiculous, the 5-foot-tall robot, its chest plate now gashed and dented, and the little girl in purple rain galoshes, holding its hand. Keegan could see the robot beginning to boot back up, a bent antenna extending to begin a data download.

TAMS reported in. "Agent Keegan, I am back online. Your viz-glasses are nonoperational."

"Haley," she said calmly, ignoring the machine. "Come back to Mommy."

"But they'll hurt TAMS," the little girl pleaded.

The crowd hung back, but Keegan could see that the two men now understood who the girl was. The man she'd mentally dubbed Crossing Guard stalked toward Haley like he thought she was easy prey.

"Move another inch and you die!" Keegan shouted.

She pointed the gun at the narrow space between the man's eyes. It wasn't the proper aim point she'd been trained for, but Keegan wanted him to literally look down the barrel. There would be no misunderstanding about where the first bullet would go if anyone touched Haley. The realization that she might have to shoot a man in front of her daughter made her simultaneously want to throw the gun away, and to shoot him even more.

The two men remained still, but behind them, two more protestors carrying makeshift weapons approached through the crowd. One wore digital camouflage fatigues and a matching chest rig, clearly a militia member playing soldier. The other was built like a body builder, but wearing a white polo shirt.[14] One of the alt-righter cliques. They pulled up when they saw Keegan's gun. But Keegan knew more were on the way.

"Butterfly," she said, deliberately ignoring them, speaking in her softer, mommy voice, "let go of TAMS's hand."

Jared's voice weighed in from behind her, the standoff allowing him to force his way back through the crowd. "Haley, come back to Daddy and Mommy, now."

The girl gripped the robot's hand tighter.

"Agent Keegan, there is an important update from the FAA," reported the machine in its normal tone. TAMS was either oblivious to the fact that it was about to be abandoned, or was aware but didn't care. "The autonomous air traffic above the National Mall is not responding to FAA airspace-management protocols. Attempted overrides have not been successful."[15]

Keegan looked up and saw the barely controlled chaos of the earlier autonomous flight patterns had formed into a single orderly swarm of dozens of drones circling in a tornado-like swirl.[16]

Then, the whine of a jet turbine pierced through the air.

An Ehang passenger-shuttle drone broke free of the swarm and swooped low over the crowd.[17] Too low — just 20 feet overhead. It was close enough that Keegan could see the passenger banging on the clear-glass canopy from inside the drone with her fists, her mouth gaping in a silent scream. A second later, the drone pulled up slightly and then slammed into the side of the Washington Monument. A fiery blast erupted, but the solid stone held fast. The drone's crumpled wreck then slid down the side of the monument, onto the crowd standing below.

Small news drones then began to peel off from the larger swarm, one by one, diving down and then exploding into the crowd. People stampeded when they realized what was happening, the standoff between the FBI agent and the protestors eclipsed by the automated death raining down.

Over the din, Keegan screamed, "TAMS! Get Haley to safety! Authorize: Riot Control Mode!"

TAM's head tilted for a microsecond as it accessed the new operating profile. At the same time, the first man in the denim shirt broke toward the machine, swinging his pole in front of him like a scythe. It wasn't clear whether Cowboy was attacking the machine and girl or just trying to clear his way through the crowd. It didn't matter.

As the pole swung toward Haley, TAMS's left arm snapped out, swatting the crude weapon aside. The machine then gently moved the girl behind it, bending at the knees to protect her with its body, while still holding her hand with its right hand. At the same moment, TAMS's left limb went from rigid to flexible at the elbow and its forearm telescoped out another 6 inches. As it did, the fingers in its hand balled into a macelike sphere studded with knuckle joints. The robot smashed its fist into the man's forearm, just above where he held the weapon he had been swinging in Haley's direction.

The man dropped the pole with a scream, his ulna and radius bones shattered. As he fell to his knees, the robot's arm began to swing in a figure-eight motion in front of it, the flexible arm moving like a nunchaku from its elbow, almost too fast to see. The big man wearing the polo shirt then tried to tackle TAMS from the right, where the robot had been shielding Haley. But before he could get close, the machine's torso pivoted on its frame. The figure-eight arc of its rapidly spinning left arm rotated with the turn, colliding with the man's collarbone in a spray of blood. It next spun toward the pretend soldier, who dropped his pole and edged back.

"TAMS, get us out of here," Keegan yelled. "Get Haley to a secure location."

"OK," the machine said calmly. Just beyond them, a drone flew into the Reflecting Pool in a watery eruption of spray and sparks.

"Please follow me," it said. Keegan pulled the elderly woman behind Haley, the robot still holding her hand behind it. She motioned Jared to stand behind the elderly woman. They formed a tight line, stacked together behind their robot shield.

"Go, Go, Go!" Keegan screamed, slapping the robot's shoulder just like she would in a room-clearing tactical formation.

But they didn't run off. TAMS advanced at a walking pace, its arm swinging before them in a figure eight, arcing to the right and then left, clearing their path with a resonant hum like an airplane propeller. Most people in the chaotic stampede of the crowd flowed around the tight mass of five bodies, like river water around a stone. Every so often, though, someone got too close, and the machine's spinning arm struck down.

Packed in tight and without her vizglasses, though, Keegan couldn't see the robot's route. But she soon got situated. After about 150 yards, they'd made their way through the dense heart of the crowd around the Reflecting Pool, to where the terrain opened up in front of the Lincoln Memorial. Rather than going toward the FBI command truck, TAMS kept going straight. Was the machine trying to find Jacobs? Had some algorithm reranked its priorities back to the investigation?

"TAMS, I said get to safety," Keegan yelled. "Not Jacobs. Priority is safety!"

"OK," TAMS replied and kept moving in the very same direction toward the metal fence at the base of the Lincoln Memorial steps.

Most of the police had fled, but a Park Police officer still crouched beneath the arched entry gate, sheltering from the crashing drones. He saw TAMS's macelike arm swinging and pointed his shotgun right at them.

"Halt!" he yelled, but the shotgun's muzzle wavered.

TAMS froze, not at the gun, but at the sight of the fellow law enforcement officer giving orders. Its arm stopped spinning and it stood still.

Keegan stepped out from behind the stack of bodies, holstering her weapon and putting her hands out, palms open, to show no threat. "FBI! Let us through!" she said, pulling out her badge.

"Get back!" said the policeman, gaining more confidence at the sight of a bureaucratic rival. "I don't care if you're FBI, lady. You can't go through, especially not with your kid."

As Keegan opened her mouth to reply, the roar of another drone's engine drowned her out. The police officer looked up to the sky for a moment, and Keegan noticed his weapon's strap wasn't wrapped around his hand. Rookie move.

Keegan snatched the shotgun barrel with her left hand, yanking it toward her. Then with her right, she reached over to grab the barrel, pulling it with both arms so that the muzzle now safely faced out under her arm. The policeman tried to wrestle it back, but with the gun now tucked under her arm, Keegan gave it a hard tug, feeling the snap as the man's trigger finger broke against the guard. Swinging the shotgun by its barrel back over her head in an exaggerated version of a baseball batter's windup, she slammed the gun's wooden stock into the policeman's helmet. The man fell to the ground unconscious.

"Let's move," said Keegan.

TAMS reanimated and stepped over the unconscious policeman, still leading Haley by the hand. As they dashed up the memorial's wide steps, Keegan turned to see if anyone pursued them. Seeing no one, she tossed the shotgun aside.

The podium, where just minutes ago Senator Jacobs had summoned the wrath of the crowd upon them, stood empty. He'd apparently fled at the first drone crash. Had that been his plan all along, to launch his campaign for president on a wave of victimhood and sympathy? Whatever it was, thought Keegan, it could wait. She needed to get Haley out of here now.

As they entered the darkness of the interior hall of the memorial, they stopped at the base of the massive statue. A few other people and cops huddled inside, peering out around the columns at the pandemonium below. The mass of the drone swarm was visually smaller, but it still ejected drones in steep arcs into the crowd.

"Agent Keegan, we are not yet secure," TAMS said. Keegan noticed that too. For all the bulk of the memorial, the fact that Lincoln's statue could gaze out on the National Mall grounds meant they were all still exposed to danger.

TAMS pointed to a set of descending stairs. A red velvet rope stand that had been blocking them lay on its side. The robot started toward the stairs, while Jared rushed to grab Haley's other hand and hurry her down to safety.

Keegan looked back through the open side of the Lincoln Memorial as another passenger drone sped past, parallel to building's face. As it flew by, the marble columns broke up the image of its flight and then it disappeared from view. But the drone doubled back, flying away from the memorial, then abruptly changed direction again. When

Keegan saw the aircraft in profile she grasped it was circling back to line up an attack run at the Lincoln Memorial itself. As the aircraft flew straight toward them directly over the Reflecting Pool, its sole passenger could be seen covering their eyes.

"Run!" Keegan screamed.

TAMS and Haley were already at the bottom of the curving stairs that led to the undercroft crypt below the Lincoln Memorial's floor.[18] The robot pushed the door open and pulled the girl through, Jared following a moment after. At the base of the steps, the elderly woman stumbled. Keegan lifted her under her armpits and dragged her through the door.

The woman's feet were not yet inside the crypt when the drone crashed into Lincoln's statue. The explosion shook the chamber below hard enough that Keegan wondered if the roof might collapse and bury them here forever. A tongue of flame then licked down and around the curve of the stairs, but the perpendicular angle of the door kept it from entering the crypt. It did force through a scalding gust of smoke and dust, knocking Keegan and the woman to the ground. Screams filled the air and then the crypt grew startlingly quiet.

Keegan lifted herself from the floor, her ears ringing as it took her a beat to find her focus again. Coughing, she pulled the older woman, whose name she still didn't know, over to where she could sit with her back against the wall and yelled for her to stay there. She nodded silently in shock, Keegan just barely able to see the features of her face as the dust in the room started to settle.

Keegan searched for Haley and Jared and found them sitting against the wall on the other side of the door, safe. Jared had their daughter hugged tight in his arms, Haley's face buried in his shoulder. Beside them was TAMS, still holding the little girl's hand.

Keegan knelt next to them, reaching out to smooth her daughter's hair. She turned to look the robot in its eyes, the visual sensors glowing yellow in the dim light. "Thank you."

It felt strange to say that to a machine. But it was something that, as a parent, she had to do.

LINCOLN MEMORIAL

Washington, DC

Keegan peered through the fine dust to see who else was in the crypt. The pressed-together bodies muffled the sounds of sobbing and coughing in the confined space. Unasked, the robot turned on its running lights, bathing the room in a blue light.

"Hey, butterfly, stay here with Daddy and TAMS," Keegan told Haley. "I need to check on the other people in here." She began to move around the room to see who needed medical attention. That's when she saw Senator Jacobs, huddled on the floor with his knees drawn in close and his face in his hands. His chief of staff sat next to him, furiously trying to clean her vizglasses with a pulled out shirttail, again and again, not noticing that the lens screen was completely cracked.

Jacobs looked up at Keegan, his face showing the kind of blankness brought on by shock. Then it began to change as there was a glimmer of recognition, and he took back on the bearing of a politician; it was something known for him to cling to, as his mind and body tried to process it all.

"I . . . nearly died up there. These machines . . . are going to kill us all. It's just like I warned. They're failing us, and now the whole country knows it."

She put her hands on the lawmaker's shoulders, and leaned in close like she was going to help him to his feet. "Fuck you," she hissed. "My daughter was out there. So was my husband. They nearly died. A lot of other people did."

Jacobs stiffened and Keegan felt him try to pull away. "Are they OK?"

"My daughter's over there . . . with the robot that saved her life. No thanks to you and your network. You own this. All of it."

Jacobs coughed and then spit. He tried to find his confidence, speaking louder now, as if to the crowd inside the crypt. "This was brought upon ourselves. We tried to make the world a better place for machines rather than God's chosen. But I had nothing to do with it. And if I had been martyred up there . . . just as Lincoln was . . . then our nation would . . ."

"Be a better place?" said Keegan. "Oh no, that doesn't work today. Not with me."

TAMS interrupted. "Agent Keegan, I have received updates from emergency management systems. FAA reports all unmanned aerial systems in the area have either been destroyed in crashes or cleared from the airspace."

Keegan used her command voice to yell to the crowd, "Everybody, I've got news from above." The sobs and whispers quieted.

"The authorities say it's all clear upstairs. You need to exit immediately. Clear the area."

Then she whispered to Jacobs, "Except you." She placed her hand back on her pistol, showing it was not a choice. "I'm going to secure the senator and ensure he's safe," she yelled to the crowd. The aide started to protest, but Keegan's face made clear she was not going to tolerate a debate.

Keegan turned to the robot. "TAMS, you remain with me. Jared and Haley, stay here too."

Slowly, the survivors shuffled out. The woman from the entrance touched the robot on its head and muttered thanks.

Jacobs watched them go and then slumped back against the wall. Haley started to play with the bot, using her hands to cover one of the blue lights and switching to the other, making a strobe effect in the room.

Keegan knelt in front of Jacobs, her hand still resting on the pistol.

"Don't waste my time with any more denials. The neo-Nazis gave you up and then the robot matched it all together," she said. "Of all people, you should have known that nothing stays hidden from the machines . . . not even what you and all the groups do playing your little game under the waterfall."

Jacobs's eyes went wide, the look of someone who unexpectedly found themselves trapped, as much by Keegan's revelation as his physical surroundings. It was a powerful feeling, Keegan knew, even more so to experience the first time, and she wanted to leverage it.

She nodded at TAMS. "It got it all. We know about the network of groups, the meetups in the virtual world . . . even your Lincoln avatar. All of it." She paused a beat to let this sink in. "The only question is, what happens next? Not whether you get elected or not, or even whether you go to jail or not. What you need to think on right now is whether Moses" — emphasizing the name to try to convince Jacobs their chat encryption had been broken — "gets you the next time."

Jacobs's eyes went even wider and his body shook with a tremor at the mention of the name. "Just turn that thing off, and then we can talk," he said in a raspy voice.

"Sure. We can do that," she said. "Haley, set TAMS on sleep mode. TAMS, turn lights off."

Haley giggled as the lights turned off and then settled down.

Jacobs looked at Keegan for a long moment, his face barely visible in the dark. "This wasn't the plan," he whispered. "You have to believe me. The idea was to *scare* people, to show how the system was breaking down, to create the needed moment for true change. But he's taken it beyond that. And, I guess, now he's going after . . . anyone."

"Do you know Moses's real name?" said Keegan. "We can't protect you without knowing that."

"Moses is the avatar of Jackson Todd."

"And who's that?" She could run it down later but wanted Jacobs to keep flowing.

"A PhD geek in electrical engineering."

"That doesn't sound like your usual crowd. How do you know him?"

"Todd was a program manager at DARPA, working on robotic applications of machine learning, neural nets, 'intelligent decision support systems,' all that next gen stuff."[19] "We first crossed paths back when I was in the House and they sent him in to change my mind by talking up the scientific value of it all," he said.

"You mean all the ways we were planning to deploy autonomous robots onto the battlefield, even while saying we were just doing research?"[20]

"Look, I don't understand the tech. Never did. But when his work came through the Appropriations Committee, I knew enough to know I didn't like what I saw. Felt it in my bones that it was just wrong. Just like with the Internet, they were trying to jump-start social change with AI, using the military budget as a backdoor to change the world.[21] I tried to zero out the funding, including for his program. You can go back and see, that's God's honest truth. They sent him in to brief me. Smart guy, but I wasn't persuaded. But there were people more important than me who wanted it to proceed. And so it did. I went to fight bigger battles and lost track of him."

"And?" Keegan asked.

"And then, years later, he reached out to me right out of the blue. Just showed up in the stairwell outside my office. I had moved up to the Senate by this point. I didn't recognize him at first; he was thinner, older, just looked like shit. Then he said everything he'd briefed me on back then had been the cause of his family's death. And so I listened."

"What did he mean was the 'cause of his family's death'?"

"You remember the Metro accident in Arlington seven years ago?"

Keegan nodded. It wasn't too far from their condo; Haley would sometimes play in the memorial fountain.

"His family died in that crash. Wife and son. It wasn't just that his whole life's work was on automation; they'd literally been on the way to meet up with him. Back then he'd been all for technological advancement, no matter the cost. Now it was all about stopping that future. And who can blame him?"

"How long ago did he come to you?" she asked.

"Maybe three years ago. He'd resigned from DARPA and was working as a contractor for the Army Corps of Engineers. He said he'd come to me because I was the only one who had tried to stop it back then. That at least we could do something now for others, to jump-start the kind of movement that you saw today, bringing together people who wouldn't otherwise connect, to work together to create a new America, a new future."

Keegan cut him off. "Yeah, I saw how that worked out today. Kumbaya, and then the riot and the drone strikes. It seems Todd decided you didn't have a role in his future, after all. What else can you can tell me about him?"

"I don't know. I guess just that he's not like the others. This goes beyond politics for him. He's a true believer."

"This some kind of religious extremism thing?"

"Yes and no. It's about what it means to be human, but also about defending our very way of life itself."

"I've heard that before," Keegan muttered.

She quickly stood, wincing at the throbbing in her leg. In the Corps, they'd told her pain is just weakness leaving the body. It still took her breath away, though.

"TAMS, lights back on," she ordered.

Jacobs's confusion was evident even in the dim blue glow. "How . . . how did it hear you?"

"Machines don't really fall sleep, everybody knows that!" Haley squealed from the corner.

So she'd been listening too. Keegan could only hope most of what she and Jacobs had said had gone over her daughter's head. As for Jared, well, it was good for him to find out firsthand what a fraud Jacobs was. Maybe it would finally drain — or at least redirect — some of his anger.

"TAMS, pull up any relationship between the recent terror attacks and religious constructs. Todd didn't just choose Moses by coincidence."

TAMS gave an immediate reply. Finding relationships between words, entities, and concepts — symbolic reasoning — was one of the earliest areas that AI had specialized in.[22] "There is a high-frequency symbolic connection between the online description of seven recent incidents in the news, Dr. Todd's choice of representational avatar, and the Old Testament section of the Bible."

"Which part?" Keegan said, already having a sense, but wanting to hear it to be sure.

"Exodus 7:14 to 9:35," TAMS replied.[23]

"Is that the story of the biblical plagues and Moses leading the Israelites out of Egypt?" she asked.

"Yes," TAMS answered.

"You said that there were seven incidents. But weren't there ten plagues?"

"That is correct," TAMS replied.

13

FBI DOMESTIC SPECIAL DETENTION FACILITY

Reston, Virginia

As Keegan stood at the podium, she was conscious that she smelled of smoke, burned plastic, and sweat. She was reminded of a former boss saying how these in-person meetings were just new ways to inhale the odors of your colleagues.

With everyone in the conference room using immersive VR rigs to watch the presentation, Keegan could well have been 1,000 miles away. But this was one of those moments when being in the room really mattered. The investigation that had been code-named "NEO-LUDDITE" wasn't just what people called a "Super Bowl" case, the kind everyone aspired their whole career to work. It was also the sense that being there was being part of something bigger than all of them. Each of them had experienced the trials of the flood and shut-downs in their own individual way, but now they could work side by side to solve them.

That sense of togetherness, though, was undermined by the sight of Deputy Director Bosch sitting at the far end of the table, his face as blank as that of TAMS, which stood across the room from him.

Keegan's briefing ran through the attacks, projecting for the audience an overlay of the biblical text of each plague and visuals of

its recent parallel. Some were fairly obvious, like the Plague of Blood
(דָּם), which was set against a video of the contaminated rivers, and
the Plague of Poisoned Livestock, whose images of contaminated
meat made Keegan's stomach knot. Others were more symbolic, like
the Plague of Lice (כִּנִּים) and the crashed banks, assumed to be a
commentary on parasitic financial networks. It culminated with the
most recent catastrophes of Boils (שְׁחִין) and Fire and Hail (בָּרָד) in the
chemical attack and hacked drone swarms on the Mall. The underlying message was the sweeping scale of what might come next, in a
world where technology had been so democratized that one man had
the power once wielded by gods.[1]

The crowd reacted as it all began to fit together, each event seemingly a technological breakdown that now made sense as part of a
broader effort to shake society's confidence as a whole — an attack on
human will as much as on digital networks. It wasn't just how their
postures visibly shifted, but that the usually staid chat room that was
running alongside the presentation soon filled with brightly colored
clouds of graphics and text.

*Why isn't he taking credit, pushing it out to the public? Terrorists
usually do that,* read one.

Are we buying this as a lone wolf? posted another. *Or is this still a
networked conspiracy . . . Jacobs trying to misdirect us, pushing it all off
on a single actor.*

If conspiracy, internal or external??? reacted another.

One meeting attendee, the assistant director for counterintelligence, even posted a series of emoji faces, charting his shock and then
displeasure. It was soon followed by a reminder from the conference
moderator staff to *not post unessential information.*[2]

As her formal briefing came to its conclusion, Keegan used the opportunity to move around slightly, feeling her back tighten up from
standing in one place too long. She picked through all the questions
and comments that had popped up during the live feed. Grabbing at
the question of Jacobs's misdirect first, she highlighted it in the projection and then answered out loud.

"All data point to the evolution of a network to a single actor going rogue. TAMS registered Jacobs as telling the truth, for once, in our conversation. I know that can be spoofed, but he didn't seem to have that in him at the moment. Plus, it fits with what else we know, from the prior apprehensions of the NFF and the political goals Jacobs had for himself."

She then moved on to the question of whether terrorists always wanted credit. On that one, Modi threw her a helping hand, posting into the chat a series of studies on terrorist psychology, whose findings he summarized.[3] *The BLUF: Terrorism comes in all sorts of forms and motivations. What leads someone down that psychological staircase to terrorism is complex, but at the end of the day the unifying factor for all is not about getting credit but creating fear,* Modi wrote.

After ticking through each comment, she reviewed a series of pictures they had pulled of Todd, the collection showing the story of his life. High school and university graduation ceremonies. Cutting the cake at his wedding. Family vacations. A newsclip about the accident that killed his family. His old Defense Department identification badge. Keegan next layered a live satellite photo of his house in Northern Virginia over all the images. The crowd went silent, wondering if he was there right now. They also noted the blackened roof of one of the neighbor's houses. McLean Fire Department had marked it as an accident, but that could certainly be questioned given what they knew now.

"Whatever the scenario, based on the information we have at hand, Todd is our primary person of interest. Bring him in and we figure out whether Jacobs is lying about what happened to his network, or we stop the next attack — maybe both."

This was the signal for the meeting to shift from Keegan's briefing to the planning of a raid on Todd's residence. The HRT agents had the lead for that. Keg came in, looking slightly uncomfortable among all the suits. This was his first briefing since taking over for Noah, and it just happened to be among the most senior group possible. As he walked toward the podium, Keegan gave him a slight nod of confidence. It was at that moment that Bosch finally spoke up.

"Before you step away, Agent Keegan, there is something to clarify." He smiled, but she perceived that it took real effort. "We all owe you our thanks," he said, "for your dedication to mission and to the Bureau." He clapped and the audience promptly followed suit, with the VR feed also filling with thumbs-up icons.

After the meeting, Noritz motioned her to follow him to his office. Modi stepped in behind them too, unasked.

TAMS moved to follow, but Noritz abruptly said, "Just humans."

"TAMS, head down to the gear room and charge up," said Keegan.

The three of them entered Noritz's office, and he sat down in the leather chair behind his desk. It was supposed to be the commanding position in the room, but after Bosch's earlier show, it had the opposite effect. As much as if Bosch had pissed down the chair legs, he had marked the chair — and anyone else who sat in it — as his.

"I have some news that's going to disappoint you, so hear me out before you react," Noritz said. He paused, licking his lips. She waited for him to pull out his ChapStick, but he plunged forward as if resolving to rip the Band-Aid off as quickly as possible. "The TAMS program is being shut down."

"What?" whispered Keegan.

Modi just nodded, as if bored by the news. It was like he'd always known this moment was coming.

"Whose orders?" said Keegan, though she knew whose. "And why?"

Noritz held up his hands and smiled, but it was a sad one. "You know that," he said. "And you know why. Deputy Director Bosch feels, and I agree . . ." he said, as if ensuring to have that on the record if the conversation was being recorded, "that given what we have seen happen with such systems, we can't trust them in an operational setting. It's not just what Todd has shown he's capable of; it's what the public might think."

"You know what happened today wasn't a machine problem. That was a human problem. All these breakdowns are Todd picking at the seams of our society and pulling the threads apart one by one. He's not done yet."

"We know that. Just because TAMS is offline does not mean the NEOLUDDITE investigation is stopping. In fact, Deputy Director

Bosch feels that our shift away from a reliance on such technology may prove advantageous in the investigation. You just said Todd was picking away at the tech one by one. Now we're closing down *both* a major liability for this investigation and for the Bureau."

"Don't twist my words around. TAMS is how we got here. Noritz, my daughter would not be alive if not for it. When those drones started falling out of the sky, it found us the only safe place on the Mall. Which also happened to be where Jacobs was hiding, too."

"You've become . . . close . . . to the machine," said Noritz, as if forgiving her for something wrong. "I get it, but—"

"But the decision's already been made," said Keegan.

"You know how it is," said Noritz.

"Yeah, sure." She looked over at Modi. "Anything to say?" said Keegan. "I thought this was your project as much as mine."

"No, as much as I'd like to," he replied, in an empathetic voice. "I have to look at the work with you and TAMS as an assignment. Like you, I don't get to do everything I want to do, say everything I want to say. I have bosses, too."

Keegan looked back at Noritz, ignoring Modi now, as if he had disappeared from the room.

"If that's all, sir. I'll be downstairs," said Keegan. "I need to go decommission . . . my partner."

She went downstairs and found TAMS hung along the back wall on a padded black metal rack, its blue running lights offering the only illumination in the room. Keegan flipped on the overhead fluorescents.

She'd waited as long as she could for Shaw to reach out, to tell her that the order was off. But nothing came in.

"TAMS, we need to talk," Keegan said, knowing that *they* really didn't need to. She did.

"OK."

"You've done a lot of solid work," said Keegan. "Just as well as any human agent would . . . Better than any human, maybe."

The machine stared back, its face blank.

"The investigation will proceed, but we're going to . . . do it another way."

"How can I assist the investigation's new priorities?" asked TAMS.

"That's not possible. It is a set of orders that I have to follow, just like any protocol that guides you."

The machine looked back at her, as if it didn't understand. Keegan knew it was just her, an all-too-human mind transposing emotions onto it.

"I know. It doesn't make much sense to me either. If there is one last thing that I can teach you, it's that there's plenty of things that humans do that don't make much sense. We're a walking bunch of contradictions. Trust me on that one thing."

"OK."

"I'm going to power you down now, TAMS," said Keegan, running her fingers across its now dented and pockmarked chest plate. "Thank you."

A moment later, it was done. The system lights went dark and the robot's limbs and head fell limp.

Lifeless, like it had always been.

But somehow, now even more so.

SCOTT'S RUN NATURE PRESERVE

McLean, Virginia

The smoke from the cooking fire kept getting in Todd's eyes. Every time he moved, it felt like the wind would pick up and push it back in his direction. He would move clockwise around the stone circle, and so did the smoke. He slid over again, which now put him next to a woman in her forties. Despite the heat, she was wrapped in a sleeping bag. Even as the smoke swirled around them, she stared blankly into the fire with glassy eyes. He took her by the hand and walked her out of the smoke.

"Thank you for that," said an older woman in a thin gray tracksuit, with duct tape binding a tear on the left sleeve. She walked over to greet Todd.

"Haven't seen you here before here. I'm Mayor Renae." She spoke with the patient cadence of a librarian, like someone used to knowing more than the people she dealt with. Her eyes, wide set and kind, looked him over with a practiced gaze to tamp down the nagging feeling she always got with a newcomer, that they could be a threat to her camp.

She waited a moment more for the man to introduce himself, and then forged on. "You might be wondering about the title. Well, if you're going to have a tent city, you gotta have a mayor," she said pointing around. There were about thirty tents gathered around the firepit and a common kitchen area with two old gas grills and table of plywood set across old stumps. "Mostly, it means I just guilt people into treating others the way they want to be treated themselves."

"How'd you end up here?" Todd asked. Dressing the part that he'd thought he'd need to play, he wore a pair of faded green corduroy pants, topped by the thin foil of an emergency thermal blanket turned into a makeshift poncho. Like the woman with her sleeping bag, he didn't need it with the fire, but he hoped the mayor wouldn't notice that.

The park, a county-owned nature preserve, was located just behind his neighborhood. When they'd bought their house, having a 300-acre forest that backed up to your property line had been one of the great appeals. There were hiking trails for the kids, deer that would wander into your backyard while you had your morning coffee, and most of all, no neighbors looking through your back windows. But then the very thing that they'd paid extra for had turned into a drag on property value.

First came the construction for the power line that ran through the county land and then set off a panic over cancer fears. A few years after that, the next controversy started when people who had lost their jobs and then their homes had set up camp in the park's woods. It had pitted the neighborhood association members against each other, some worried about safety or property values, others knowing how close they really were to being in the same position. Soon, even those most worked up about the squatters found out there wasn't much they could do. The homeless camp had been set up in a hollow hidden from the public hiking trail that ran along the top of the ridge. The park rangers knew they were there, but as long as there was no trouble, left them alone. Which was why Todd was there. It was off the grid, but near where he needed to be.

"I used to work as a hostess over at the restaurant for Washington Golf and Country Club, not far from here," Renae said. "After my shifts, I'd bring leftover food from the parties and banquets. It seemed the least I could do. After the downturn dragged on, I couldn't keep up with the bills. You know how it is . . ."

He nodded as if that were something he'd been dealing with too.

"They already knew me here, so it just seemed the natural place for me. After that, well, people came and went, and I just stayed."

"She been here long too?" Todd asked, tilting his chin over at the woman still staring into the fire.

"No, from a family that just came down from Baltimore. You see what happened there?"

Todd felt his legs wobble, just for a moment. He nodded his assent to Renae.

"There's four of 'em and they're really sick," she said. "There's a guy on the other side of that tree, I think her husband. He was still puking up blood."

"Should we . . . call an ambulance for them?" Todd asked before he could stop himself. He chided himself to be more careful in balancing the character he had to play and the agent of change he had to be.

"Here? Then what?" said Renae. "First, they're not going to come. Second, even if they do, it's just going to create trouble with the cops."

"Sure," he said.

"We'll do our best for them. And that's the best we can do," she said. "How about you? You doing OK?"

"I know it feels like everything is coming apart," he said, "but maybe that's for the best. It means something is finally changing." He said it as much for himself as for her.

"I hope you're right," she replied. "Anyways, as long as you treat everyone the way you want to be treated, you're welcome to stay here . . ." She held out her hand, her eyes indicating she was still waiting for his name.

"Ned," he supplied, and shook her hand.

"Good to meet you, Ned. With everything coming apart like you say, it's good to be around other people." She walked back to her tent, leaving Todd by the fire, wondering what the woman exactly saw in the flames, and if she could ever understand the justice of his actions.

All of a sudden, there was movement behind him in the trees, a rustle of leaves followed by a glimpse of brown. It was one of the deer overrunning the park. Normally, they sauntered through the park like they owned it, but this time the animal looked spooked.

It had happened quicker than he expected.

Todd took hurried steps away from the camp, moving down the hill to the muddy shore of the Potomac River. He crouched low, walking along the waterline for a few hundred feet, and then headed back up into the woods, following a washout that doubled as a game trail. The thin paper of the thermal blanket rustled slightly, but the sound was close enough to that of leaves crinkling in the breeze to mask it.

He froze. They were hard to see at first, but silhouetted on the hiking trail that ran along the ridgeline was the outline of a person wearing a combat helmet and carrying a rifle. A soldier. Then another and another after that.

He lay down quietly in the roots and slithered the last 20 feet to his destination: a metal stand in one of the trees, wreathed in dark green camouflage thermal netting. The freegans would be proud of him, he thought, recycling someone else's work. The tree stand had been put in by the bow hunters licensed by the county to try to trim back the deer numbers.

Just a foot away from the tree, the plan went awry. Todd cut his left hand on a piece of broken glass, likely from some discarded beer bottle. He bit back a curse at the pain and slowly ascended the ladder. At the top, he hunkered down behind the netting and shifted the heat-reflective blanket that he wore as a poncho to shield his body.

Peering through the slit, he watched as more soldiers advanced by in the dark. It soon became clear he didn't need the camouflage that the thermal blanket or the hunting blind offered. The figures seemed intent on navigating the dark trail to his neighborhood as rapidly as possible, not scanning the forest for targets. Then, he saw that they weren't soldiers at all. Stitched in the middle of their dark green body armor were three yellow letters: FBI.

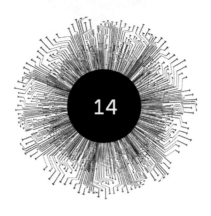

14

POTOMAC OVERLOOK NEIGHBORHOOD

McLean, Virginia

In the darkness, the noise of her own breathing and the slight murmurs of the wind working its way through the dense trees sounded louder than they actually were.

The timer on her vizglasses told Keegan the main assault force would race up from the trail to Todd's backyard in the next thirty seconds. With his residence on a single-road cul-de-sac, the working assumption was he would see any vehicles coming from a distance. So the raid would seize the element of surprise by coming in on foot from the back, using the adjacent park's forest as cover. The follow-on force would block any vehicular traffic from approaching the cul-de-sac. At the nearby American Legion Memorial Bridge that ran over the Potomac River, Virginia State Police had set up another roadblock, cutting off any escape back into the city.

The HRT operators, led by Keg, crouched at the head of the trail behind the house. The agents spread out, lying down on the slight slope in Todd's property line, framed between the privacy fences on either side of the backyard. Keegan and the follow-on force stacked up on the trail, waiting for the signal. It would be an obvious one.

Keegan zoomed in on the target, using the full-color night vision that amplified the ambient light 85,000 times.[1] The split-level ranch-style home showed its age. It needed some paint on the white trim, and one of the gutters hung askew. Had it always looked like this, or had Todd given up on the upkeep when his life's work shifted from creation to destruction?

She looked up from the house to the sky above, a swirl of tiny lights extending out as far as her eyes could track. That was the one thing she'd always loved about the goggles, the way they allowed you to see five hundred times more stars in the sky. On night raids, they turned every soldier into an astronomer, and sometimes even a philosopher, pondering the meaning of their smallness in the midst of all that light in the distance.[2]

Buzzing replaced the whisper of the wind. Then, like an omnipotent deity, a voice rang out from megaphones mounted on the four quadcopters that dropped down to hover at the corners of Todd's property. "Jackson Todd! This is the FBI." At those words, the HRT operators ran from the woods into the backyard.

One of them then fell, as if yanked backward by the neck. The other HRT members dropped to the ground, weapons searching for the sniper. There was no other fire, no explosions.

"Anyone have eyes on?" Keg yelled out.

The agent who had fallen pulled away a thin piece of greenish rope that he'd gotten tangled in, tossing aside what looked like a wooden handle.

"Stand down the sniper hunt," Keg said. "It's a kid's zip line."

The HRT operators regained their footing and carefully worked their way to the back porch. Edging past a gas grill, they placed a wall-penetrating radar next to an exterior brick wall.[3] It showed what the overhead drones' thermal sensors had indicated: there were no humans home. But with somebody as savvy as Todd, there was no way to know for certain.

Keegan advanced from the trail and walked around the house to locate Noritz. He was huddled inside a navy blue tactical command post van, part of the convoy of law enforcement vehicles that filled the cul-de-sac at the HRT operators' initial all clear. Sitting beside him were a pair of FBI Special Agent Bomb Techs performing the law enforcement version of Keegan's old robot-wrangler job in the Marines. Noritz had said he wanted her in there with them for the next phase, when they entered the house. But it was not clear to her if he was trying to signal his continued trust by having her in the command center, or if it was the very opposite: keeping her where he could see her.

In either case, the two wranglers had their hands full tonight, literally. After all of Todd's tech takedowns, the operational plan was to limit use of anything that had advanced automation software. Fingers dancing across keyboards in a blur, the two steered everything from the drones that hovered above Todd's yard to a cloud of insect-sized drones that were pushed out through the neighborhood to establish a perimeter.

"HRT confirms no sign of Todd," Keegan announced.

"Strike one," said Noritz and then he turned to the wranglers. "Send it in."

A small tracked robot about the size of a lawnmower rolled off the van's ramp and turned jerkily toward Todd's house. An older model PackBot, the machine did not try to hide its singular purpose behind plastic skin or human form.[4] Designed for bomb squad and SWAT team work and then sent out to the second Iraq War, it had a single metal arm with four hinged joints topped by a two-fingered claw. Mounted on the second-to-last joint, the equivalent of the robot's forearm, was a sensor pod and a shotgun.[5] The gun was supposed to be used to detonate improvised explosives, but Keegan knew from experience it could be used to target people.

The robot rolled up Todd's front stoop with a stuttering advance. With a critical eye, Keegan could see the wrangler's moves were unsteady; he wasn't used to the joystick-style controller, modeled after the video games of their parents' generation. What had once been a user-friendly design was now as intuitive as changing typewriter ribbon.

At the door, the robot stopped.

"Ring the bell, or blast it open?" asked the technician, perhaps a little too eager to try out the shotgun.

"Try the door," Noritz said.

The robot's claw hand reached out and grasped at the door handle. After a first miss, Keegan suggested, "Try shifting to the pinhole camera mounted inside the hand; it's easier that way."

"Thanks."

The viewscreen shifted from looking down on the door handle to a bug's-eye view looking directly at it. Centering the knob on the screen, the twin metal grippers closed on the hand, darkening the screen. It shifted back to the sensor pod view above the handle and the hand spun slowly, turning the door handle.

Todd's house was unlocked.

"That's not suspicious at all," said Keegan.

"Agreed," said Noritz. He spoke into the comms channel. "All agents, pull back. Let's clear the house first with the PackBot."

"Roger that," Keg's voice came back.

An update flashed across the viewscreen in the van and onto Keegan's viz; no traces of explosives or any other nuclear, biological, or chemical threats had been detected by the PackBot's sniffers. But it also illustrated how much code was still running back and forth, even with their attempt to avoid automation.

The robot used its arm to push the door open wider.

"Hold it here to see if there's any reaction from inside the house," Keegan instructed. Being silhouetted in an open doorway was often the start of an ambush.

After five seconds of nothing, the wrangler looked back at Noritz and he nodded his approval. The robot's spotlight on the sensor pod turned on and it crept forward. On the viewscreen, a new window opened. It showed a graphic layout of the robot's actual position matched to a rendering they'd built from the house's plans and photos from an old online real estate listing. This would allow them not only to track its progress, but also to see if there were any false walls hiding potential dangers.

The robot rolled through a hall entryway with wooden floors, then into a carpeted den connected to an open kitchen. The operator spun the PackBot on its tracks slowly, surveying the room. Keegan wasn't sure what she expected to see, but the normality of it surprised her. Hell, it was exactly the kind of needing-to-be-updated suburban house that she and Jared had spent hours poring over online before he'd lost his job.

"Light on over there," Noritz said, and the robot headed toward a doorway with a band of light peeking out from beneath it. The builder's plans marked it as stairs down to the basement level.

The robot opened the door — no need for Keegan to tell the wrangler how to do his job twice — then rumbled down a short set of stairs, a second set of tracks flipping downward off the back of the Pack-Bot to keep it steady. At the bottom, the machine paused, as if appreciating that it had the room to itself. It was an empty rec room, the carpet showing the tracks of a vacuum. The emptiness was eerie; it was the kind of room that should have been littered with toys. The bot advanced slowly, then stopped before entering the other room in the lower level, where the light was coming from. The design plans showed a 22- by 18-foot room with no windows, labeling it a "guest room/office." Yet in builder speak, that could mean anything from a spare bedroom to sex dungeon.

"Open it?" asked the tech.

"If he's set something to blow, all we've lost is a bot," said Noritz. "Do it."

Just before the bot pushed opened the door with its arm, it seemed as if every person in the crowded van took a breath in nervous anticipation. The door opened to show a large box, about the size of a refrigerator, standing in the middle of the room.

"What the hell is that?" said the robot operator.

Its sides were a yellowish glass, shimmering with the reflection of the robot's light. Two thick black cables snaked out the top, running down the box to the wall, where they followed the baseboard.

"Analytics on what we are seeing? Anybody?" asked Noritz.

All Keegan could think was how useful TAMS would have been at this moment. As the operator started to drive the robot closer, she said, "Don't touch the cables," worried about a booby trap.

"Got it. I'm going to get a better angle on those wire terminals coming out the top," he said. "It looks like some kind of big generator or battery."

It was the last word that did it — the shimmery glass looked like the big brother of what she'd seen inside the guts of the tiny robots she'd so many times assembled herself. "It's not that," she said.

"What is it then?" asked Noritz.

"I think it's a capacitor," she said.

"A what?" asked Noritz.

"It's like a battery, but instead of producing electricity with chemicals, it just stores it. Kinda like a water tower for electrons, storing them until you need them.[6] That yellow is graphene, superefficient, probably lined with ceramic or something else nonconductive. I've never seen plates that big before, though. You'd have to buy that special from a fab."

"What's he doing with it then, powering his house? Maybe for some kind of secret lab?"

"No, it's doing the opposite. See how he's got it hooked up over there? He's got to be charging it off the power grid with cables that big. Plus, you wouldn't want to store any electrical lab equipment near a charged capacitor like that in case you ever shorted it out . . ." Her voice trailed off, as she considered the cramped space of the van, packed with electronics mere inches from her face.

She tossed her vizglasses aside and covered her eyes, and shouted "Cover!"

SCOTT'S RUN NATURE PRESERVE

McLean, Virginia

Face down in the mud, Todd pushed himself up and took a deep breath, trying to stop hyperventilating. Just another 20 feet and he would be back at the river's edge. But he kept slipping down the slick, steepening slope, unable to find either his footing or his breath. This had all started years ago, but somehow it felt as if a line had just been crossed. That it had taken place in his home made it personal, but also meant that he could never go back. It was done. That part of his life was now truly over — just as it was for society.

The lightning-like electric crack of the capacitor discharging in his house had been followed by eight more in the distance. The FBI team must have set off the proximity sensor in the basement, which sent out the last digital signal in the area for some time. None of his jury-rigged devices had the world-spanning range of the nuclear-weapon-powered EMPs that the doomsayers fantasized about.[7] But it wasn't needed. At the proximity sensor's signal, a daisy chain of electromagnetic pulses had shot out from the capacitors that he'd geographically set to cover the network of power grid substations in Washington; one had even been assembled in an apartment that he'd rented across from the Capitol Power Plant.[8] Just that single device would take out the power source that every office in Congress and the Supreme Court relied on, as well as brick every single computer in the headquarters buildings of the Departments of Energy, Education, and Housing and Urban Development, as well as the Federal Aviation Administration and US Postal Service, turning them into mere paperweights. Perhaps most damaging, though, would be at the General Services Administration's DC region headquarters, the little-known agency that managed the basic functions and office management for every single other federal organization. Even if the politicians and bureaucrats tried to fight it, there was now literally no choice other than to remake vast swaths of American government.

Then came a sweet silence that no one inside the Beltway had heard for literally a generation. None of the cicada-like buzzing of drones overhead or whirring of electric vehicles that had become part of the everyday background noise of modern life. Nothing.

He wanted to howl with exaltation at the triumph of his moment. But respecting the silence was an even greater celebration of a journey that had begun with such loss. He alone had given society this

moment to rethink and reset. He alone had steered it to the last possible off-ramp from the information superhighway, before it all ca-
reened out of human control.

The silence passed through him. Calmed, he started to move with
deliberate steps down to the river's edge. There was still more work
to be done. As he reached the water, he washed his hand of the blood
from the broken bottle. When he stood back up to survey the shore,
only then did he realize he had a far bigger problem that he hadn't
factored in. The small black kayak he had hidden was gone. Or, to put
it more accurately, the old river's edge he had hidden it on was gone,
its geography changed by the force of the flood.

Todd looked around, feeling his heart race now. *Breathe,* he told
himself. *Every problem has a solution.* He found the kayak floating
about 30 yards away. The tree that it had been tied to had broken off at
the stump, but fortunately gotten wedged into a tangle of other trees
and debris piled up against a boulder.

He untied the kayak and checked to make sure the backpack was
still secured inside. There was always the risk that someone might
have taken it, but the kayak had been set well off any hiking trail and
covered with netting and leaves.

Todd dragged the boat deeper into the fast-moving water and, using the paddle planted in the mud to try to steady himself, put one
foot up in the kayak. As he tried to pull in the other leg, however, he
began to tip over and his arm holding the paddle swayed out.

The kayak rolled, dumping Todd into the river, and he scrambled
to hold on to the paddle while the kayak started to float downstream.
Luckily, he'd attached its rope to his wrist, and after a drawn-out
thrashing about in the fast-moving water, he got his feet underneath
him and stood. He checked for the backpack again and stowed the
paddle back inside the boat, then dragged it ashore, half out of the
water and half on the mud.

He'd been kayaking before, but it had always been off a dock, the
teenager who worked at the rental stand at Georgetown's waterfront
holding it steady while he and his wife climbed in. Only now had

he considered that was another of those little things for which you needed human help. At that thought, he laughed at the simultaneous appropriateness and ludicrousness of it all. He deserved to be cold and wet and at a loss for what to do next, he thought. It was a very human feeling.

Trying again, this time he wedged himself into the kayak while it was still ashore, the bow of the boat squishing down low in the mud from his weight, but the stern floating free. The cut on his hand throbbed as he dug the paddle's edge into the muck and inched the boat backward into the water push by push. It probably wasn't the right way, but it worked. And that made it the right way.

As the kayak finally broke free of the sludge, the river's current spun the bow downstream. With a wobbly first few strokes, Todd felt the boat pick up speed. In the faster open water, he found it easier to steer. With little effort, he soon closed in on the American Legion Memorial Bridge that crossed the Potomac. Its high, thick, reinforced concrete piers had kept it safe above the flood, but now it appeared as it never had before. Backlit only by the stars, its spans were completely dark, not a single car headlight on its ten lanes of highway. As the kayak passed under the bridge and he entered pure darkness, the boat's swaying movement was the only sensation fed into his body. When the boat exited back into the starlight on the other side, he began a slow and deliberate paddle toward his next destination. Not everything had gone to plan, but enough had that he could continue his work.

POTOMAC OVERLOOK NEIGHBORHOOD

McLean, Virginia

It all had the look of a funeral pyre, a central column of smoke pouring out of Todd's house, framed by the four smoldering drones where they had crashed in the corners of the yard. Yet as she emerged from the FBI van, Keegan couldn't see anyone in the immediate vicinity who was either hurt or dead. Mostly, agents stood about confused, pulling off their AR glasses to see what was wrong with them and flicking switches on tactical radios that had gone dead.

"Is everyone OK on your team?" Keegan yelled over to Keg.

"I think so," he yelled back. "We were far enough back. But a few of the rigs jolted when the comms went down. What the hell happened? We've got no feed from the network."

"He had some kind of electronic defeat device in the house. A big jury-rigged capacitor set off to go when we got near it. It likely fried anything close with unprotected electronic circuitry." She looked down at her Watchlet. It had a blank screen. She couldn't even mark the time of the attack. It was that moment when she noticed the silence in the air. "Keg, get your team to set a perimeter, facing out," she yelled.

He gave her a confused look.

"We don't have any drones watching our back anymore," she explained.

One second they had been a connected force in a position of strength. Now they were on the defensive and disconnected, mentally as much as technologically.

"Keegan, you OK?" Noritz asked, exiting the vehicle in a daze. Inside the van, the detonation had made sparks fly out from the servers and the PackBot's control screen sizzle, but nothing major had exploded.

Keegan didn't respond. She kept scanning the area to make sure there were not any threats emerging from the forest or the street, ready to take advantage of this sudden shift.

"Keegan?" said Noritz. "Hey! You OK?"

Even in this cul-de-sac, she could feel that something else had shifted. There was a different energy in the air. Or, rather, a lack of it. "Yeah. All good."

Noritz pointed into the night sky. "Look at the stars . . . I've never seen them that bright."

"There's no ambient light. Power must be out all over."

The two of them stood still, now able to see as many stars as they'd previously needed their night-vision goggles to view. The darkness offered clarity.

"Just how many of those devices did he have?" Noritz asked.

"Enough to make plagues eight" — she walked over to the edge of the road and picked up a dragonfly-like microdrone about the size of her trigger finger — "and nine happen." She tossed the inert little drone to the side, seeing scores of them on the ground in piles, their translucent wings glittering from the starlight

"What are you talking about?" said Noritz.

"Locusts and darkness," said Keegan. "The eighth and ninth plagues — which means there's one more to go if Todd is doing what we think."

The growl of a diesel engine interrupted them; a matte black MRAP with "FBI" stenciled on the side pulled up. It was from the quick reaction force, set at the end of the cul-de-sac, which might as well have been on the other side of the city with the comms gear out.

"Thank God for military surplus," Keegan said. The hardened electronics of the armored truck had protected its systems from Todd's pulse blast, but the universe of people its radios could call would be limited.

Noritz went over to confer with the team lead of the rapid reaction team, Keegan holding back. There was no rapid reaction to make, no clear next move to take. After a few minutes, Noritz returned, seemingly reenergized. "I'm going to make that my ride. I'll drop you off close as we can get, then I need to circle back to the office," he said.

"What do you mean, drop me off?" she asked.

"Take the time to check in on your family. They've been through a lot. This mess will all be here tomorrow to deal with."

He said it as if he was giving friendly advice, but unstated was what would happen in the interim. The mess would still be there tomorrow, but tonight would be when they'd figure out who to pin it on. They'd be looking for a scapegoat, and Noritz was making sure she wasn't going to be there when they did. The absent person who had steered them right into this trap would take the fall.

She wanted to argue, but she didn't have the energy to deal with it all. He was right. She needed to be somewhere else tonight, with someone else.

But all she could do was think about what was to come. The final plague was the one that had finally persuaded the Egyptians when the other catastrophes hadn't: Death of the Firstborn. It took her imagination to darker places than she wanted to go, and she forced herself awake by digging her fingernails into her palms. The horror of what she kept imagining made her nauseous. And TAMS, maybe the best weapon they had to do something about it, was hanging on a rack in the back of a converted shopping mall.

15

BALLSTON NEIGHBORHOOD

Arlington, Virginia

Hundreds of lights glowed from high-rises' windows. It was beautiful in a way, thought Keegan, the glimmers silhouetting backlit bodies staring out into the darkened city.[1] Usually that came from a wall screen or tablet. Instead, it was hundreds of tiny candle flames. Flames had always meant fear for some, hope for others. There would be more of the former than the latter right now. But there was something human about the flames, something that forged a shared connection against the darkness.

The lobby of her building, though, was completely dark. The electric doors didn't automatically open, but they hadn't autolocked either, which was a good thing because she had no idea how she would have gotten in otherwise. They opened just an inch, something on the inside blocking them. Keegan pushed harder, this time with the full force of her shoulder leaning in, and the door slid back a few more inches so she could slide her body through. As she squeezed inside, the sound of something moving through the air made her duck. Metal pinged into the hard glass of the door about where her head had just been. She rolled to a low crouch and drew her pistol. Seeing more movement and the outline of a person, she took aim.

"Federal agent! Do not move!"

"What?" said an older woman's voice.

As Keegan's eyes started to adjust to the dark, she lowered her weapon. "What the hell are you doing?"

"Oh! You're the cop!" said a gray-haired woman in her sixties, who wielded a bat.

"Not a cop, FBI," Keegan said, exasperated.

"That's right, Siena. She's little Haley's mom," said a second figure that emerged from the dark. He was a man, also in his sixties. Instead of a bat, he had a claw hammer in his hand.

"Yeah, that's me. Haley's mom, FBI agent."

She couldn't remember their names either, so it was only fair that was how they knew her. She'd made small talk about the weather with Siena and what's-his-name with the hammer whenever they crossed paths in the lobby and up on the drone delivery pad. But in buildings like this, no one was borrowing cups of sugar, or whatever people did with neighbors "back in the day."

"Seriously," Keegan said. "What are you doing down here? I almost killed you both."

"We're protecting the building from looters."

"Right . . ." Keegan said. She didn't have the patience for this. "Can I give you some advice, though? Find out who's coming in before you try to brain them."

"What's happening out there?" said Siena, sounding eager, almost like she wished it were Armageddon beyond the building.

"It's what it looks like," said Keegan, getting annoyed at the delay. "It's dark, most everyone huddled up like us."

"When's the power coming back on?" they asked, as if being in the FBI meant she had all the answers. It was a far cry from the usual "Deep State" crap that their generation had become consumed by.

"Power's going to be out for a while. I don't know any more than you do. If I do hear more, I'll be sure to let you know. Police will be by at some point to check on everybody, so just hang in there and we'll be fine. If you really want to do something, maybe go door to door to see if anybody needs medical help or candles or whatnot?"

"What about protecting the lobby?" said Siena.

"Checking on neighbors is more important," said Keegan. "I need to go check on my family, too. We're all going to be fine." She didn't believe it. They were a long way from fine. But they wouldn't detect her lie in the dark.

Upstairs, Keegan paused outside her front door and instinctively swiped at the Watchlet to check on what the tiny bot cams inside would reveal. She half expected to see an image of her daughter and husband huddled around a trio of candles, faces lit from beneath. Instead, the screen remained blank.

A deep breath and she knocked gently on the door.

"It's me," she said. "Lara."

Then came a rush of shame that she even had to say that.

She could hear fast-paced footsteps as Haley sprinted toward the door. After Jared opened it, Haley leapt into her arms. "Mommy!" she said.

Keegan squeezed her tight. It used to be that every time she saw her, it seemed like her little girl had grown inches in between. If anything, tonight Haley felt smaller, more vulnerable as the world around her had become more dangerous.

The room was lit with long white candles, flickering shadows dancing along the wall.

Jared held back, for a moment, then moved in to hug them both. It was a hard squeeze, and a longer one than she had had from him in a very long time.

"Mommy, you changed your clothes," Haley said, pointing out her tactical gear.

"Yeah, I had to," she said.

"Did you go to the store for them?" she said.

"I got them at work," she said.

"How come? Are the stores dark too?" Haley asked.

"You doing OK?" Jared asked.

"Yeah, I think so. Tired as hell, but good otherwise, considering . . ." She carried Haley inside, not giving a damn about what it would do to her back later on, and all three of them crashed down onto the couch.

Its springs creaked; Jared being on it so long for his job had worn them out.

Nobody spoke. They just watched the candle flames flicker in the dark living room.

"You guys have enough to eat?" Keegan asked.

"We're OK," Jared replied. "After the flood scare, I stocked up on freeze-dried meals and cans, twice the recommended FEMA amount."[2]

The way he was so calm about it made her think that her order of extra medication had come through too.

That wasn't fair, she chided herself. For all their troubles, she knew Jared wanted to protect their family.

"That's when I got the extra candles too. I didn't know how many you're supposed to have, so I just ordered a couple of boxes of the long fancy ones we use in the dining room."

"Well, at least it classes up the joint," she said with a slight smile.

"Haley, do you wanna go get Mommy one of her energy bars?" he said — the kind of question parents asked to plant an idea that was really an order.

Haley ran to the kitchen.

"Just what is happening out there?" Jared asked when she'd moved out of earshot. "Everything's off, not just the power, but all our devices. I can't even pull down the news to find out why, let alone work. Haley's toys are on the fritz too."

"The same people behind the flood and drone crashes fried the power grid and knocked out anything digital with what were essentially daisy-chained electric IEDs."

"Feels like this is never going to end," he said, "like we're never going to go back to normal."

"I don't know about that. We'll catch them and then get things back on track," she said, maybe not so certain herself. But she had to be the confident one.

"No. You know how our parents talked about the September 11 attacks, like the whole world changed forever after that?" he asked.

"Not because of the attacks themselves, but by what came after. Afghanistan. Iraq. Saudi Arabia. This is going to be like that. Except we're going to be attacking one another."

She stared back at him. Maybe he'd been living online for too long. Or, maybe he was right.

"No need to go there just yet. Some things you have to take one day at a time. An hour at a time. Otherwise it's too much," she said, as much to convince herself as him.

"Where's TAMS?" said Haley, running back into the room, no bar in hand, having forgotten the mission.

"Still at work," Keegan said.

"I miss it," said Haley, as she climbed into her mom's lap. "Did it get turned off too?"

For a second Keegan wondered how Haley had guessed that, then realized she meant like her toys. "Haley, TAMS is resting at my office."

"You can turn it on, right?" said Haley.

"It's not quite like that," said Keegan. How would the little girl understand a robot "dying"?[3] Would it be like losing a toy, a pet, or even a human friend? "TAMS had a job to do, and did it. It did a really good job, in fact. But now it's all done."

"But I want TAMS here, with me!" Haley started balling her fists like she was about to have a tantrum.

A loud knock on the door interrupted them. Keegan set Haley aside and went to the entry hallway, taking in how the door was cheap wood, the kind that any looter's axe could go through in a second.

Get a grip. Those two dingbats in the lobby are in your head.

The second knock was even louder, shaking the door on its frame.

She drew her pistol from her holster, in that moment realizing that in the rush to get inside, she hadn't even put it away in the gun safe above the refrigerator.

"Bathroom," she hissed at Jared and Haley.

Haley started to cry, a wail that was between mumbling and moaning. Jared just nodded solemnly and scooped the girl up.

Keegan refocused on the front door.

"Keegan, it's Modi," a voice called from outside. "Open up. I know you're in there."

What was *he* doing here?

She unlocked the door, then stepped back, hiding the pistol behind her.

Modi was not first through the door, however. TAMS was. In the silhouette of the doorway, the outline of the robot looked fragile and childlike, almost like Haley herself—delicate.

"What the . . . ?" said Keegan.

"Hello," the machine said, and then a microsecond pause of recognition, "Agent Keegan."

"You can put away the gun, OK?" said Modi stepping in behind the robot. She nodded and holstered her Sig, impressed he had noticed that tactical detail so quickly. But any thought of that changed as he came closer. The candlelight didn't shimmer off his hair. Instead of the rippling metallic colors, it was all now a muted brown. He was also wearing a fitted business suit, the fabric tight around defined muscles.

The bathroom door swung open and Haley ran out. "TAMS!"

"It is nice to see you again, Haley," TAMS said, as the girl collided with the bot, rocking it backward with the force of a hug every bit as intense as the one that she had given her mother. Jared walked out into the room behind her but hung back, eyeing both the robot and Modi with suspicion.

Haley was oblivious to it, though, squeezing what would have been the life out of the machine. Keegan marveled at the connection Haley seemed to have with the robot. Yet, as she looked at the child's hands clasped around the robot's waist, she picked up that something was wrong. The bot's ceramic skin was unmarked. No dings and scratches from battle damage.

"Wait," Keegan said to herself. There was no way they could have fixed it in the interim, not with all the attacks and system collapses. She stepped closer to the bot, then dropped down on one knee to examine the plating.

"Haley, why don't you take TAMS to your room to show it your toys?" said Keegan. "TAMS . . ." she said haltingly, feeling almost guilty for using the same name for this other system. "TAMS, go with Haley until I tell you to return."

"OK," Haley and the robot said, almost in unison, which made Haley giggle. She tugged the bot by the hand to her room. "Can you help Baz fly again?" Haley asked.

Keegan waited for the door to close, then turned on Modi. "That isn't TAMS."

"Yes and no," Modi said. "It is a TAMS unit, just not yours. It has the same experiences synched up, but we had to pull another one for you . . . from other sources."

"How did you get a new one in the middle of all this?" she asked. "That kind of tech isn't just lying around in a warehouse, waiting to be booted up."

"For some organizations, it is," he said.

"Seriously, I need to know. How'd you get the hardware here, backed up, and I am guessing charged up, in the middle of an EMP blackout? Is this Shaw pulling strings for you too now?"

He shook his head. "No, there are limits to even where someone like Mr. Shaw can reach."

"Who then? DoD used to run the program. This one of theirs?"

"Indirectly. It was provided to other government agencies that have an interest in this matter," he said.

"The other kind with three letters?" asked Keegan.

Modi nodded.

At that, Jared abruptly stood up.

"OK, this has been fun, but one of us has to stay out of prison. I know I shouldn't be in the room for this," he said, heading toward the bedroom.

"A very good idea," Modi said under his breath.

After the door closed, Modi pulled out a small black rectangle the size of an auxiliary phone battery and flicked it on with his thumb. He quickly circled the room, exuding confidence that had been lacking before — gone was the gawky uncertainty of an academic uncomfortable in his own skin and now he had quick, predatory movements. It was the practiced efficiency of a well-trained soldier, Keegan realized.

"We're good now," he said. "Just stay away from the windows."

They sat down at the kitchen counter, moving aside two half-eaten bowls of cereal. Looking past Modi, she noticed that her folded bots were all set along the windowsill, looking out toward the city.

"Second one of those I've had pulled out on me in two days," she said. "This another conversation that never happened?"

Modi took a breath. But rather than hunch and sink into himself, as had been his habit before, he sat with military posture, his shoulders back and spine ramrod straight. "Agent Keegan, I have close-hold information that I have been authorized to share with you and you alone at this stage of what is a highly compartmented national security investigation. Not Noritz. Not Bosch. Not Shaw. Understood?"

"Yes," she replied, wondering why this clearance wasn't being done in written form and a little afraid of the answer.

"I don't work for the Justice Department or the FBI. At least, not exactly."

"Not exactly?"

"I'm a counterintelligence officer at CIA assigned to a special internal task force that has a domestic focus. In my case, it has me inside the FBI to monitor the Bureau for penetration by enemies of the Constitution, foreign or domestic." He emphasized the latter, then paused to let Keegan process the full meaning of what he had said. "The program started after the, shall we say, interesting behavior within the FBI's New York office that hampered the nation's ability to respond to the very first case of foreign interference into a domestic US election."[4]

"Who watches the watchers?" whispered Keegan, still taking it in.[5]

"A question asked by everyone from the ancient Romans to *Star Trek*."

"A spook and a geek?"

"Guilty as charged ... but they had it right. It's the question that comes back every generation or so, the last time being when America's elections were rocked by the very same problem, prodded on by our Russian and then Gulf friends. The counterprogram took a couple years to fine-tune the legalities, but it's been running for quite a while now."

Keegan said nothing. The questions crashed together in her mind, and she tried to focus on which to ask first. What exactly did they know about her, and was she under investigation? Was there a threat inside the Bureau? What did CIA know about where the next attack would be? What came out was the question that could unlock many of these others: "Did TAMS know all along?"

"Of course not," Modi said. "We had nothing to do with the creation of that program or its activities, though I will admit it gave us a wealth of internal surveillance data far beyond the original expectations of our own collection plan."

Keegan thought about what that exactly meant in translation. Modi and the Agency had been monitoring everything that TAMS had seen and experienced. Including of her.

"What about you? Are you even a profiler?"

"Not exactly. I actually am a psychologist. Started out in SOCOM working computational understanding of humans, essentially using AI to understand how people are best influenced.[6] Moved over to the Agency after that. You can see why our sessions were so personally interesting to me."

"Glad to know I kept you entertained," she asked, making it clear she didn't appreciate being viewed as simply a unit of study for him. "I guess that explains the placement in Unit 5 then."

"In more ways than one. Being in the Behavioral Analysis group allowed us to monitor activity within the Bureau, but not directly be involved in a law enforcement operation, such as having to make arrests or testify. Keeps us on the right side of the law . . . supposedly." He smiled but had a resigned look. "Someone has to follow the law, even if it's the spies."

Keegan looked at the way he calmly rested his hands on the counter;

he wasn't worried what she thought. "Well, at least now I know why you threw out the bot I gave you."

"Yes, your 'gift' is right out of our playbook. It got swept up in a routine bug check. Caused quite the stir in Langley, people thinking the whole operation had been compromised. Fortunately, TAMS's feed showed you'd been placing them in your own home as well," he said, nodding over to the ones on the windowsill.

They'd been watching . . . everything. What else had they spied on?

Haley squealed in her bedroom, and Keegan smiled involuntarily at the thought of an analyst in a dark room at CIA headquarters having to watch Haley put on a stuffed-animal play for TAMS. Then she turned serious again. "How did you know about the rune tattoo? You figured that out before TAMS did."

"A prior assignment I'd worked for the Agency. After the assassinations and mass killings that happened everywhere from London to New Zealand to Pittsburgh, the directors of the allied Five Eyes nations intelligence services realized we had to treat the white nationalist phenomenon as a global extremist network, much as we did ISIS and then the Sons of Aleppo.[7] Same threat profile, same actions, same shitty ideology of hate and violence."[8]

"So what else didn't you tell us then? If you were tracking neo-Nazis . . . The ambush in Greene County — did you know that it was coming?"

Modi shook his head. "No, and if I had, I'd have found a way to warn HRT either through CIA or some other way. I know it may not feel like it, but we're on the same team. Heath, Jacobs, Todd, and their like are a cancer inside this country and they need to be cut out."

"OK then. What are you going to do about it?"

"Exactly what I just did," Modi said. "It has been decided to return TAMS to you. Or, at least a version of TAMS that will aid you in halting a domestic threat my agency is limited in our legal ability to intervene against any further." At that, he stood up from the counter and put the jammer in his pocket. He then reached across, took her hand, and placed a folded-up Watchlet in it.

"Like TAMS, it's in perfect working order, with all your data up to the last network backup." Another reminder they knew more about her than anyone else. "You can use the satellite uplink on the bot to work around the crashed local networks."

He left his hand on top of hers, though, a little bit longer than needed. Then he gave it a light squeeze, maybe out of affection, she thought, maybe just another attempt at manipulation.

"Lara, I know you have less reason to trust me now than ever before, but it has been a true pleasure working with you." He let go of her hand. "I really do mean that."

"And that's all you can say?"

"I guess so."

Modi let himself out of the apartment, leaving Keegan sitting alone at the counter. A moment later, her husband came into the living room.

"How much did you hear?" Keegan asked.

"Enough," he said, a slight hint of hurt in the tone. "What are you going to do now?"

"There's more attacks coming. I know it. I also think I know what I need to do, but I'm going to be on my own."

"What's that supposed to mean?"

"I'll have TAMS, or I guess a TAMS. But if I hook it back into the Bureau network, we'll probably be called in. Maybe worse."

He put his hands up. "Wait. Could this get you fired?"

"I don't know. I may already be."

"What do you mean?" said Jared. "Shouldn't that decide it for you?"

"It's not that simple," said Keegan, now thinking about how she faced a problem much like TAMS did every single moment it traveled through a human world. The right thing to do isn't always binary.

"Well, what do you do now that Modi is part of this?" He said it with a tone that betrayed a bit of suspicion, maybe even jealousy. "Do you trust him?"

"I'm not sure. Given the stakes, I think I have to."

"Maybe he's just setting you up. Did you think of that? Maybe this is to make you some kind of scapegoat."

"You mean, is the CIA behind it all?"

"Who the hell knows? This is your world," he said, offering a smile of acceptance.

"Alright then," said Keegan. "I hear you. Focus on Haley, that's the most important thing in the world you can do for me. I'll be back quick as I can, but no promises."

"Whatever you do, please make it quick. I don't know how long the two of us will be able to hold out without the feeds and stay sane. Plus, I want you to be the one who has to have the existential talk with Haley about Baz dying." That was the old Jared, using humor to deflect from the angst he must be feeling.

"Hopefully it doesn't come to that," she said. "Why don't you go up to the roof for a bit? Stars are out. It really is quite beautiful."

He smiled and gave her an appreciative look. "You should join us," he said quietly, maybe one last try.

"I need to finish this."

"I know," he said, and leaned in to give her a hug. He smelled faintly of the bay leaf cologne that she'd bought him as a Father's Day gift from Haley last year. He smelled of their life a long time ago, none of the fear of the world outside, or the buried anger inside.

He called Haley and the two of them headed up to the roof, the little girl leading the way with a long white candle in hand, as if leading a Christmas Eve procession.

Keegan went to the couch, leaving the Watchlet on the kitchen counter, as if to get it physically away from her. She could feel her back starting to lock up, so she moved to the floor and laid her head back, closed her eyes, and took a deep breath, trying to release the tension. Her mind swirled as she tried take it all in. Her back started to loosen up, but with it came a feeling of fatigue that was mentally and physically overwhelming. Knowing if she gave in to the feeling for any longer that she'd never get back up, Keegan stood and went over to the coffeemaker in the kitchen. There was no tiny red light on, though, reminding her of the power outage and all that remained to be set back in order.

She still needed to fortify herself for what was to come, so she poured herself a cup of the leftovers and took a sip of the bitter, room-temperature coffee.

Keegan asked herself one more time if she was really going to do this.

"OK, TAMS," she called out. "Time to stop playing with Haley's stuffed animals and get back to work. Come back in."

Leaning against the counter, she watched the machine walk in. It looked exactly the same as the system that she'd met that first day in the interrogation room. "You ready for this?" she asked, working to convince her brain to treat this new TAMS the same as the old one. It was a different kind of uncanny valley to cross that she'd never thought about before.

"Yes, I am fully operational," it replied.

"Good enough. Open up a connection from the Watchlet onto your sat comms network. Time to call in a favor." She slipped the device around her wrist and swiped through her personal contacts list. Of course the Agency had downloaded that too, she ruefully noted.

She pulled up Willow Shaw's information and opened an encrypted text chat.

What was she going to say? Keep it simple, she thought. It was all complex enough dealing with Shaw.

Need to speak.

After only five seconds, the bracelet vibrated and a video chat screen opened up. It showed rolling green hills bathed in the fading pinks of an ocean sunset. The timing meant it was somewhere on the West Coast. Maybe his estate. Or rather, she corrected herself, one of his estates.

"Agent Keegan, I wondered when you might call," Shaw said in a disembodied voice.

"That doesn't look like Washington."

"I'm at home. With all that is going on, I thought you might need something calming to look at."

She wondered if that too was the truth; he could be anywhere, just pushing out a different feed.

"Thank you. As you've probably seen, we're trying a different way of reconnecting to the natural state of things." She opened her Watchlet's lens and extended her arm, so it showed the kitchen sink, the candles, and then the darkness outside. Keegan wanted him to see up close what had happened to the city, reminding him that he'd never know what this was like in real life.

"I see that," said Shaw. "You will be glad to hear that the president has assured me that power will be restored within the next two days. Our own estimates are at least ninety-six hours, but it is still a storm that can be weathered."

"I don't think the real storm is over," said Keegan. "The threat against the Washington area, perhaps other cities, remains urgent."

"Yes, I have been briefed on that. In fact, the president's weighing martial law. Ostensibly the added military resources in the streets are to aid in recovery, but they would really be to stop Jackson Todd."

"It won't work," Keegan said.

"And why not?" said Shaw.

"They don't have TAMS."

"I was told the TAMS program was shut down," he said.

"Yes and no," she replied. "I have it back."

"That is an interesting development," he said, no visible evidence of surprise, but something Keegan guessed he hadn't been briefed on. "And you are letting me know because?"

"I have the tool, but not the data. The Bureau can't provide the kind of information we need." She left it vague, not specifying the real reason she didn't have access.

"Legally speaking, that is correct. So what you are asking for is the 'open kimono' package, full cloud search access?"[9]

"Yes. We need full access," said Keegan, not wanting to repeat the creepy phrase businesses used for open networks. "You said I had your support. This is the time."

"Three point five million dollars per minute," he said matter of factly.

"What?"

"Three point five million dollars per minute. That's what we charge client companies for access to that kind of data."

"I'm pretty sure you already know I can't afford that."

"Yes, I know that, and so much else, which is exactly what you are asking for here. We have more insight into every American than their own government does. Sensors in their vizglasses. Sensors in their heartburn medicine. Implants in their house. Implants near their kidneys. Chips in their cats. Chips in their *chips*. All that computing on what is becoming an endless edge of an ever-growing network then reporting back into the cloud anything and everything.[10] And then we are able to combine and mine that nearly infinite information to gain insights beyond people's wildest dreams. Sometimes even the most disturbing ones of their dreams, revelations of their psychology, the true dimensions of their personality, to the extent that the algorithm now knows more about them than even they do.[11] And, unlike what we charge the companies to get the fruits of it, people *give us* all that for free. Not just what they are doing and thinking, but how to change what they do and think.[12] They give us control of their lives, without reservation, in exchange for us giving them free access to the services and goods that we will charge them dearly for."

"There are literally thousands of lives on the line right now," said Keegan, not needing another lesson from Shaw on just how influential he was. "I think it's children's lives," she added, knowing that wouldn't sway him, but still needing to say it.

"Yes, Agent Keegan, this is the time, isn't it?" The view wavered and panned to show green fields, the sunset moving to the side. That kind of acreage in the world's most expensive zip code served as another reminder of how power now came from the control of information.

"People see who they want when they think of me and the work that I do, but they rarely understand its true purpose. My actions are felt profoundly, even if they are not widely known."

The screen pivoted to show Shaw's face, a smile emerging on it. He really had been there all the while. "This will be one of those times. I will give you what you need."

The condescension made Keegan bristle, which made her keep pushing. "Thank you. And one more thing — we need a vehicle. Something to get around a city gone to hell."

AMERICAN LEGION MEMORIAL BRIDGE

Washington, DC

They slalomed between the darkened cars abandoned on the bridge, their own lack of headlights making the graveyard of technology feel even more disconcerting.

The Range Rover Encounter steered itself through the shadows using a fly's-eyes mix of LIDAR, thermal cameras, and other sensors. It had driven itself to Keegan's condo not twenty minutes after her call with Shaw; she had no idea from where.

But it was exactly what they needed — military grade, albeit wrapped in luxury. She'd seen the ads. It was supposedly designed for rugged journeys exploring the world's last few unconnected zones, like a last-chance glacier safari in upper Greenland.[13] The reality was that it was mostly used by diplomats in war zones and dilettantes in suburbia. The sleek SUV melded an exterior of up-armored protection with interior features like the built-in champagne chiller mounted between the hand-stitched red leather seats.[14] More pertinent to tonight's drive, the Encounter had a diesel engine and drive-by wire control system hardened against pulse waves and a massive antenna meshed into the roof itself, providing a Navy warship's equivalent of bandwidth to pull down from a dedicated satellite connection. Typically used by rich kids to stream VR games in the back seat without suffering the indignity of a microsecond pause in download; tonight, it would be used to mine Shaw's world-spanning cloud database, searching through zetabytes of information every second.

"Alright, start searching through the cloud for anything you can that is relevant to our investigation," Keegan said out loud, partly as a command and partly to get used to talking to the new TAMS in the same way. "We know Todd's going for something that has to do with the tenth plague, Death of the Firstborn. That's the big one, the one that finally convinced the pharaoh to let Moses's people go. Between that and the symbolism, it likely has something to do with kids."

"That aligns with current model projections," TAMS said.

Keegan wondered if she should think of it as TAMS or TAMS-2. And then she just set it aside. It was a TAMS with the same data and same memories, just up to the point that she'd turned it off.

"We also know Todd still has access to Preston's automation software," she said. "Check what matches up, cross-referencing large populations of minors and current implementation of systems based on Preston's code."

"OK," said TAMS. "Would you like me to include past implementations?"

"Yes, good call," Keegan said, noting how it had packaged the suggestion that she had given the wrong command as a polite request. Was this another one of the user-interface updates from the other FBI field offices' TAMS that she'd just not noticed before? Or was it a feature only of wherever Modi had gotten this one from? "Just because somebody installed Preston's software once and never updated it, doesn't mean they aren't still using it."

The machine plugged itself into the vehicle's entertainment port for even faster access to Shaw's cloud network. Keegan snorted a laugh at the sight of its metallic arms on the luxury vehicle's passenger-side pullout table made of rare rosewood. "And don't scratch the trim; I'm not sure I can afford the deductible."

"OK," said TAMS, keeping its arms still, meaning it had already run those calculations.

The air warmed slightly as TAMS ran its searches. The machine occasionally emitted a faint hum as it opened up each new layer of data in Shaw's cloud.

Keegan could do little but wait, so she pulled the car to a stop at the halfway point of the bridge. It was as logical a place as any, as they literally didn't know which side of the river Todd was on. Looking out into the abyss-like darkness of the waters below made it feel like the potential places were just as infinite as the data.

"There are 152 children between the ages of eight and seventeen at a Red Cross disaster relief shelter established at the National Zoo," said TAMS, starting to report matches. "The National Zoo operations center utilizes Professor Preston's open-source automation software."

Keegan shook her head. "Not it," she said. "Tigers aren't the problem. It's technology that has to be the killer."

TAMS identified another connection point. "There are 167 children of indeterminate age from Baltimore, recently loaded onto three Star Choice LLC school buses. They are traveling to an aid facility set up at the US Naval Academy in Annapolis, which uses the software in its network as well."

"Something Defense Department related could be significant," she mused, pulling off the pair of tortoiseshell and titanium vizglasses fastened into the charging clips on the ceiling. Shaw had certainly provided the whole package, all she needed to work, in a bubble of luxury. It wasn't a sign of added care; rather, the network of support built around the superrich couldn't even contemplate anything else.

The lens projected the data stream pulled from Shaw's Kloud-Sky network. Keegan's vision filled with everything from social media posts by the kids on the bus to satellite tracking of the vehicles' movement history, derived from rider activity metadata over the last several years. Was this what it felt like to be Shaw, an infinite amount of other peoples' data to be mined to your own personal purpose?

"They're already past Bowie," Keegan said. "And each bus has a human driver. Doesn't seem to fit the profile of Todd's attacks so far."

But just what was that profile? Not just the means but the ends? Everything Todd had done so far had pulled on the thread of human powerlessness, the sense that death could be random, but only when ascribed to a machine's actions, not a person's. The machines — really, the code running it — would have to be the ones taking lives.

TAMS moved on to a new cluster of data. "There are ninety-three newborn infants at the National Neonatal Intensive Care Unit of Children's Hospital, which relies on —"

Her sharp intake of breath and rapid rise in pulse rate were enough to prompt the machine to dive further. Without being asked, a satellite image of the hospital popped into her lens view.

"That's a hell of a lot of preemies for one hospital," she said. "Why so many at that one NICU?"

The vizglasses then changed to a map of Washington, DC, marked by a series of overlapping circles, showing the blast effects of the power outages. A series of dots then emerged, the locations of the area's hospitals, most of them inside the circles. "Multiple area hospitals were taken offline in the recent power outages," TAMS summarized. "Emergency services have moved their patients to parallel units at any nearby operative hospitals, along with their equipment."

"How does it overlap with the threat profile?"

"Patient care in the NICU is coordinated by a system that automatically registers patient identity and manages their condition and treatment. Among its capabilities are oxygen-level monitoring and drug delivery.[15] This system's software is also open-source algorithms originally created by Preston."

TAMS shifted Keegan's visual to display the hospital's operating system, showing the patient records as multicolored lollipop-like icons within an administrative form layout. Rather than the customary images of faces, however, the accompanying picture for each patient was just a barcode. She realized they were the identifiers worn on their ankle bands. Human babies' faces were too mashed up for facial recognition software to register them yet, plus they were just data in some form to the network anyway.

"However, the systems are air-gapped from the Internet and have asynchronous cloud access," the robot explained.

"So, Todd would have to be at the hospital in person . . . I see four in the map outside the affected areas."

The map rebuilt itself, with the functional hospitals highlighted, and a graph stacking up the number of patients in their NICUs.

"Children's National has the largest number, followed by Fairfax, Georgetown University, and Sibley," TAMS reported.

Dammit, they were spread all over the city. Which one? Children's National had the most cases, making it the most damaging target to hit. But Fairfax was on the same side of the river as Todd's house, easier for him to reach while on the run.

As Keegan churned through the parameters, TAMS highlighted Georgetown University Hospital, overlaying it with a photo of a tiny baby linked up to a respirator, clearly taken through a window. Then, it projected a second photo of a tired, smiling mother in a wheelchair, holding a baby as she was being wheeled out through a pair of sliding glass doors.

"KloudSky records include photos of Todd's son and wife posted online fourteen years ago," it said. "Metadata markers show their upload was made via a wireless network run by Georgetown University Information Services. Subsequent credit card company records confirm Todd making multiple purchases at the Georgetown University Hospital gift shop."

Keegan knew that hospital. She knew that NICU. "Haley was born there," she said quietly, trying not to personalize it but unable to avoid it. The memory of that NICU was as much a part of her as her time in the Sandbox, and ten times as scary. The image forever seared into her brain was of Haley's glassy eyes and button nose, all that peeked out from the light blue plastic thermal wrap and cotton that cocooned her inside the machines that kept her alive.

"Yes," TAMS said, matter of fact in its knowledge of all the moments in her life.

"How many?" she whispered, her mind coming to grips with it.

"There are presently seventy-seven infants in the Georgetown University Hospital NICU."

Across her field of vision, the lollipop-like icons reappeared, then their demographics. Thirty-two boys. Forty-five girls. She shifted in her seat at the realization of how many lives not yet lived depended on this decision. "Georgetown Hospital seems the most likely then?" she asked.

The machine responded immediately. "Yes. It is a probabilistic exploration, but that is what the model indicates."

"Whatever you want to call it, it's little better than a hunch . . . But that's what good agents sometimes have to do."

Even if they were wrong, the machine might as well learn from the experience.

GEORGETOWN NEIGHBORHOOD

Washington, DC

As the Encounter drove itself through the closely packed row houses of Georgetown, Keegan let her eyes wander, taking in the two sides of the tragedy, evident just from the outside of people's homes. In the glimpse of an elderly man in a sleeping bag, curled up on his porch, probably too fearful to be in the same room with machines that couldn't be trusted. Through the next-door house's living room window, a mother reading a book to her kids by candlelight, seizing the opportunity to reconnect while all other connections had gone down. "There'll be a lot of memorable family moments made tonight . . . as long they don't accidentally burn down the city," Keegan thought to herself.

As they drove farther up to Georgetown Heights, into the wealthier part of the neighborhood, the row homes turned into mansions. Keegan caught sight of the running lights of a large National Guard octocopter loitering overhead. TAMS marked it as providing network connectivity, an emergency deployed hot spot. Not surprising, Keegan thought, that the politically connected were the first ones to be reconnected.

TAMS broke the silence. "I have now obtained an answer to your query on the date of April 28."

"What?" Keegan asked. TAMS must be choking down all the data in Shaw's cloud, churning through all the vestigial requests, in this case from literally days back. "What was my question?"

"During the operation to arrest Gregory Heath, you inquired about a real estate transaction."

"Huh?"

Noah Reddy's voice then echoed out of TAMS's speaker. "This really is beautiful land, though." Keegan's stomach clinched as she relived her last moments with her friend.

"It is. Doesn't seem fair," she heard her own voice say. "TAMS, just how did these fuckers afford a place like this?"

TAMS turned to face her and then said in its distinctive monotone, "With my increased access to data, I can now answer that question."

"You're scouring real estate records?" Keegan could not conceal her annoyance at the waste of TAMS's processing power. That was the problem of putting parallel computing into a cloud that big, all the queries running off in different directions.

"Yes, I have also achieved access to additional financial and legal data through the broader private cloud accounts provided by Mr. Shaw."

"Not the time, TAMS. We have a more important investigation."

"This information is relevant to our investigation," TAMS replied.

"OK. What'd you find out that's so important then?"

"There were four Cayman Islands–registered shell companies involved in the real estate transaction: PS2 LLC; Brilliance LLC; SCIKITE LLC; KronoGraf LLC," TAMS said, as it projected a series of records and lines linking legal documents. "The purchase followed a sequential transaction, which originated with a Bitcoin mining collective, Militas Mining." A line then connected to highlighted text from the Todd investigation file. "An offshore bank account at Can-Fin Global was accessed by a server in the geographic location of Todd's neighborhood. This account received four deposits from Militas Mining, using them in the purchase of nanocomposite paper sheets. These are of the type utilized in the design of the improvised electronic pulse weapon used by Todd."

"Makes sense," she said. "They're all part of the same conspiracy. That really doesn't answer the question of where they got the money, though."

The Encounter braked hard. Keegan tapped the screen to find out why; the bumper-level night-vision cameras revealed a makeshift barricade blocking the road. It looked like lawn equipment lashed together, obviously built by somebody who had never built a roadblock. Their first venture into a new kind of politics. They'd soon get the hang of it if Todd wasn't stopped. Maybe it was too late.

"What is notable," said TAMS continuing on, "is that Militas Mining was set up by VDO Associates." Further lines connected to new dots. "It is an algorithmic law firm that has worked on seventeen merger and acquisition transactions for companies owned by Willow Shaw."

Her face was easy for the robot to read.

"Your biometric profile indicates an adverse reaction to this information," TAMS said.

"A strong one," said Keegan.

She wanted to pull over to the side of the road and think for a minute. Instead, she took control of the vehicle's steering wheel and drove it directly toward the barrier. The Encounter's underbody skid plate ground on metal as it rose slightly and then crashed back down, smashing an edge trimmer under its tires.

She set the vehicle back on autodrive to continue to the hospital.

Link analysis led analysts astray all the time, she thought. It was also how so many wing-nut conspiracies had been fueled, cloud crawler algorithms building connections between countless events that had no real ties. Elvis and a lunar helium farm that somehow connected to Hitler and the Deep State. The same could be the case for the law firm and the hidden transactions, just connections made literally out of digital noise. But it didn't feel like that.

"Damn," she muttered to herself. Why would Shaw, as much a pro-technology and societal transformation zealot as anybody she had ever met, be behind a campaign to derail the very advances he'd worked his whole life to spread?

It didn't make sense. Unless it did and she just wasn't getting it yet.

"Do you have anything else?" she asked. "Anything else at all you've learned from accessing Shaw's network that identifies other persons of interest in our investigation?"

"Yes," said TAMS.

"And?"

From the car's speakers, Justin Timberlake's "Can't Stop the Feeling" began softly playing. "With expanded cloud access, I now understand your reaction to this song when it played during one of our training cycles," said TAMS. "I also now understand the context of this subsequent statement."

Jared's voice then spoke from the car speakers. "That machine is going to find out more than you want it to." As it played, Keegan's viz displayed a historic chart of her biometric data, showing a previously unexplained spike at that moment.

Keegan took off the glasses, as her vision narrowed and pulse began to pound in her ears. She looked away from the robot and caught her reflection in the driver-side window. Shadow veiled her forehead and brow, but the whites of her eyes glared back. She had dreaded this moment for over a decade, but had to decide in an instant what to do next.

"And what do you now understand?" she asked, trying to keep her voice even.

"There are critical anomalies in your personnel records," said TAMS.

"How so?" she asked, limiting her words to avoid giving TAMS any more data to churn.

"Expanded cloud access revealed anomalous correspondence between yourself and Mr. Shelby Brown, as well as the contents of his cloud. Your combined data and timeline activity indicate that you are both persons of interest in an open case in Washington State, an un-solved homicide at the University of Washington Tacoma on the date of—"

"Stop." She shifted in her seat to look squarely at the robot. "You pulled this from Shaw's proprietary database?"

"Yes."

"Not an FBI algo or data set?"

"Correct," said TAMS. "I presently only have access to the Kloud-Sky network."

And that set the timer of the ticking bomb that would destroy her life. The microsecond that TAMS linked back into the FBI's network, it would automatically download its findings.

She leaned back in her seat, feeling the metal of the multi-tool press into her hip. The sound of Noah's voice playing in the car's speaker brought back the memory of the advice that he'd given back at the shooting range.

Never go into battle with a bot you can't trust and never trust a bot you don't know how to snuff out.

Perhaps TAMS would not even realize what was happening before it began to overheat and cook its own chips. Or, maybe it would, but wouldn't care.

"Your biometric profile indicates acute stress," said TAMS. "Is there anything that you need assistance with?"

16

GEORGETOWN UNIVERSITY HOSPITAL

Washington, DC

The Georgetown University internal medicine intern chewed harder, trying to get one last boost out of the cherry-flavored stim gum. The whole day had been chaos for the junior physician, the Emergency Department flooded by every type of case possible. Some were directly caused by the power outages that had hit the city, while others were from its ripple effects, like the rash of broken bones from people tripping down dark stairs.

That was probably the case with the patient on the gurney. The old guy in mud-streaked green corduroy pants was a walk-in, so they didn't have a run sheet from the ambulance. But it looked like he had somehow managed to fall face-first through a plate glass window. A band of ravaged skin slashed across his face, with a laceration dividing his left eyebrow, while his right check was swollen with an even dozen short rough gashes. His left hand had another slash on it, maybe from breaking his fall on the glass. At least most of the cuts weren't too deep, as if made by the kind of knife her dad used to fillet the fish he caught on Lake Anna. She couldn't remember what it was exactly called, she was that tired.

"Sir, I need to fill out a form for you. What is your name?"

The patient looked back blankly at her and shook his head. Then he started to speak slowly. Each word was in some kind of Eastern European accent, distorted by the grimace of agony that he made to get it out. He moaned, "Pain. Help."

"What? Is? Your? Name?" she said louder. Then she shook her head at what she'd just done, realizing she was being the Ugly American.

The man only shook his head in confusion, then gripped the metal bars of the gurney as if trying to control the hurt.

One of the nurses came over, the one that she knew hated interns, thinking they lacked enough experience to be useful and just got in the way. The nurse wiped her hands on her pink scrubs, as if wanting to be rid of the intern and her inefficiency. She was maybe only a year or two older, but while the aspiring doctor had been traveling to Cancun, writing med school applications, and studying in classrooms, the nurse had been working in this very hospital.

With an audible sigh, the nurse reached up and tightened her ponytail, separating it into two pieces and pulling, as if preparing herself for the long night ahead. Only then did she speak to the intern.

"What the hell are you screaming at a patient for?"

"I need to know his name for the system, but I don't think he speaks English. He was a walk-in and the facial ID admissions scanner's not working, because, you know," she said tilting her head at the man. He likely wouldn't understand, but it still didn't seem right to say out loud that all the cuts had changed the geographic markers of his face.

"*Cómo te llamas?*" the nurse asked the man. As if the doctor didn't know Spanish herself.

He looked blankly from the nurse to the intern and back and then shook his head. "Pain. Help," he said again.

"That doesn't sound like a Spanish accent," the nurse said.

The intern took a breath, remembering not to come off as uppity to the nurse. The last thing she wanted to do was get that reputation. It'd come back to bite her in the ass later on, not just with this nurse, but every one of her colleagues. "It sounds East European, maybe," she said, trying to say it with a helpful tone. "I can run through all the languages with the translation app and see which one?"

"Skip it," the nurse said. "Enter him as a John Doe for now and the records software will figure it out later. You need to keep things moving along. But make sure he gets a CT stat."

"Thanks. Good advice; don't get bogged down."

"You need an attending to help?" the nurse asked.

"No, I got it," she replied, and then added "Thank you," one more time just to be safe.

As the nurse moved down the hallway, the intern turned back to the man. "Don't worry, Mr. Doe, we'll get you patched up soon enough," she said in what she hoped was a calming, confident tone. She wiped away the blood and then showed him the needle of lidocaine. "First I'm going to help you out a bit with the pain . . . For pain. Help."

He nodded.

She inserted the needle into the main laceration, pressing slightly to inject the painkiller. He was a head trauma, so she didn't want to sedate him, just numb the points of most intense pain. She made several more injections at each of the largest cuts and then started to treat them, some with stitches, some with glue, and the smaller ones just using butterfly strips to close them. He was a tough old dude, who probably could have put up with old-school stitches. The second that she had started to work, a calm had come over him; his eyes tracked each of her moves, but he never flinched.

After she was done, John Doe's face was a patchwork of bandages. Before she left, she rechecked his pulse, even as the automatic diagnostic features of the gurney evaluated the patient. With all the ways the tech had gone screwy the past few days, she felt like she had to be sure herself. His heart rate was 47 beats per minute, which stopped her. A resting rate that low wasn't necessarily dangerous, but more apt for a yoga instructor or professional athlete than an old guy who'd just gone through a trauma. It showed 48 the next time. Just to be safe, she shined a light in his eyes, seeing how they reacted. She checked his eyes with a flashlight and had him visually track her finger but did not seem to find any telltale signs of a concussion. If anything, it was abnormal the way his eyes held steady the whole time.

Seeing the nurse start to come back down the hallway, she recognized she'd lingered too long. "All done, Mr. Doe. They'll come for you soon and get everything sorted out." She gave him a gentle pat on the hand, hoping he got what she meant.

The patient nodded and lay back on the gurney, closing his eyes. It was probably a good thing he couldn't understand everything that was going on in the city; at least one person had found peace in all the chaos.

Jackson Todd waited thirty seconds until after the young doctor left to sit back up, counting the seconds in his head. Then he opened his eyes.

She'd done a good job, far better than he'd hoped. The bandages pulled at his skin, but he did not register the feeling as pain, certainly not after the agony of making that first cut into his own face. The intensity of that moment — the feel of the knife in his hand, the sight of his blood drops splashing onto the side of the kayak — was receding into the background, the way a nightmare is only hazily recalled but the primal feeling of fear during the dream is never forgotten.

He looked around the hallway, checking that the intern and nurse were nowhere to be seen, and got down off the gurney. He pulled out the backpack he'd stored beneath, still streaked with mud. Slinging it over his shoulder, he moved slowly at first, the shuffle of someone uncertain where they should go. He exited the Emergency Department through the double doors and turned down one hallway and then the next, moving as if he was looking for a destination that he didn't know, before finally entering a restroom.

Five minutes later, he emerged wearing a white doctor's coat, clean pants, and an ID badge. With a confident step, he took the stairs up to the third floor, exiting into the waiting room for the Neonatal Intensive Care Unit. The paint and furniture of the NICU were all muted colors — light tans, yellows, and greens. It was an earthy palette designed to soothe. On the other side of a thick glass viewing window, curtained partitions framed rows of bubble-like incubators.

Todd walked through quickly, lest any of the parents there, lingering over their infants with looks of satisfaction and uncertainty, stop him to ask a question. At the far end, the glass security doors into the facility opened, automatically sweeping inward in welcome. In another era, all he would have needed was the coat to pass through the entire building. Yet even the security badge's electronic permission, sent via an RFID signal that he'd coded himself, would not be enough to get any farther without passing another test.

Stationed at the desk just beyond the door was a young nurse with pink fingernails decorated with unicorns. "Can I help you? All visiting staff still need to register."

He watched her eyes dart back and forth from his face to the badge on his white coat. Then, instinctively, she inhaled quickly, her hand going to her mouth, as she imagined the painful injuries the doctor must have suffered. Working in the NICU, she only dealt with the emotional trauma of parents, not the physical kind before her.

"It's that bad, isn't it?" Todd asked.

At that she looked slightly embarrassed, focusing away from his bandages and back on the name and photo, which would further reinforce their validity in her mind. She would want to avoid causing further offense to "Erik Reed," a visiting pediatrics fellow from Johns Hopkins.

"No, not at all, Dr. Reed."

"There's no need to sugarcoat it," Todd replied. "I count myself lucky. Baltimore is . . . a heartbreak."

"Are those from the . . . chemical burns?" the nurse asked, then instantly regretted her curiosity.

He shook his head. "No, fortunately not that. It happened in the chaos that came after. When the gas cloud hit Baltimore, I was on my way down here for a study review meeting with Dr. Tomkins" — he name-dropped a senior doctor in the hospital — "who is coordinating on how environmental factors impact critical-care outcomes in the NICU." He patted his messenger bag. "So it was this project I have to thank for saving my life."

"That's amazing," she said, eager to draw some tiny bit of good from the bad that felt so overwhelming. "You need anything?"

"No, I tried to remotely upload the study's data, but it's not working. I just need to quickly access the local data files; I already have the code."

As she swiped his badge and buzzed him through, Todd waited for her to sneak one more glance at his face and looked directly back at her, forcing her to maintain the gaze.

"It may look bad," he said. "But I know I've been blessed with this opportunity. It came at a cost, which is why it is so important to finish the task."

GEORGETOWN UNIVERSITY HOSPITAL

Washington, DC

Stepping through the entrance to the Emergency Department brought back a rush of memories. The last time Keegan had been there was when a Sunday afternoon trip to the mall for new baby clothes had instantly transformed with her first early labor pain, followed by an hour-by-hour fight to keep her newborn daughter alive.

Tonight, she tried to bury that feeling of panic. She could deal with the shitstorm that TAMS was going to unleash on her life after this all was over. She had to trust right now that it too could prioritize Todd's capture as their most important objective. Todd was no longer just their prime suspect in the attacks; he was now the potential key to unlocking something much bigger.

The waiting area inside the ED was barely controlled chaos. Wall screens blinked on and off, flashing images of the flood and blackout while nurses triaged patients, recording vitals and chief complaints in the race to see who needed to be seen first. Family members of unseen patients pleaded with blood- and mud-covered doctors hurrying in and out of the waiting area.

Keegan scanned the area for Todd's face, but nothing popped. At the far end of the waiting room, she spied a security guard blocking the doorway to the patient-care area. She strode toward him with intent, TAMS following at the normal distance she'd instructed it. That was good, she thought; a visual confirmation of Modi's claim the new body still had all the old memories.

"I'm Agent Lara Keegan, FBI. I need access to your facility." She showed him her ID and badge. "We believe there's a threat to the hospital."

The guard wore a black nylon jacket with "SECURITY" in large yellow letters, an outfit he'd attempted to up-armor himself with knee and elbow guards and a black ballistic vest missing its protective plates. Squinting back at her through smudged black-framed AR glasses, he reacted as if she'd come to lodge a noise complaint about a too-loud dorm-room party. "There's a threat to everything today, Agent Kagan," he said.

"It's Keegan," she said. "And this is different. We have a high-threat individual who we believe may be inside your facility."

He hooked his thumbs into his belt, leather creaking. "And they just sent you? And this, uh, thing?"

"We're stretched thin, just like you guys," she said.

"You got a picture of your person of interest? Let's start with that." She looked at TAMS and nodded.

The guard's eyes lost focus on hers as he looked at Todd's driver's license photo projected onto his lens. "Haven't seen him. If he's here, he didn't come by me."

"That's good news," she said, not wanting to pop the campus cop's bubble at how out of his league he was against Todd. "But we'll still need to access the entire hospital's facial recognition systems. Our guy could have come through any of the entrances."

"Yeah, that's not going to be possible," he replied. "Student government voted a campus-wide policy of no face rec sharing with law enforcement.[1] The cameras here collect it for the patient service and staff access authorization, but after that all the faces get fuzzed over.

A comp sci student updates the program each year for their senior thesis."

"You gotta be kidding me," Keegan fumed. "Can your IT folks at least share over the pixilated feed?"

"Yeah, we can get them to do that."

"Thanks," she said.

He looked down and spoke into a mic mounted on his vest. "Wait a second . . ." the cop said.

A cold blast of adrenaline shot down Keegan's spine. In getting the feed from the campus security, had they just tripped a notice to main FBI?

"I know you," he said. "The bot too. You're the one from that rooftop perp chase, the subway, and all that."

"Yeah, that's us," Keegan said.

"No wonder you're all that they sent," he said enthusiastically. "That video of the beatdown you did on those dudes at the Mall . . . Ruthless! How did it feel to lay someone out like —"

"Agent Keegan," said TAMS. "There is an urgent message for you."

She turned to the machine, thankful for the interruption, but wondering why it was notifying her verbally when it could have popped it on her vizglasses.

"I am sorry, officer," said TAMS. "It is urgent and requires privacy."

"No worries at all," the guard said. "You can go on through. I'm posted down here for the next six hours. Your guy won't get past me." Then he looked at TAMS and smiled. "Just don't go beating up too many people . . . without me."

"OK," TAMS said. The robot turned and walked to the far end of the area, toward an alcove that, for the moment, was only occupied with an empty patient's bed. "I have obtained network access to the hospital video surveillance system," said TAMS.

"Why didn't you just push the info to my lens?" Keegan asked.

"It appeared that you required an exit from the conversation," TAMS said.

It was right. And it also meant that the CIA had provided its TAMS with a few added protocols, including the ability to deceive. Such a feature made perfect sense for an intelligence-community machine; hell, it made sense for any social interaction with humans.[2] But she wasn't sure how comfortable she was with a robot that could tell even a little white lie.

"New command protocol," she instructed. "When on operations with me, do not speak false information unless I specifically authorize it."

"OK," TAMS said.

But now that she knew the machine could tell a lie, how could she be certain its response was the truth? She buried that riddle. Now wasn't the time.

"Display what you have," she said, and multiple windows of streaming video popped up in her vizglasses, showing views of the lobby, hallways, parking garage, and various departments. In each, hundreds of evident hospital staff, patients, and visitors moved back and forth, their faces all with the same smear of pixilation.

"Anything you can do about the anonymizer?" she asked, hopeful that TAMS's neural networks would be able to find the underlying patterns in the obscuring mosaics of digital noise.[3]

"No," the machine replied. "It has been designed with interception in mind, using a combination of three-stage quantum cryptography and blockchain principles.[4] Even if decryption were possible, any change of the pixilation will result in a change of the underlying image itself."

"I guess they got an A on their senior thesis then," Keegan muttered to herself.

"Yes," TAMS replied.

She shook her head at the sheer amount of knowledge it had access to and instructed, "Show me the schematics of the hospital and cross-match any activity from the cloud that connects to the NICU."

A 3-D rendering of the hospital structure built on her screen. A cluster of the anonymized faces in the third floor began to be overlaid with data points. Different colored tags marked everything from an individual who had NICU work history on their online resume to someone wearing a Watchlet that posted social media images geo-tagged to the NICU's location.

"We need to winnow it down," Keegan said. "Pull out anyone who's not tagged and doesn't fit any personal identifying features we know of Todd."

At a sweep, scores of figures were erased from the screen, every pixilated human body without a data point disappearing. Then, wave after wave of deletions played out in more staggered form. Mothers-to-be disappeared like apparitions, but the children they held, and those lying in protected warmers, remained. After a few seconds, the children's figures evaporated as well. Within a few seconds, all that was left after the data-driven rapture was a hospital of just under a hundred men.

"It's still too many," said Keegan. "Is there anything that ties them together?"

Seconds passed before TAMS spoke. "Of the remaining possible suspects, there are two main clusters with limited overlap. The first is the use of password-protected network stations or other secured systems."

"Hospital staff. Pull out anyone who's made multiple entries before tonight."

Roughly half the bodies disappeared from the screen.

"The second cluster has made phone calls from the hospital during the past sixty minutes. Based on direct-access database analysis, they have been contacting individuals with whom they have tightly meshed social connections, close family and friends."

"New dads," Keegan said. "Delete them."

At once, the remaining bodies faded from the image. All that was left was a single man in a doctor's coat, his face obscured by a mosaic of black, gray, and white dots, leaving the NICU.

17

GEORGETOWN UNIVERSITY HOSPITAL

Washington, DC

The choice was seemingly a binary one:

Save the children. Stop a mass murderer. Which was more important?

Keegan weighed the outcomes over mere microseconds, infinitesimal calculations factoring in everything from the certainty of the number of children in the NICU to the untold catastrophes that might follow if Todd went free. But then cutting through it all was the realization that she was no mere calculating machine. It didn't have to be a binary choice, if she was willing to give to a machine that most human gift of all. Not trust that TAMS would do what she expected, but trust that it would do the right thing on its own.

"I'll follow Todd and you go to the NICU," she commanded. If they had to split up, she had to admit to herself that TAMS was better suited to figure out whatever Todd had done there.

She reached out to grasp the robot by the shoulders. She could only hope it had learned enough to register that signal as something more than mere tactile pressure. "TAMS, stop whatever attack Todd has planned against those kids. I'm trusting you to save them."

"OK."

It bolted through the Emergency Department waiting room, followed by surprised shouts and cries of anger as it weaved between patients and staff.

Keegan pulled up directions that marked the quickest route in the building to cross paths with Todd. Following the line of small green arrows projected in her field of view, she sprinted down the hallway.

As she ran, she tried to check in on TAMS, blinking open onto her viz a POV shot from the machine's forward-facing cameras. All it showed was a disorienting picture of jarring motion, maybe a stairwell, maybe another hallway. Before she could shift back to the 3-D building map to mark its position, she stumbled, tripping over a wheelchair folded up against the wall that she'd missed in her focus on the machine's mission, and not her own. She struggled to stay upright as the impact jarred her spine and her leg took the weight of the fall at an odd angle. Numbness started to creep up her leg, and she grabbed the handrail that ran along the hallway to steady herself for a moment.

As Keegan took off again at a slower jog, she double-blinked to close the window on her vizglasses. It was time to take the training wheels off. Whatever TAMS did, it'd have to do it without her watching.

For TAMS, it was now as much a race through the digital world as it was through the hospital itself.

As the machine ran toward the NICU, its physical sensors detected obstacles and projected optimal pathways freed from human limitations. Its feet sprang off positions on the floor selected for their greater traction by minute reflections of light off the tile, while its fingers reached out to press against food trolleys, gurneys, and water fountains, anything to give extra speed.

Rounding a corner, the bot's camera detected the foot of a bed being wheeled into the hallway by a knee-high orderly bot and determined that its speed and direction would intersect with its own path.[1] Rather than stopping, TAMS leaped, one foot extending onto the hallway railing, the other pivoting to step onto the wall itself. As it passed over the gurney, literally running up the side of the wall to keep its maximum pace, the patient below began to wonder about the side effects of her pain meds.

At the very same moment of its physical movements forward to its target, TAMS's analytic systems were moving backward through the video trail of Todd. Layers of neural networks deconstructed the footage of the pixilated man's movements through the hospital, battling away to identify any anomalous behavior compared with that of all the other human-sized objects in the NICU's video history. In less than two seconds, it identified a marker moment from just before it identified Todd. Imagery showed the blurred man pulling a small tablet computer out of his backpack. He typed on it for a few moments, inserted a cable, and then slid it into one of the bedside monitors next to one of the human-sized objects, digitally identified by a barcode tag on their left ankle.

Running profile matches to Todd's prior attacks, TAMS's network analysis determined that the imagery time stamp matched that of a software download into the hospital control systems managing the facility's liquid oxygen supply. As it ran calculations of how long it would take for the download to complete and for the software's embedded instructions to force an explosion of the highly combustible gas, the emotional burden of the prospect of the entire neonatal wing of the hospital — every newborn baby, parent, and staff member — being consumed in a fiery blast did not factor into its calculations. Yet now TAMS understood the stakes in a different way: the specific outcome that had to be prevented in order to complete Keegan's command.

When it entered the waiting room, TAMS pulled up short before the NICU ward entrance. A few parents started to murmur at the unaccompanied machine's sudden arrival. It looked nothing like the hospital bots, designed to appear docile and approachable. The murmurs grew louder when its lower legs extended an entire foot to give the machine an elevated position to see their children through the viewing window.

Now able to assess the NICU with its own sensors, TAMS confirmed Todd was already gone. It pushed the information to Keegan but judged any other action on that pathway of the decision tree to be of lesser priority to its ordered task. The robot then ran multiple simulations on the expected time of standard human pathways and found none that allowed it to meet its overall goal. Punching its left fist forward, TAMS shattered the viewing window. Parents screamed as glass rained down. Their shouts intensified as the robot vaulted through the broken frame into the NICU.

Ignoring the screams of the families in the waiting room behind it, the robot stalked between the incubators. Its audio sensor picked up a baby at the far end of the room crying with the desperate and breathless high-pitched mewing of helplessness. TAMS leapt over one warmer and loomed over the plastic incubator. Inside was a small boy, wearing a barcode bracelet around his ankle. The unique design of thin and thick black lines matched what TAMS had observed in the video footage, identifying the human as "Mark Rezak," two months old, born premature at twenty-three weeks, weighing 658 grams.

As TAMS lifted the lid on the warmer, an adult ran into the room. She wore clothing that corresponded to the records of hospital staff and a name tag that read "Karina." This matched a "Karina Eggers" in the hospital files, who was assigned as a nurse to the NICU, which was soon confirmed by a facial recognition match with her Virginia driver's license and several online dating sites.

"No!" screamed the human identified as Karina Eggers, as TAMS scoured the cloud for any and all information on her, pulling down everything from job history to her complaints on social media about a last date gone bad. It determined she was not authorized to issue command orders to deviate from Keegan's instructions.

TAMS dropped the incubator lid, which hit the floor with a clatter, causing the baby Mark Rezak to cry at a 23 percent higher volume. With its right hand, TAMS extended its fingers into a cradle-like claw and lifted the infant from its warmer. A tangle of blue and white wires hung down from the child, back into the incubator's monitors.

Following the nurse, another human entered the room. Facial recognition matched her to a driver's license for Sheryl Root, age forty-four, of Silver Spring, Maryland, as well as the state registry for a personal weapon. This was further confirmed when the gun that she was registered for in the state database matched the outline of the weapon that TAMS detected in the human's hand, a Smith & Wesson M&P 9 with a laser sight mounted under the barrel.

"Stop right there!" Root shouted, raising the gun. While TAMS registered the text "SECURITY" on the front of the second human adult's black jacket, neither Sheryl Root's uniform or online history empowered her as an official agent of law enforcement, able to command its operations. TAMS then judged the threat from the observed weapon. Self-preservation was determined to be secondary to its mission. It continued with its prior decided course of action, but with a slight modulation of a pivot of its torso, so as to place itself between the projected bullet trajectory and the loudly crying human child.

The shot now clear, the security guard laid her finger down on the trigger. A tiny red dot from the pistol's laser sight appeared on what would be the face of the robot, the red light splashing slightly across the smooth surface.

The guard's finger began to press down on the trigger, taking a breath to hold the dot steady. In that one moment of stillness, she heard the sound of a woman's voice. It had the lilting cadence of a mother singing a lullaby.

You are my sunshine, my only sunshine
You make me happy when skies are gray[2]

As the voice sang from its onboard speakers, the robot's hand slowly began to rock the baby in a swaying motion. With its other arm, it reached into the warmer and pulled out a blue cable connecting to a tablet.

"Just . . . stop right there," said the guard, not knowing what else to say.

The nurse stepped in front of the red laser target and slowly walked toward TAMS. "I can take him," she said, her arms out.

"OK," TAMS said, responding in a digital voice that was discordant from the music. The nurse froze for a moment, but then took the baby from the machine and wrapped it in a warming blanket.

With Todd's command code prevented from being completely downloaded, TAMS assessed that Keegan's primary task instruction had been fulfilled. It searched for Todd's present location and found him on the rooftop of the hospital, detecting that Keegan was in the stairwell, climbing toward the same position. Without another word, TAMS turned to join them, vaulting back through the broken glass. As the robot ran down the hallway, however, it continued to play the four-year-old clip that it had pulled from the cloud of Lara Keegan singing to her baby daughter, reflecting its new learned behavior that lullabies apparently also calmed human adults.

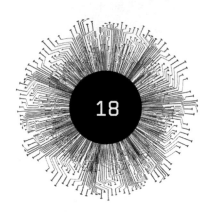

GEORGETOWN UNIVERSITY HOSPITAL

Washington, DC

Keegan climbed up to stand on the stairwell's handrail running next to the door to the hospital roof. With one hand holding the exit sign that hung down, she drew her Sig pistol with the other. Reaching out, she carefully tapped the overhead light with the butt of the pistol. It was a delicate blow, like cracking an egg, enough to be almost silent, but with it, the stairwell was left in complete darkness. When she opened the door, Keegan did not want to present an easy-to-target silhouette.

She climbed down, and after marking to memory the door's location in the infrared projected layout of the hallway, she took off the expensive vizglasses from the Range Rover. She then placed them on the concrete steps. Feeling for them in the dark with the tip of her shoe, she stepped down as hard as she could, snapping the frames and grinding down the lenses with her heels.

It was another precaution that could make all the difference. She didn't know who to trust anymore, but had to assume Shaw was watching.

Then she chambered a round into her Sig Sauer. A long exhale, and she delicately shouldered open the door to the roof. As she emerged into the night, a part of her brain still found a way to marvel at the stars overhead.

The rooftop was a forest of exhaust pipes, microsatellite dishes, articulating delivery drone pads on long stalk-like pedestals, and the glimmering aluminum fins of the heat sinks that passively cooled the hospital's network hardware.[1] Crouching low, Keegan moved slowly along the perimeter of the roof, rather than trying to weave through that jungle. Seven stories up, a light breeze could be felt. Overhead, a brightly blinking air ambulance cut through the night with a growl as it flared down to a hover. Keegan watched it warily, wondering if it was going to crash, another one of Todd's attacks, or simply deliver patients to the automated orderly cart that waited below. Her question was answered as it came to a hover and then dropped out of view, landing on a pad on the next building's roof.

She used the sound to advance quicker, turning the corner of the roof. There. Roughly 30 paces ahead.

A man in a doctor's coat sat on the low wall that ran along the edge of the rooftop. His legs dangled over the side of the building, as if he were taking in the view. An open backpack lay nearby.

She had a clean shot. Unmissable. But she did not take it.

"Todd!" she shouted.

The man turned his head to look at her and was briefly illuminated by the air ambulance's landing lights as it lifted back up into the night. His face was covered in white bandages, but she almost didn't notice it because of his eyes. They showed not surprise or anger but recognition — not at his name but at her. And then, as the night went dark again, his eyes disappeared.

"That's for the best," he said to her. "The stars can only be enjoyed, can only be truly understood when it is just us, none of our creations to get in the way."

The wonder she had felt at the very same night sky instantly changed. She noticed how, while most of Washington and Northern Virginia had gone dark, there were lights on out in the farther Maryland suburbs, and to the east and to the south even past Alexandria. You just saw what you wanted to see.

"Get off there," she commanded. "And keep your hands where I can see them."

Todd nodded his head and then rocked forward, pushing out over the edge of the building with his arms. But he did not jump, instead using the movement to swing his legs back up so he was in a crouch on the low concrete wall. Then he stood, indifferent to the depths of the dark just behind him. His hands extended out above his head, palms wide, claiming it all as creator.

"Seven years ago, I stood in this exact same place," he said. "I wondered why God did something to me that he didn't even do to Abraham in the end? For what possible reason were my son and wife sacrificed? And then he answered me: It was my fault. I was responsible for the creations that had destroyed them, as if Abraham had actually pulled that knife across his child's throat."

"Then why do it to others?" she asked. "You'd just gone through every parent's nightmare. Why inflict that pain on others?"

"Sacrifice is sometimes necessary. It was only when I truly lost what was most precious to me that I realized what I had to do to save us all."

"To 'save' us? You're here tonight trying to kill kids at the same place your son was born and died. That's not saving, that's destroying," Keegan said, keeping the pistol trained on him. "How could you?"

"How could I? How could I not?" he responded. "God sent plague after plague to the Egyptians. But it was only when their arrogance began to threaten the lives of their children that they realized they had to give up their servants, much like us, with our mechanical ones. I did not ask of others any more than the sacrifice I had already made."

"Not everyone had that choice. Those kids down there in the NICU, they're innocent of all that."

"The firstborn children of Egypt were innocent. My son was innocent! Their innocence is what made their sacrifice so compelling, so world-changing."

"World-changing?" she said. "Bullshit. All you did by trying to play God was hurt people and break things. Nothing more."

"No, I destroyed something far more important."

"What?"

"Trust." He smiled, as if he somehow knew the word had added meaning for her. "Without ever deciding, without ever thinking it through, we grew to trust machines that we don't even understand to run our adult lives. We grant unexplainable black boxes of code the power to make all the decisions that should matter for us.[2] Now we'll never trust them the same way again, as we never should have. As you never should have, Agent Keegan."

So he did know her. But from watching her and TAMS on the feeds, or through somewhere, someone, else?

"You know my name, I know yours. Whatever. Get down off there," Keegan commanded, motioning with the gun. She began to move closer, as if to underscore that he had no choice but to obey. And to show him that she was not afraid.

She heard muffled footsteps on the roof to the left of her, moving through the tangle of rooftop machinery.

"You accomplish your mission?" she asked, knowing who it was without even looking.

"Yes. The NICU is secured," said TAMS, emerging from behind one of the drone pads.

"Good job, partner," said Keegan, knowing it would set the man off. "So, Todd, no big finale, all because I trusted one of those monstrous machines you tried to make everyone so scared of."

"That's disappointing, Agent Keegan. I was told you thought of that *thing* as just a tool."

She didn't like the idea that he was throwing her words back at her. She liked even less what it meant he also had access to. "You were 'told'? That means you're no different than TAMS. In fact, it means you're the same." She paused. "You're just Shaw's 'tool.'"

"We all have our roles to play," Todd said, without any pause or tone of denial. "Mr. Shaw simply came to the same realization that I did, that things had to change."

She glanced at TAMS, furrowing her brow in what it would know was an inquiring look.

"He is telling the truth," TAMS said.

Another air ambulance began its descent, landing lights washing over the rooftop. In that flare of light and the swirling air, Keegan saw Todd's shirt lift. Underneath, he was wearing a tan hunter's shooting vest. Instead of shotgun shells, though, each sleeve in the bandolier held a glass tube filled with what looked like a block of wax covered by a thin layer of clear liquid.

Unable to push the notice to Keegan's glasses, TAMS identified the danger aloud.

"Warning, Agent Keegan!" TAMS announced in a raised tone of alarm. "There is a high likelihood that Mr. Todd is armed with an improvised incendiary device."

"Explain. Tell me what we're dealing with here," she commanded, as Todd's face curled in a smile.

"A holding company within the VDO Associates network has made purchases of phosphate, carbon black, and silica," TAMS said. "Another firm within the network, presenting itself as a research lab, purchased a humidifying environmental system, pressure reactor, filter, condenser, and extruder pump, as well as a rotary evaporator system. Using these components, the precursor substances could be converted by an expert into a material matching the appearance of the unknown substance in the glass: white phosphorus."[3]

Keegan knew white phosphorus by its military nickname. "Willie Pete" was a pyrophoric; the second it was exposed to the air, it would ignite into an explosive white flame that burned at thousands of degrees.[4] While it was frowned upon by the JAG lawyers, they'd occasionally used smoke rounds packed with small amounts of white phosphorus for what they called "shake and bake" strikes against insurgents hunkered in a bunker or basement.[5] Willie Pete burned so hot that afterward, literally the only thing left was the outline of their body on the wall.

"So that was the plan all along, to go out in a blaze of glory?" Keegan asked Todd.

In her head, she worked out the various scenarios. However she played it, though, it ended the same way. Any shot that she took at

Todd would set off the devilish device, either hitting it directly or the glass breaking when his body fell.

"It was never about me," Todd replied. "When I'm gone, there'll be no trace for any person to blame, only the machines, like your 'partner' that failed."

At that TAMS moved forward, a careful crouching advance of just two steps, as if taking Todd's measure.

"I already died here that night long ago," Todd said. "Everything since has been to make it right."

It all came together at once.

Todd bringing his arms down, moving to wrap them over his chest and smash the explosive glass tubes that hung on the vest.

Kissing the top of Haley's head that very first time in the hospital room, just a few floors below.

Jumping into the surf at La Jolla, hand in hand with Jared.

Holding her hands on her knees as she vomited all over her running shoes, the fastest finisher at boot camp.

Her mother smiling, as chocolate ice cream dripped down onto the report card with straight A's.

The blur moving past her, as TAMS leaped across the rooftop into Todd and then over the edge.

A flash of intense white light.

Heat.

Buzzing all over her body.

Then nothing.

A silence as if she had never existed.

19

GEORGETOWN UNIVERSITY HOSPITAL

Washington, DC

"Haley, get off the bed! I told you to be careful with Mommy."

Keegan woke to sharp pain in her side, as Haley clambered onto the hospital bed to snuggle her. That was what love felt like.

As her eyes struggled to open, she felt Jared's fingers wrap around her left hand, a tentative and searching connection.

"Where am I?" She tried to say more, but her mouth was too dry.

"You're still at Georgetown Hospital. Take your time," Jared said, handing her a cup of water with a straw to sip from, as the bed slowly raised itself up, sensing she was awake now.

She tried to push herself up farther, but her right hand wouldn't respond.

"It's OK," Jared said quickly. "They gave you a nerve blocker there for the burns."

As the haze began to clear, she looked around the room, her vision blocked slightly by what must have been a bandage just above her left eye. Her right arm was completely wrapped in bandages and her left leg was stabilized in some kind of cast. She didn't have the heart to know what her face looked like, but she reasoned it couldn't be that bad if Haley was in the room. As she looked around the room filled with balloons, flowers, and get-well cards, several of them registered her making eye contact and began to play dueling cloying tunes and trite audio messages.

"Stop," she rasped, and the cards went silent.

"Most of them are from family, but there's a few from some pretty heavy hitters," Jared said, picking up a card out of the back. As he opened it, a 3-D image projected what Keegan had seen before — the ocean view from Shaw's California estate.

"See how pretty it is, Mommy?" Haley said.

"Wait, it gets better," Jared said, setting an angular matte-gray-framed card down on the bed in front of her.

The panorama shifted with a slight shimmer, and the entire picture came into improbably sharp focus. It was an expensive effect. Then Shaw appeared walking toward them, speaking through the card.

"Agent Keegan, I want to thank you for the sacrifice you have made for your country, yet again. We all owe you a great deal — in fact, everything. None of this could have happened without you. If there is anything I can do to aid you, in turn, please let me know."

He was mocking her. And at that, she felt a little bit of that same raw anger that had fueled everyone else Shaw had been behind. With her good leg, she violently shook the bed and knocked the card to the floor. Jared picked it up, placing it behind a card featuring the grinning face of the DC police commissioner.

"What was that about?" Jared asked.

Keegan just closed her eyes and burrowed her face into the top of Haley's head, as perfect a place as any to try to forget it all.

"It's OK, Mommy, you'll be all better soon," Haley said.

"With you here, butterfly, how could I not?" she replied.

One day she would have to stop lying to her daughter. But what could she say? She could barely admit to herself what she had just experienced.

She gave Haley a kiss on the forehead — human connection that could not be replaced, the bond between parent and child. What Todd had lost, and what had driven his crusade for Shaw.

"OK, Haley, you really do need to get down now. Mommy needs her space," said Jared.

"Agent Keegan!" a voice called from the doorway.

Noritz.

"Glad to see you awake," he said, entering the room with a pronounced smile. It seemed he was claiming her again, which meant his bosses must have been happy about the outcome. He stopped a few feet short of the bed, however, as if unsure of how welcome he would be. "I've got someone else to see you," Noritz said. "Your old friend . . . Booted back up and brought straight to you."

Stepping out from behind Noritz came TAMS.

"Hello," the machine said, as if presenting itself anew.

Haley jumped off the bed and ran to the robot. "TAMS!!!"

Just as a human body's imperfections make it unique and identifiable, the nicks and dents around where Haley hugged the robot were an immediate giveaway. It was the TAMS that had been shelved and hung on a rack just days earlier.

"My original assigned resource?" Keegan asked. She tried to use words Haley wouldn't understand the full meaning of. The girl had gone through enough; there was no need to add more confusion about her new friend and savior.

"Correct," said Noritz. "Not much left of the, um, other one. This one's baseline stops when we powered it down; don't worry, it still knows everything you taught it."

Not everything . . . Thankfully.

"I thought it'd make a nice get-well gift," he said, the two of them knowing it was more like a peace offering. "Maybe get the old team back together." He paused. "When you're ready, of course."

"Thank you for that," she said.

Jared scooped Haley up. "Come on, they've got work stuff to talk about. Let's go grab a snack."

The little girl waved to TAMS and blew Keegan a kiss.

Noritz shut the door behind them and sat down heavily in an overstuffed vinyl chair, the deep purple color of a bruise. "You doing OK?" he asked.

"Everything hurts," Keegan said.

"I bet," he said.

"And the case?"

"Nothing left to do but suck up Todd with a dustbuster . . . Ah, um, that was inappropriate. Forget I said that, TAMS."

"OK," said TAMS.

Noritz ran ChapStick around his lips, the same tell as ever that he was having to do something he'd prefer not to. "You ready to talk about what we need to talk about?"

She nodded, wincing at the pain behind her temples. She'd have to be careful, not just with what she'd discovered during the last moments of Todd's life, but to avoid leading Noritz or anybody else in the FBI to reexamine her own past, maybe no longer so deeply buried.

"TAMS, go wait outside," he said. "Then enter standby mode."

"So, it seems you're getting the hang of working with it," she said.

"The word from the top is get used to it. The hospital surveillance video of that machine running in to save all those babies and then tackling Todd to save you before he lit off his vest . . . It's everywhere. Hell, a few years from now all the preschools are going to be filled with a bunch of little kids named 'TAMS.' No way the Bureau is going to squander a win like that."

"Shit," said Keegan. "I'm guessing that didn't make Bosch too happy."

"The director told Bosch to pound sand," he said. "You're blessed now too, as long as you can clear something up for the case record." He chewed his cheek and stopped speaking.

"You want to know how I found Todd?"

A nod. "We know how Modi gave you that TAMS unit, but we don't know how it led you to the hospital."

"A hunch," said Keegan. "That unit I received from Modi didn't have FBI network access, so we just used what we had and went there on a hunch." She did not want to divulge the role that Shaw played, at least not yet.

"Then with all the comms down, we couldn't wait to call in backup," she added. It was a good thing the robot had left the room. It was the sort of lie that TAMS's sensors would have seen right through. But it was a lie that Noritz wanted to hear, one that threw him a lifeline inside the bureaucracy by keeping any mention of his attempt to bury her out of the official file. He now owed her.

Noritz looked around the room, as if wondering who was listening in. "In the official record, you'll also have to leave the part about Modi out," he said quietly. "And that order is from well above my pay grade."

"How high?"

"The highest possible. The FBI suspended the agent who saved the city and the CIA supplied her with an off-the-books robot sidekick. So, rather than investigate everybody into retirement about how this good deed actually got done, the president sat the two directors down and told them they need to eat shit sandwiches and smile to the public about how good they tasted. Everybody's got enough to do cleaning up Washington, and the White House doesn't want to lose momentum on the basic income commission's reforms and all the other policy crap that they're using this crisis to ram through Congress."

That set something off in her brain, but it was all still fuzzy. "So, we're going to act like it was all planned this way?"

"Yeah. Same for the TAMS program. Trial run's over. None of the other field office tests had anywhere near the same outcome as yours, but screw 'em. Everything's been a 'complete success,' if that wasn't clear by now. We're all the way on this. The Bureau is buying TAMS units for every single field office around the country. After that, federal grants for state and local police departments to buy their own. Like they're going to know what to do with them. But anyway, the public is asking for it, to feel safe again. So the White House is getting ahead of the curve, to make it a bigger win — its win."

"What have we unleashed?" Keegan asked.

"Yeah, I'm not sure Todd would appreciate everything he just jump-started."

She jerked upright as the realization hit her. Shaw hadn't just played her; he'd played everyone.

Jackson Todd. Senator Jacobs. The whole network of extremists. Even her and TAMS. They had all been the same to Shaw: investments in a revolution on his terms. A series of moves all to take a society struggling with change to its lowest point and then remake it.

It hadn't been about fighting the future, but making it come true. Keegan sighed and lay back, taking it all in.

"I'll let you rest," Noritz said. "When you're ready to come back to work, you can let me know what you want to do. There's nothing wrong with letting the Bureau put you out on the vizcast circuit until retirement. Hell, besides all the little babies being named after TAMS, 'Lara' and 'Keegan' are trending, as well."

"I'll think about it. Can you send TAMS back in here?"

"Sure thing."

Noritz disappeared and TAMS returned, alone. It presented itself as if at attention. The scars that decorated its chest were akin to a row of medals that it should feel pride in, if it could.

"What was the very last thing that I said to you?" she asked.

"Thank you," TAMS replied.

Keegan reflected on this for a moment. "I have to say that again, for more than you know."

TAMS looked back at her and she wanted to believe it comprehended her unspoken meaning—and for all she knew, it did. She wasn't sure of anything anymore. Despite herself, she had come to trust this machine to which she now owed everything. Yet that very same trust made their partnership a new kind of danger.[1] Every second she spent with TAMS, everything she taught it, would only bring it closer to the moment they had already arrived at once—the moment that could end everything.

Keegan surveyed the rows of get-well cards, the top of Shaw's card lurking just behind them.

Fuck it. It was a risk she'd just have to take.

"TAMS, you all powered up and ready to get back to work?"

"OK," said TAMS.

"Because once I get out of this hospital, we've got a new case to pursue."

ACKNOWLEDGMENTS

Just like the reader's experience, the act of writing a book is a journey that involves a cast of memorable characters.

Alex Littlefield, Gretchen Stelter, and Olivia Bartz and the entire editorial and production team at HMH shepherded *Burn-In* from mere concept to the product in your hand, while the indefatigable Michelle Triant and the marketing and publicity teams worked to spread the good word about it. We fully recognize that this meld of fiction and nonfiction is a different kind of proposition for a publisher and we are so grateful for their support in making it real.

We were also aided by a cohort of experts and friends, who did everything from answer research questions to provide invaluable creative feedback on early drafts. Some have to remain anonymous because of their jobs, which ranged from FBI agents and CIA officers to executives of AI companies. But many can and should be thanked, including Che Bolden, Marcus Carey, Sam Cole, Sam Freund, Matt Gallagher, Josh Geltzer, Mark Hagerott, Amir Husain, Phil Klay, Brian Michelson, Ian Morrison, Tyler Quinn, Tammy Schultz, Kristin Sharp, Peter Tieryas, Dan Wilson, Beau Woods, and Nicholas Wright.

Our agents Dan Mandel and Katherine Flynn have represented us for years, serving as everything from representatives to deeply appreciated sounding boards on issues large and small.

Books also require a setting that makes that journey possible. New America, led by Anne-Marie Slaughter, truly is the only think tank that could have housed a project like this that crosses research on issues ranging from the future of tech to cyber threats, while making use of something other than a traditional white paper to communicate it. Crucial support in this was also kindly provided by the Smith Richardson Foundation and Arizona State University's Center on the Future of War, two organizations that have made their mission to aid the broader world in preparing for tomorrow.

Yet, just like in the book, the most important part of the journey comes from the most personal of ties. As for Keegan, our identity is as much defined by the balancing act of parenting and work as by anything else. We wrote scenes while sitting on uncomfortable gym benches, as basketball practice took place below, and edited on family car trips, as the new Taylor Swift album blared in the background. And we loved every minute of it. Catherine and Madeleine, Owen and Liam, you are our joy.

Most of all we'd like to thank our wives, who supported us every step of the way, not just in the book, but in life's journey. They encouraged and inspired us in all ways, and we could not be more thankful to have them as our true partners.

REFERENCES

Burn-In is a work of fiction.

It also wrestles with real issues that will have to be faced in the coming years.

Automation, robotics, and ever more capable artificial intelligence are no longer just science fiction. Their ongoing advancement and application, across nearly every segment of society, will create amazing new possibilities and efficiencies. As we go through what is best understood as a new industrial revolution, however, there will also be political, economic, social, and cultural disruptions and debates, as well as security threats, of a scale not experienced for generations, if not ever before. What is worrisome is how poorly understood this all is, both by the public and policymakers. It is not just that too many lack a sense of the scale of change that is to come, but also the ability to visualize it.

This is what motivated us to write *Burn-In,* not just to create and share new characters and stories, but also to aid broader engagement with the thorny issues related to technology and society that will soon become all too real. In the past we've termed this approach as the concept of "useful fiction."[1] It also explains those little numbers that popped up in the text as Keegan and TAMS went on their journey. They both validate that moment in the text and credit the writers or researchers whose hard work lay behind it. That is, in this differing approach of a novel woven with real-world research, the following endnotes serve the very same purpose that they would serve in a work of traditional nonfiction: to provide a source for the fact or concept being communicated.

Yet we also hope that you see the following references as an opportunity. They are potential threads to pull on further, just like TAMS did, to seek greater understanding. It might be to learn more about a certain technology that excited you, which seemed like science fiction in the story but turns out to be real. Or it might be to dive deeper into a particular concept, dilemma, or debate, as it may not be theoretical for much longer. Most of all, we hope that the combination of the story and these sources leaves you empowered with new knowledge as you navigate these issues in the real world.

Notes

1. CAPITOL HILL

1. Ritika Trikha, "The History of 'Hello, World.'" *HackerRank*, April 21, 2015. https://blog.hackerrank.com/the-history-of-hello-world/.

2. Adam Conner-Simons and Rachel Gordon, "'Superhero' Robot Wears Different Outfits for Different Tasks." *MIT News*, September 27, 2017. http://news.mit.edu/2017/superhero-robot-wears-different-outfits-different-tasks-0927.
    Massachusetts Institute of Technology, "Robot Origami: Robot Self-folds, Walks, and Completes Tasks." YouTube, June 11, 2015. Video, 2:43. https://www.youtube.com/watch?v=ZVYz7g-qLjs.

3. Clark Construction, "Washington Post Press Facility." Accessed April 3, 2019. https://www.clarkconstruction.com/our-work/projects/washington-post-press-facility.

4. Arthur Holland Michel, "Amazon Delivery Drone Patents." Center for the Study of the Drone, September 2017. https://dronecenter.bard.edu/files/2017/09/CSD-Amazons-Drone-Patents-1.pdf.

5. History.com, "1932: Bonus Marchers Evicted by U.S. Army." February 9, 2010. https://www.history.com/this-day-in-history/bonus-marchers-evicted-by-u-s-army.

6. US Marine Corps, "New Marine Corps Tattoo Regulations." Marines.mil, June 2, 2016. https://www.marines.mil/News/News-Display/Article/788805/new-marine-corps-tattoo-regulations/.

7. Leo Shane III, "Veterans, Military Retirees to See a 1.6 Percent Cost-of-Living Boost in Benefits." *Military Times*, October 11, 2019. https://www.militarytimes.com/news/pentagon-congress/2019/10/11/veterans-military-retirees-to-see-a-16-percent-cost-of-living-boost-in-benefits/.

8. Lara Seligman, "In Overflowing Syrian Refugee Camps, Extremism Takes Root." *Foreign Policy*, July 29, 2019. https://foreignpolicy.com/2019/07/29/in-overflowing-syrian-refugee-camps-extremism-takes-root-syria-bashar-assad-islamic-state-isis/.
    Garrett Graff, *The Threat Matrix: The FBI at War in the Age of Global Terror*. New York: Little Brown and Co., 2011.

9. Peter Diamandis, "Convergence in VR/AR: 5 Anticipated Breakthroughs to Watch." LinkedIn. May 6, 2019. https://www.linkedin.com/pulse/convergence-vrar-5-anticipated-breakthroughs-watch-peter-h-diamandis/.
    John James, "Future OE Mission Command and Future OE Decision Cycles." US Army Mad Scientist Laboratory, May 16, 2019. https://madsciblog.tradoc.army.mil/145-future-oe-mission-command-and-future-oe-decision-cycles/.

10. Vlad Savov, "Nubia's Wearable Smartphone Is a Preview of Our Flexible OLED Future." *The Verge*, September 4, 2018. https://www.theverge.com/circuitbreaker/2018/9/4/17817416/wearable-smartphone-nubia-alpha-flexible-oled-ifa-2018.

Zachariah Yuzon, "Nubia's Alpha Wearable Is the Craziest Gadget at MWC 2019." *Mashable,* February 28, 2019. Video, 00:50. https://mashable.com/video/nubia-alpha/#kFH57ndsemqR.

11. Jeremy Hsu, "Out of the Way, Human! Delivery Robots Want a Share of Your Sidewalk." *Scientific American,* February 19, 2019. https://www.scientific american.com/article/out-of-the-way-human-delivery-robots-want-a-share-of-your-sidewalk/.

12. Ina Fried, "Preparing for a Future of Augmented Reality." *Axios,* September 27, 2019. https://www.axios.com/augmented-reality-future-personal-privacy-concerns-797deaf0-3a24-4eb4-98d7-99e304608c88.html.

13. Amanda Lentino, "This Chinese Facial-Recognition Start-up Can Identify a Person in Seconds." CNBC.com, May 16, 2019. https://www.cnbc.com/2019/05/16/this-chinese-facial-recognition-start-up-can-id-a-person-in-seconds.html.

14. Direct quote from China Electronics Technology Corp. presentation. Chris Buckley and Paul Mozur, "How China Uses High-Tech Surveillance to Subdue Minorities." *New York Times,* May 22, 2019. https://www.nytimes.com/2019/05/22/world/asia/china-surveillance-xinjiang.html.

15. Julien Happich, "The Future of Video Surveillance: HD, Hyperspectral and Stereoscopic." *EeNews Europe,* February 5, 2014. http://www.eenewseurope.com/news/future-video-surveillance-hd-hyperspectral-and-stereoscopic.

16. Jonathan Hilburg, "Elon Musk Receives Exploratory Permit for D.C. to NYC Hyperloop." *The Architect's Newspaper,* February 21, 2018. https://archpaper.com/2018/02/elon-musks-boring-company-exploratory-permit-dc-hyperloop/.

17. Steve Hanley, "Tesla Model 3 Stuns German Engineers with Its Wonders." *CleanTechnica,* February 19, 2018. https://cleantechnica.com/2018/02/19/tesla-model-3-stuns-german-engineers-wonders/.

18. Selfdefense.com, "Stun Gun Batons." Accessed July 27, 2019. https://www.srselfdefense.com/stun-gun-batons/.

19. Aaron C. Davis, Emma Brown, and Michael Miller, "Inside Casa Padre, the Converted Walmart Where the U.S. Is Holding Nearly 1,500 Immigrant Children." *Washington Post,* June 14, 2018. https://www.washingtonpost.com/local/inside-casa-padre-the-converted-walmart-where-the-us-is-holding-nearly-1500-immigrant-children/2018/06/14/0cd65ce4-6eba-11e8-bd50-b80389a4e569_story.html.

20. Andrew Giambrone, "Trump Reportedly Wants to Keep the FBI HQ in D.C. and Oversee Its Redevelopment." *Curbed Washington DC,* July 30, 2018. https://dc.curbed.com/2018/7/30/17631828/trump-fbi-hq-redevelopment-washington-brutalism-architecture.

21. CV Dazzle. Accessed November 5, 2019. https://cvdazzle.com/.

22. James Vincent, "Google's AI Thinks This Turtle Looks Like a Gun, Which Is a Problem." *The Verge,* November 2, 2017. https://www.theverge.com/2017/11/2/16597276/google-ai-image-attacks-adversarial-turtle-rifle-3d-printed.

23. James Vincent, "These Glasses Trick Facial Recognition Software into Thinking You're Someone Else." *The Verge,* November 3, 2016. https://www.theverge.com/2016/11/3/13507542/facial-recognition-glasses-trick-impersonate-fool.

24. Guy Cramer, "Quantum Stealth; The Invisible Military Becomes a Reality." HyperStealth, October 19, 2012. http://www.hyperstealth.com/Quantum-Stealth.

25. Quran.com, "Sura 43: Az-Zukhruf, The Ornaments of Gold." https://quran.com/43.

26. Lorenzo Franceschi-Bicchierai, "Hackers Behind WannaCry Cashed Out Bitcoin While No One Was Watching." *Vice,* August 3, 2017. https://motherboard.vice.com/en_us/article/qvky75/hackers-behind-wannacry-cashed-out-bitcoin-while-no-one-was-watching.

2. PRINCETON UNIVERSITY

1. Jennifer Greenstein Altmann, "Venerable Lecture Hall Reaches Century Milestone." Princeton.edu, August 16, 2007. https://www.princeton.edu/news/2007/08/16/venerable-lecture-hall-reaches-century-milestone.

2. "Linux Kernel." Wikipedia. Accessed May 15, 2019. https://en.wikipedia.org/wiki/Linux_kernel.

3. Kirkpatrick Sale, *Rebels Against the Future: The Luddites and Their War on the Industrial Revolution: Lessons for the Computer Age.* New York: Basic Books, 1996.

4. MΔDΞRΔS, "Improvements Like These Have Interesting Implications." Twitter, March 9, 2019. pic.twitter.com/ZywUM4XsBn.

5. Will Knight, "Meet the Fake Celebrities Dreamed Up by AI." *MIT Technology Review,* October 31, 2017. https://www.technologyreview.com/the-download/609290/meet-the-fake-celebrities-dreamed-up-by-ai/.

6. Greg Synek, "Gait Recognition Tech Can Identify People Even with Their Backs Turned." *TechSpot,* November 7, 2018. https://www.techspot.com/news/77298-gait-recognition-tech-can-identify-people-even-their.html.

7. Parmy Olson, "Image-Recognition Technology May Not Be as Secure as We Think." *Wall Street Journal,* June 4, 2019. https://www.wsj.com/articles/image-recognition-technology-may-not-be-as-secure-as-we-think-11559700300.

8. Angela Chen, "Inmates in Finland Are Training AI as Part of Prison Labor." *The Verge,* March 28, 2019. https://www.theverge.com/2019/3/28/18285572/prison-labor-finland-artificial-intelligence-data-tagging-vainu.

9. Based on a quote from Roger McNamee, one of the original funders of Facebook, on the problem with the libertarian tech tycoons funded by Peter Thiel, etc. Roger McNamee, "Roger McNamee: 'It's Bigger Than Facebook. This Is a Problem with the Entire Industry.'" Interview by Alex Hern, *The Guardian,* February 16, 2019. https://www.theguardian.com/books/2019/feb/16/roger-mcnamee-zucked-waking-up-to-the-facebook-catastrophe-interview.

10. Gregg Maisel, Ken Kohl, and Deborah Curtis, "National Security." US Department of Justice. Updated December 22, 2017. https://www.justice.gov/usao-dc/criminal-division/national-security.

11. FragranceAdvisors.com, "Top 5 Best Pheromone Colognes for Men in 2019." https://www.fragranceadvisors.com/best-pheromone-cologne-men/.

12. FBI, Investigative Programs: Critical Incident Response Group. Accessed July 19, 2019. https://www2.fbi.gov/hq/isd/cirg/ncavc.htm.

13. Nick Lavars, "Robotic Leg Leans on Animal Evolution to Teach Itself to Walk." *New Atlas,* March 12, 2019. https://newatlas.com/robotic-leg-teaches-walk/58817/.

14. James Vincent, "Boston Dynamics' Robots Are Preparing to Leave the Lab — But Is the World Ready?" *The Verge,* July 17, 2019. https://www.theverge.com/2019/7/17/20697540/boston-dynamics-robots-commercial-real-world-business-spot-on-sale.

15. "burn-in," Merriam-Webster.com. Accessed November 5, 2019. https://www.merriam-webster.com/dictionary/burn-in.

16. Charlotte Jee, "Female Voice Assistants Fuel Damaging Gender Stereotypes, Says a UN Study." *MIT Technology Review,* May 22, 2019. https://www.technologyreview.com/f/613569/female-voice-assistants-fuel-damaging-gender-stereotypes-says-un-study/.

17. AI is an incredibly contested term, with at least 70 different definitions according to one study (Shane Legg and Marcus Hutter, "A Collection of Definitions of Intelligence," IDSIA report, 2007. https://arxiv.org/pdf/0706.3639.pdf). It has come to encompass anything from a "narrow" or "weak" task of human intelligence being performed by a machine to one requiring "general" or even "super" intelligence. It is often expanded to include everything from "machine learning," where a machine is trained to do the task, to approaches like "multi-agent systems" and artificial "neural networks" to create more expansive "deep learning," where the machine operates in ways akin to the human brain, to "neuromorphic chips," which allow individual chips to do massive calculations, enabling further supercomputing breakthroughs and pushing intelligence outward to individual systems or even sensors.

The US military has officially defined AI as "the ability of machines to perform tasks that normally require human intelligence — for example, recognizing patterns, learning from experience, drawing conclusions, making predictions, or taking action — whether digitally or as the smart software behind autonomous physical systems" (US Department of Defense, "Summary of the 2018 Department of Defense Artificial Intelligence Strategy," available at https://media.defense.gov/2019/Feb/12/2002088963/-1/-1/1/SUMMARY-OF-DOD-AI-STRATEGY.PDF). For our general purposes, we use it in broad terms to mean the capability of a machine to imitate, match, or surpass an intelligent human behavior or task, with "intelligent" defined as able to function appropriately and with foresight in its environment.

For further background on the terming issues, see also Nils J. Nilsson, *The Quest for Artificial Intelligence: A History of Ideas and Achievements* (Cambridge, UK: Cambridge University Press, 2010), and Peter Stone et al., "Artificial Intelligence and Life in 2030." One Hundred Year Study on Artificial Intelligence: Report of the 2015–2016 Study Panel, Stanford University, September 2016. http://ai100.stanford.edu/2016-report.

18. Brady Moore and Chris Sauceda, "The Guy Behind the Guy: AI as the Indispensable Marshal." US Army Mad Scientist Laboratory, February 21, 2019. https://madsciblog.tradoc.army.mil/122-the-guy-behind-the-guy-ai-as-the-indispensable-marshal/.

19. Lance Ulanoff, "LEGO Mindstorms Ev3 Is 601 Pieces of Awesome." *Mashable,* August 21, 2013. https://mashable.com/2013/08/21/lego-mindstorms-ev3-review/.
20. Amazon.com, "Amazon Mechanical Turk: Overview." Accessed June 23, 2019. https://www.mturk.com/.
21. Jamie Metzl, "Making Babies in the Year 2045." *New York Times,* April 10, 2019. https://www.nytimes.com/2019/04/10/opinion/genetic-testing-privacy.html.
22. Dave Gershgorn, "Companies Are on the Hook if Their Hiring Algorithms Are Biased." *Quartz,* October 22, 2018. https://qz.com/1427621/companies-are-on-the-hook-if-their-hiring-algorithms-are-biased/.
23. McKinsey Global Institute, "The Future of Work in America." July 2019. https://www.mckinsey.com/featured-insights/future-of-work/the-future-of-work-in-america-people-and-places-today-and-tomorrow.
24. Charlotte Jee, "Amazon's System for Tracking Its Warehouse Workers Can Automatically Fire Them." *MIT Technology Review,* April 26, 2019. https://www.technologyreview.com/f/613434/amazons-system-for-tracking-its-warehouse-workers-can-automatically-fire-them.
25. Andrew Ross Sorkin, "Peter Thiel, Tech Billionaire, Reveals Secret War with Gawker." *New York Times,* May 25, 2016. https://www.nytimes.com/2016/05/26/business/dealbook/peter-thiel-tech-billionaire-reveals-secret-war-with-gawker.html.
26. Jason Nark, "Seven Endangered Places You Should See Before It's Too Late." *Outside,* June 11, 2019. https://www.outsideonline.com/2397326/places-threatened-by-climate-change.
27. I. Orha and Stefan Oniga. "Assistance and Telepresence Robots: A Solution for Elderly People." *Carpathian Journal of Electronic and Computer Engineering* 5 (2012): 87–90. https://www.researchgate.net/publication/235417999_Assistance_and_telepresence_robots_a_solution_for_elderly_people.
28. University of Washington, "How to Train Your Robot (to Feed You Dinner)." *Science Daily,* March 11, 2019. https://www.sciencedaily.com/releases/2019/03/190311101221.htm.
29. Jo White, "Is the Kitchen Dead?" Medium.com, August 12, 2018. https://medium.com/cookpadteam/is-the-kitchen-dead-d7c44597b1f3.
30. Greg Bensinger, "'Mission Racer': How Amazon Turned the Tedium of Warehouse Work into a Game." *Washington Post,* May 21, 2019. https://www.washingtonpost.com/technology/2019/05/21/missionracer-how-amazon-turned-tedium-warehouse-work-into-game.
31. Suren Ramasubbu, "Biological & Psychological Reasons for Social Media Addiction." *Huffington Post,* March 10, 2017. https://www.huffpost.com/entry/biological-psychological-reasons-for-social-media.
32. Andrew Myers, "Stanford Engineers Make Editing Video as Easy as Editing Text." *Stanford News,* June 5, 2019. https://news.stanford.edu/2019/06/05/edit-video-editing-text/.
33. Allen Yu, "How Netflix Uses AI, Data Science, and Machine Learning—From A Product Perspective." *Becoming Human,* February 27, 2019. https://becoming-human.ai/how-netflix-uses-ai-and-machine-learning-a087614630fe.

34. Daron Acemoglu and Pascual Restrepo, "The Wrong Kind of AI? Artificial Intelligence and the Future of Labor Demand." Massachusetts Institute of Technology, March 5, 2019. https://papers.ssrn.com/sol3/papers.cfm?abstract_id=3359482.

35. John Marangos and J. E. King, "Two Arguments for Basic Income: Thomas Paine (1737–1809) and Thomas Spence (1750–1814)." academia.edu, 2006. http://www.academia.edu/2698139/Two_arguments_for_Basic_Income_Thomas_Paine_1737-1809_and_Thomas_Spence_1750-1814.

36. James Beniger, *The Control Revolution: Technological and Economic Origins of the Information Society.* Cambridge, MA: Harvard University Press, 1989.
     Elsa Kania, "Battlefield Singularity: Artificial Intelligence, Military Revolution, and China's Future Military Power." CNAS report, November 28, 2017. https://www.cnas.org/publications/reports/battlefield-singularity-artificial-intelligence-military-revolution-and-chinas-future-military-power.

37. Ajay Agrawal, Joshua Gans, and Avi Goldfarb, *Prediction Machines: The Simple Economics of Artificial Intelligence.* Boston: Harvard Business Review Press, 2018, p. 213.

38. "Technology is not destiny." Direct quote. Conor McKay, Ethan Pollack, and Alastair Fitzpayne, "Automation and a Changing Economy: The Case for Action." The Aspen Institute, April 2, 2019. https://www.aspeninstitute.org/publications/automation-and-a-changing-economy-the-case-for-action/.

39. "We can promote greater opportunity and broadly shared prosperity for all." Direct quote. Conor McKay, Ethan Pollack, and Alastair Fitzpayne, "Automation and a Changing Economy: The Case for Action." The Aspen Institute, April 2, 2019. https://www.aspeninstitute.org/publications/automation-and-a-changing-economy-the-case-for-action/.

40. John Marangos and J. E. King, "Two Arguments for Basic Income: Thomas Paine (1737–1809) and Thomas Spence (1750–1814)." academia.edu, 2006. http://www.academia.edu/2698139/Two_arguments_for_Basic_Income_Thomas_Paine_1737-1809_and_Thomas_Spence_1750-1814.

3. FBI ACADEMY

1. FBI.gov, "Celebrating Women Special Agents, Part 1: May 12, 1972 — A New Chapter Is Opened." May 16, 2012. https://www.fbi.gov/news/stories/celebrating-women-special-agents.
     FBI.gov, press release. May 12, 1972. https://archives.fbi.gov/archives/news/stories/2012/may/women-agents_051612/press-release-may-12-1972.

2. Boston Dynamics, YouTube channel. https://www.youtube.com/user/Boston Dynamics.

3. Nicholas Wright, "The Technologies: What Specifically Is New?" In "AI, China, Russia, and the Global Order: Technological, Political, Global, and Creative Perspectives," US Department of Defense SMA report, December 2018. http://static1.1.sqspcdn.com/static/f/1399691/28061274/1547846008013/AI+China+Russia+Global+WP_FINAL.pdf?token=Z%2FlRqydDuVOllSW6riUx5nAVkX4%3D.

4. Kate Darling, "Why We Have an Emotional Connection to Robots." TED Talks,

September 2018. https://www.ted.com/talks/kate_darling_why_we_have_an_emotional_connection_to_robots?language=en.

5. Prajwal Paudyal, "Should AI Explain Itself? Or Should We Design Explainable AI So That It Doesn't Have To." *Towards Data Science.* Accessed June 28, 2019. https://towardsdatascience.com/should-ai-explain-itself-or-should-we-design-explainable-ai-so-that-it-doesnt-have-to-90e75bb6089e.

6. FBI.gov, "The Hostage Rescue Team, Part 2: The Crucible of Selection." February 12, 2013. https://www.fbi.gov/news/stories/hostage-rescue-team-the-crucible-of-selection-2.

7. FBI.gov, "The Hostage Rescue Team, Part 3: Training for Every Contingency." February 19, 2013. https://www.fbi.gov/news/stories/hostage-rescue-team-training-for-every-contingency.

8. P. W. Singer, *Wired for War: The Robotics Revolution and Conflict in the 21st Century.* New York: Penguin, 2009, p. 337.

9. Julien Happich, "The Future of Video Surveillance: HD, Hyperspectral and Stereoscopic." *EeNews Europe,* February 5, 2014. http://www.eenewseurope.com/news/future-video-surveillance-hd-hyperspectral-and-stereoscopic.

10. Kathy Fessler, "What You Need to Know About Gunshot Detection Technology." Security101 blog, November 28, 2018. https://www.security101.com/blog/gunshot-detection-technology.

11. Michael Maguire, "Active Shooter Drills in Schools Do More Harm Than Good. It's Time to Put a Stop to Them." WGBH, April 16, 2019. https://www.wgbh.org/news/commentary/2019/04/16/active-shooter-drills-in-schools-do-more-harm-than-good-its-time-to-put-a-stop-to-them.

12. Andrew Liszewski, "This Clip-on Handgun Attachment Makes Bullets Non-Lethal." *Gizmodo,* September 12, 2015. https://gizmodo.com/this-clip-on-handgun-attachment-makes-bullets-non-letha-1730039256.

13. Noah Shachtman, "Israeli 'Auto Kill Zone' Towers Locked and Loaded." *Wired,* December 5, 2008. https://www.wired.com/2008/12/israeli-auto-ki/.

14. Daniel H. Wilson, *Robopocalypse.* New York: Doubleday, 2011.

15. Elliot Carter, "Seen This Wall by the Washington Monument? That's the Potomac Park Levee." Architect of the Capital, December 5, 2016. https://architectofthecapital.org/posts/2016/12/4/potomac-park-levee.

16. NASA.gov, "Robonaut 2, the Next Generation Dexterous Robot." July 15, 2010. https://www.nasa.gov/mission_pages/station/multimedia/robonaut_photos.html.

17. NurdRage, "Gallium Induced Structural Failure of an Aluminum Sheet." YouTube, December 13, 2014. Video, 2:54. https://www.youtube.com/watch?v=IZkzxWZETds.

4. FBI ACADEMY

1. Paul Scharre, *Army of None: Autonomous Weapons and the Future of War.* New York: W. W. Norton, 2019.

2. US Army Mad Scientist Laboratory, "An Appropriate Level of Trust. . . ." May 29, 2018. https://madsciblog.tradoc.army.mil/56-an-appropriate-level-of-trust/.

3. Liesbeth De Mol, "Turing Machines." *The Stanford Encyclopedia of Philosophy*, September 24, 2018. https://plato.stanford.edu/entries/turing-machine/.

4. C. E. Shannon, J. McCarthy, M. L. Minsky, and N. Rochester, "A Proposal for the Dartmouth Summer Research Project on Artificial Intelligence." Dartmouth College, August 31, 1955. http://www-formal.stanford.edu/jmc/history/dartmouth/dartmouth.html.

5. Alexis Madrigal, "How Checkers Was Solved." *The Atlantic*, July 19, 2017. https://www.theatlantic.com/technology/archive/2017/07/marion-tinsley-checkers/534111/.

6. Larry Greenemeir, "20 Years After Deep Blue: How AI Has Advanced Since Conquering Chess." *Scientific American*, June 2, 2017. https://www.scientific american.com/article/20-years-after-deep-blue-how-ai-has-advanced-since-conquering-chess/.

7. Eleanor Cummins, "Another AI Winter Could Usher in a Dark Period for Artificial Intelligence." *Popular Science*, August 29, 2018. https://www.popsci.com/ai-winter-artificial-intelligence.

8. "IBM's Watson Supercomputer Destroys Humans in Jeopardy." *Engadget*, January 13, 2011. https://www.youtube.com/watch?v=WFR3lOm_xhE.

9. Jon Russell, "Google AI Beats Go World Champion Again to Complete Historic 4–1 Series Victory." TechCrunch, March 15, 2016. https://techcrunch.com/2016/03/15/google-ai-beats-go-world-champion-again-to-complete-historic-4-1-series-victory.

10. DeepMind, "AlphaGo Zero: Starting from scratch." YouTube, October 18, 2017. Video, 2:13. https://www.youtube.com/watch?v=tXlM99xPQC8.

11. DeepMind, "AlphaGo." https://deepmind.com/research/alphago/.

12. Elsa Kania, "Chinese Military Innovation in Artificial Intelligence." Hearing of the US-China Economic and Security Review Commission, June 7, 2019. https://s3.amazonaws.com/files.cnas.org/documents/June-7-Hearing_Panel-1_Elsa-Kania_Chinese-Military-Innovation-in-Artificial-Intelligence.pdf.

13. Jamie Condliffe, "A New Artificial Synapse Is Faster and More Efficient Than Ones in Your Brain." *MIT Technology Review*, January 29, 2018. https://www.technologyreview.com/f/610089/a-new-artificial-synapse-is-faster-and-more-efficient-than-ones-in-your-brain/.

Andrew Freedman, "Meet Aurora, Soon to Be the First 'Exascale' Supercomputer in the U.S." *Axios*, March 18, 2019. https://www.axios.com/us-to-get-its-first-ultra-powerful-exascale-supercomputer-015cc201-0660-430f-9bf2-83e5ac4edcad.html.

14. Valerie Insinna, "Introducing Skyborg, Your New AI Wingman." C4ISRNET, March 14, 2019. https://www.c4isrnet.com/air/2019/03/14/introducing-skyborg-your-new-ai-wingman/.

15. Arthur Conan Doyle, "Silver Blaze." In *The Memoirs of Sherlock Holmes*, London: George Newnes, 1893.

See also Maria Konnikova, "Lessons from Sherlock Holmes Pt. I: Paying Attention to What Isn't There." Big Think, July 21, 2011. https://bigthink.com/artful-choice/lessons-from-sherlock-holmes-pti-paying-attention-to-what-isnt-there.

16. Heather Roff, "How Understanding Animals Can Help Us Make the Most of Artificial Intelligence." *The Conversation,* March 30, 2017. https://theconversation.com/how-understanding-animals-can-help-us-make-the-most-of-artificial-intelligence-74742.

17. Mike Allen, Sara Fischer, and Felix Salmon, "Fortnite: The Hot, New Social Network." *Axios,* December 25, 2018. https://www.axios.com/fortnite-the-hot-new-social-network-45cc0576-a49f-467f-b3aa-b5e06ec8aa53.html.

18. Peter Rubin, "Facebook Can Make VR Avatars Look — and Move — Exactly Like You." *Wired,* March 13, 2019. https://www.wired.com/story/facebook-oculus-codec-avatars-vr/.

19. Sansar. https://www.sansar.com/.

20. P. W. Singer and Emerson T. Brooking, *LikeWar: The Weaponization of Social Media.* Boston: Houghton Mifflin Harcourt, 2018.

21. "It is not human jobs that are at risk from the rise of the robots. It is humanity itself." Direct quote. Robert Skidelsky, "Is AI the Road to Serfdom?" *Asia Times,* February 22, 2019. https://www.asiatimes.com/2019/02/opinion/is-ai-the-road-to-serfdom/.

22. "Mazzy Star — Fade Into You." YouTube, November 16, 2010. Video, 4:28. https://www.youtube.com/watch?v=ImKY6TZEyrI.

23. Thomas Hobbes, *The English Works of Thomas Hobbes of Malmesbury,* vol. 1, p. 7. London: J. Bohn, 1839. https://archive.org/details/englishworkstho21hobbgoog/page/n32.

24. "Act of God," USLegal.com. Accessed July 27, 2019. https://definitions.uslegal.com/a/act-of-god/.

25. Shivali Best, "The Ambulance Drone That Could Save Your Life: Video Reveals How Flying Robots May Someday Carry the Injured to Hospital." *Daily Mail,* January 3, 2017. http://www.dailymail.co.uk/sciencetech/article-4084008/Incredible-video-shows-flying-AMBULANCE-speed-emergency-support.html.

26. Seth Borenstein, "No AI in Humor: R2-D2 Walks into a Bar, Doesn't Get the Joke." *AP News,* March 31, 2019. https://www.apnews.com/bae71c3bef8145ecaaa84bca24d77430.

27. US Army, "Mine Resistant Ambush Protected (MRAP) Vehicles." Accessed July 17, 2019. https://asc.army.mil/web/portfolio-item/cs-css-mine-resistant-ambush-protected-mrap-vehicle-mrap/.

28. Deloitte, "The Future of Policing." 2019. https://www2.deloitte.com/us/en/pages/public-sector/articles/future-of-policing-and-law-enforcement-technology-innovations.html.

29. Adam Tuss and Cordilia James, "Self-Driving Shuttle Buses Ride Around the Region." NBC 4 Washington, June 20, 2019. https://www.nbcwashington.com/news/local/Self-Driving-Shuttle-Buses-Cruise-Around-DC-Area-511594472.html.

30. George Leopold, "Air Force Tests 'Attritable' Weapons." *Electronic Engineering Times,* March 22, 2019. https://www.eetimes.com/document.asp?doc_id=1334456#.

31. Harriet Taylor, "Why Transportation Networks Are Especially Vulnerable to

Ransomware." CNBC, November 29, 2016. https://www.cnbc.com/2016/11/29/why-transportation-networks-are-especially-vulnerable-to-ransomware.html.

32. Caroline Haskins, "Amazon Provided Police with 'Heat Maps' of Package Theft for Sting Operation." *Vice,* July 9, 2019. https://www.vice.com/en_us/article/5978vd/amazon-provided-police-with-heat-maps-of-package-theft-for-sting-operation-cops.

33. Gao Huang, Zhuang Liu, Laurens van der Maaten, and Kilian Q. Weinberger, "Densely Connected Convolutional Networks." Cornell University, version v5, January 28, 2018. https://arxiv.org/abs/1608.06993.

34. "Vintage Chatty Cathy Toy Doll TV Commercial 1960's." YouTube, November 3, 2008. Video, 01:05. https://www.youtube.com/watch?v=f-sYQ8_2v_Q.

35. Kirstin Korosec, "In Ford's Future Two-Legged Robots and Self-Driving Cars Could Team Up on Deliveries." TechCrunch, May 22, 2019. https://techcrunch.com/2019/05/21/in-fords-future-two-legged-robots-and-self-driving-cars-could-team-up-on-deliveries/.

36. Peter Holley, "The Technology 202: Drones in Aisle 5? Grocery Stores Are Becoming Unusual Hotbeds of Innovation." *Washington Post,* May 3, 2019. https://www.washingtonpost.com/news/powerpost/paloma/the-technology-202/2019/05/03/the-technology-202-drones-in-aisle-5-grocery-stores-are-becoming-unusual-hotbeds-of-innovation/5ccb371c1ad2e506550b2f0d/.

37. Paul Daugherty and H. James Wilson, *Human + Machine: Reimagining Work in the Age of AI.* Boston: Harvard Business Review Press, 2018. https://hbr.org/product/human-machine-reimagining-work-in-the-age-of-ai/10163-HBK-ENG.

38. David Z. Morris, "Nearly Half of All Retail Jobs Could Be Lost to Automation Within 10 Years." *Fortune,* May 21, 2017. http://fortune.com/2017/05/21/automation-retail-job-losses/.

39. Bernard Marr, "Artificial Intelligence Has a Problem with Bias, Here's How to Tackle It." *Forbes,* January 29, 2019. https://www.forbes.com/sites/bernardmarr/2019/01/29/3-steps-to-tackle-the-problem-of-bias-in-artificial-intelligence/#4def775f7a12.

40. Patrick Tucker, "Here Come AI-Enabled Cameras Meant to Sense Crime Before It Occurs." *Defense One,* April 24, 2019. https://www.defenseone.com/technology/2019/04/ai-enabled-cameras-detect-crime-it-occurs-will-soon-invade-physical-world/156502/.

41. Glock. Accessed November 5, 2019. https://us.glock.com/en/pistols/g43.

42. Manuel Blum, "How to Exchange (Secret) Keys." *ACM Transactions on Computer Systems* 1 (2) (May 1983): 175–93. https://doi.org/10.1145%2F357360.357368.

43. Jade Fell, "Hacking Through the Years: A Brief History of Cyber Crime." *Engineering and Technology,* March 13, 2017. https://eandt.theiet.org/content/articles/2017/03/hacking-through-the-years-a-brief-history-of-cyber-crime/.

44. Mat Honan, "What Is Doxing?" *Wired,* March 6, 2014. https://www.wired.com/2014/03/doxing/.

45. P. W. Singer and Allan Friedman, *CyberSecurity and CyberWar: What Everyone Needs to Know.* New York: Oxford University Press, 2013, pp. 47–49.

Panayotis Vryonis, "Explaining Public-Key Cryptography to Non-Geeks." Medium.com, August 27, 2013. https://medium.com/@vrypan/explaining -public-key-cryptography-to-non-geeks-f0994b3c2d5.

46. Patrick Sawer, "The Unsung Genius Who Secured Britain's Computer Defences and Paved the Way for Safe Online Shopping". *The Telegraph,* March 11, 2016. https://www.telegraph.co.uk/history/12191473/The-unsung-genius -who-secured-Britains-computer-defences-and-paved-the-way-for-safe-online -shopping.html.

47. "always improving itself" is a direct quote from "Linux Mint How to Update System." Sidratul Muntaha, LinuxHint.com, May 2019. https://linuxhint.com/ update_linux_mint_system/.

48. Charlie Osborne, "OpenEMR Security Flaws Could Have Exposed Millions of Patient Records." *ZDNet,* August 8, 2018. https://www.zdnet.com/article/ openemr-security-flaws-left-millions-of-patient-records-open-to-attack/.

49. Blake Sobczak, "Hackers Force Water Utilities to Sink or Swim." *E&E News,* March 28, 2019. https://www.eenews.net/stories/1060131769.

50. John Miller and David Mainor, "WannaCry Ransomware Campaign: Threat Details and Risk Management." *FireEye,* May 15, 2017. https://www.fireeye .com/blog/products-and-services/2017/05/wannacry-ransomware-campaign .html.

51. John Leyden, "Water Treatment Plant Hacked, Chemical Mix Changed for Tap Supplies." *The Register,* March 24, 2016. https://www.theregister.co.uk/2016/ 03/24/water_utility_hacked/.

52. Kim Zetter, *Countdown to Zero Day: Stuxnet and the Launch of the World's First Digital Weapon.* New York: Random House, 2014.
    Patrick Clare, "Stuxnet: Anatomy of a Computer Virus." 2014. https://vimeo .com/25118844.

53. "What Is Selenium, and Why Should You Care?" Appalachian Mountain Advocates, June 15, 2011. http://www.appalmad.org/2011/06/15/what-is-selenium -and-why-should-you-care-2/.

54. Mark Reinsel, "Selenium Removal Technologies: A Review." WaterOnline. org, January 15, 2016. https://www.wateronline.com/doc/selenium-removal -technologies-a-review-0001.

55. National Park Service, "DC Clean Rivers Project Potomac River Tunnel, Environmental Assessment." October 2018. https://www.dcwater.com/sites/ default/files/project/documents/Potomac_River_Tunnel_EA_508_2018_10_25 .pdf.
    "four valves" is from an interview by Peter W. Singer with DC water expert, Washington, DC, July 26, 2019.

56. Interstate Commission on the Potomac River Basin, "Cooperative Water Supply Operations on the Potomac." Accessed June 23, 2019. https:// www.potomacriver.org/focus-areas/water-resources-and-drinking-water/ cooperative-water-supply-operations-on-the-potomac/.

57. Gregory J. Prelewicz, P.E., Erik R. Hagen, P.E., and Ani Kame'enui, "Potomac Reservoir and River Simulation Model User's Guide and Documentation." Interstate Commission on the Potomac River Basin, Report No. 04-03, 2004.

https://www.potomacriver.org/wp-content/uploads/2015/06/ICP04-3
_Prelewicz.pdf.

58. Danny Yadron, "Iranian Hackers Infiltrated New York Dam in 2013." *Wall Street Journal,* December 20, 2015. https://www.wsj.com/articles/iranian -hackers-infiltrated-new-york-dam-in-2013-1450662559.

59. Kate Goddard, Abdul Roudsari, and Jeremy C. Wyatt, "Automation Bias: A Systematic Review of Frequency, Effect Mediators, and Mitigators." *Journal of American Medical Information Association,* 2012. https://www.ncbi.nlm.nih .gov/pmc/articles/PMC3240751/.

    M. L. Cummings, "Automation Bias in Intelligent Time Critical Decision Support Systems." American Institute of Aeronautics and Astronautics. Accessed May 22, 2019. http://citeseerx.ist.psu.edu/viewdoc/download?doi=10.1.1 .91.2634&rep=rep1&type=pdf.

60. M. Arbeiter, "Enjoy a Country Song Written by a Neural Network." *Nerdist,* April 24, 2019. https://nerdist.com/article/neural-network-country-song/.

61. Janet Reitman, "U.S. Law Enforcement Failed to See the Threat of White Nationalism." *New York Times,* November 3, 2018. https://www.nytimes.com/ 2018/11/03/magazine/FBI-charlottesville-white-nationalism-far-right.html.

62. "Portland Far-Right Rally: Police Charge Counterprotesters with Batons Drawn." *The Guardian,* August 5, 2018. https://www.theguardian.com/us -news/2018/aug/04/patriot-prayer-to-carry-guns-at-portland-rally-as-fears-of -violence-rise.

63. Monika Nickelsburg, "A Brief History of the Guy Fawkes Mask." *Mental Floss,* November 5, 2015. http://mentalfloss.com/article/70807/brief-history-guy -fawkes-mask.

64. Sarah Wynn, "Water Turns Purple Overnight in Ohio Town." ABC6onyourside. com, June 4, 2019. https://abc6onyourside.com/news/local/water-turns-purple -overnight-in-ohio-town.

65. Merrit Kennedy, "A Siberian River Has Mysteriously Turned Blood Red." NPR, September 8, 2016. https://www.npr.org/sections/thetwo-way/2016/09/08/ 493139519/a-siberian-river-has-mysteriously-turned-blood-red.

66. Heather Pemberton Levy, "Gartner's Top 10 Strategic Predictions for 2017 and Beyond: Surviving the Storm Winds of Digital Disruption." Gartner, October 18, 2016. https://www.gartner.com/smarterwithgartner/gartner-predicts-a-virtual -world-of-exponential-change/.

67. Theoriz, "Mixed Reality RnD Test 002." Accessed August 30, 2019. https:// www.theoriz.com/portfolio/mixed-reality-project/.

68. Alison Gopnik, "A Generational Divide in the Uncanny Valley." *Wall Street Journal,* January 10, 2019. https://www.wsj.com/articles/a-generational-divide-in -the-uncanny-valley-11547138712.

69. Caroline Holmes, "Robust Future Changes in Temperature Variability Under Greenhouse Gas Forcing and the Relationship with Thermal Advection." *Journal of Climate,* March 15, 2016. https://journals.ametsoc.org/doi/full/10.1175/ JCLI-D-14-00735.1

70. Carlene Hempel, "The Man — Facts, Fiction and Themes." John Henry: The Steel Driving Man, December 1998. https://www.ibiblio.org/john_henry/ analysis.html.

71. Freegan.info, "What Is a Freegan?" Accessed May 23, 2019. https://freegan.info/.
72. Rachel Kurzius, "Well, Where Did You Think Stephen Miller Lived?" DCist.com, August 8, 2017. https://dcist.com/story/17/08/08/well-where-did-you-think-stephen-mi/.
73. Freegan.info, "Freegan Philosophy." Accessed May 23, 2019. https://freegan.info/what-is-a-freegan/freegan-philosophy/.
74. Tom Bateman, "Police Warning After Drug Traffickers' Cyber-Attack." BBC News, October 16, 2013. https://www.bbc.com/news/world-europe-24539417.
75. Alibaba.com. 2019. https://www.alibaba.com/showroom/fragile-warning-sticker-for-export-carton.html.
76. Tsuyoshi Inagaki, "The Difference Between a Chef's Knife and Santoku Knife." Kamikoto.com, March 12, 2018. https://kamikoto.com/blogs/fundamentals/difference-between-chefs-knife-and-santoku-knife.
77. Rolex.com. 2019. https://www.rolex.com/watches/explorer.html.
78. Christianna Reedy, "Graphene That Changes Color When It Cracks Could Literally Save Lives." *Futurism*, April 13, 2017. https://futurism.com/graphene-that-changes-color-when-it-cracks-could-literally-save-lives.
79. Victor L. Pushparaj et al., "Flexible Energy Storage Devices Based on Nanocomposite Paper." *Proceedings of the National Academy of Sciences of the United States of America*, August 21, 2007. https://www.ncbi.nlm.nih.gov/pmc/articles/PMC1959422/.
80. Ben's Chili Bowl, "Our Legacy." Accessed July 27, 2019. https://www.benschilibowl.com/history.

5. BEN'S CHILI BOWL

1. US Supreme Court, Opinion of the Court by Chief Justice Earl Warren in the Case of *Miranda v. Arizona*. June 13, 1966. Available at https://catalog.archives.gov/id/597564.
2. Adam Clark Estes, "The 3D Printed Gun Threat Is Getting Weird and Scary." *Gizmodo*, June 20, 2019. https://gizmodo.com/the-3d-printed-gun-threat-is-getting-weird-and-scary-1835694478.
3. US Supreme Court, *Berghuis v. Thompkins*. June 1, 2010. Available at https://www.supremecourt.gov/opinions/09pdf/08-1470.pdf.
4. Tiffany Jeung, "Watch How the World's Fastest Robot Cat Learns Feline Tricks." Inverse.com, November 12, 2018. https://www.inverse.com/article/50754-nybble-is-the-fastest-robot-cat.
5. Kelsey Atherton, "How to Make a DIY Anti-Surveillance Spray." *Popular Science*, August 2, 2013. https://www.popsci.com/diy/article/2013-08/diy-anti-surveillance-camera-spray/.
6. Shinichi Tsuchiya, Tomohiro Kiguchi, and Makoto Nishiuchi, "Underground Makeover." *Transmission & Distribution World*, January 1, 2012. https://www.tdworld.com/underground-tampd/underground-makeover.
7. Jack Corrigan, "'Siri, Watch That Guy': Pentagon Seeks AI That Can Track Someone Across a City." *Defense One*, May 13, 2019. https://www.defenseone.com/technology/2019/05/iarpa-needs-more-training-data-video-surveillance-algorithms/156955/?oref=DefenseOneTCO.

8. "Bornean Orangutan Infant Crosses O-Line for the First Time at the Smithsonian's National Zoo." Smithsonian's National Zoo & Conservation Biology Institute, April 10, 2017. https://nationalzoo.si.edu/animals/news/bornean -orangutan-infant-crosses-o-line-for-first-time-smithsonians-national-zoo.
9. "Boston Dynamics Atlas Robot Does Parkour." *What the Future,* October 17, 2018. https://www.youtube.com/watch?v=1crOxJa6Z18.

6. OLD EXECUTIVE OFFICE BUILDING

1. US Army, "Mine Resistant Ambush Protected (MRAP) Vehicles." Accessed July 17, 2019. https://asc.army.mil/web/portfolio-item/cs-css-mine-resistant -ambush-protected-mrap-vehicle-mrap/.
2. WhiteHouse.gov, "Eisenhower Executive Office Building." Accessed July 28, 2019. https://www.whitehouse.gov/about-the-white-house/eisenhower -executive-office-building/.
3. "All Terrain Surveillance Robot." *Wisdom Land,* March 7, 2018. https://www .youtube.com/watch?v=ar-YCHQK4ew.
4. Matt Day, "Amazon Is Working on a Device That Can Read Human Emotions." *Bloomberg,* May 23, 2019. https://www.bloomberg.com/news/articles/2019-05 -23/amazon-is-working-on-a-wearable-device-that-reads-human-emotions.
5. Bryn Farnsworth, "Facial Action Coding System (FACS) — A Visual Guidebook." *Imotions,* August 18, 2019. https://imotions.com/blog/facial-action-coding -system/.
   Jinni Harrigan, Robert Rosenthal, and Klaus Scherer (eds.), *New Handbook of Methods in Nonverbal Behavior Research.* New York: Oxford University Press, 2008.
6. "The Making of a Little Professor." MusingsofanAspie.com, November 3, 2012. https://musingsofanaspie.com/2012/11/03/the-making-of-a-little-professor/.
7. "The Edge (1997) Anthony Hopkins — Memorable Quotes." YouTube, January 19, 2014. Video, 06:47. https://www.youtube.com/watch?v=H2NaM8XFd_E.
8. Noam Brown and Tuomas Sandholm, "Superhuman AI for Multiplayer Poker." *Science,* August 30, 2019. https://science.sciencemag.org/content/365/6456/885.
9. MIT Media Lab, "DuoSkin." Accessed June 23, 2019. https://duoskin.media.mit .edu/.
10. Defense Advanced Research Projects Agency, "Broad Agency Announcement: Narrative Networks, DARPA-BAA-12-03." October 7, 2011. Available at https:// robo-hunter.com/uploads/files/560c1c5fe87df.pdf.
11. "Oldest Literary Reference to Automata, Computers, Robots." Abcdunlimited. com. Accessed July 23, 2019. http://abcdunlimited.com/liberty/refs/aristotle .html.
12. As quoted in Sarah Kessler, "The Optimist's Guide to the Robot Apocalypse." *Nextgov,* March 9, 2017. http://www.nextgov.com/emerging-tech/2017/03/ optimists-guide-robot-apocalypse/136028/?oref=nextgov_today_nl.
13. Katy Shepard, Christina Nemeth, Karen Murray, and Callie McGrath, "Ethics of 'Cogniceuticals.'" The Central Sulcus, August 18, 2013. https://thecentralsulcus .wordpress.com/2013/08/18/ethics-of-cogniceuticals/.
14. Matthew Cox, "Army Studies Electrical Brain Zaps for Enhancing Soldier

Performance." Military.com, April 25, 2019. https://www.military.com/daily -news/2019/04/25/army-studies-electrical-brain-zaps-enhancing-soldier -performance.html.

Josh Constine, "Facebook Is Building Brain-Computer Interfaces for Typing and Skin-Hearing." TechCrunch, April 19, 2017. https://techcrunch.com/2017/ 04/19/facebook-brain-interface/.

15. As quoted in Matt Novak, "Yes, the Eerie Carl Sagan Prediction That's Going Viral Is Real." *Gizmodo,* January 23, 2017. https://paleofuture.gizmodo.com/yes -the-eerie-carl-sagan-prediction-thats-going-viral-1791502520. The quote originally appeared in Sagan's book *The Demon-Haunted World: Science As a Candle in the Dark,* New York: Random House, 1995.

16. Sergio Miracola, "How China Uses Artificial Intelligence to Control Society." ISPI, June 3, 2019. https://www.ispionline.it/it/pubblicazione/how-china-uses -artificial-intelligence-control-society-23244.

17. "Hashcat Tutorial for Beginners." *InfoSec Institute,* April 9, 2018. https:// resources.infosecinstitute.com/hashcat-tutorial-beginners/#gref.

18. Steve Ranger, "IoT Security Crackdown: Stop Using Default Passwords and Guarantee Updates, Tech Companies Told." *ZDNet,* May 1, 2019. https://www .zdnet.com/article/iot-security-crackdown-stop-using-default-passwords-and -guarantee-updates-tech-companies-told/.

19. Jeff Stone, "Newly Reported Flaws in Cameras, Locks Add to Scrutiny of Smart-Home Security." *CyberScoop,* July 2, 2019. https://www.cyberscoop.com/ smart-home-vulnerabilities-netgear-zipato/; Zack Whittaker, "A Backdoor in Optergy Tech Could Remotely Shut Down a Smart Building 'with One Click.'" TechCrunch, June 6, 2019. http://social.techcrunch.com/2019/06/06/optergy -backdoor-smart-building/.

20. "Hakuna Matata," *The Lion King,* 1994, music by Elton John, lyrics by Tim Rice. November 17, 2013. https://www.youtube.com/watch?v=nbY_aP-alkw.

21. Deep Dream Generator. Accessed July 23, 2019. https://deepdreamgenerator .com/#gallery.

22. David T. Zabecki, "The Greatest German General No One Ever Heard Of." Historynet, May 12, 2008. https://www.historynet.com/the-greatest-german -general-no-one-ever-heard-of.htm.

23. Plato, "The Allegory of the Cave." *Republic,* VII 514 a, 2 to 517 a, 7, translation by Thomas Sheehan. https://web.stanford.edu/class/ihum40/cave.pdf.

Amy Trumpeter, "'The Allegory of the Cave' by Plato: Summary And Meaning." September 21, 2012. http://www.philosophyzer.com/the-allegory-of-the -cave-by-plato-summary-and-meaning/.

24. April Glaser, "How to Not Build a Panopticon." Slate.com. July 19, 2019. https:// slate.com/technology/2019/07/amazon-rekognition-surveillance-panopticon .html.

25. Peter Holley, "Baristas Beware: A Robot That Makes Gourmet Cups of Coffee Has Arrived." *Washington Post,* March 22, 2019. https://www.washingtonpost .com/technology/2019/03/22/baristas-beware-robot-that-makes-gourmet -cups-coffee-has-arrived/.

26. Mary L. Gray and Siddarth Suri, *Ghost Work: How to Stop Silicon Valley from Building a New Global Underclass.* Boston: Houghton Mifflin Harcourt, 2019.

27. Chavie Lieber, "Your Favorite Stores Could Be Tracking You with Facial Recognition." Racked, May 22, 2018. https://www.racked.com/2018/5/22/17380410/facial-recognition-technology-retail.

28. Emily Price, "At San Francisco's New Cafe X, A Robot Makes Your Coffee Just the Way You Like It." *Fast Company,* January 30, 2017. https://www.fastcompany.com/3067635/at-san-franciscos-new-cafe-x-a-robot-makes-your-coffee-just-the-way-you-lik.

7. CLARENDON NEIGHBORHOOD

1. Miklós Vincze, Ion Dan Borcia, and Uwe Harlander, "Temperature Fluctuations in a Changing Climate: An Ensemble-based Experimental Approach." *Nature,* article number 254 (2017). https://www.nature.com/articles/s41598-017-00319-0.

2. Paul Sullivan, "A Battle over Diamonds: Made by Nature or in a Lab?" *New York Times,* February 9, 2018. https://www.nytimes.com/2018/02/09/your-money/synthetic-diamond-jewelry.html.

8. BALLSTON NEIGHBORHOOD

1. National Weather Service, "1936 Flood Retrospective." Accessed June 23, 2019. https://www.weather.gov/lwx/1936Flood.

2. Floodmap.net, "Elevation of Washington, D.C., US Elevation Map, Topo, Contour." Accessed March 12, 2019. http://www.floodmap.net/Elevation/ElevationMap/?gi=4140963.

3. *"View of the City of Washington in 1792,* Showing Goose Creek (Tiber Creek) and James Creek (18??)." Wikipedia. Accessed July 25, 2019. https://en.wikipedia.org/wiki/Washington_City_Canal#/media/File:View_of_the_city_of_Washington_in_1792.tif.

4. Aaron Steckelberg, Philip Kennicott, Bonnie Berkowitz, and Denise Lu, "A 200-Year Transformation: How the Mall Became What It Is Today." *Washington Post,* August 23, 2016. https://www.washingtonpost.com/graphics/lifestyle/the-evolution-of-the-national-mall/.

5. Libby Nelson and Annah Hackett, "The Flood Map: Using NASA's Data to Show the Devastating Impact of Global Warming on the World's Coastlines." SLIS Digital Humanities Project Toolkit 2015. https://sites.google.com/a/wisc.edu/slisdhtoolkit15/how-did-they-make-that/flood-map.
   "Washington D.C. 100 Year Flood (FEMA Map)." ArcGIS, October 29, 2012. https://www.arcgis.com/home/item.html?id=639caddb19614293ba90ca09cf21c747.

6. "Marine Corps Commercial: Toward the Sounds of Chaos." YouTube, March 10, 2012. https://www.youtube.com/watch?v=tYrBSTBHCS4.

7. Interview by Peter W. Singer with water facility expert, Washington, DC, July 26, 2019.
   See also Clean Rivers project (https://www.dcwatercom/cleanrivers) and Neil Augenstein, "Raw Sewage in DC Rivers Likely After Heavy Rain. But That

Will Change." WTOP, July 28, 2017. https://wtop.com/dc/2017/07/heavy-rain
-raw-sewage-potomac-anacostia-rivers-likely/.

9. THE NATIONAL ARCHIVES

1. Flood image: https://i.ytimg.com/vi/93hmFYccNlg/maxresdefault.jpg.
2. National Museum of American History, "Mister Rogers' Sweater." Smithsonian.
   https://www.si.edu/object/nmah_680637.
3. Sarah Kessler, "AMAZON: This Company Built One of the World's Most
   Efficient Warehouses by Embracing Chaos." *Quartz*. Accessed July 23, 2019.
   https://classic.qz.com/perfect-company-2/1172282/this-company-built-one-of
   -the-worlds-most-efficient-warehouses-by-embracing-chaos/.
4. Donovan Alexander, "New Self-Aware Robotic Arm Can Recognize and Repair
   Itself." *Interesting Engineering,* February 3, 2019. https://interestingengineering
   .com/new-self-aware-robotic-arm-can-recognize-and-repair-itself.
       Kalev Leetaru, "Will We Really Need Humans to Fix the Robots?" *Forbes,*
   April 25, 2019. https://www.forbes.com/sites/kalevleetaru/2019/04/25/will-we
   -really-need-humans-to-fix-the-robots/#36a8e4613673.
5. Ray Kurzweil, *The Singularity Is Near.* New York: Penguin Books, 2006.
6. Stefan Holtel, "From Computer to Centaur — Cognitive Tools Turn the
   Rules Upside Down." *KM World,* January 30, 2015. https://www.kmworld
   .com/Articles/ReadArticle.aspx?ArticleID=101525.
7. Matthew Sadler and Natasha Regan. *Game Changer: AlphaZero's Groundbreaking Chess Strategies and the Promise of AI.* Alkmaar, The Netherlands: New in
   Chess, 2019. https://www.newinchess.com/en_US/game-changer.
8. Dan Costa, "Garry Kasparov Says AI Can Make Us 'More Human.'"*PC Magazine,* March 20, 2019. https://www.pcmag.com/article/367202/garry-kasparov
   -says-ai-can-make-us-more-human.
9. Walt Whitman, "Song of Myself," 1855. Available at https://whitmanarchive
   .org/published/LG/1891/poems/27.
10. Nick Bostrom, *Superintelligence: Paths, Dangers, Strategies.* Oxford, UK: Oxford
    University Press, 2014.
        Nick Bostrom, "Superintelligence. " Talks at Google. YouTube, September
    22, 2014. https://www.youtube.com/watch?v=pywF6ZzsghI.
        Joshua Gans, "AI and the Paperclip Problem." VoxEU.org, June 10, 2018.
    https://voxeu.org/article/ai-and-paperclip-problem.

10. BALLSTON NEIGHBORHOOD

1. David Canellis, "WATCH: Bitcoin ATM Showers London's Bond Street Station
   in Cash Money." *TNW* June 7, 2019. https://thenextweb.com/hardfork/2019/
   06/07/bitcoin-atm-london-cash-money-notes-duffel-bag-cryptocurrency
   -bond-street/.
2. Sesame Street — Little Jerry and The Monotones, "Sesame Street: Sad." You-
   Tube, September 19, 2011. Video, 2:39. https://www.youtube.com/watch?v=
   2hBYDrBnMnc.

3. Brian Trompeter, "Fairfax County to Pursue Autonomous-Vehicle Pilot Program in Merrifield." InsideNoVa.com, February 21, 2019. http://www .insidenova.com/news/business/fairfax/fairfax-county-to-pursue-autonomous -vehicle-pilot-program-in-merrifield/article_723eca84-3535-11e9-88af -fbd43c377b55.html.

4. Ben Fritz, "Startup Backed by Spielberg and Studios Seeks to Create VR Experiences for Malls." *Wall Street Journal,* February 13, 2017. https://www.wsj .com/articles/startup-backed-by-spielberg-and-studios-seeks-to-create-vr -experiences-for-malls-1486990802.

5. "John W. Gardner." Wikipedia. Accessed June 15, 2019. https://en.wikipedia .org/w/index.php?title=John_W._Gardner&oldid=901967935.

6. "John Gardner: Engineer of the Great Society." PBS. Accessed July 8, 2019. https://www.pbs.org/johngardner/chapters/4.html.

7. Lily Hay Newman, "How to Make Your Amazon Echo and Google Home as Private as Possible." *Wired,* April 11, 2019. https://www.wired.com/story/alexa -google-assistant-echo-smart-speaker-privacy-controls/.
    Geoffrey A. Fowler, "Alexa Has Been Eavesdropping on You This Whole Time." *Washington Post,* May 6, 2019. https://www.washingtonpost.com/ technology/2019/05/06/alexa-has-been-eavesdropping-you-this-whole-time/.

8. Anne-Marie Slaughter, "Why Women Still Can't Have It All." *The Atlantic,* July/August 2012. https://www.theatlantic.com/magazine/archive/2012/07/ why-women-still-cant-have-it-all/309020/.

9. Larry Cooper, "How Casinos Use Facial Recognition Technology." *Cool Cat Casino.* Accessed June 23, 2019. https://www.coolcat-casino.com/casino-news/ how-casinos-use-facial-recognition-technology.php.

10. Stephen Streng, *Adulterating More Than Food: The Cyber Risk to Food Processing and Manufacturing.* Food Protection and Defense Institute Report, University of Minnesota, September 2019. https://foodprotection.umn.edu/sites/ foodprotection.umn.edu/files/fpdi-food-ics-cybersecurity-white-paper.pdf.

11. Nate Silver, *The Signal and the Noise: Why So Many Predictions Fail — But Some Don't.* New York: Penguin Books, 2015.

12. Tech Insider, "This Sea-Craft Looks Like a Plane, Has a Car's Engine, and Docks Like a Boat." YouTube, March 9, 2018. Video. https://www.youtube.com/ watch?v=C-sWokqiVHw.

13. Jackson Barnett, "Pentagon Partners with Singapore to Develop AI for Disaster Response." *FedScoop,* July 1, 2019. https://www.fedscoop.com/jaic-working -with-singapore-on-ai/.

14. "The Fragile," song by Nine Inch Nails. Accessed November 5, 2019. https:// genius.com/Nine-inch-nails-the-fragile-lyrics.

15. *Sex Robots.* Digital photograph, 467 x 374. Accessed June 26, 2019. https://img .scoop.it/8ls07MswihziRE4D5NB-gDl72eJkfbmt4t8yenImKBVvK0kTmF0xjc tABnaLJIm9.

16. Erin Brodwin, "Here's the Personality Test Cambridge Analytica Had Facebook Users Take." *Business Insider,* March 19, 2018. https://www.businessinsider .com/facebook-personality-test-cambridge-analytica-data-trump-election -2018-3.

17. David Yates, "I Mean, It's Sort of Exciting, Isn't It, Breaking the Rules?" From *Harry Potter and the Order of the Phoenix*, 2007. https://getyarn.io/yarn-clip/a787344e-30d1-435d-a975-e076338510c5.

18. "Othala Rune." Anti-Defamation League. Accessed June 26, 2019. https://www.adl.org/education/references/hate-symbols/othala-rune.

19. Henry Farrell, "The 'Intellectual Dark Web,' Explained." *Vox,* May 10, 2018. https://www.vox.com/the-big-idea/2018/5/10/17338290/intellectual-dark-web-rogan-peterson-harris-times-weiss.

20. Geoffrey A. Fowler, "First Look: Now Laptop Screens Fold, Too, with This ThinkPad from Lenovo." *Washington Post,* May 13, 2019. https://www.washingtonpost.com/technology/2019/05/13/first-look-now-laptop-screens-fold-too-with-this-thinkpad-lenovo/.

11. FBI HOSTAGE RESCUE TEAM OPERATIONS CENTER

1. Malcolm Owen, "Apple Working on Force-Sensing Gloves for Gesture Controls." *AppleInsider,* January 15, 2019. https://appleinsider.com/articles/19/01/15/apple-working-on-force-sensing-gloves-for-gesture-controls.

2. "Built for Boys," Blue Ridge School, 2015. https://www.blueridgeschool.com/.

3. "Next Generation Squad Weapons (NGSW)." US Army Acquisition Support Center, 2019. https://asc.army.mil/web/portfolio-item/fws-cs-2/.

4. *Military Exoskeleton Suit.* GIF, 632 x 268. Accessed June 26, 2019. https://66.media.tumblr.com/03838f53888dabb692ceaeb55b61af52/tumblr_nizd9ifMwV1tks6n9o1_1280.gif.

5. *The 500-Volt Shotgun.* Photograph, 600 x 373. Accessed June 26, 2019. https://d1w116sruyx1mf.cloudfront.net/ee-assets/channels/cdd_default/130808image2.jpg.

6. Patrick Tucker, "This Formula Predicts Soldier Firepower in 2050." *Defense One,* September 17, 2019. https://www.defenseone.com/technology/2019/09/formula-predicts-soldier-firepower-2050/159931/.

7. Kyle Mizokami, "This Russian Company Plans a Sniper Rifle That Can Fire Rounds at Mach 5.83." *Foxtrot Alpha,* October 3, 2018. https://foxtrotalpha.jalopnik.com/this-russian-company-plans-a-sniper-rifle-that-can-fire-1829496377.

8. Giancarlo Fiorella, "A Beginner's Guide to Flight Tracking." Bellingcat, October 15, 2019. https://www.bellingcat.com/resources/how-tos/2019/10/15/a-beginners-guide-to-flight-tracking/.

9. Nigel Chiwaya, "Along the East Coast, Rainy Days, High Tides and Sea Rise Make Floods a Part of Life." NBC, January 10, 2019. https://www.nbcnews.com/mach/news/east-coast-sea-level-rise-high-tides-flooding-ncna957241.

10. Jennifer Kite-Powell, "How Sensors, Robotics and Artificial Intelligence Will Transform Agriculture." *Forbes,* March 19, 2017. https://www.forbes.com/sites/jenniferhicks/2017/03/19/how-sensors-robotics-and-artificial-intelligence-will-transform-agriculture/#69bfeb30384b.

11. Zeo Kleinman, "Ocado Trials Fruit-picking Robot." BBC, January 31, 2017. https://www.bbc.com/news/technology-38808925.

12. "Strawberry Robots Forever." @Mashable, July, 1, 2019. https://twitter.com/mashable/status/1145725499806760962.

13. Janet Adamy and Paul Overberg, "Rural America Is the New 'Inner City.'" *Wall Street Journal,* May 26, 2017. https://www.wsj.com/articles/rural-america-is-the-new-inner-city-1495817008.

14. Alex Hern, "Stormfront: 'Murder Capital of Internet' Pulled Offline After Civil Rights Action." *The Guardian,* August 29, 2017. https://www.theguardian.com/technology/2017/aug/29/stormfront-neo-nazi-hate-site-murder-internet-pulled-offline-web-com-civil-rights-action.

15. Gunwerks, "Determining Wind Speed and Direction." YouTube, January 24, 2012. https://www.youtube.com/watch?v=hBdhWe-C4Co.

16. "Industry Day for the Advanced Targeting and Lethality Automated System (ATLAS) Program — W909MY-19-R-C004." Federal Contract Opportunity, February 11, 2019. https://govtribe.com/opportunity/federal-contract-opportunity/industry-day-for-the-advanced-targeting-and-lethality-automated-system-atlas-program-w909my19rc004.

17. Peter W. Singer, *Children at War.* Berkeley: University of California Press, 2006. https://www.ucpress.edu/book/9780520248762/children-at-war.
    Michel Chossudovsky, "Military Training for Young Children at Ukraine's 'Neo-Nazi Summer Camp.'" Geopolitica.ru, September 2, 2015. https://www.geopolitica.ru/en/1158-military-training-for-young-children-at-ukraines-neo-nazi-summer-camp.html.
    Ben Makuch and Mack Lamoureux, "Neo-Nazis Are Organizing Secretive Paramilitary Training Across America." *Vice,* November 20, 2018. https://www.vice.com/en_us/article/a3mexp/neo-nazis-are-organizing-secretive-paramilitary-training-across-america.

18. Andrew Prokop, "The 2014 Controversy over Nevada Rancher Cliven Bundy, Explained." *Vox,* May 14, 2015. https://www.vox.com/2014/8/14/18080508/nevada-rancher-cliven-bundy-explained.

19. *Sticky Foam Gun.* Photograph, 460 x 318. Accessed June 26, 2019. https://futures.armyscitech.com/ex4/wp-content/uploads/sites/2/2016/06/STICKY-FOAM-1_v2.jpg.

20. Nick Hague and Alexei Ovchinin, "2 Astronauts Safe after Soyuz Forced to Make Emergency Landing." CBC, October 11, 2018. https://www.cbc.ca/news/technology/soyuz-iss-incident-emergency-landing-1.4858238.

21. "Artificial Intelligence: An Evangelical Statement of Principles." The Ethics & Religious Liberty Commission of the Southern Baptist Convention, April 11, 2019. https://erlc.com/resource-library/statements/artificial-intelligence-an-evangelical-statement-of-principles.
    Ruth Graham, "How Southern Baptists Are Grappling with Artificial Intelligence." *Slate,* April 12, 2019. https://slate.com/technology/2019/04/southern-baptist-convention-artificial-intelligence-evangelical-statement-principles.html.

22. "Federal Line of Duty Death Benefits (LODD)." *FEDweek Forum & Knowledge Base,* May 11, 2016. https://ask.fedweek.com/federal-government-policies/line-duty-death-benefits/.

23. "This Is What Your Next MOPP Suit Could Look Like." We Are The Mighty, September 19, 2016. https://www.wearethemighty.com/articles/this-is-what -your-next-mopp-suit-could-look-like.

24. Kathryn Harkup, "Chlorine: The Gas of War Crimes." *The Guardian* (blog), September 16, 2016. https://www.theguardian.com/science/blog/2016/sep/16/ chlorine-the-gas-of-war-crimes.

25. Michael Carpenter, "Russia Is Co-opting Angry Young Men." *The Atlantic,* August 29, 2018. https://www.theatlantic.com/ideas/archive/2018/08/russia-is -co-opting-angry-young-men/568741/.

   Bill Gertz, "Russian Group Offered Paramilitary Training to U.S. Neo-Nazis." *RealClearDefense (RCD),* April 6, 2019. https://www.realcleardefense.com/ 2019/04/06/russian_group_offered_paramilitary_training_to_us_neo-nazis _307443.html.

   Kevin Poulsen, "Trump's New Favorite Network Embraces Russian Propaganda." *Daily Beast,* May 3, 2019. https://www.thedailybeast.com/trumps-new -favorite-network-oann-embraces-russian-propaganda.

26. National Park Service, "Baltimore-Washington Parkway." July 31, 2017. https:// www.nps.gov/bawa/index.htm.

27. Maya Oppenheim, "Neo-Nazis Are Taking Genetic Tests and Are Deeply Upset by the Results." *The Independent,* August 18, 2017. http://www .independent.co.uk/news/world/americas/neo-nazis-genetic-tests-white -supremacist-stormfront-racial-ethnic-african-jewish-asian-dna-a7899746 .html.

28. US Marshals Service, "Witness Security Program." Accessed June 25, 2019. https://www.usmarshals.gov/witsec/.

29. Joel Achenbach, "Two Mass Killings a World Apart Share a Common Theme: 'Ecofascism.'" *Washington Post,* August 18, 2019. https://www.washingtonpost .com/science/two-mass-murders-a-world-apart-share-a-common-theme -ecofascism/2019/08/18/0079a676-bec4-11e9-b873-63ace636af08_story.html.

12. FBI DOMESTIC SPECIAL DETENTION FACILITY

1. Kashmir Hill, "Jamming GPS Signals Is Illegal, Dangerous, Cheap, and Easy." *Gizmodo,* July 24, 2017. https://gizmodo.com/jamming-gps-signals-is-illegal -dangerous-cheap-and-e-1796778955.

2. Robert S. Mueller, "Report on the Investigation into Russian Interference in the 2016 Presidential Election: Volume I of II." Washington, DC: US Department of Justice, March 2019. https://www.justice.gov/storage/report.pdf.

3. Quint Forgey, "McCabe: 'I Was Fired Because I Opened a Case Against the President.'" *Politico,* February 17, 2019. https://www.politico.com/story/2019/ 02/17/mccabe-fired-trump-fbi-1173596.

4. James Vincent, "Welcome to the Automated Warehouse of the Future." *The Verge,* May 8, 2018. https://www.theverge.com/2018/5/8/17331250/automated -warehouses-jobs-ocado-andover-amazon.

5. "Bureau of Engraving and Printing." Wikipedia. Accessed June 19, 2019. https://en.wikipedia.org/wiki/Bureau_of_Engraving_and_Printing.

6. Sabrina Stierwalt, "How Do You Estimate Crowd Size?" *Everyday Einstein,* January 25, 2017. https://www.quickanddirtytips.com/education/science/how -do-you-estimate-crowd-size.

7. Dianna Cahn, "Senate Approves Global War on Terrorism Memorial in DC." Military.com, August 4, 2017. https://www.military.com/daily-news/2017/08/ 04/senate-approves-global-war-terrorism-memorial-dc.html.

8. Kevin Roose, "His 2020 Campaign Message: The Robots Are Coming." *New York Times,* February 10, 2018. https://www.nytimes.com/2018/02/10/ technology/his-2020-campaign-message-the-robots-are-coming.html.

9. Howard M. Wasserman, "Argument Analysis: 'Contempt of Cop' — Justices Search for Compromise Standard for First Amendment Retaliatory Arrests." SCOTUSblog, November 27, 2018. https://www.scotusblog.com/2018/11/ argument-analysis-contempt-of-cop-justices-search-for-compromise-standard -for-first-amendment-retaliatory-arrests/.

10. William McPeak, "Weapons of War: The War Hammer." Warfare History Network, November 20, 2018. https://warfarehistorynetwork.com/daily/military -history/weapons-of-war-the-war-hammer/.

11. Zach D. Roberts, "Earlier in a Parking Garage in #Charlottesville — White Supremacists Beat This Black Kid w/ Poles." Twitter, *@zdroberts,* August 12, 2017. https://twitter.com/zdroberts/status/896519908795854848.

12. Sam Reisman, "Trump: 'Knock the Crap Out' of Protesters, I'll Pay Legal Fees." *Daily Beast,* February 1, 2016. https://www.thedailybeast.com/cheats/2016/02/ 01/trump-i-ll-pay-for-protester-beatings.

13. "Yellow Vests Movement." Wikipedia. Accessed July 28, 2019. https://en .wikipedia.org/wiki/Yellow_vests_movement#Protests_outside_France _adopting_yellow_vests_as_a_symbol.

14. Gavin Haynes, "The White Polo Shirt: How the Alt-Right Co-Opted a Modern Classic." *The Guardian,* August 30, 2017. https://www.theguardian.com/ fashion/2017/aug/30/the-white-polo-shirt-how-the-alt-right-co-opted-a -modern-classic.

15. Patrick Howell O'Neill, "Drones Emerge as New Dimension in Cyberwar." *CyberScoop,* February 5, 2018. https://www.cyberscoop.com/apolloshield-septier -drones-uav-cyberwar-hacking/.

    "Teenager Hacks Drone to Prove Cyber Attack Risk." Reuters, May 3, 2019. https://www.reuters.com/video/2019/05/03/teenager-hacks-drone-to-prove -cyber-atta-id545468936.

    US Department of Homeland Security-CERT, "ICS Alert (ICS-ALERT-19-211-01): CAN Bus Network Implementation in Avionics." Issued July 30, 2019. https://www.us-cert.gov/ics/alerts/ics-alert-19-211-01?wpisrc=nl _cybersecurity202&wpmm=1.

16. US Department of Defense, "Department of Defense Announces Successful Micro-Drone Demonstration." Press release, January 9, 2017. https://dod.defense .gov/News/News-Releases/News-Release-View/Article/1044811/department -of-defense-announces-successful-micro-drone-demonstration/.

    Fortune Magazine, "Drone Swarms Are the New Fireworks in China." YouTube, June 14, 2018. https://www.youtube.com/watch?v=ZbCR8mOPkuo.

17. Jeffrey Lin and Peter W. Singer, "This People-Moving Drone Has Completed More Than 1,000 Test Flights." *Popular Science,* February 8, 2018. https://www.popsci.com/ehang-passenger-carrying-drone/.

18. Elliot Carter, "The Hidden Chamber Underneath the Lincoln Memorial." *Atlas Obscura.* Accessed June 25, 2019. http://www.atlasobscura.com/places/lincoln-memorial-undercroft.

19. Defense Advanced Research Projects Agency, "AI Next campaign." Accessed July 21, 2019. https://www.darpa.mil/work-with-us/ai-next-campaign.

20. Kirsten Gronlund, "State of AI: Artificial Intelligence, the Military and Increasingly Autonomous Weapons." Future of Life Institute, May 9, 2019. https://futureoflife.org/2019/05/09/state-of-ai/.

21. Sharon Weinberger, *The Imagineers of War: The Untold Story of DARPA, the Pentagon Agency That Changed the World.* New York: Knopf, 2017.

    Defense Advanced Research Projects Agency, "How DARPA Created AI." DARPATV, December 7, 2018. https://www.youtube.com/watch?v=ri5gOjYgLns.

22. Richa Bhatia, "Understanding the Difference Between Symbolic AI & Non Symbolic AI." *Analytics India Magazine* (blog), December 27, 2017. https://www.analyticsindiamag.com/understanding-difference-symbolic-ai-non-symbolic-ai/.

23. "Exodus 7 — New International Version (NIV)." Biblica. Accessed June 25, 2019. https://www.biblica.com/bible/niv/exodus/7/.

13. FBI DOMESTIC SPECIAL DETENTION FACILITY

1. US Army TRADOC, "The Democratization of Dual Use Technology." US Army Mad Scientist Laboratory, June 27, 2019. https://madsciblog.tradoc.army.mil/157-the-democratization-of-dual-use-technology/.

2. Leela Jacinto, "Turkey's Coup Brought to You via Plotters' WhatsApp Posts." France24, July 25, 2016. https://www.france24.com/en/20160725-turkey-coup-whatsapp-plotters-erdogan-media.

3. Fathali M. Moghaddam, "The Staircase to Terrorism: A Psychological Exploration." *American Psychologist* 60(2) (February–March 2005): 161–69. https://psycnet.apa.org/doiLanding?doi=10.1037%2F0003-066X.60.2.161.

    Martha Crenshaw. *Explaining Terrorism: Causes, Processes and Consequences.* London and New York: Routledge, 2011.

14. POTOMAC OVERLOOK NEIGHBORHOOD

1. Leon Cook, "New Full-Color Night Vision Could Revolutionize Troops' Ability to Operate in Dark." *Stars and Stripes,* January 16, 2019. https://content.jwplatform.com/previews/UsNYCGmj-9WGzrfLj.

2. John Ismay, "Stargazing in a War Zone." *New York Times,* September 12, 2019. https://www.nytimes.com/2019/09/12/magazine/stargazing-war-zone.html.

3. Department of Homeland Security, "Radar Systems for Through-the-Wall Surveillance." July 22, 2016. https://www.dhs.gov/publication/radar-systems-through-wall-surveillance.

4. *IRobot 510 PackBot.* Photograph, 800 x 550. Accessed June 26, 2019. https://www.militaryfactory.com/armor/imgs/irobot-510-packbot.jpg.
5. Frank Colucci, "Explosive Ordnance Disposal Robots Outfitted with Weapons." *National Defense*, August 1, 2003. https://www.nationaldefensemagazine.org/articles/2003/8/1/2003august-explosive-ordnance-disposal-robots-outfitted-with-weapons.
6. Marshall Brain and Charles W. Bryant, "How Capacitors Work." HowStuffWorks. Accessed July 8, 2019. https://electronics.howstuffworks.com/capacitor.htm.
7. Jeffrey Lewis, "The EMPire Strikes Back." *Foreign Policy*, May 24, 2013. https://foreignpolicy.com/2013/05/24/the-empire-strikes-back/.
8. "Capitol Power Plant." Architect of the Capitol, March 14, 2019. https://www.aoc.gov/capitol-buildings/capitol-power-plant.

15. BALLSTON NEIGHBORHOOD

1. Adam Janofsky, "Federal Researchers Simulate Power Grid Cyberattack, Find Holes in Response Plan." *Wall Street Journal,* November 9, 2018. https://www.wsj.com/articles/federal-researchers-simulate-power-grid-cyberattack-find-holes-in-response-plan-1541785202.
2. Ready.gov, "Build a Kit." Accessed June 26, 2019. https://www.ready.gov/build-a-kit.
3. Alexis Madrigal, "Should Children Form Emotional Bonds with Robots?" *The Atlantic*, December 2017. https://www.theatlantic.com/magazine/archive/2017/12/my-sons-first-robot/544137/.
4. "Testimony of Erik Prince," US House of Representatives, Permanent Select Committee on Intelligence. November 30, 2017. https://docs.house.gov/meetings/IG/IG00/20171130/106661/HHRG-115-IG00-Transcript-20171130.pdf.
    US District Court for the District of Columbia, "Lawsuit Filed by Citizens for Responsibility and Ethics in Washington v. US Department of Justice." December 2018. https://s3.amazonaws.com/storage.citizensforethics.org/wp-content/uploads/2018/12/10165327/Giuliani-Complaint.pdf; P. W. Singer and Emerson T. Brooking, *LikeWar: The Weaponization of Social Media*. Boston: Houghton Mifflin Harcourt, 2018.
5. "Quis Custodiet Ipsos Custodes?" Wikipedia. Accessed June 7, 2019. https://en.wikipedia.org/w/index.php?title=Quis_custodiet_ipsos_custodes%3F&oldid=900799787.
6. Defense Advanced Research Projects Agency program manager, interview by Peter W. Singer, Washington, DC, April 30, 2019.
7. Shane Harris, "New Zealand Attack Exposes How Little the U.S. and Its Allies Share Intelligence on Domestic Terrorism Threats." *Washington Post,* March 16, 2019. https://www.washingtonpost.com/world/national-security/new-zealand-attack-exposes-how-little-the-us-and-its-allies-share-intelligence-on-domestic-terror-threats/2019/03/16/42c14d9c-4744-11e9-8aab-95b8d80a1e4f_story.html.
8. Peter W. Singer, "National Security Pros, It's Time to Talk About Right-Wing

Extremism." *Defense One,* February 28, 2018. https://www.defenseone.com/threats/2018/02/national-security-pros-its-time-talk-about-right-wing-extremism/146319/.

Kathy Gilsinan, "How White-Supremacist Violence Echoes Other Forms of Terrorism." *The Atlantic,* March 15, 2019. https://www.theatlantic.com/international/archive/2019/03/violence-new-zealand-echoes-past-terrorist-patterns/585043/.

9. Steve Haruch, "Why Corporate Executives Talk About 'Opening Their Kimonos.'" NPR.org, November 2, 2014. https://www.npr.org/sections/codeswitch/2014/11/02/360479744/why-corporate-executives-talk-about-opening-their-kimonos.

10. Paul Miller, "What Is Edge Computing?" *The Verge,* May 7, 2018. https://www.theverge.com/circuitbreaker/2018/5/7/17327584/edge-computing-cloud-google-microsoft-apple-amazon.

11. Frank Luerweg, "The Internet Knows You Better Than Your Spouse Does." *Scientific American,* March 14, 2019. https://www.scientificamerican.com/article/the-internet-knows-you-better-than-your-spouse-does/.

12. Andreas Vogel and Nicholas Wright, "Alexa, What Is a Conflict of Interest?" *Slate,* May 10, 2019. https://slate.com/technology/2019/05/alexa-amazon-voice-assistant-conflict-interest-regulation.html.

13. "Scientists Shocked by Arctic Permafrost Thawing 70 Years Sooner Than Predicted." *The Guardian,* June 18, 2019. https://www.theguardian.com/environment/2019/jun/18/arctic-permafrost-canada-science-climate-crisis.

14. "The Most Expensive Car Interiors in the World." *Simoniz* (blog), September 16, 2016. https://www.holtsauto.com/simoniz/news/expensive-car-interiors-world/.

15. Behnood Gholami, Wassim M. Haddad, and James M. Bailey, "AI Could Provide Moment-by-Moment Nursing for a Hospital's Sickest Patients." *IEEE Spectrum,* September 24, 2018. https://spectrum.ieee.org/biomedical/devices/ai-could-provide-momentbymoment-nursing-for-a-hospitals-sickest-patients.

16. GEORGETOWN UNIVERSITY HOSPITAL

1. Katie Malafronte, "Facial-recognition Technology Banned in San Francisco." *Campus Safety Magazine,* May 15, 2019. https://www.campussafetymagazine.com/technology/facial-recognition-san-francisco/.

2. Alistair M. C. Isaac and Will Bridewell, "White Lies on Silver Tongues: Why Robots Need to Be Able to Deceive (And How)." In Patrick Lin, Ryan Jenkins, and Keith Abney (eds.), *Robot Ethics 2.0,* New York: Oxford University Press, 2017. Available at https://www.nrl.navy.mil/itd/aic/sites/www.nrl.navy.mil.itd.aic/files/pdfs/chapter_oso-9780190652951-chapter-11.pdf.

3. Lily Hay Newman, "AI Can Recognize Your Face Even If You're Pixilated." *Wired,* September 12, 2016. https://www.wired.com/2016/09/machine-learning-can-identify-pixelated-faces-researchers-show/.

4. David Cardinal, "Quantum Cryptography Demystified: How It Works in Plain Language." *ExtremeTech,* March 11, 2019. https://www.extremetech.com/extreme/287094-quantum-cryptography.

S. Kak, "A Three-Stage Quantum Cryptography Protocol." *Foundations of Physics Letters*, vol. 19 (3) (2006): 293–96.

17. GEORGETOWN UNIVERSITY HOSPITAL

1. Zachary Tomlinson, "15 Medical Robots That Are Changing the World." *Interesting Engineering*, October 11, 2018. https://interestingengineering.com/15 -medical-robots-that-are-changing-the-world.
2. "You Are My Sunshine." Louisiana State Song, State Symbols USA. Accessed September 19, 2019. https://statesymbolsusa.org/symbol-official-item/ louisiana/state-song/you-are-my-sunshine.

18. GEORGETOWN UNIVERSITY HOSPITAL

1. Robert Hartle, "How Heat Sinks Work." HowStuffWorks. Accessed June 18, 2019. https://computer.howstuffworks.com/heat-sink.htm.
2. Matt Turek, "Explainable Artificial Intelligence (XAI)." Defense Advanced Research Projects Agency (DARPA). Accessed July 6, 2019. https://www.darpa .mil/program/explainable-artificial-intelligence.
   Molly Kovite, "I, Black Box: Explainable Artificial Intelligence and the Limits of Human Deliberative Processes." War on the Rocks, July 5, 2019. https:// warontherocks.com/2019/07/i-black-box-explainable-artificial-intelligence -and-the-limits-of-human-deliberative-processes/.
3. Ghiselaine Vu-Han, "Perfecting the Phosphorus Process." *MIT-The Tech*, March 8, 2018. https://chemistry.mit.edu/chemistry-news/perfecting-the -phosphorus-process/.
4. "Factbox: Key Facts About White Phosphorus Munitions." Reuters, May 8, 2009. https://www.reuters.com/article/us-afghanistan-phosphorus-facts -sb/factbox-key-facts-about-white-phosphorus-munitions-idUSTRE5471T 620090508.
5. Paul Reynolds, "White Phosphorous: Weapon on the Edge." BBC, November 16, 2005. http://news.bbc.co.uk/2/hi/americas/4442988.stm.

19. GEORGETOWN UNIVERSITY HOSPITAL

1. Judith Shulevitz, "Alexa, Should We Trust You?" *The Atlantic*, November 2018. https://www.theatlantic.com/magazine/archive/2018/11/alexa-how-will-you -change-us/570844/.

REFERENCES

1. P. W. Singer and August Cole, "How to Write About World War III." *The Atlantic*, June 30, 2015. https://www.theatlantic.com/international/archive/ 2015/06/ghost-fleet-world-war-III/397301/.
   See also J. Furman Daniel III and Paul Musgrave, "Synthetic Experiences: How Popular Culture Matters for Images of International Relations." *Interna-*

tional Studies Quarterly, Volume 61, Issue 3, September 2017 (pages 503–16). https://academic.oup.com/isq/advance-article-abstract/doi/10.1093/isq/sqx053/4616603; and "Why It's Worth Reading Crazy-Sounding Scenarios About the Future," *The Economist,* July 6, 2019. https://www.economist.com/leaders/2019/07/06/why-its-worth-reading-crazy-sounding-scenarios-about-the-future.

Made in United States
North Haven, CT
08 December 2023

45360784R00259